ADRIFT
on the
HAUNTED SEAS

The Best Short Stories of
William Hope Hodgson

"Few can equal him..." —H. P. Lovecraft

ACKNOWLEDGEMENTS

Thanks go to Richard Bleiler, who provided an eleventh-hour copy of the original magazine version of one of the stories included herein; to Jane Frank, for sharing her Hodgson research; and to Jim Rockhill, for comments and opinions. A special thanks goes to R. Alain Everts, who generously shared with me several years ago the results of his own research into Hodgson's life and bibliography.

ADRIFT
on the
HAUNTED SEAS

The Best Short Stories of William Hope Hodgson

Edited and with an Introduction by Douglas A. Anderson

Cold Spring Press

Cold Spring Press

P.O. Box 284, Cold Spring Harbor, NY 11724
E-mail: Jopenroad@aol.com

Introduction and compilation Copyright © 2005
by Douglas A. Anderson

ISBN 1-59360-049-6
Library of Congress Control No. 2005925490

Contents

Introduction

WILLIAM HOPE HODGSON'S writings demonstrate a remarkable engagement with the sea and with the sailor's life. His entire literary output consists of four novels, over one hundred short stories, and just over ninety poems—two of these novels are sea stories, while over seventy of the short stories and around forty of the poems concern the sea.

Hodgson's most important works are the four novels and the short stories collected in this volume, at least three of which are true masterpieces. Of the novels, *The Boats of the 'Glen Carrig'* (1907) tells of the three lifeboats from a shipwreck and their adventures in the mysterious Sargasso Sea. *The House on the Borderland* (1908) concerns an isolated house on the west coast of Ireland which is attacked by beings from another dimension. *The Ghost Pirates* (1909) is the account of a ship assaulted by strange phenomena and mysterious creatures from the sea. *The Night Land* (1912) is a brilliant piece of imagination, set on earth in the far future after the sun has burnt itself out, where small bastions of humanity struggle in the endless darkness.

During his lifetime, some of his short stories were collected in *Carnacki, the Ghost-Finder* (1913), *Men of the Deep Waters* (1914), *The Luck of the Strong* (1916) and *Captain Gault* (1917). After his death in 1918, his wife arranged for the publication of two slim volumes of his poetry, *The Calling of the Sea* (1920) and *The Voice of the Ocean* (1921), the latter a single long metaphysical poem about the sea. Over the last forty years the bulk of Hodgson's surviving manuscripts have been published, and his unreprinted works collected in various small press volumes, edited by Sam Moskowitz and others.

Hodgson's short stories exhibit a range of types— from simple adventures and romances to the imaginative fantasies of haunted derelicts and mysterious sea creatures that are his trademark characteristics. This collection brings together the very best of his short stories, together with a sampling of his poetry. It includes a variety of his sea horrors along with two non-fantastic pieces: "On the Bridge," a journalistic story written immediately after the sinking of the Titanic which attempts to show some of the various factors which contributed to the tragedy, and the suspenseful nonfiction story "Through the Vortex of a Cyclone," which is based on Hodgson's own experiences at sea.

William Hope Hodgson, known familiarly as "Hope," was born on 15 November 1877 at Blackmore End, Essex, the second of twelve children of an Anglican clergyman. He moved frequently as a child, eventually attending a boarding school in Margate, from which he ran away at the age of thirteen with the intention of going to sea. His desire was initially resisted by his father, but eventually, through the intervention of an uncle, young Hope was apprenticed as a cabin boy for a period of four years beginning on 28 August 1891. After completing his apprenticeship in 1895, he attended a school in Liverpool to study for his mate's certificate. This was the last formal schooling Hodgson had, after which he returned to the sea.

What did Hodgson do at sea? His duties, first and foremost—during various watches these might include pulling the braces (i.e., the ropes which regulate the position of the sails), furling and unfurling the sails, walking the pigs while the pigsty was being washed out, scrubbing the decks, repairing sails, etc. These duties were no doubt hard work, but Hodgson filled his spare time with other more pleasant activities: reading books, weaving mats out of ship's rope, and taking photographs of rare sea phenomenon—photographs he developed onboard in a makeshift darkroom. Being small (he was not quite 5 feet 6 inches tall), he became obsessed with physical training, weight-lifting with dumbbells and working out with a punching bag. He boxed with ship-mates, and learned Judo. In a 1901 interview with a newspaper, he explained the origins of his interest in physical culture:

> "I was driven to the development of my muscles at a very early age. I went to sea when thirteen, and being a little chap with a very ordinary physique, had the misfortune to serve under a second mate of the worst possible type. He was brutal, and although I can truthfully say I never gave him just cause, he singled me out for ill-treatment. He made my life so miserable that in the end I summoned sufficient courage to retaliate, and 'went for him'. It was for all the world like a fight between a mastiff and a terrier, for he was power and knew how to punish. Of course I took a merciless thrashing, but I remember how proud I was the next day when I was arraigned before the captain for insubordination to see that I had left my mark."

In 1898, he dove into shark-infested waters in order to save the life of a fellow sailor who had fallen overboard. Hodgson was awarded a bronze medal by the Royal Humane Society for his courage. The following year he gave up the life of the sea. In an article in *The Grand Magazine* in September 1905, Hodgson responded to the editor's question of "Is the Mercantile Navy Worth Joining?" with a resounding "no:"

INTRODUCTION

"Why am I not at sea? I am not at sea because I object to bad treatment, poor food, poor wages, and worse prospects. I am not at sea because very early I discovered that it is a comfortless, wearyful, and thankless life—a life compact of hardness and sordidness such as shore people can scarcely conceive. I am not at sea because I dislike being a pawn with the sea for a board and the ship owners for players."

Towards the end of this article, Hodgson summed up what he had learned in his time at sea:

"It is a life of hardness, broken sleep, loneliness, separation, and discomfort. It is indeed a thankless life, without even the common rewards of industry. It leads neither to fame nor wealth, nor, save in exceptional cases, to a sufficiency upon which to retire; and finally the officers of the mercantile marine have not that poor consolation of their Naval brethren, a certain social position. The shore-dwellers scarcely recognise any difference between the mercantile marine officer and the poor wretch they have most atrociously designated the *common sailor*."

He returned to his family, who were now living in Blackburn, Lancashire, and there he opened W. H. Hodgson's School of Physical Culture. He also dabbled with the writing of articles on physical culture for magazines. After only a few years, the school failed, and in August 1902 Hodgson turned to the writing of fiction. Over the next three years, Hodgson wrote his four novels, and numerous short stories, but received literally hundreds of rejections from magazine and book publishers. He persevered, but as he grew aware that the market would not at that time accept his most imaginative writings, he strove to be more commonplace.

His novels, when finally published, made very little money. But the early twentieth century was part of the golden age for short story writers, with a very large number of fiction magazines that paid well for popular fiction. Hodgson worked for the market, developing a number of series characters—including Thomas Carnacki, an occult detective, and more successfully, Captain Gault, a smuggler who exercises great imagination in circumventing customs agents.

Perhaps Hodgson's most enduring cycle is not based on a character but a place—the Sargasso Sea, a snare of weed-patched sea in the mid-Atlantic, long a legend to sailors. The Sargasso Sea became known to readers in Jules Verne's *Twenty Thousand Leagues Under the Sea* (1869), and in subsequent books like Thomas Janvier's *In the Sargasso Sea* (1898), but Hodgson invested the place with horrors of his own devising, and built a kind of mythos around it. The Sargasso Sea enters into several of Hodgson's stories, including "The Voice in the Dawn," "From the Tideless Sea" (in two parts), "The Finding of the Graiken," and "The Mystery of the Derelict." It figures also in Hodgson's novel, *The Boats of the 'Glen Carrig'*.

Hodgson gradually found success with his short stories. In 1913, he married and moved with his wife to the south coast of France. After the outbreak of the First World War, he returned to England, where he enlisted. He attended the University of London's Officer's Training Corps, and in July 1915 was commissioned as a Lieutenant in the Royal Field Artillery. Hodgson suffered a broken jaw in June of the following year when he was thrown from a horse, and he was sent home to his family on medical leave. He passed the medical board in March 1917 and was recommissioned. He was sent to the front later in the year, where he served heroically, but on 19 April 1918, on the eastern slope of Mount Kemmel near Ypres in Belgium, he was killed by the direct hit of a German artillery shell. He was forty years old.

Hodgson's literary legacy is secure. He had imitators from early on. Adrian Ross's (Arthur Reed Ropes's) 1914 novel *The Hole in the Pit* shows the unmistakeable influence of Hodgson, while Philip M. Fisher's "Fungus Isle" (in *Argosy All-Story Weekly*, 27 October 1923) shows clearly its inspiration in Hodgson's classic story "The Voice in the Night". Some of Dennis Wheatley's writings, particularly the novel *Uncharted Seas* (1938), filmed bizarrely by Hammer Studios in 1968 under the title *The Lost Continent*, reflect Wheatley's own admiration for Hodgson.

Throughout the 1930s and 1940s, Hodgson's writings were championed in the United States by bibliophile H. C. Koenig, who loaned his rare Hodgson first editions to various members of the Lovecraft circle, including August Derleth, who afterwards reprinted several of Hodgson's works under his Arkham House imprint.

In the 1940s, Ellery Queen celebrated Hodgson's stories of the occult detective Carnacki by naming the book *Carnacki, the Ghost-Finder* (1913) as number 53 (chronologically) of the one hundred most important books in the field of the detective short story. More recently, the unwritten adventures of Carnacki (which are alluded to by Hodgson) have subsequently been recorded by A. F. Kidd and Rick Kennett, and collected in their book *No. 472 Cheyne Walk* (1992; expanded 2002).

A reprint of "The Voice in the Night" in the July 1954 issue of *Playboy* magazine was followed by its appearance in *Alfred Hitchcock Presents: Stories They Wouldn't Let Me Do on TV* (1957), no doubt sparking the filming of the story for the N.B.C. television series *Suspicion* (1957-59), a rival to the more famous C.B.S. show, *Alfred Hitchcock Presents* (1955-62). Broadcast 24 March 1958, it starred James Coburn, James Donald, Patrick Macnee, and Barbara Rush.

Hodgson's novel *The House on the Borderland* figures significantly in the plot of Iain Sinclair's postmodern novel *Radon Daughters* (1994). And stories modeled on Hodgson's Sargasso Sea have been written in recent years by John B. Ford and Simon Clark. Andy W. Robertson currently maintains a website devoted to *The Night Land*, and has edited a volume of tribute fiction, *William Hope Hodgson's Night Lands Volume I: Eternal Love* (2003).

INTRODUCTION

Of Hodgson himself, a choice remembrance was left by one of his literary friends, A. St. John Adcock, editor of *The Bookman*:

"There was something curiously attractive in his breezy, forceful, eager personality; his dark eyes were wonderfully alert and alive; he was wonderfully and restlessly alive and alert in all his mind and body. He was emphatic and unrestrained in his talk, but would take the sting out of an extravagant denunciation of some inartistic popular author, or of some pestilent critic, and the egotism out of some headlong confession of his own belief in himself with the pleasantest boyish laugh that brushed it all aside as the mere spray and froth of a passing thought. His dark, handsome features were extraordinarily expressive; they betrayed his emotions as readily as his lips gave away whatever happened to rise in his mind. Always he had the courage of his opinions and no false modesty; it never seemed to occur to him to practise politic subterfuges; and it was this absolute candour and naturalness that compelled you to like him and before long strengthened your liking into a friendly affection."

Douglas A. Anderson

On the Bridge

(The 8 to 12 watch, and ice was in sight at nightfall)

IN MEMORY OF
APRIL 14, 1912.
LAT. 41 deg. 16 min. N.
LONG. 50 deg. 14 min. W.

Two-bells has just gone. It is nine o'clock. You walk to wind'ard and sniff anxiousiy. Yes, there it is, unmistakably, the never-to-be-forgotten smell of ice . . . a smell as indescribable as it is unmistakable.

You stare, fiercely anxious (almost incredibly anxious), to wind'ard, and sniff again and again. And you never cease to peer, until the very eye-balls ache, and you curse almost insanely because some door has been opened and lets out a shaft of futile and dangerous light across the gloom, through which the great ship is striding across the miles.

For the least show of light about the deck, "blinds" the officer of the watch temporarily, and makes the darkness of the night a double curtain of gloom, threatening hatefully. You curse, and 'phone angrily for a steward to go along and have the door shut or the window covered, as the case may be; then once again to the dreadful strain of watching.

Just try to take it all in. You are, perhaps, only a young man of twenty-six or twenty-eight, and you are in sole charge of that great bulk of life and wealth, thundering on across the miles. One hour of your watch has gone, and there are three to come, and already you are feeling the strain. And reason enough, too; for though the bridge-telegraph pointer stands at HALF-SPEED, you know perfectly well that the engine-room has its private orders, and speed is not cut down at all.

And all around, to wind'ard and to loo'ard, you I can see the gloom pierced dimly in this place and that, everlastingly, by the bursts of phosphorescence from breaking sea-crests. Thousands and tens of thousands of times you see this . . . ahead, and upon either beam. And you sniff, and try to distinguish between the coldness of the half-gale and the peculiar and what I might term the "personal," brutal, ugly Chill-of-Death that comes stealing down to you through the night, as you pass some ice-hill in the darkness.

And then, those countless bursts of dull phosphorescence, that break out eternally from the chaos of the unseen waters about you, become suddenly things of threatening, that frighten you; for any one of them may mean broken water about the unseen shore of some hidden island of ice in the night . . . some half-submerged, inert Insensate Monster-of-Ice, lurking under the wash of the seas, trying to steal unperceived athwart your hawse.

You raise your hand instinctively in the darkness, and the cry "HARD A STARBOARD!" literally trembles on your lips; and then you are saved from making an over-anxious spectacle of yourself; for you see now that the particular burst of phosphorescence that had seemed so pregnant of ICE, is nothing more than anyone of the ten thousand other bursts of sea-light, that come and go among the great moundings of the sea-foam in the surrounding night.

And yet there is that infernal ice-smell again, and the chill that I have called the Chill-of-Death, is stealing in again upon you from some unknown quarter of the night. You send word forrard to the look-outs, and to the man in the "nest," and redouble your own care of the thousand humans who sleep so trustfully in their bunks beneath your feet . . . trusting you—a young man—with their lives . . . with everything. They, and the great ship that strides so splendid and blind through the Night and the Dangers of the Night, are all, as it were, in the hollow of your hand . . . a moment of inattention; and a thousand deaths upon the head of your father's son! Do you wonder that you watch, with your very heart seeming dry with anxiety, on such a night as this!

Four bells! Five bells! Six bells! And now there is only an hour to go; yet, already, you have nearly given the signal three times to the Quartermaster to "port" or "starboard," as the case may be; but each time the conjured terror of the night, the dree, suggestive foam-lights, the infernal ice-smell, and the Chill-of-Death have proved to be no true Prophets of Disaster in your track.

Seven bells! My God! Even as the sweet silver sounds wander fore and aft into the night, and are engulfed by the gale, you see something close upon the starboard bow. . . . A boil of phosphorescent lights, over some low-lying, sea-buried thing in the darkness. Your night-glasses are glaring at it; and then, even before the various look-outs can make their reports, you KNOW. "My God!" your spirit is crying inside of you. "My God!" But your human voice is roaring words that hold life and death for a thousand sleeping souls: —"HARD A STARBOARD!" "HARD A STARBOARD!" The man in the Wheel-house leaps at your cry . . . at the fierce intensity of it; and then, with a momentary loss of nerve, *whirls the wheel the wrong way.* You make one jump, and are into the Wheelhouse. The glass is tinkling all about you, and you do not know in that instant that you are carrying the frame of the shattered Wheel-house door upon your shoulders. Your fist takes the frightened helmsman under the jaw, and your free hand grips the spokes, and dashes the wheel round toward you, the engine roaring, away in its appointed place. Your junior has already flown to his post at the telegraph, and the engine-room is answering the order you have flung at him as you leapt for the Wheel-house. But YOU . . . why, you are staring, half-mad, through the night, watching the monster bows swing to port, against the mighty background of the night. . . . The seconds are the beats of eternity, in that brief, tremendous time. . . . And then, aloud to the wind and the night, you mutter, "Thank God!" For she has swung clear. And below you the thousand sleepers sleep on.

A fresh Quartermaster has "come aft" (to use the old term) to relieve the other, and you stagger out of the Wheel-house, becoming conscious of the inconvenience of the broken woodwork around you. Someone, several people, are assisting you to divest yourself of the framework of the door; and your junior has a queer little air of respect for you, that, somehow, the darkness is not capable of hiding.

You go back to your post then; but perhaps you feel a little sick, despite a certain happy elation that stimulates you.

Eight bells! And your brother officer comes up to relieve you. The usual formula is gone through, and you go down the bridge steps, to the thousand sleeping ones.

Next day a thousand passengers play their games and read their books and talk their talks and make their usual sweepstakes, and never even notice that one of the officers is a little weary-looking.

The carpenter has replaced the door; and a certain Quartermaster will stand no more at the wheel. For the rest, all goes on as usual, and no one ever knows. . . . I mean no one outside of official circles, unless an odd rumour leaks out through the stewards.

And a certain man has no deaths to the name of his father's son.

And the thousand never know. Think of it, you people who go down to the sea in floating palaces of steel and electric light. And let your benedictions fall silently upon the quiet, grave, neatly-uniformed man in blue upon the bridge. You have trusted him unthinkingly with your lives; and not once in ten thousand times has he ever failed you. Do you understand better now?

The Voice in the Night

It was a dark, starless night. We were becalmed in the Northern Pacific. Our exact position I do not know; for the sun had been hidden during the course of a weary, breathless week, by a thin haze which had seemed to float above us, about the height of our mastheads, at whiles descending and shrouding the surrounding sea.

With there being no wind, we had steadied the tiller, and I was the only man on deck. The crew, consisting of two men and a boy, were sleeping forrard in their den; while Will—my friend, and the master of our little craft—was aft in his bunk on the port side of the little cabin.

Suddenly, from out of the surrounding darkness, there came a hail:—

"Schooner, ahoy!"

The cry was so unexpected that I gave no immediate answer, because of my surprise.

It came again—a voice curiously throaty and inhuman, calling from somewhere upon the dark sea away on our port broadside:—

"Schooner, ahoy!"

"Hullo!" I sung out, having gathered my wits somewhat. "What are you? What do you want?"

"You need not be afraid," answered the queer voice, having probably noticed some trace of confusion in my tone. "I am only an old—man."

The pause sounded oddly; but it was only afterwards that it came back to me with any significance.

"Why don't you come alongside, then?" I queried somewhat snappishly; for I liked not his hinting at my having been a trifle shaken.

"I—I—can't. It wouldn't be safe. I—" The voice broke off, and there was silence.

"What do you mean?" I asked, growing more and more astonished. "Why not safe? Where are you?"

I listened for a moment; but there came no answer. And then, a sudden indefinite suspicion, of I knew not what, coming to me, I stepped swiftly to the binnacle, and took out the lighted lamp. At the same time, I knocked on the deck with my heel to waken Will. Then I was back at the side, throwing the yellow funnel of light out into the silent immensity beyond our rail. As I did so, I heard a slight, muffled cry, and then the sound of a splash as though someone had dipped oars abruptly. Yet I cannot say that I saw anything with certainty; save, it seemed to me, that with the first flash of the light, there had been something upon the waters, where now there was nothing.

"Hullo, there!" I called. "What foolery is this!"

But there came only the indistinct sounds of a boat being pulled away into the night.

Then I heard Will's voice, from the direction of the after scuttle:—

"What's up, George?"

"Come here, Will!" I said.

"What is it?" he asked, coming across the deck.

I told him the queer thing which had happened. He put several questions; then, after a moment's silence, he raised his hands to his lips, and hailed:—

"Boat, ahoy!"

From a long distance away there came back to us a faint reply, and my companion repeated his call. Presently, after a short period of silence, there grew on our hearing the muffled sound of oars; at which Will hailed again.

This time there was a reply:—

"Put away the light."

"I'm damned if I will," I muttered; but Will told me to do as the voice bade, and I shoved it down under the bulwarks.

"Come nearer," he said, and the oar-strokes continued. Then, when apparently some half-dozen fathoms distant, they again ceased.

"Come alongside," exclaimed Will. "There's nothing to be frightened of aboard here!"

"Promise that you will not show the light?"

"What's to do with you," I burst out, "that you're so infernally afraid of the light?"

"Because—" began the voice, and stopped short.

"Because what?" I asked quickly.

Will put his hand on my shoulder.

"Shut up a minute, old man," he said, in a low voice. "Let me tackle him." He leant more over the rail.

"See here, Mister," he said, "this is a pretty queer business, you coming upon us like this, right out in the middle of the blessed Pacific. How are we to know what sort of a hanky-panky trick you're up to? You say there's only one of you. How are we to know, unless we get a squint at you—eh? What's your objection to the light, anyway?"

As he finished, I heard the noise of the oars again, and then the voice came; but now from a greater distance, and sounding extremely hopeless and pathetic.

"I am sorry—sorry! I would not have troubled you, only I am hungry, and— so is she."

16

The voice died away, and the sound of the oars, dipping irregularly, was borne to us.

"Stop!" sung out Will. "I don't want to drive you away. Come back! We'll keep the light hidden, if you don't like it."

He turned to me:—

"It's a damned queer rig, this; but I think there's nothing to be afraid of?"

There was a question in his tone, and I replied.

"No, I think the poor devil's been wrecked around here, and gone crazy."

The sound of the oars drew nearer.

"Shove that lamp back in the binnacle," said Will; then he leaned over the rail, and listened. I replaced the lamp, and came back to his side. The dipping of the oars ceased some dozen yards distant.

"Won't you come alongside now?" asked Will in an even voice. "I have had the lamp put back in the binnacle."

"I—I cannot," replied the voice. "I dare not come nearer. I dare not even pay you for the—the provisions."

"That's all right," said Will, and hesitated. "You're welcome to as much grub as you can take—" Again he hesitated.

"You are very good," exclaimed the voice. "May God, Who understands everything, reward you—" It broke off huskily.

"The—the lady?" said Will, abruptly. "Is she—"

"I have left her behind upon the island," came the voice.

"What island?" I cut in.

"I know not its name," returned the voice. "I would to God—!" it began, and checked itself as suddenly.

"Could we not send a boat for her?" asked Will at this point.

"No!" said the voice, with extraordinary emphasis. "My God! No!" There was a moment's pause; then it added, in a tone which seemed a merited reproach:—

"It was because of our want I ventured—Because her agony tortured me."

"I am a forgetful brute," exclaimed Will. "Just wait a minute, whoever you are, and I will bring you up something at once."

In a couple of minutes he was back again, and his arms were full of various edibles. He paused at the rail.

"Can't you come alongside for them?" he asked.

"No—I *dare not*," replied the voice, and it seemed to me that in its tones I detected a note of stifled craving—as though the owner hushed a mortal desire. It came to me then in a flash, that the poor old creature out there in the darkness, was *suffering* for actual need of that which Will held in his arms; and yet, because of some unintelligible dread, refraining from dashing to the side of our little schooner, and receiving it. And with the lightning-like conviction, there came the knowledge that the Invisible was not mad; but sanely facing some intolerable horror.

"Damn it, Will!" I said, full of many feelings, over which predominated a vast sympathy. "Get a box. We must float off the stuff to him in it."

This we did—propelling it away from the vessel, out into the darkness, by means of a boathook. In a minute, a slight cry from the Invisible came to us, and we knew that he had secured the box.

A little later, he called out a farewell to us, and so heartful a blessing, that I am sure we were the better for it. Then, without more ado, we heard the ply of oars across the darkness.

"Pretty soon off," remarked Will, with perhaps just a little sense of injury.

"Wait," I replied. "I think somehow he'll come back. He must have been badly needing that food."

"And the lady," said Will. For a moment he was silent; then he continued:—

"It's the queerest thing ever I've tumbled across, since I've been fishing."

"Yes," I said, and fell to pondering.

And so the time slipped away—an hour, another, and still Will stayed with me; for the queer adventure had knocked all desire for sleep out of him.

The third hour was three parts through, when we heard again the sound of oars across the silent ocean.

"Listen!" said Will, a low note of excitement in his voice.

"He's coming, just as I thought," I muttered.

The dipping of the oars grew nearer, and I noted that the strokes were firmer and longer. The food had been needed.

They came to a stop a little distance off the broadside, and the queer voice came again to us through the darkness:—

"Schooner, ahoy!"

"That you?" asked Will.

"Yes," replied the voice. "I left you suddenly; but—but there was great need."

"The lady?" questioned Will.

"The—lady is grateful now on earth. She will be more grateful soon in—in heaven."

Will began to make some reply, in a puzzled voice; but became confused, and broke off short. I said nothing. I was wondering at the curious pauses, and, apart from my wonder, I was full of a great sympathy.

The voice continued:—

"We—she and I, have talked, as we shared the result of God's tenderness and yours—"

Will interposed; but without coherence.

"I beg of you not to—to belittle your deed of Christian charity this night," said the voice. "Be sure that it has not escaped His notice."

It stopped, and there was a full minute's silence. Then it came again:—

"We have spoken together upon that which—which has befallen us. We had thought to go out, without telling any, of the terror which has come into our—lives. She is with me in believing that to-night's happenings are under a special ruling, and that it is God's wish that we should tell to you all that we have suffered since—since—"

"Yes?" said Will softly.

"Since the sinking of the *Albatross*."

"Ah!" I exclaimed involuntarily. "She left Newcastle for 'Frisco some six months ago, and hasn't been heard of since."

"Yes," answered the voice. "But some few degrees to the North of the line she was caught in a terrible storm, and dismasted. When the day came, it was found that she was leaking badly, and, presently, it falling to a calm, the sailors took to the boats, leaving—leaving a young lady—my fiancée—and myself upon the wreck.

"We were below, gathering together a few of our belongings, when they left. They were entirely callous, through fear, and when we came up upon the deck, we saw them only as small shapes afar off upon the horizon. Yet we did not despair, but set to work and constructed a small raft. Upon this we put such few matters as it would hold including a quantity of water and some ship's biscuit. Then, the vessel being very deep in the water, we got ourselves on to the raft, and pushed off.

"It was later, when I observed that we seemed to be in the way of some tide or current, which bore us from the ship at an angle; so that in the course of three hours, by my watch, her hull became invisible to our sight, her broken masts remaining in view for a somewhat longer period. Then, towards evening, it grew misty, and so through the night. The next day we were still encompassed by the mist, the weather remaining quiet.

"For four days we drifted through this strange haze, until, on the evening of the fourth day, there grew upon our ears the murmur of breakers at a distance. Gradually it became plainer, and, somewhat after midnight, it appeared to sound upon either hand at no very great space. The raft was raised upon a swell several times, and then we were in smooth water, and the noise of the breakers was behind.

"When the morning came, we found that we were in a sort of great lagoon; but of this we noticed little at the time; for close before us, through the enshrouding mist, loomed the hull of a large sailing-vessel. With one accord, we fell upon our knees and thanked God; for we thought that here was an end to our perils. We had much to learn.

"The raft drew near to the ship, and we shouted on them to take us aboard; but none answered. Presently, the raft touched against the side of the vessel, and, seeing a rope hanging downwards, I seized it and began to climb. Yet I had much ado to make my way up, because of a kind of grey, lichenous fungus which had seized upon the rope, and which blotched the side of the ship, lividly.

"I reached the rail and clambered over it, on to the deck. Here I saw that the decks were covered, in great patches, with grey masses, some of them rising into nodules several feet in height; but at the time I thought less of this matter than of the possibility of there being people aboard the ship. I shouted; but none answered. Then I went to the door below the poop deck. I opened it, and peered in. There was a great smell of staleness, so that I knew in a moment that nothing living was within, and with the knowledge, I shut the door quickly; for I felt suddenly lonely.

"I went back to the side where I had scrambled up. My—my sweetheart was still sitting quietly upon the raft. Seeing me look down she called up to know whether there were any aboard of the ship. I replied that the vessel had the appearance of having been long deserted; but that if she would wait a little I would see whether there was anything in the shape of a ladder by which she could ascend to the deck. Then we would make a search through the vessel together. A little later, on the opposite side of the decks, I found a rope side-ladder. This I carried across, and a minute afterwards she was beside me.

"Together, we explored the cabins and apartments in the after-part of the ship; but nowhere was there any sign of life. Here and there, within the cabins themselves, we came across odd patches of that queer fungus; but this, as my sweetheart said, could be cleansed away.

"In the end, having assured ourselves that the after portion of the vessel was empty, we picked our ways to the bows, between the ugly grey nodules of that strange growth; and here we made a further search, which told us that there was indeed none aboard but ourselves.

"This being now beyond any doubt, we returned to the stern of the ship and proceeded to make ourselves as comfortable as possible. Together, we cleared out and cleaned two of the cabins; and after that, I made examination whether there was anything eatable in the ship. This I soon found was so, and thanked God in my heart for His goodness. In addition to this, I discovered the whereabouts of the fresh-water pump, and having fixed it, I found the water drinkable, though somewhat unpleasant to the taste.

"For several days we stayed aboard the ship, without attempting to get to the shore. We were busily engaged in making the place habitable. Yet even thus early, we became aware that our lot was even less to be desired than might have been imagined; for though, as a first step, we scraped away the odd patches of growth that studded the floors and walls of the cabins and saloon, yet they returned almost to their original size within the space of twenty-four hours, which not only discouraged us, but gave us a feeling of vague unease.

"Still, we would not admit ourselves beaten, so set to work afresh, and not only scraped away the fungus, but soaked the places where it had been, with carbolic, a can-full of which I had found in the pantry. Yet, by the end of the week the growth had returned in full strength, and, in addition, it had spread to other places, as though our touching it had allowed germs from it to travel elsewhere.

"On the seventh morning, my sweetheart woke to find a small patch of it growing on her pillow, close to her face. At that, she came to me, so soon as she could get her garments upon her. I was in the galley at the time, lighting the fire for breakfast.

"'Come here, John,' she said, and led me aft. When I saw the thing upon her pillow, I shuddered, and then and there we agreed to go right out of the ship and see whether we could not fare to make ourselves more comfortable ashore.

"Hurriedly, we gathered together our few belongings, and even among these, I found that the fungus had been at work; for one of her shawls had a little lump of it growing near one edge. I threw the whole thing over the side, without saying anything to her.

"The raft was still alongside, but it was too clumsy to guide, and I lowered down a small boat that hung across the stern, and in this we made our way to the shore. Yet, as we drew near to it, I became gradually aware that here the vile fungus, which had driven us from the ship, was growing riot. In places it rose into horrible, fantastic mounds, which seemed almost to quiver, as with a quiet life, when the wind blew across them. Here and there, it took on the forms of vast fingers, and in others it just spread out flat and smooth and treacherous. Odd places, it appeared as grotesque stunted trees, seeming extraordinarily kinked and gnarled— The whole quaking vilely at times.

"At first, it seemed to us that there was no single portion of the surrounding shore which was not hidden beneath the masses of the hideous lichen; yet, in this, I found we were mistaken; for somewhat later, coasting along the shore at a little distance, we descried a smooth white patch of what appeared to be fine sand, and there we landed. It was not sand. What it was, I do not know. All that I have observed, is that upon it the fungus will not grow; while everywhere else, save where the sand-like earth wanders oddly, path-wise, amid the grey desolation of the lichen, there is nothing but that loathsome greyness.

"It is difficult to make you understand how cheered we were to find one place that was absolutely free from the growth, and here we deposited our belongings. Then we went back to the ship for such things as it seemed to us we should need. Among other matters, I managed to bring ashore with me one of the ship's sails, with which I constructed two small tents, which, though exceedingly rough-shaped, served the purpose for which they were intended. In these, we lived and stored our various necessities, and thus for a matter of some four weeks, all went smoothly and without particular unhappiness. Indeed, I may say with much of happiness—for—for we were together.

"It was on the thumb of her right hand, that the growth first showed. It was only a small circular spot, much like a little grey mole. My God! how the fear leapt to my heart when she showed me the place. We cleansed it, between us, washing it with carbolic and water. In the morning of the following day she showed her hand to me again. The grey warty thing had returned. For a little while, we looked at one another in silence. Then, still wordless, we started again to remove it. In the midst of the operation she spoke suddenly.

"'What's that on the side of your face, Dear?' Her voice was sharp with anxiety. I put my hand up to feel.

"'There! Under the hair by your ear. A little to the front a bit.' My finger rested upon the place, and then I knew.

"'Let us get your thumb done first,' I said. And she submitted, only because she was afraid to touch me until it was cleansed. I finished washing and disinfecting her thumb, and then she turned to my face. After it was finished we sat together and talked awhile of many things for there had come into our lives sudden, very terrible thoughts. We were, all at once, afraid of something worse than death. We spoke of loading the boat with provisions and water, and making our way out on to the sea; yet we were helpless, for many causes, and—and the growth had attacked us already. We decided to stay. God would do with us what was His will. We would wait.

"A month, two months, three months passed and the places grew somewhat, and there had come others. Yet we fought so strenuously with the fear that its headway was but slow, comparatively speaking.

"Occasionally, we ventured off to the ship for such stores as we needed. There, we found that the fungus grew persistently. One of the nodules on the maindeck became soon as high as my head.

"We had now given up all thought or hope of leaving the island. We had realised that it would be unallowable to go among healthy humans, with the thing from which we were suffering.

"With this determination and knowledge in our minds, we knew that we should have to husband our food and water; for we did not know, at that time, but that we should possibly live for many years.

"This reminds me that I have told you that I am an old man. Judged by the years this is not so. But—but—"

He broke off; then continued somewhat abruptly:—

"As I was saying, we knew that we should have to use care in the matter of food. But we had no idea then how little food there was left, of which to take care. It was a week later, that I made the discovery that all the other bread tanks—which I had supposed full—were empty, and that (beyond odd tins of vegetables and meat, and some other matters) we had nothing on which to depend, but the bread in the tank which I had already opened.

"After learning this, I bestirred myself to do what I could, and set to work at fishing in the lagoon; but with no success. At this I was somewhat inclined to feel desperate, until the thought came to me to try outside the lagoon, in the open sea.

"Here, at times, I caught odd fish; but, so infrequently, that they proved of but little help in keeping us from the hunger which threatened. It seemed to me that our deaths were likely to come by hunger, and not by the growth of the thing which had seized upon our bodies.

"We were in this state of mind when the fourth month wore out. Then I made a very horrible discovery. One morning, a little before midday, I came off from the ship with a portion of the biscuits which were left. In the mouth of her tent, I saw my sweetheart sitting, eating something.

"'What is it, my Dear?' I called out as I leapt ashore. Yet, on hearing my voice, she seemed confused, and, turning, slyly threw something towards the edge of the little clearing. It fell short, and a vague suspicion having arisen within me, I walked across and picked it up. It was a piece of the grey fungus.

"As I went to her, with it in my hand, she turned deadly pale; then a rose red.
"I felt strangely dazed and frightened.

"'My Dear! My Dear!' I said, and could say no more. Yet, at my words, she broke down and cried bitterly. Gradually, as she calmed, I got from her the news that she had tried it the preceding day, and—and liked it. I got her to promise on her knees not to touch it again, however great our hunger. After she had promised, she told me that the desire for it had come suddenly, and that, until the moment of desire, she had experienced nothing towards it, but the most extreme repulsion.

"Later in the day, feeling strangely restless, and much shaken with the thing which I had discovered, I made my way along one of the twisted paths—formed by the white, sand-like substance—which led among the fungoid growth. I had, once before, ventured along there; but not to any great distance. This time, being involved in perplexing thought, I went much further than hitherto.

"Suddenly I was called to myself, by a queer hoarse sound on my left. Turning quickly, I saw that there was movement among an extraordinarily shaped mass of fungus, close to my elbow. It was swaying uneasily, as though it possessed life of its own. Abruptly, as I stared, the thought came to me that the thing had a grotesque resemblance to the figure of a distorted human creature. Even as the fancy flashed into my brain, there was a slight, sickening noise of tearing, and I saw that one of the branch-like arms was detaching itself from the surrounding grey masses, and coming towards me. The head of the thing—a shapeless grey ball, inclined in my direction. I stood stupidly, and the vile arm brushed across my face. I gave out a frightened cry, and ran back a few paces. There was a sweetish taste upon my lips where the thing had touched me. I licked them, and was immediately filled with an inhuman desire. I turned and seized a mass of the fungus. Then more, and—more. I was insatiable. In the midst of devouring, the remembrance of the morning's discovery swept into my mazed brain. It was sent by God. I dashed the fragment I held to the ground. Then, utterly wretched and feeling a dreadful guiltiness, I made my way back to the little encampment.

"I think she knew, by some marvellous intuition which love must have given, so soon as she set eyes on me. Her quiet sympathy made it easier for me, and I told her of my sudden weakness; yet omitted to mention the extraordinary thing which had gone before. I desired to spare her all unnecessary terror.

"But, for myself, I had added an intolerable knowledge, to breed an incessant terror in my brain; for I doubted not but that I had seen the end of one of those men who had come to the island in the ship in the lagoon; and in that monstrous ending, I had seen our own.

"Thereafter, we kept from the abominable food, though the desire for it had entered into our blood. Yet, our drear punishment was upon us; for, day by day, with monstrous rapidity, the fungoid growth took hold of our poor bodies. Nothing we could do would check it materially, and so—and so—we who had been human, became—Well, it matters less each day. Only—only we had been man and maid!

"And day by day, the fight is more dreadful, to withstand the hunger-lust for the terrible lichen.

"A week ago we ate the last of the biscuit, and since that time I have caught three fish. I was out here fishing to-night when your schooner drifted upon me out of the mist. I hailed you. You know the rest, and may God, out of His great heart, bless you for your goodness to a—a couple of poor outcast souls."

There was the dip of an oar—another. Then the voice came again, and for the last time, sounding through the slight surrounding mist, ghostly and mournful.

"God bless you! Good-bye!"

"Good-bye," we shouted together, hoarsely, our hearts full of many emotions. I glanced about me. I became aware that the dawn was upon us.

The sun flung a stray beam across the hidden sea; pierced the mist dully, and lit up the receding boat with a gloomy fire. Indistinctly I saw something nodding between the oars. I thought of a sponge—a great, grey nodding sponge—The oars continued to ply. They were grey—as was the boat—and my eyes searched a moment vainly for the conjunction of hand and oar. My gaze flashed back to the—head. It nodded forward as the oars went backward for the stroke. Then the oars were dipped, the boat shot out of the patch of light, and the—the thing went nodding into the mist.

Grey Seas Are Dreaming of My Death

I know grey seas are dreaming of my death,
Out on grey plains where foam is lost in sleep,
Where one damp wind wails on continually,
And no life lives in the forgotten air.

And change the mood, and Ha! the fierce winds howl,
And the unforgotten hissing of the foam
Pours out of heaven's bowl;
And oh! my home
Lifts up its voice in one tremendous chaunt—
Greeting! Oh, Greeting!
Ye souls of dust in weary lands
Shall never know that greeting.

Death's purple shadow tinges all the grey;
And we of those grey waters know it well;
We know that he is come, and not in vain;
One must go hence, passing in his pain.

Ayhie! Yoi! But oh! the mood doth change,
The sea doth lift me high on living mountains;
As a mother guards her babe
So the fierce hills round me range,
And a Voice goes on and on in mighty laughter—
The joyous call of Strength which doth enguard me.
Ayhie! Yoi! all the splendour of the sea
Doth guard me from the slaughter.
Oh! men in weary lands
Lift up your hearts and hands,
And weep ye are not me,
Child of all the sea,

Out upon the foam among the fountains
And the glory
And the magic of this water world
Where in childhood I was hurled.
Weep, for I am dying in my glory;
And the foam swings round and sings,
And the grey seas chaunt; and the whitened hills are falling;
And I am dying in my glory, dying—
Dying, dying, dying.

Out of the Storm

"Hush!" said my friend the scientist, as I walked into his laboratory. I had opened my lips to speak; but stood silent for a few minutes at his request.

He was sitting at his instrument, and the thing was tapping out a message in a curiously irregular fashion—stopping a few seconds, then going on at a furious pace.

It was during a somewhat longer than usual pause that, growing slightly impatient, I ventured to address him.

"Anything important?" I asked.

"For God's sake, shut up!" he answered back in a high, strained voice.

I stared. I am used to pretty abrupt treatment from him at times when he is much engrossed in some particular experiment; but this was going a little too far, and I said so.

He was writing, and, for reply, he pushed several loosely-written sheets over to me with the one curt word, "Read!"

With a sense half of anger, half of curiosity, I picked up the first and glanced at it. After a few lines, I was gripped and held securely by a morbid interest. I was reading a message from one in the last extremity. I will give it word for word:—

"John, we are sinking! I wonder if you really understand what I feel at the present time—you sitting comfortably in your laboratory, I out here upon the waters, already one among the dead. Yes, we are doomed. There is no such thing as help in our case. We are sinking—steadily, remorselessly. God! I must keep up and be a man! I need not tell you that I am in the operator's room. All the rest are on deck—or dead in the hungry thing which is smashing the ship to pieces.

"I do not know where we are, and there is no one of whom I can ask. The last of the officers was drowned nearly an hour ago, and the vessel is now little more than a sort of breakwater for the giant seas.

"Once, about half an hour ago, I went out on to the deck. My God! the sight was terrible. It is a little after midday; but the sky is the color of mud—do you understand?—gray mud! Down from it there hang vast lappets of clouds. Not such clouds as I have ever before seen; but monstrous, mildewed-looking hulls. They

27

show solid, save where the frightful wind tears their lower edges into great feelers that swirl savagely above us, like the tentacles of some enormous Horror.

"Such a sight is difficult to describe to the living; though the Dead of the Sea know of it without words of mine. It is such a sight that none is allowed to see and live. It is a picture for the doomed and the dead; one of the sea's hell-orgies—one of the THING'S monstrous gloatings over the living—say the alive-in-death, those upon the brink. I have no right to tell of it to you; to speak of it to one of the living is to initiate innocence into one of the infernal mysteries—to talk of foul things to a child. Yet I care not! I will expose, in all its hideous nakedness, the death-side of the sea. The undoomed living shall know some of the things that death has hitherto so well guarded. Death knows not of this little instrument beneath my hands that connects me still with the quick, else would he haste to quiet me.

"Hark you, John! I have learnt undreamt of things in this little time of waiting. I know now why we are afraid of the dark. I had never imagined such secrets of the sea and the grave (which are one and the same).

"Listen! Ah, but I was forgetting you cannot hear! I can! The Sea is—Hush! the Sea is laughing, as though Hell cackled from the mouth of an ass. It is jeering. I can hear its voice echo like Satanic thunder amid the mud overhead—It is calling to me! call—I must go—The sea calls!

"Oh! God, art Thou indeed God? Canst Thou sit above and watch calmly that which I have just seen? Nay! Thou art no God! Thou art weak and puny beside this foul THING which Thou didst create in Thy lusty youth. *It* is *now* God—and I am one of its children.

"Are you there, John? Why don't you answer! Listen! I ignore God; for there is a stronger than He. My God is here, beside me, around me, and will be soon above me. You know what that means. It is merciless. *The sea is now all the God there is!* That is one of the things I have learnt.

"Listen! IT is laughing again. God is *it*, not He.

"It called, and I went out on to the decks. All was terrible. IT is in the waist—everywhere. IT has swamped the ship. Only the forecastle, bridge and poop stick up out from the bestial, reeking THING, like three islands in the midst of shrieking foam. At times gigantic billows assail the ship from both sides. They form momentary arches above the vessel—arches of dull, curved water half a hundred feet towards the hideous sky. Then they descend—roaring. Think of it! You cannot.

"There is an infection of sin in the air: it is the exhalations from the *Thing*. Those left upon the drenched islets of shattered wood and iron are doing the most horrible things. The THING is teaching them. Later, I felt the vile informing of its breath; but I have fled back here—to pray for death.

"On the forecastle, I saw a mother and her little son clinging to an iron rail. A great billow heaved up above them—descended in a falling mountain of brine.

It passed, and they were still there. The *Thing* was only toying with them; yet, all the same, it had torn the hands of the child from the rail, and the child was clinging frantically to its Mother's arm. I saw another vast hill hurl up to port and hover above them. Then the Mother stooped and bit like a foul beast at the hands of her wee son. She was afraid that his little additional weight would be more than she could hold. I heard his scream even where I stood—it drove to me upon that wild laughter. It told me again that God is not He, but IT. Then the hill thundered down upon those two. It seemed to me that the *Thing* gave a bellow as it leapt. It roared about them churning and growling; then surged away, and there was only one— the Mother. There appeared to me to be blood as well as water upon her face, especially about her mouth; but the distance was too great, and I cannot be sure. I looked away. Close to me, I saw something further—a beautiful young girl (her soul hideous with the breath of the *Thing*) struggling with her sweetheart for the shelter of the charthouse side. He threw her off; but she came back at him. I saw her hand come from her head, where still clung the wreckage of some form of headgear. She struck at him. He shouted and fell away to leeward, and she—smiled, showing her teeth. So much for that. I turned elsewhere.

"Out upon the *Thing*, I saw gleams, horrid and suggestive, below the crests of the waves. I have never seen them until this time. I saw a rough sailorman washed away from the vessel. One of the huge breakers snapped at him!—Those things were teeth. *It* has teeth. I heard them clash. I heard his yell. It was no more than a mosquito's shrilling amid all that laughter; but it was very terrible. There is worse than death.

"The ship is lurching very queerly with a sort of sickening heave—

"I fancy I have been asleep. No—I remember now. I hit my head when she rolled so strangely. My leg is doubled under me. I think it is broken; but it does not matter—

"I have been praying. I— I— What was it? I feel calmer, more resigned, now. I think I have been mad. What was it that I was saying? I cannot remember. It was something about—about—God. I— I believe I blasphemed. May He forgive me! Thou knowest, God, that I was not in my right mind. Thou knowest that I am very weak. Be with me in the coming time! I have sinned; but Thou art all merciful.

"Are you there, John? It is very near the end now. I had so much to say; but it all slips from me. What was it that I said? I take it all back. I was mad, and—and God knows. He is merciful, and I have very little pain now. I feel a bit drowsy.

"I wonder whether you are there, John. Perhaps, after all, no one has heard the things I have said. It is better so. The Living are not meant—and yet, I do not know. If you are there, John, you will—you will tell *her* how it was; but not—not—Hark! there was such a thunder of water overhead just then. I fancy two vast seas have met in mid-air across the top of the bridge and burst all over the vessel. It must be soon now—and there was such a number of things I had to say! I can hear voices in the wind. They are singing. It is like an enormous dirge—

"I think I have been dozing again. I pray God humbly that it be soon! You will not—not tell *her* anything about, about what I may have said, will you, John? I mean those things which I ought not to have said. What was it I did say? My head is growing strangely confused. I wonder whether you really do hear me. I may be talking only to that vast roar outside. Still, it is some comfort to go on, and I will not believe that you do not hear all I say. Hark again! A mountain of brine must have swept clean over the vessel. She has gone right over on to her side. . . . She is back again. It will be very soon now—

"Are you there, John? Are you there? It is coming! The Sea has come for me! It is rushing down through the companionway! It—it is like a vast jet! My God! I am dr-own-ing! I—am—dr—"

The Voice in the Dawn

To those who have cast doubt upon the reality of the great Sargasso Sea, asserting that the romantic features of this remarkable sea of weed have been greatly exaggerated, I would point out that this mass of weed lurking in the central parts of the Atlantic Ocean is a fluctuating quantity, not confined strictly to an area, but moving bodily for many hundred of miles according to storms and prevailing winds, though always within certain limits.

Thus it may be that those who have gone in search of it, and not having found it where they expected, have therefore foolishly considered it to be little more than a myth built around those odd patches and small conglomerations of the weed which they may have chanced across. And all the time, somewhere to the north or south, east or west, the great shifting bulk of the weed has lain quiet and lonesome and impassable—a cemetery of lost ships and wrack and forgotten things. And so my story will prove to all who read.

I was, at the time of this happening, a passenger in a large barque of eight hundred and ninety tons, bound down to the Barbadoes. We had very fine, light weather for the first twenty days out, with the wind variable, giving the men a great deal of work with the yards.

On the twenty-first day, however, we ran into strong weather, and at nightfall Captain Johnson shortened sail right down to the main topsail, and hove to the vessel.

I questioned him concerning his reason for doing this, as the wind was not extraordinarily heavy. He took me down into the saloon, and there, by the aid of diagrams, showed me that we were within the eastern fringe of a great cyclone which was coming up northward from the vicinity of the Line, but trending constantly westward in its progress. By heaving to the vessel as he had done, he allowed the cyclone to continue its Westward journey, leaving us free. If, however, he had continued to run the ship on, then he would have ended by running us right into the heart of the storm, where we might have been very easily dismasted or even sunk; for the fury of these storms is prodigious if one comes truly within their scope.

The captain gave me his opinion and reasons for supposing that this storm, of which we felt no more than the fringe, as it were, was a cyclone of quite unusual violence and extent. He assured me also that when daylight came on the morrow there would most probably be a certain proof of this, in the great masses of floating weed and wrack that we should be likely to encounter. These weed masses, he informed me, were torn from the Great Eddy of the Atlantic Ocean, where enormous quantities of it were gathered, extending—broken and unbroken—for many hundreds of miles. A place to be avoided by all reasonable navigators.

Now, it all turned out as the captain had foretold. The storm eased hourly through the night as the cyclone drew off into the westward sea; so that ere the dawn had come we lay upon water somewhat broken by the swell of the departed storm, yet almost lacking even a light breath of wind.

At midnight I went below for sleep; but was again on deck in a few hours, being restless. I found Captain Johnson there walking with the mate, and after greeting him I went over to the lee rail to watch the coming of the dawn which even then made some lightness in the eastward sky. It came with no more than moderate quickness, for we had not yet come into the tropics, and I watched very earnestly because the dawn-light has always held for me a strange attraction.

There grew first in the east a pale shimmering of light, very solemn, coming so quietly into the sky, it might have been a ghost-light spying secretly upon the sleeping world. And then, even as I took account of this thing, there went a spreading of gentle rose hues to the northward, and upon this a dull orange light in the mid-sky. Presently there was a great loom of greenness, most wondrous, in the upper sky, and from this green and aerial splendour of utter quietness there dropped curtains of lemon that enticed the sight to peer through their mystery into the lost distance, so that my thoughts were all very far from this world.

And the lights grew and strengthened as if they had a great pulse, and the wonder of the dawn-lights beat steadily upon the eye in an ever-continuing brightness, until all the eastward sky was full of a pale and translucent lemon, flaked athwart with clouds of transparent greyness and gentle silver. And in the end there came a little light upon the sea, very solemn and dreary, making all that vast ocean but a greater mystery.

And, surely, as I looked outward upon the sea, there was something that broke the faint looming of light upon the waters, but what it was I could not at first see. Out of the mists of the lost horizon there climbed, presently, a little golden glory, so that I knew the sun had near come out of the dark. And the golden light made a halo in that part of the far world, sending a ray across the mystery of the dark waters. Then I saw somewhat more plainly the thing that had lain upon the sea between me and the far lights of the dawn. It was a great, low-seeming island in the midst of the loneliness of the ocean. Yet, as I knew well from the charts, there was no proper island in these parts; and I conceived, therefore, that this thing must be an island of the weed, of which the captain had spoken the previous day.

"Captain Johnson," I called to him softly, because there seemed so great a quietness beyond the ship—"Captain Johnson. Bring the glasses."

And presently we were spying across the vanishing dark at this floating land of the storm.

Now, as we looked earnestly across all that quiet greyness of the sea at the dim-seen island, I became doubly filled with the mystery and utter hush of the dawn-time, and of the lights and of the lesson of the morning which is told silently at each dawn over the world. I seemed to hear newly and with great plainness each sound and vague noise that was about me; so that the gentle creaking of the masts and gear was as a harsh calling across that quiet, while the sea made hollow and dank sounds against the wet sides of the ship, and the noise of one walking on the fo'cas'le was a thing that made all the vessel seem to resound emptily.

But when I listened to the far-off parts of the sea, even whilst I looked with solemn feelings at that ghostly island half seen in the dawn, it was as if no sound had ever been out there except it might be some damp wind that wandered forlorn in the distance of the ocean.

And by all this you will understand something of the mood that had come upon me; and, indeed, I think this mood was not mine alone; for the captain was very quiet, and said little, looking constantly towards the grey gloom of the island in the dawn.

And then, as the sun cast the first beam of light clear over the mists of the hid horizon there came a little thin noise out of all the dawn of the world. It was as if I heard a small voice far off in the miles, coming to me out of an infinite distance:

"Son of Man!"

"Son of Man!"

"Son of Man!"

I heard it very faint and lost—seeming in all that mystery of the eastward sea, drifting out of the quiet of the dawn. Towards the east there was only emptiness and greyness, and the quiver of the dawn-shine, and the first rays of the morning upon the silver-grey shimmer of the sea. Only these things, and the low-lying stretch of the weed island, maybe half a mile to the eastward—a desolate shadow, quiet upon the water.

I set my hand to my ear and listened, looking at the captain; he likewise listening, having looked first well through his glasses. But now he stared at me, half questioning with his eyes.

The sun stood up over the edge of the grey, glimmering ocean like a roadway of flame, broken midway by the dull stretch of the weed-island. And in that moment the sound came again:

"Son of Man!"

"Son of Man!"

"Son of Man!" Out of morning light that made glows in the eastward sea. Far and faint and lonesome was the voice, and so thin and ethereal it might have been a ghost calling vaguely out of the scattering greynesses—the shadow of a voice amid the fleeting shadows.

I stared round at all the sea, and, surely, on every side it was studded with islets of weed, clearly seen upon the silver of the morning sea through the quiet miles into the horizons. As I looked this way and that way with something of astonishment, there came again to my hearing a faint sound, as if I heard a thin, attenuated piping in the east, coming very incredible and far-off sounding and unreal over the hush of the water. Shrill and dree and yet vague it was; and presently—heard it no more.

The captain and I looked often at one another during this time; and again we searched the width of the eastward sea, and the desolateness of the long, low island of the weed; but there was nowhere anything that might lead us to an understanding of this thing that bewildered us.

The mate also had stood near to us listening, and had heard the strange thin, faint calling and piping; but he, likewise, had no knowledge or understanding by which we might judge the thing.

While we were drinking our morning coffee Captain Johnson and I discoursed upon this mysterious happening, and could in nowise come any the nearer to an understanding, unless it was some lone derelict held in the weed of the great island that lay Eeastward of us. This was, in truth, a proper enough explanation, if only we might set proof upon it; and to this end the captain ordered one of the boats to be lowered, and a large crew to man the boat, and each man to be armed with a musket and a cutlass. Moreover, he sent down into the boat two axes and three double-edged whale-pikes or lances, with six feet blades, very keen and as broad as my palm.

To me he dealt a brace of pistols, and likewise a brace to himself, and the two of us had our knives. And by all of these things you can see, as I have told, that he had known previous adventures with the weed, and that he had knowledge of dangers that were peculiar thereto.

We put out presently in the clear morning light towards the great island of the weed that lay to the eastward. And this island was, maybe, nearly two miles long, and, as we found, something more than half of a mile broadwise, or, as the sailors named it, "in the beam." We came to it pretty quickly, and Captain Johnson bid the men back-water when we were some twenty fathoms off from the mid-most part, which was opposite to the ship. Here we lay awhile, and looked through our glasses at the weed, searching it all ways, but saw nowhere any sign of derelict craft, nor aught that spoke of human life.

Yet of the life of sea animals there was no end; for all the weed, upon the outer edges, seemed a-crawl with various matters; though at first we had not been able to perceive these, because of the similarity in colour with the yellowness of the weed, which was very yellow in the light outward fronds spreading out upon the waters. Inward of the mass of the island I saw that there went a dark and greener shading of the yellow, and there I discovered that this green darkness was the colour of the great weed stems that made up the bulk of the island, like so many great cables and serpents of a yellow green, very dank and gloomy, wandering amid their twistings and turnings and vast entanglements that made so huge and dreary a labyrinth.

After we had made a pretty good survey of that part, we turned to the northward, and Captain Johnson bid the men pull slowly along the coast of that great island of weed. In this wise we went a good mile, until we came to the end, where we set the boat to the eastward, so as to come round to the other side. And all the while as we went forward the captain and I made constant observations of the island and of the sea about it, using our glasses to the purpose.

This way I saw a thousand matters to give me cause for interest and wonder; for the weed all about the borders of the island had living creatures a-move within amid the fronds, and the sea showed frequently in this place and the glitter of strange fish, very plentiful and various.

Now, I took a particular heed to note the many creatures that lived amid the weed; for I was always interested in the weed-sea, from the many accounts which I had heard concerning it, both from Captain Johnson and from other men of the sea that had been ship-masters in my voyages. And surely these islands and gatherings together of the weed had been rent from that great weed-sea which Captain Johnson spoke of always as the Great Eddy. As I have said, I took very good heed to note what manner of creatures lived in the weed, and in this way I perceived presently that there were more crabs than aught else, so far as the power of my glasses could show me; for there were crabs in every place, and all of them yellow in the top parts as the weed. And some were as small as my thumb top, and many were less, I suppose, had I been closer to discover them; but others crawling amid the weed fronds must have spread a great foot across the back, and were all yellow, so that, save when they moved, they might lie hidden entirely by matching the shades of the weed in which they lived.

We had pulled round the northward end of the island, and found it, as I have told, something more than half a mile wide, or, maybe, three-quarters for all that we could be sure. And here let me tell concerning the height of the island above the sea, which we judged now, being very low down in the boats and looking upward at the weed, to be about twenty or twenty-five feet good above the ocean, the greatest height being in the middle parts, inland as it were of the island, looking as if it had been a low, thick wood with the greater trees in the centre, and all lost in jungle of strange, creeping plants. And this is the best likeness I can give of that island to any landward thing.

Having pulled round the north end of the island, we made southward all along the western coast of the weed, being minded to go entirely about it, and chance discovering the cause and the place of that strange calling in the dawn. And, indeed, it was a dree place to by by; for constantly we would open out some dark, cavern-place of dark green and gloom that went inward of the weed, amid those great stems. And often there seemed to be things moving therein, and always there was a quietness in all that desolate waste save when some small wind played strangely across it, making the yellow fronds of the weed stir a little in this place and that with little sighings of sound, as if doleful beings lurked in all that mass of quiet darkness. And when the little wind had gone away over the sea there came a double silence by the contrast, so that I was glad that the boat was kept well off from the weed.

In this way, with growing caution and quietness because of the dreeness of that dank and lonesome island, which had begun now to affect our spirits somewhat, we went downward to the south along that coast of the westward side of the island. And as we went a greater and a greater hush and caution came upon us, so that the men scarcely dipped their oars with any sound, but pulled daintily, each one staring very keen and tensely into the shadows within that mighty mass of weed.

It chanced that one of the men ceased suddenly to pull upon his oar, looking very eagerly and fearfully at something that he perceived amid the gloom that lurked among the monstrous stems of the weed. And at that, every man ceased likewise to work upon his oar, and peered fearfully into the dark places of the weed, being assured that the man saw something very dreadful.

The captain made no attempt to chide the men, but stared himself, as even as I did, to see what manner of thing it was that the man saw. And presently each one discovered the thing for himself. But at the first it seemed only as if we peered at a great and ugly bunching of the weed-stems, far inward from the edge of the island; but in a little while the thing grew plainer to the eye, and we saw that it was some kind of a devil-fish or octopus lying among the weed, very quiet, and shaded with the same gloom and colour as the weed which was its home. The thing was enormous, as my eyes told me, seeming to spread all ways among the weed.

Captain Johnson got up out of the stern of the boat, and called in a low voice to the men to dip their oars very gently, so as to have way upon the boat again. And this they did with great care, while the captain steered the boat outward awhile from the island, and we became presently happier in our minds as we drew afar off from so dreadful and horrible a brute.

In this way we pulled nearly a good mile southward, keeping well from the shore of the island, and soon we saw the weed come outward in something of a ness or cape from the main body. We came round this with a fair offing, and found the shore of the island ran inward in a deep bay, and in the weed in the bight of the bay we saw something that made us suppose we had discovered the place whence came that unnatural calling in the dawn; for there was the hull of a vessel, all mastless, in among the weed near the edge, yet not very plain to be seen, because it was so hidden and smothered by the weed.

We were all vastly excited at this, and the captain bid the men give way with heartiness, and, indeed, we lost suddenly the fear of lurking monsters which had before made us so quiet and cautious. And because the men set their strength into the oars, we came very soon to the bight of the bay where lay the derelict ship and found that she was no more than, maybe, a dozen yards or so inward of the weed, which was pretty low and flat in that place around her; but beyond the ship the weed was piled up very dark and gloomy for twenty feet high and more, and growing all over her.

We paused now, wondering how we should best come up to the ship. And all the time, while the captain considered, I spied through my glasses at the wreck, having little hope that we should find any aboard of her; for it was plain to me now how old she was, and all crumbled with time and weather, and the weed girting her in all parts, seeming to grow through the wood of her sides, though this was very incredible. Yet so we found it to be when we came near her. Afterwards I searched the weed all near her, to see whether there was any monster fish about, Captain Johnson doing the same, but we found nothing. And the captain then gave orders to put the boat in among the weed, and we cut our way through the low weed to the side of the ship.

Now, as we made way through the weed, it amazed us to see how much life had been hidden there, very still, for all the weed now about the boat was a-swarm with small crabs, running along the fronds and smaller stems, while the water that showed between the growths of the weed was full of living things—great shrimps that seemed bigger than prawns, darting a thousand ways at once, and coloured fish that passed very swiftly. From the weed itself numberless insects of a peculiar kind jumped like a flea, only that they were a hundred times greater. And twice and thrice, as we put the boat through the weed, we disturbed great crabs that were lain there sullen or waiting for their prey. One of them, as big across the back as a dish-cover, which caught at the oar of one of the men with its pincers and nipped the thin wood of the blade through quick and cleanly. Afterwards it went away, rough and active, shaking the weed in its passage, which will show you the vigour and strength that was in the creature.

In a few minutes we had cut a way into the ship, using the axes and the men's knives and the oars; but the cutlasses the captain would not have used on the wood because they were weapons and to be kept as such.

When we came close in upon the ship we found that the weed grew completely through her side, as though the weed had rooted in the wood of her. And we were all somewhat astonished at this thing, and many another which we discovered, for when we came to clamber up her side, we found the wood had gone soft and rotted to a sponginess, so that we could kick our shod toes into the wood, and thereby make each an immediate ladder upwards.

When we came to the top level of the hulk, and could look aboard, there was nothing to her but the shell of her sides and of her bows and stern; for all the decks were gone, and the beams that had held the decks were part missing, and few of those which remained were complete. The bottom of the ship was rotted nigh out of her so that the weed came upward in plenty that way with the water showing down below very gloomy and dark. And the weed grew through the sides of the vessel, or over the rails, just as it had seemed to suit the convenience of the strange vegetable, if I may call it so.

It was very dismal looking downward into that desert hull which had been upheld from its sinking by the grip of the weed through a hundred or, maybe, two hundred years. When I asked the captain about this, he set her age to be something more than four hundred years, speaking learnedly concerning the rotted stern and bow and the way and set of the frame-timbers; so that it was plain to me that he had considerable knowledge on such matters.

Presently, because there was nothing more to be done, we came down again to the boat, kicking our toes into the soft hull of the old ship for our footholds. And before we left her I broke away a lump of one of her smaller timbers for a memento of the adventure.

And after that we backed out from the weed, glad to be free of it now that the lust of adventure had somewhat died out of us, and the memory of what lurked therein still strong upon us. So we made the complete round of that island, which was more than seven good miles in all to circumnavigate. And afterwards we pulled to our own ship with very good appetites for our breakfast, as you may think.

All that day it remained calm, and often I turned my glass upon the weed islets that studded the sea in other parts; but none was very great or high, though I reminded myself that they would have appeared higher had we approached them in a boat. And this we found to be true; for we used that afternoon to go from one small islet to another, in the boat; and crabs and fish and small living things we found in plenty but never any sign of a wreck or of human life.

We returned to our ship in the evening, and had much talk upon the strangeness of that calling that had come to us in the dawn; but no reasonable explanation could we make. And presently I went to my bed, being weary by the lack of rest on the night that had passed.

I was wakened in the early morn by the captain shaking me, and when I had come properly to my senses he told me to hasten on deck, that it was still calm and they had heard the voice again in the dawn that was just breaking.

On hearing this I made speed to go with Captain Johnson on deck, and here, upon the poop, I found the second mate with his glass, staring eastward across the sea towards the weed-island which was barely seen save as a vague shadow, low upon the water.

The second mate held up his hand to us and whispered "Hist!" and we all fell to listening; but there came no sound for a time, and meanwhile I was greatly aware of the very solemn beauty of the dawn; for the eastward sky seemed lost in waters of quiet emerald, from a strange and apparent green to a translucence of shimmering green that surely stretched to the very borders of the Eternal, in palest lights that carried the consciousness through ethereal deeps of space until the soul went lost through the glimmering dawn, greeting unknown spirits.

And this is but a clumsy wording of the way that the holiness of that dim light and wonder hushed my very being with a silent happiness. Then, even as I came to this condition of mind, out of the eastward sea and of all that quiet of the dawn, there came again that far attenuated voice:

"Son of Man!"

"Son of Man!"

"Son of Man!" Coming faint and thin, and incredible out of the utter stillness of the wonder and silent glamour of the east. The green of the lower sky faded even as we listened, breathless, and upward there stole the stain of purple lights that blended into a growing bloom of fire-clouds in the middle and lower sky, and so to warmer lights and then to the silver-grey paling of the early morning. And still we waited.

Presently, eastward, there came a golden warmth upward into the pearl quiet of the lower sky, and the edge of the sun rose up calm and assured out of the mists, casting a roadway of light over the sea. And in that moment the far, lost voice came again:

"Son of Man!"

"Son of Man!"

"Son of Man!" Drifting to us strangely over the hushed sea, seeming to come out of immense and infinite distances—a voice thin and lonesome, as might be thought to be the call of a spirit crying in the morning. As we looked at one another, questioning wordless things, there came a vague, impossible piping far away and away over the sea, to be presently lost again in the quietness. And we were all agog to know what it might portend.

After breakfast that day Captain Johnson ordered the boat to be lowered, and put a large crew into her, all armed as before. Then we put off to the weed-island; but before we left the ship the Captain had dismounted the smaller ship's bell that was upon the poop, and this we had with us in the boat, also his speaking trumpet.

All that morning we spent circumnavigating the great weed-island again, and at each hundred fathoms I beat upon the bell, and the Captain sent his voice inland, speaking through the trumpet, and asking whether there were any derelict ship with lost humans hid in the heart of the weed. Yet whether his voice carried through the weed or was smothered we could not know, but only of this could we be certain, that there came never an answer out of all that desolation of the weed, neither to the bell nor to our callings.

In this way we went full round about that island, and naught came of it, save once when we were very near inshore, I saw a truly monstrous crab, double as big as any I had ever seen, far in among the great weed stems; and the crab was dark hued as though to match the darker colour of that inward weed; and by this I judged that it lived far inward amid the gloom of the centre parts of that strange island.

And truly, as I thought, what could we do, even though we found a ship far inward of the weed; for how could any man face a monstrous thing like that, and surely there would be multitudes of such brutes in the middle part of the island, taking no count of the devil-fish which also inhabited the weed of that desolate and lonesome island.

In the end we came back to our own ship, having passed again that doleful hulk within the edge of the weed-island; and I remember how I thought of the long centuries that had gone since that old craft was lost.

When we came back to the ship Captain Johnson went up the mainmast, and I with him; and from the crosstrees we made a further examination, through the glasses, of the inward parts of the great island; but the weed went everywhere in a riot of ugly yellow, and in this place and that the colour changed to a dull, greenish hue where the weed was hidden from the light.

And presently we ceased to spy upon the island; for the over-arching and entanglement of those monstrous fronds would have hidden with ease a great fleet of ships, if the same had been lacking their masts.

Now, whether there was a ship hidden in all that desolation of weed, who shall say? And if there had been a ship hidden, and caught far inward of that weed and all overgrown with it, how was it likely that any living being was aboard of her? For you must bear in mind the human needs of any that would be so held; and further you must remember the monstrous brutes that roamed in that great bulk of the weed.

And, again if there had been a ship inward of that weed and a living human still within her, why should he make that strange crying in the dawn, over the sea, and yet give no answer to our callings? On all this I have pondered a thousand times and oft, but have no ready answer to myself, save that there might have been some poor mad soul, yet holding off desperately from death through the lonesome years, in a lost ship hidden within that weed.

This is the only explanation that I have found to come anywhere near the need of my reasoning. And, truly, it would be strange if such an one could be anything but a lonesome madman, greeting each dawn with wild and meaningless words and singings that might seem to be of meaning to a poor demented brain.

But whether this was so or whether there was some matter in the adventure beyond our indifferent knowledge, I cannot altogether decide. I can only tell you that, in the dawn of the third day of that calm, we heard again that far and strange calling, coming to us through the hush and the greyness, out of the eastward sea where the weed-island lay. Very thin and lonesome was the cry:

"Son of Man!"

"Son of Man!"

"Son of Man!" coming to us in a long drawn out attenuation of sound, as if out of an immense distance. The dawn was ruddy, showing plain signs of wind; yet before the wind came down upon us the upward edge of the sun rose above the black-gloomed horizon, very sombre seeming and bearded with the wind-haze. The sea had gone leaden, and the sun threw a roadway of crimson light upon us, very grand yet somewhat dreary, and in that moment we heard the far, faint voice again for the last time:

"Son of Man!"

"Son of Man!"

"Son of Man!" And afterwards that vague, attenuated piping that had grown so weak-sounding we scarcely knew whether we heard it or not; for the coming of the wind made a little, almost unperceived, noise over the sea. And presently the wind darkened the northward sea, and our sails filled as the yards were swung by the sailors. And we sailed beyond the long desolation of the great weed-island, and continued our voyage, leaving the mystery of the voice to the hush of the sea and the companionship of its constant mystery.

The Haunted *Jarvee*

"Seen anything of Carnacki lately?" I asked Arkright when we met in the City.

"No," he replied. "He's probably off on one of his jaunts. We'll be having a card one of these days inviting us to No. 472, Cheyne Walk, and then we'll hear all about it. Queer chap that."

He nodded, and went on his way. It was some months now since we four—Jessop, Arkright, Taylor and myself—had received the usual summons to drop in at No. 472 and hear Carnacki's story of his latest case. What talks they were! Stories of all kinds and true in every word, yet full of weird and extraordinary incidents that held one silent and awed until he had finished.

Strangely enough, the following morning brought me a curtly worded card telling me to be at No. 472 at seven o'clock prompt. I was the first to arrive, Jessop and Taylor soon followed, and just before dinner was announced Arkright came in.

Dinner over, Carnacki, as usual, passed round his smokes, snuggled himself down luxuriously in his favourite arm-chair and went straight to the story we knew he had invited us to hear.

"I've been on a trip in one of the real old-time sailing ships," he said without any preliminary remarks. "The *Jarvee*, owned by my old friend, Captain Thompson. I went on the voyage primarily for my health, but I picked on the old *Jarvee* because Captain Thompson had often told me there was something queer about her. I used to ask him up here whenever he came ashore, and try to get him to tell me more about it, you know; but the funny thing was he never could tell me anything definite concerning her queerness. He seemed always to *know*, but when it came to putting his knowledge into words it was as if he found that the reality melted out of it. He would end up usually by saying that you saw things, and then he would wave his hands vaguely; but further than that he never seemed able to pass on the knowledge of something strange which he had noticed about the ship, except odd outside details.

"'Can't keep men in her, no-how,' he often told me. 'They get frightened, and they see things and they feel things. An' I've lost a power o' men out of her. Fallen from aloft, you know. She's getting a bad name.' And then he'd shake his head very solemn.

41

"Old Thompson was a brick in every way. When I got aboard I found that he had given me the use of a whole empty cabin opening off my own as my laboratory and workshop. He gave the carpenter orders to fit up the empty cabin with shelves and other conveniences according to my directions, and in a couple of days I had all the apparatus, both mechanical and electric, with which I had conducted my other ghost-hunts, neatly and safely stowed away; for I took a great deal of gear with me, as I intended to interest myself by examining thoroughly into the mystery about which the captain was at once so positive and so vague.

"During the first fortnight out I followed my usual methods of making a thorough and exhaustive search. This I did with the most scrupulous care, but found nothing abnormal of any kind in the whole vessel. She was an old wooden ship, and I took care to sound and measure every casement and bulkhead; to examine every exit from the holds, and to seal all the hatches. These, and many other precautions I took; but at the end of the fortnight I had neither seen anything nor found anything.

"The old barque was just, to all seeming, a healthy, average old-timer, jogging along comfortably from one port to another. And save for an indefinable sense of what I could now describe as 'abnormal peace' about the ship I could find nothing to justify the old captain's solemn and frequent assurances that I would see soon enough for myself. This he would say often as we walked the poop together; afterwards stopping to take a long, expectant, half-fearful look at the immensity of the sea around.

"Then on the eighteenth day something truly happened. I had been pacing the poop as usual with old Thompson, when suddenly he stopped and looked up at the mizzen royal which had just begun to flap against the mast. He glanced at the wind-vane near him; then ruffled his hat back and stared at the sea.

"'Wind's droppin', mister. There'll be trouble to-night,' he said. 'D'you see yon?' And he pointed away to windward.

"'What?' I asked, staring with a curious little thrill that was due to more than curiosity. 'Where?'

"'Right off the beam,' he said. 'Comin' from under the sun.'

"'I don't see anything,' I explained, after a long stare at the wide-spreading silence of the sea, that was already glassing into a dead calm surface now that the wind had died.

"'Yon shadow fixin',' said the old man, reaching for his glasses.

"He focussed them and took a long look, then passed them across to me and pointed with his finger. 'Just under the sun,' he repeated. 'Comin' towards us at the rate o' knots.' He was curiously calm and matter-of-fact; and yet I felt that a certain excitement had him in the throat, so that I took the glasses eagerly and stared according to his directions.

"After a minute I saw it—a vague shadow upon the still surface of the sea that seemed to move towards us as I stared. For a moment I gazed fascinated, yet ready every moment to swear that I saw nothing, and in the same instant to be assured that there was truly *something* out there upon the water, apparently coming towards the ship.

"'It's only a shadow, captain,' I said at length.

"'Just so, mister,' he replied simply. 'Have a look over the stern to the norrard.' He spoke in the quietest way, as a man speaks who is sure of all his facts and who is facing an experience he has faced before, yet who salts his natural matter-of-factness with a deep and constant excitement.

"At the captain's hint I turned about and directed the glasses to the northward. For a while I searched, sweeping my aided vision to and fro over the greying arc of the sea.

"Then I saw the thing plain in the field of the glass—a vague something, a shadow upon the water and the shadow seemed to be moving towards the ship.

"'That's queer,' I muttered, with a funny little stirring at the back of my throat.

"'Now to the west'ard, mister,' said the captain, still speaking in his peculiar level way.

"I looked to the westward, and in a minute I picked up the thing—a third shadow that seemed to move across the sea as I watched it.

"'My God, captain,' I exclaimed, 'what does it mean?'

"'That's just what I want to know, mister,' said the captain. 'I've seen 'em before and thought sometimes I must be going mad. Sometimes they're plain an' sometimes they're scarce to be seen, an' sometimes they're like livin' things, an' sometimes they're like nought at all but silly fancies. D'you wonder I couldn't name 'em proper to you?'

"I did not answer; for I was staring now expectantly towards the south along the length of the barque. Afar off on the horizon my glasses picked up something dark and vague upon the surface of the sea, a shadow it seemed which grew plainer.

"'My God!' I muttered again. 'This is real. This—' I turned again to the eastward.

"'Comin' in from the four points, ain't they,' said Captain Thompson and he blew his whistle.

"'Take them three r'yals off her,' he told the mate, 'an' tell one of the boys to shove lanterns up on the sherpoles. Get the men down smart before dark,' he concluded as the mate moved off to see the orders carried out.

"'I'm sendin' no men aloft to-night,' he said to me. 'I've lost enough that way.'

"'They may be only shadows, captain, after all,' I said, still looking earnestly at that far-off grey vagueness on the eastward sea. 'Bit of mist or cloud floating low.' Yet though I said this I had no belief that it was so. And as for old Captain Thompson, he never took the trouble to answer, but reached for his glasses which I passed to him.

"'Gettin' thin an' disappearin' as they come near,' he said presently. 'I know; I've seen 'em do that oft an' plenty before. They'll be close round the ship soon; but you nor me won't see them, nor no one else; but they'll be there. I wish 'twas mornin'. I do that!'

"He had handed the glasses back to me and I had been staring at each of the oncoming shadows in turn. It was as Captain Thompson had said. As they drew nearer they seemed to spread and thin out and presently to become dissipated into the grey of the gloaming so that I could easily have imagined that I watched merely four little portions of grey cloud, expanding naturally into impalpableness and invisibility.

"'Wish I'd took them t'gallants off her while I was about it,' remarked the old man presently. 'Can't think to send no one off the decks to-night, not unless there's real need.' He slipped away from me and peered at the aneroid in the skylight. 'Glass steady, anyhow,' he muttered as he came away, seeming more satisfied.

"By this time the men had all returned to the decks and the night was down upon us, so that I could watch the queer, dissolving shadows which approached the ship.

"Yet as I walked the poop with old Captain Thompson, you can imagine how I grew to feel. Often I found myself looking over my shoulder with quick, jerky glances; for it seemed to me that in the curtains of gloom that hung just beyond the rails there must be a vague, incredible thing looking inboard.

"I questioned the captain in a thousand ways; but could get little out of him beyond what I knew. It was as if he had no power to convey to another the knowledge which he possessed, and I could ask no one else; for every other man in the ship was newly signed on, including the mates, which was in itself a significant fact.

"'You'll see for yourself, mister,' was the refrain with which the captain parried my questions, so that it began to seem as if he almost *feared* to put anything he knew into words. Yet once, when I had jerked round with a nervous feeling that something was at my back he said calmly enough: 'Naught to fear, mister, whilst you're in the light an' on the decks.' His attitude was extraordinary in the way in which he *accepted* the situation. He appeared to have no personal fear.

"The night passed quietly until about eleven o'clock, when suddenly and without one atom of warning a furious squall burst on the vessel. There was something monstrous and abnormal in the wind; it was as if some power were using the elements to an infernal purpose. Yet the captain met the situation calmly. The helm was put down, and the sails shaken while the three t'gallants were lowered. Then the three upper topsails. Yet still the breeze roared over us, almost drowning the thunder which the sails were making up in the night.

"'Split 'em to ribbons!' the captain yelled in my ear above the noise of the wind. 'Can't help it. I ain't sendin' no men aloft to-night unless she seems like to shake the sticks out of her. That's what bothers me.'

"For nearly an hour after that, until eight bells went at midnight, the wind showed no signs of easing, but breezed up harder than ever. And all the while the skipper and I walked the poop, he ever and again peering up anxiously through the darkness at the banging and thrashing sails.

"For my part I could do nothing except stare round and round at the extraordinarily dark night in which the ship seemed to be embedded solidly. The very feel and sound of the wind gave me a sort of constant horror; for there seemed to be an unnaturalness rampant in the atmosphere. But how much this was the effect of my over-strung nerves and excited imagination, I cannot say. Certainly, in all my experience, I had never come across anything just like what I felt and endured through that peculiar squall.

"At eight bells, when the other watch came on deck, the captain was forced to send all hands aloft to make the canvas fast, as he had begun to fear that he would actually lose his masts if he delayed longer. This was done, and the barque snugged right down.

"Yet, though the work was done successfully, the captain's fears were justified in a sufficiently horrible way, for as the men were beginning to make their way in off the yards there was a loud crying and shouting aloft, and immediately afterwards a crash down on the main deck, followed instantly by a second crash.

"'My God! Two of 'em!' shouted the skipper, as he snatched a lamp from the forrard binnacle. Then down on to the main deck. It was as he had said. Two of the men had fallen, or—as the thought came to me—been thrown from aloft, and were lying silent on the deck. Above us in the darkness I heard a few vague shouts followed by a curious quiet, save for the constant blast of the wind, whose whistling and howling in the rigging seemed but to accentuate the complete and frightened silence of the men aloft. Then I was aware that the men were coming down swiftly, and presently one after the other came with a quick leap out of the rigging and stood about the two fallen men, with odd exclamations and questions, which always merged off instantly into new silence.

"And all the time I was conscious of a most extraordinary sense of oppression and frightened distress and fearful expectation; for it seemed to me, standing there near the dead in that unnatural wind, that a power of evil filled all the night about the ship, and that some fresh horror was imminent.

"The following morning there was a solemn little service, very rough and crude, but undertaken with a nice reverence, and the two men who had fallen were tilted off from a hatch-cover and plunged suddenly out of sight. As I watched them vanish in the deep blue of the water an idea came to me, and I spent part of the afternoon talking it over with the captain, after which I passed the rest of the time until sunset was upon us in arranging and fitting up a part of my electrical apparatus. Then I went on deck and had a good look round. The evening was beautifully calm and ideal for the experiment which I had in mind; for the wind had died away with a peculiar suddenness after the death of the two men, and all that day the sea had been like glass.

"To a certain extent I believed that I comprehended the primary cause of the vague, but peculiar manifestations which I had witnessed the previous evening, and which Captain Thompson believed implicitly to be intimately connected with the death of the two sailormen.

45

"I believed the origin of the happenings to lie in a strange but perfectly understandable cause, *i.e.*, in that phenomenon known technically as 'attractive vibrations.' Harzam, in his monograph on 'Induced Hauntings,' points out that such are invariably produced by 'induced vibrations,' that is, by temporary vibrations set up by some outside cause.

"This is somewhat abstruse to follow out in a story of this kind; but it was on a long consideration of these points that I had resolved to make experiments, to see whether I could not produce a counter or 'repellent' vibration, a thing which Harzam had succeeded in producing on three occasions, and in which I have had a partial success once; failing only because of the imperfectness of the apparatus I had aboard.

"As I have said, I can scarcely follow the reasoning further in a brief record such as this; neither do I think it would be of interest to you who are interested only in the startling and weird side of my investigations. Yet I have told you sufficient to show you the germ of my reasonings, and to enable you to follow intelligently my hopes and expectations in sending out what I hoped would prove 'repellent' vibrations.

"Therefore it was that, when the sun had descended to within ten degrees of the visible horizon, the captain and I began to watch for the appearance of the shadows. Presently, under the sun, I discovered the same peculiar appearance of a moving greyness which I had seen on the preceding night, and almost immediately Captain Thompson told me that he saw the same to the south.

"To the north and east we perceived the same extraordinary thing, and I at once set my electric apparatus at work, sending out the strange repelling force to the dim, far shadows of mystery which moved steadily out of the distance towards the vessel.

"Earlier in the evening the captain had snugged the barque right down to her topsails; for, as he said, until the calm went he would risk nothing. According to him, it was always during calm weather that the extraordinary manifestations occurred. In this case he was certainly justified; for a most tremendous squall struck the ship in the middle watch, taking the fore upper topsail right out of the ropes.

"At the time when it came I was lying down on a locker in the saloon; but I ran up on to the poop as the vessel canted under the enormous force of the wind. Here I found the air pressure tremendous and the noise of the squall stunning. And over it all and through it all, I was conscious of something abnormal and threatening that set my nerves uncomfortably acute. The thing was not natural.

"Yet, despite the carrying away of the topsail, not a man was sent aloft.

"'Let 'em all go!' said old Captain Thompson. 'I'd have shortened her down to the bare sticks if I'd done all I wanted!'

"About two a.m. the squall passed with astonishing suddenness, and the night showed clear above the vessel. From then onward I paced the poop with the skipper, often pausing at the break to look along the lighted main deck. It was on one of these occasions that I saw something peculiar. It was like a vague flitting of an impossible shadow between me and the whiteness of the well-scrubbed decks. Yet, even as I stared, the thing was gone and I could not say with surety that I had seen anything.

"'Pretty plain to see, mister,' said the captain's voice at my elbow. 'I've only seen that once before an' we lost half of the hands that trip. We'd better be at 'ome, I'm thinkin'. It'll end in scrappin' her, sure.'

"The old man's calmness bewildered me almost as much as the confirmation his remark gave that I had really seen something abnormal floating between me and the deck eight feet below us.

"'Good lord, Captain Thompson,' I exclaimed, 'this is simply infernal!'

"'Just that,' he agreed. 'I said, mister, you'd see if you'd wait. And this ain't the half. You wait till you sees 'em looking like little black clouds all over the sea round the ship, and movin' steady with the ship. All the same, I ain't seen 'em aboard but the once. Guess we're in for it.'

"'How do you mean?' I asked. But though I questioned him in every way I could get nothing satisfactory out of him.

"'You'll see, mister. You wait an' see. She's a queer un.' And that was about the extent of his further efforts and methods of enlightening me.

"From then on through the rest of the watch I leaned over the break of the poop, staring down at the main-deck, and odd whiles taking quick glances to the rear. The skipper had resumed his steady pacing of the poop; but now and again he would come to a pause beside me and ask calmly enough whether I had seen any more of 'them there.'

"Several times I saw the vagueness of something drifting in the lights of the lanterns, and a sort of wavering in the air in this place and that, as if it might be an attenuated something having movement, that was half-seen for a moment, and then gone before my brain could record anything definite.

"Towards the end of the watch, however, both the captain and I saw something very extraordinary. He had just come beside me and was leaning over the rail across the break. 'Another of 'em there,' he remarked in his calm way, giving me a gentle nudge and nodding his head towards the port side of the main-deck, a yard or two to our left.

"In the place he had indicated there was a faint, dull shadowy spot seeming suspended about a foot above the deck. This grew more visible and there was movement in it and a constant, oily-seeming whirling from the centre outwards. The thing expanded to several feet across, with the lighted planks of the deck showing vaguely through. The movement from the centre outwards was now becoming very distinct, till the whole strange shape blackened and grew more dense, so that the deck below was hidden.

"Then as I stared with the most intense interest there went a thinning movement over the thing, and almost directly it had dissolved, so that there was nothing more to be seen than a vague rounded shape of shadow, hovering and convoluting dimly between us and the deck below. This gradually thinned out and vanished, and we were both of us left staring down at a piece of the deck where the planking and pitched seams showed plain and distinct in the light from the lamps that were now hung nightly on the sherpoles.

"'Mighty queer that, mister,' said the captain meditatively as he fumbled for his pipe. 'Mighty queer.' Then he lit his pipe and began again his pacing of the poop.

"The calm lasted for a week with the sea like glass and every night without warning there was a repetition of the extraordinary squall, so that the captain had everything made fast at dusk, and waited patiently for a trade wind.

"Each evening I experimented further with my attempts to set up 'repellent' vibrations; but without result. I am not sure whether I ought to say that my meddling produced *no* result; for the calm gradually assumed a more unnatural permanent aspect whilst the sea looked more than ever like a plain of glass, bulged anon with the low oily roll of some deep swell. For the rest, there was by day a silence so profound as to give a sense of unrealness; for never a sea-bird hove in sight, whilst the movement of the vessel was so slight as scarce to keep up the constant creak, creak of spars and gear, which is the ordinary accompaniment of a calm.

"The sea appeared to have become an emblem of desolation and freeness, so that it seemed to me at last that there was no more any known world, but just one great ocean going on for ever into the far distances in every direction. At night the strange squalls assumed a far greater violence, so that sometimes it seemed as if the very spars would be ripped and twisted out of the vessel; yet fortunately no harm came in that wise.

"As the days passed I became convinced at last that my experiments were producing very distinct results; though the opposite to those which I hoped to produce, for now at each sunset a sort of grey cloud resembling light smoke would appear far away in every quarter, almost immediately upon the commencement of the vibrations, with the effect that I desisted from any prolonged attempt and became more tentative in my experiments.

"At last, however, when we had endured this condition of affairs for a week, I had a long talk with old Captain Thompson and he agreed to let me carry out a bold experiment to its conclusion. It was to keep the vibrations going steadily at full power from a little before sunset until the dawn, and to take careful notes of the results.

"With this in view, all was made ready. The royal and t'gallant yards were sent down, all the sails stowed, and everything about the decks made fast. A sea anchor was rigged out over the bows, and a long line of cable veered away. This was to ensure the vessel coming head to wind should one of those strange squalls strike us from any quarter during the night.

"Late in the afternoon the men were sent into the fo'c'sle, and told that they might please themselves and turn in, or do anything they liked; but that they were not to come on deck during the night whatever happened. To ensure this the port and starboard doors were padlocked. Afterwards I made the first and the eighth signs of the Saaamaaa Ritual opposite each door-post, connecting them with triple lines crossed at every seventh inch. You've dipped deeper into the science of magic than I have, Arkright, and you will know what that means. Following this I ran a wire entirely around the outside of the fo'c'sle and connected it up with my machinery, which I had erected in the sail-locker aft.

"'In any case,' I explained to the captain, 'they run practically no risk other than the general risk which we may expect in the form of a terrific storm-burst. The real danger will be to those who are 'meddling.' The 'path of the vibrations' will make a kind of 'halo' round the apparatus. I shall have to be there to control and I'm willing to risk it; but you'd better get into your cabin and the three mates must do the same.'

"This the old captain refused to do and the three mates begged to be allowed to stay and 'see the fun.' I warned them very seriously that there might be a very disagreeable and unavoidable danger, but they agreed to risk it; and I can tell you I was not sorry to have their companionship.

"I set to work then, making them help where I needed help, and so presently I had all my gear in order. Then I led my wires up through the skylight from the cabin, and set the vibrator dial and trembler-box level, screwing them solidly down to the poop-deck, in the clear space that lay between the foreside of the skylight and the lid of the sail locker.

"I got the three mates and the captain to take their places close together, and I warned them not to move whatever happened. I set to work then, alone, and chalked a temporary pentacle about the whole lot of us, including the apparatus. Afterwards I made haste to get the tubes of my electric pentacle fitted all about us, for it was getting on to dusk. As soon as this was done I switched on the current into the vacuum tubes, and immediately the pale sickly glare shone dull all about us, seeming cold and unreal in the last light of the evening.

"Immediately afterwards I set the vibrations beating out into all space and then I took my seat beside the control board. Here I had a few words with the others, warning them again whatever they might hear or see not to leave the pentacle, if they valued their lives. They nodded to this, and I knew that they were fully impressed with the possibility of the unknown danger that we were meddling with.

"Then we settled down to watch. We were all in our oilskins, for I expected the experiment to include some very peculiar behaviour on the part of the elements, and so we were ready to face the night. One other thing I was careful to do, and that was to confiscate all matches, so that no one should forgetfully light his pipe; for the light rays are 'paths' to certain of the Forces.

"With a pair of marine glasses I was staring round at the horizon. All around, but miles away in the greying of the evening, there seemed to be a strange, vague darkening of the surface of the sea. This became more distinct, and it seemed to me presently that it might be a slight, low-lying mist far away about the ship. I watched it very intently, and the captain and the three mates were doing likewise through their glasses.

"'Coming in on us at the rate o' knots, mister,' said the old man in a low voice. 'This is what I call playin' with 'ell. I only hope it'll all come right.' That was all he said, and afterwards there was absolute silence from him and the others through the strange hours that followed.

"As the night stole down upon the sea we lost sight of the peculiar incoming circle of mist, and there was a period of the most intense and oppressive silence to the five of us, sitting there watchful and quiet within the pale glow of the electric pentacle.

"A while later there came a sort of strange, noiseless lightning. By noiseless I mean that while the flashes appeared to be near at hand and lit up all the vague sea around, yet there was no thunder; neither, so it appeared to me, did there seem to be any *reality* in the flashes. This is a queer thing to say, but it describes my impressions. It was as if I saw a representation of lightning rather than the physical electricity itself. No, of course, I am not pretending to use the word in its technical sense.

"Abruptly a strange quivering went through the vessel from end to end, and died away. I looked fore and aft, and then glanced at the four men, who stared back at me with a sort of dumb and half-frightened wonder, but no one said anything. About five minutes passed with no sound anywhere except the faint buzz of the apparatus and nothing visible anywhere except the noiseless lightning, which came down, flash after flash, lighting the sea all around the vessel.

"Then a most extraordinary thing happened. The peculiar quivering passed again through the ship and died away. It was followed immediately by a kind of undulation of the vessel, first fore and aft and then from side to side. I can give you no better illustration of the strangeness of the movement on that glass-like sea than to say that it was just such a movement as might have been given her had an invisible, giant hand lifted her and toyed with her, canting her this way and that with a certain curious and rather sickening rhythm of movement. This appeared to last about two minutes, so far as I can guess, and ended with the ship being shaken, up and down several times, after which there came again the quivering, and then quietness.

"A full hour must have passed during which I observed nothing, except that twice the vessel was faintly shaken, and the second time this was followed by a slight repetition of the curious undulations. This, however, lasted but a few seconds and afterwards there was only the abnormal and oppressive silence of the night, punctured time after time by these noiseless flashes of lightning. All the time I did my best to study the appearance of the sea and atmosphere around the ship.

"One thing was apparent, that the surrounding wall of vagueness had drawn in more upon the ship, so that the brightest flashes now showed me no more than about a clear quarter of a mile of ocean around us, after which the sight was just lost in trying to penetrate a kind of shadowy distance, that yet had no depth in it; but which still lacked any power to arrest the vision at any particular point so that one could not know definitely whether there was anything there or not; but only that one's sight was limited by some phenomenon which hid all the distant sea. Do I make this clear?

"The strange, noiseless lightning increased in vividness, and the flashes began to come more frequently. This went on till they were almost continuous, so that all the near sea could be watched with scarce an intermission. Yet the brightness of the flashes seemed to have no power to dull the pale light of the curious detached glows that circled in silent multitudes about us.

"About this time I became aware of a strange sense of breathlessness. Each breath seemed to be drawn with difficulty, and presently with a sense of positive distress. The three mates and the captain were breathing with curious little gasps, and the faint buzz of the vibrator seemed to come from a great distance away. For the rest there was such a silence as made itself known like a dull, numbing ache upon the brain.

"The minutes passed slowly and then, abruptly, I saw something new. There were grey things floating in the air about the ship which were so vague and attenuated that at first I could not be sure that I saw anything; but in a while there could be no doubt that they were there.

"They began to show plainer in the constant glare of the quiet lightning, and growing darker and darker they increased visibly in size. They appeared to be but a few feet above the level of the sea, and they began to assume humped shapes.

"For quite half an hour, which seemed indefinitely longer, I watched those strange humps like little hills of blackness floating just above the surface of the water, and moving round and round the vessel with a slow, everlasting circling that produced on my eyes the feeling that it was all a dream.

"It was later still that I discovered still another thing. Each of those great vague mounds had begun to oscillate as it circled round about us. I was conscious at the same time that there was communicated to the vessel the beginning of a similar oscillating movement, so very slight at first that I could scarcely be sure she so much as moved.

"The movement of the ship grew with a steady oscillation, the bows lifting first and then the stern, as if she were pivoted amidships. This ceased, and she settled down on to a level keel with a series of queer jerks as if her weight were being slowly lowered again to the buoying of the water.

"Suddenly there came a cessation of the extraordinary lightning, and we were in an absolute blackness with only the pale sickly glow of the electric pentacle above us, and the faint buzz of the apparatus seeming far away in the night. Can you picture it all? The five of us there, tense and watchful, and wondering what was going to happen.

"The thing began gently—a little jerk upward of the starboard side of the vessel; then a second jerk, then a third and the whole ship was canted distinctly to port. It continued in a kind of slow rhythmic tilting, with curious timed pauses between the jerks, and suddenly, you know, I saw that we were in absolute danger, for the vessel was being capsized by some enormous Force in the utter silence and blackness of that night.

"'My God, mister, stop it!' came the captain's voice, quick and very hoarse. 'She'll be gone in a moment! She'll be gone!'

"He had got on to his knees and was staring round and gripping at the deck. The three mates were also gripping at the deck with their palms to stop them from sliding down the violent slope. In that moment came a final tilting of the side of the vessel and the deck rose up almost like a wall. I snatched at the lever of the vibrator and switched it over.

"Instantly the angle of the deck decreased as the vessel righted several feet with a jerk. The righting movement continued with little rhythmic jerks until the ship was once more on an even keel.

"And even as she righted I was aware of an alteration in the tenseness of the atmosphere, and a great noise far off to starboard. It was the roaring of wind. A huge flash of lightning was followed by others and the thunder crashed continually overhead. The noise of the wind to starboard rose to a loud screaming, and drove towards us through the night. Then the lightning ceased and the deep roll of the thunder was lost in the nearer sound of the wind, which was now within a mile of us, and making a most hideous, bellowing scream. The shrill howling came at us out of the dark and covered every other sound. It was as if all the night on that side were a vast cliff, sending down high and monstrous echoes upon us. This is a queer thing to say, I know, but it may help you to get the feeling of the thing; for that just describes exactly how it felt to me at the time—that queer, echoey, empty sense above us in the night; yet all the emptiness filled with sound on high. Do you get it? It was most extraordinary, and there was a grand something about it all as if one had come suddenly upon the steeps of some monstrous lost world.

"Then the wind rushed out at us and stunned us with its sound and force and fury. We were smothered and half-stunned. The vessel went over on to her port side merely from pressure of the wind on her naked spars and side. The whole night seemed one yell, and the foam roared and snowed over us in countless tons. I have never known anything like it. We were all splayed about the poop, holding on to anything we could, while the pentacle was smashed to atoms so that we were in complete darkness. The storm-burst had come down on us.

"Towards morning the storm calmed, and by evening we were running before a fine breeze; yet the pumps had to be kept going steadily, for we had sprung a pretty bad leak, which proved so serious that we had to take to the boats two days later. However, we were picked up that night, so that we had only a short time of it. As for the *Jarvee*, she is now safely at the bottom of the Atlantic, where she had better remain for ever."

Carnacki came to an end, and tapped out his pipe.

"But you haven't explained," I remonstrated. "What made her like that? What made her different from other ships? Why did those shadows and things come to her? What's your idea?"

"Well," replied Carnacki, "in my opinion she was a *focus*. That is a technical term which I can best explain by saying that she possessed the 'attractive vibration'— that is the power to draw to her any psychic waves in the vicinity, much in the way of a medium. The way in which the 'vibration' is acquired—to use a technical term again—is, of course, purely a matter for supposition. She may have developed it during the years, owing to a suitability of conditions; or it may have been in her ('of her' is a better term) from the very day her keel was laid. I mean the direction in which she lay, the condition of the atmosphere, the state of the 'electric tensions,' the very blows of the hammers, and the accidental combining of materials suited to such an end—all might tend to such a thing. And this is only to speak of the *known*. The vast *unknown* it is vain even to speculate upon in a brief chatter like this.

"I would like to remind you here of that idea of mine that certain forms of so-called 'hauntings' may have their cause in the 'attractive vibrations.' A building or a ship—just as I have indicated—may develop 'vibrations,' even as certain materials in combination under the proper conditions will certainly develop an electric current.

"To say more in a talk of this scope is useless. I am more inclined to remind you of the glass which will vibrate to a certain note struck upon a piano, and to silence all your worrying questions with that simple little unanswered one: What *is* electricity? When we've got that clear, it will be time to take the next step in a more dogmatic fashion. We are but speculating on the coasts of a strange country of mystery. In this case, I think the next best step for you all will be home and bed."

And with this terse ending, in the most genial way possible, Carnacki ushered us out presently on to the quiet chill of the Embankment, replying heartily to our various good-nights.

From the Tideless Sea (First Part)

The Captain of the schooner leant over the rail, and stared for a moment, intently.

"Pass us them glasses, Jock," he said, reaching a hand behind him.

Jock left the wheel for an instant, and ran into the little companionway. He emerged immediately with a pair of marine-glasses, which he pushed into the waiting hand.

For a little, the Captain inspected the object through the binoculars. Then he lowered them, and polished the object glasses.

"Seems like er water-logged barr'l as sumone's been doin' fancy paintin' on," he remarked after a further stare. "Shove ther 'elm down er bit, Jock, an' we'll 'ave er closer look at it."

Jock obeyed, and soon the schooner bore almost straight for the object which held the Captain's attention. Presently, it was within some fifty feet, and the Captain sung out to the boy in the caboose to pass along the boathook.

Very slowly, the schooner drew nearer, for the wind was no more than breathing gently. At last the cask was within reach, and the Captain grappled at it with the boathook. It bobbed in the calm water, under his ministrations; and, for a moment, the thing seemed likely to elude him. Then he had the hook fast in a bit of rotten-looking rope which was attached to it. He did not attempt to lift it by the rope; but sung out to the boy to get a bowline round it. This was done, and the two of them hove it up on to the deck.

The Captain could see now, that the thing was a small water-breaker, the upper part of which was ornamented with the remains of a painted name.

"H—M—E—B—" spelt out the Captain with difficulty, and scratched his head. "'ave er look at this 'ere, Jock. See wot you makes of it."

Jock bent over from the wheel, expectorated, and then stared at the breaker. For nearly a minute he looked at it in silence.

"I'm thinkin' some of the letterin's washed awa'," he said at last, with considerable deliberation. "I have ma doots if ye'll be able to read it."

"Hadn't ye no better knock in the end?" he suggested, after a further period of pondering. "I'm thinkin' ye'll be lang comin' at them contents otherwise."

"It's been in ther water er thunderin' long time," remarked the Captain, turning the bottom side upwards. "Look at them barnacles!"

Then, to the boy:—

"Pass erlong ther 'atchet outer ther locker."

Whilst the boy was away, the Captain stood the little barrel on end, and kicked away some of the barnacles from the underside. With them, came away a great shell of pitch. He bent, and inspected it.

"Blest if ther thing ain't been pitched!" he said. "This 'ere's been put afloat er purpose, an' they've been mighty anxious as ther stuff, in it shouldn't be 'armed."

He kicked away another mass of the barnacle-studded pitch. Then, with a sudden impulse, he picked up the whole thing and shook it violently. It gave out a light, dull, thudding sound, as though something soft and small were within. Then the boy came with the hatchet.

"Stan' clear!" said the Captain, and raised the implement. The next instant, he had driven in one end of the barrel. Eagerly, he stooped forward. He dived his hand down and brought out a little bundle stitched up in oilskin.

"I don' spect as it's anythin' of valley," he remarked. "But I guess as there's sumthin' 'ere as'll be worth tellin' 'bout w'en we gets 'ome."

He slit up the oilskin as he spoke. Underneath, there was another covering of the same material, and under that a third. Then a longish bundle done up in tarred canvas. This was removed, and a black, cylindrical shaped case disclosed to view. It proved to be a tin canister, pitched over. Inside of it, neatly wrapped within a last strip of oilskin, was a roll of papers, which, on opening, the Captain found to be covered with writing. The Captain shook out the various wrappings; but found nothing further. He handed the MS. across to Jock.

"More 'n your line 'n mine, I guess," he remarked. "Jest you read it up, an' I'll listen."

He turned to the boy.

"Fetch ther dinner erlong 'ere. Me an' ther Mate'll 'ave it comfortable up 'ere, an' you can take ther wheel. Now then, Jock!"

And, presently, Jock began to read.

"The Losing of the *Homebird*"

"The 'Omebird!" exclaimed the Captain. "Why, she were lost w'en I wer' quite a young feller. Let me see—seventy-three. That were it. Tail end er seventy-three w'en she left 'ome, an' never 'eard of since; not as I knows. Go a'ead with ther yarn, Jock."

"It is Christmas eve. Two years ago today, we became lost to the world. Two years! It seems like twenty since I had my last Christmas in England. Now, I suppose, we are already forgotten—and this ship is but one more among the missing! My God! to think upon our loneliness gives me a choking feeling, a tightness across the chest!

"I am writing this in the saloon of the sailing ship, *Homebird*, and writing with but little hope of human eye ever seeing that which I write; for we are in the heart of the dread Sargasso Sea—the Tideless Sea of the North Atlantic. From the stump of our mizzen mast, one may see, spread out to the far horizon, an interminable waste of weed—a treacherous, silent vastitude of slime and hideousness!

"On our port side, distant some seven or eight miles, there is a great, shapeless, discoloured mass. No one, seeing it for the first time, would suppose it to be the hull of a long lost vessel. It bears but little resemblance to a sea-going craft, because of a strange superstructure which has been built upon it. An examination of the vessel herself, through a telescope, tells one that she is unmistakably ancient. Probably a hundred, possibly two hundred, years. Think of it! Two hundred years in the midst of this desolation! It is an eternity.

"At first we wondered at that extraordinary superstructure. Later, we were to learn its use—and profit by the teaching of hands long withered. It is inordinately strange that we should have come upon this sight for the dead! Yet, thought suggests, that there may be many such, which have lain here through the centuries in this World of Desolation. I had not imagined that the earth contained so much loneliness, as is held within the circle, seen from the stump of our shattered mast. Then comes the thought that I might wander a hundred miles in any direction—and still be lost.

"And that craft yonder, that one break in the monotony, that monument of a few men's misery, serves only to make the solitude the more atrocious; for she is a very effigy of terror, telling of tragedies in the past, and to come!

"And now to get back to the beginnings of it. I joined the *Homebird*, as a passenger, in the early part of November. My health was not quite the thing, and I hoped the voyage would help to set me up. We had a lot of dirty weather for the first couple of weeks out, the wind dead ahead. Then we got a Southerly slant, that carried us down through the forties; but a good deal more to the Westward than we desired. Here we ran right into a tremendous cyclonic storm. All hands were called to shorten sail, and so urgent seemed our need, that the very officers went aloft to help make up the sails, leaving only the Captain (who had taken the wheel) and myself upon the poop. On the main-deck, the cook was busy letting go such ropes as the Mates desired.

"Abruptly, some distance ahead, through the vague sea-mist, but rather on the port bow, I saw loom up a great black wall of cloud.

"'Look, Captain!' I exclaimed; but it had vanished before I had finished speaking. A minute later it came again, and this time the Captain saw it.

"'O, my God!' he cried, and dropped his hands from the wheel. He leapt into the companionway, and seized a speaking trumpet. Then out on deck. He put it to his lips.

"'Come down from aloft! Come down! Come down!' he shouted. And suddenly I lost his voice in a terrific mutter of sound from somewhere to port. It was the voice of the storm—shouting. My God! I had never heard anything like it! It ceased as suddenly as it had begun, and, in the succeeding quietness, I heard the whining of the kicking-tackles through the blocks. Then came a quick clang of brass upon the deck, and I turned quickly. The Captain had thrown down the trumpet, and sprung back to the wheel. I glanced aloft, and saw that many of the men were already in the rigging, and racing down like cats.

"I heard the Captain draw his breath with a quick gasp.

"'Hold on for your lives!' he shouted, in a hoarse, unnatural voice.

"I looked at him. He was staring to windward with a fixed stare of painful intentness, and my gaze followed his. I saw, not four hundred yards distant, an enormous mass of foam and water coming down upon us. In the same instant, I caught the hiss of it, and immediately it was a shriek, so intense and awful, that I cringed impotently with sheer terror.

"The smother of water and foam took the ship a little foreside of the beam, and the wind was with it. Immediately, the vessel rolled over on to her side, the sea-froth flying over her in tremendous cataracts.

"It seemed as though nothing could save us. Over, over we went, until I was swinging against the deck, almost as against the side of a house; for I had grasped the weather rail at the Captain's warning. As I swung there, I saw a strange thing. Before me was the port quarter boat. Abruptly, the canvas-cover was flipped clean off it, as though by a vast, invisible hand.

"The next instant, a flurry of oars, boats' masts and odd gear flittered up into the air, like so many feathers, and blew to leeward and was lost in the roaring chaos of foam. The boat, herself, lifted in her chocks, and suddenly was blown clean down on to the main-deck, where she lay all in a ruin of white-painted timbers.

"A minute of the most intense suspense passed; then, suddenly, the ship righted, and I saw that the three masts had carried away. Yet, so hugely loud was the crying of the storm, that no sound of their breaking had reached me.

"I looked towards the wheel; but no one was there. Then I made out something crumpled up against the lee rail. I struggled across to it, and found that it was the Captain. He was insensible, and queerly limp in his right arm and leg. I looked round. Several of the men were crawling aft along the poop. I beckoned to them, and pointed to the wheel, and then to the Captain. A couple of them came towards me, and one went to the wheel. Then I made out through the spray the form of the Second Mate. He had several more of the men with him, and they had a coil of rope, which they took forrard. I learnt afterwards that they were hastening to get out a sea-anchor, so as to keep the ship's head towards the wind.

"We got the Captain below, and into his bunk. There, I left him in the hands of his daughter and the steward, and returned on deck.

"Presently, the Second Mate came back, and with him the remainder of the men. I found then that only seven had been saved in all. The rest had gone.

"The day passed terribly—the wind getting stronger hourly; though, at its worst, it was nothing like so tremendous as that first burst.

"The night came—a night of terror, with the thunder and hiss of the giant seas in the air above us, and the wind bellowing like some vast Elemental beast.

"Then, just before the dawn, the wind lulled, almost in a moment; the ship rolling and wallowing fearfully, and the water coming aboard—hundreds of tons at a time. Immediately afterwards it caught us again; but more on the beam, and bearing the vessel over on to her side, and this only by the pressure of the element upon the stark hull. As we came head to wind again, we righted, and rode, as we had for hours, amid a thousand fantastic hills of phosphorescent flame.

"Again the wind died—coming again after a longer pause, and then, all at once, leaving us. And so, for the space of a terrible half hour, the ship lived through the most awful, windless sea that can be imagined. There was no doubting but that we had driven right into the calm centre of the cyclone—calm only so far as lack of wind, and yet more dangerous a thousand times than the most furious hurricane that ever blew.

"For now we were beset by the stupendous Pyramidal Sea; a sea once witnessed, never forgotten; a sea in which the whole bosom of the ocean is projected towards heaven in monstrous hills of water; not leaping forward, as would be the case if there were wind; but hurling upwards in jets and peaks of living brine, and falling back in a continuous thunder of foam.

"Imagine this, if you can, and then have the clouds break away suddenly overhead, and the moon shine down upon that hellish turmoil, and you will have such a sight as has been given to mortals but seldom, save with death. And this is what we saw, and to my mind there is nothing within the knowledge of man to which I can liken it.

"Yet we lived through it, and through the wind that came later. But two more complete days and nights had passed, before the storm ceased to be a terror to us, and then, only because it had carried us into the seaweed laden waters of the vast Sargasso Sea.

"Here, the great billows first became foamless; and dwindled gradually in size as we drifted further among the floating masses of weed. Yet the wind was still furious, so that the ship drove on steadily, sometimes between banks, and other times over them.

"For a day and a night we drifted thus; and then astern I made out a great bank of weed, vastly greater than any which hitherto we had encountered. Upon this, the wind drove us stern foremost, so that we over-rode it. We had been forced some distance across it, when it occurred to me that our speed was slackening. I guessed presently that the sea-anchor, ahead, had caught in the weed, and was holding. Even as I surmised this, I heard from beyond the bows a faint, droning, twanging sound, blending with the roar of the wind. There came an indistinct report, and the ship lurched backwards through the weed. The hawser, connecting us with the sea-anchor, had parted.

"I saw the Second Mate run forrard with several men. They hauled in upon the hawser, until the broken end was aboard. In the meantime, the ship, having nothing ahead to keep her "bows on," began to slew broadside towards the wind.

I saw the men attach a chain to the end of the broken hawser; then they paid it out again, and the ship's head came back to the gale.

"When the Second Mate came aft, I asked him why this had been done, and he explained that so long as the vessel was end-on, she would travel over the weed. I inquired why he wished her to go over the weed, and he told me that one of the men had made out what appeared to be clear water astern, and that—could we gain it—we might win free.

"Through the whole of that day, we moved rearwards across the great bank; yet, so far from the weed appearing to show signs of thinning, it grew steadily thicker, and, as it became denser, so did our speed slacken, until the ship was barely moving. And so the night found us.

"The following morning discovered to us that we were within a quarter of a mile of a great expanse of clear water—apparently the open sea; but unfortunately the wind had dropped to a moderate breeze, and the vessel was motionless, deep sunk in the weed; great tufts of which rose up on all sides, to within a few feet of the level of our main-deck.

"A man was sent up the stump of the mizzen, to take a look round. From there, he reported that he could see something, that might be weed, across the water; but it was too far distant for him to be in any way certain. Immediately afterwards, he called out that there was something, away on our port beam; but what it was, he could not say, and it was not until a telescope was brought to bear, that we made it out to be the hull of the ancient vessel I have previously mentioned.

"And now, the Second Mate began to cast about for some means by which he could bring the ship to the clear water astern. The first thing which he did, was to bend a sail to a spare yard, and hoist it to the top of the mizzen stump. By this means, he was able to dispense with the cable towing over the bows, which, of course, helped to prevent the ship from moving. In addition, the sail would prove helpful to force the vessel across the weed. Then he routed out a couple of kedges. These, he bent on to the ends of a short piece of cable, and, to the bight of this, the end of a long coil of strong rope.

"After that, he had the starboard quarter boat lowered into the weed, and in it he placed the two kedge anchors. The end of another length of rope, he made fast to the boat's painter. This done, he took four of the men with him, telling them to bring chain-hooks, in addition to the oars—his intention being to force the boat through the weed, until he reached the clear water. There, in the marge of the weed, he would plant the two anchors in the thickest clumps of the growth; after which we were to haul the boat back to the ship, by means of the rope attached to the painter.

"'Then,' as he put it, 'we'll take the kedge-rope to the capstan, and heave her out of this blessed cabbage heap!'

"The weed proved a greater obstacle to the progress of the boat, than, I think, he had anticipated. After half an hour's work, they had gone scarcely more than some two hundred feet from the vessel; yet, so thick was the stuff, that no sign could we see of them, save the movement they made among the weed, as they forced the boat along.

"Another quarter of an hour passed away, during which the three men left upon the poop, paid out the ropes as the boat forged slowly ahead. All at once, I heard my name called. Turning, I saw the Captain's daughter in the companionway, beckoning to me. I walked across to her.

"'My father has sent me up to know, Mr. Philips, how they are getting on?'

"'Very slowly, Miss Knowles,' I replied. 'Very slowly indeed. The weed is so extraordinarily thick.'

"She nodded intelligently, and turned to descend; but I detained her a moment.

"'Your father, how is he?' I asked.

"She drew her breath swiftly.

"'Quite himself,' she said; 'but so dreadfully weak. He—'

"An outcry from one of the men, broke across her speech:—

"'Lord 'elp us, mates! wot were that!'

"I turned sharply. The three of them were staring over the taffrail. I ran towards them, and Miss Knowles followed.

"'Hush!' she said, abruptly. 'Listen!'

"I stared astern to where I knew the boat to be. The weed all about it was quaking queerly—the movement extending far beyond the radius of their hooks and oars. Suddenly, I heard the Second Mate's voice:—

"'Look out, lads! My God, look out!'

"And close upon this, blending almost with it, came the hoarse scream of a man in sudden agony.

"I saw an oar come up into view, and descend violently, as though someone struck at something with it. Then the Second Mate's voice, shouting: —

"'Aboard there! Aboard there! Haul in on the rope! Haul in on the rope—!' It broke off into a sharp cry.

"As we seized hold of the rope, I saw the weed hurled in all directions, and a great crying and choking swept to us over the brown hideousness around.

"'Pull!' I yelled, and we pulled. The rope tautened; but the boat never moved.

"'Tek it ter ther capsting!' gasped one of the men.

"Even as he spoke, the rope slackened.

"'It's coming!' cried Miss Knowles. 'Pull! Oh! Pull!'

"She had hold of the rope along with us, and together we hauled, the boat yielding to our strength with surprising ease.

"'There it is!' I shouted, and then I let go of the rope. There was no one in the boat.

"For the half of a minute, we stared, dumfounded. Then my gaze wandered astern to the place from which we had plucked it. There was a heaving movement among the great weed masses. I saw something waver up aimlessly against the sky;

it was sinuous, and it flickered once or twice from side to side; then sank back among the growth, before I could concentrate my attention upon it.

"I was recalled to myself by a sound of dry sobbing. Miss Knowles was kneeling upon the deck, her hands clasped round one of the iron uprights of the rail. She seemed momentarily all to pieces.

"'Come! Miss Knowles,' I said, gently. 'You must be brave. We cannot let your father know of this in his present state.'

"She allowed me to help her to her feet. I could feel that she was trembling badly. Then, even as I sought for words with which to reassure her, there came a dull thud from the direction of the companionway. We looked round. On the deck, face downward, lying half in and half out of the scuttle, was the Captain. Evidently, he had witnessed everything. Miss Knowles gave out a wild cry, and ran to her father. I beckoned to one of the men to help me, and, together, we carried him back to his bunk. An hour later, he recovered from his swoon. He was quite calm, though very weak, and evidently in considerable pain.

"Through his daughter, he made known to me that he wished me to take the reins of authority in his place. This, after a slight demur, I decided to do; for, as I reassured myself, there were no duties required of me, needing any special knowledge of ship-craft. The vessel was fast; so far as I could see, irrevocably fast. It would be time to talk of freeing her, when the Captain was well enough to take charge once more.

"I returned on deck; and made known to the men the Captain's wishes. Then I chose one to act as a sort of bo'sun over the other two, and to him I gave orders that everything should be put to rights before the night came. I had sufficient sense to leave him to manage matters in his own way; for, whereas my knowledge of what was needful, was fragmentary, his was complete.

"By this time, it was near to sunsetting, and it was with melancholy feelings that I watched the great hull of the sun plunge lower. For awhile, I paced the poop, stopping ever and anon to stare over the dreary waste by which we were surrounded. The more I looked about, the more a sense of lonesomeness and depression and fear assailed me. I had pondered much upon the dread happening of the day, and all my ponderings led to a vital questioning:— What was there among all that quiet weed, which had come upon the crew of the boat, and destroyed them? And I could not make answer, and the weed was silent—dreadly silent!

"The sun had drawn very near to the dim horizon, and I watched it, moodily, as it splashed great clots of red fire across the water that lay stretched into the distance across our stern. Abruptly, as I gazed, its perfect lower edge was marred by an irregular shape. For a moment, I stared, puzzled. Then I fetched a pair of glasses from the holdfast in the companion. A glance through these, and I knew the extent of our fate. That line, blotching the round of the sun, was the conformation of another enormous weed bank.

"I remembered that the man had reported something as showing across the water, when he was sent up to the top of the mizzen stump in the morning; but, what it was, he had been unable to say. The thought flashed into my mind that it had been only *just* visible from aloft in the morning, and now it was in sight from the deck. It occurred to me that the wind might be compacting the weed, and driving the bank which surrounded the ship, down upon a larger portion. Possibly, the clear stretch of water had been but a temporary rift within the heart of the Sargasso Sea. It seemed only too probable.

"Thus it was that I meditated, and so, presently, the night found me. For some hours further, I paced the deck in the darkness, striving to understand the incomprehensible; yet with no better result than to weary myself to death. Then, somewhere about midnight, I went below to sleep.

"The following morning, on going on deck, I found that the stretch of clear water had disappeared entirely, during the night, and now, so far as the eye could reach, there was nothing but a stupendous desolation of weed.

"The wind had dropped completely, and no sound came from all that weed-ridden immensity. We had, in truth, reached the Cemetery of the Ocean!

"The day passed uneventfully enough. It was only when I served out some food to the men, and one of them asked whether they could have a few raisins, that I remembered, with a pang of sudden misery, that it was Christmas day. I gave them the fruit, as they desired, and they spent the morning in the galley, cooking their dinner. Their stolid indifference to the late terrible happenings, appalled me somewhat, until I remembered what their lives were, and had been. Poor fellows! One of them ventured aft at dinner time, and offered me a slice of what he called 'plum duff.' He brought it on a plate which he had found in the galley and scoured thoroughly with sand and water. He tendered it shyly enough, and I took it, so graciously as I could, for I would not hurt his feelings; though the very smell of the stuff was an abomination.

"During the afternoon, I brought out the Captain's telescope, and made a thorough examination of the ancient hulk on our port beam. Particularly did I study the extraordinary superstructure around her sides; but could not, as I have said before, conceive of its use.

"The evening, I spent upon the poop, my eyes searching wearily across that vile quietness, and so, in a little, the night came—Christmas night, sacred to a thousand happy memories. I found myself dreaming of the night a year previous, and, for a little while, I forgot what was before me. I was recalled suddenly—terribly. A voice rose out of the dark which hid the main-deck. For the fraction of an instant, it expressed surprise; then pain and terror leapt into it. Abruptly, it seemed to come from above, and then from somewhere *beyond* the ship, and so in a moment there was silence, save for a rush of feet and the bang of a door forrard.

"I leapt down the poop ladder, and ran along the main-deck, towards the fo'cas'le. As I ran, something knocked off my cap. I scarcely noticed it *then*. I reached the fo'cas'le, and caught at the latch of the port door. I lifted it and pushed; but the door was fastened.

"'Inside there!' I cried, and banged upon the panels with my clenched fist.

"A man's voice came, incoherently.

"'Open the door!' I shouted. 'Open the door!'

"'Yes, Sir—I'm com—ing, Sir,' said one of them, jerkily.

"I heard footsteps stumble across the planking. Then a hand fumbled at the fastening, and the door flew open under my weight.

"The man who had opened to me, started back. He held a flaring slush-lamp above his head, and, as I entered, he thrust it forward. His hand was trembling visibly, and, behind him, I made out the face of one of his mates, the brow and dirty, clean-shaven upper lip drenched with sweat. The man who held the lamp, opened his mouth, and gabbered at me; but, for a moment, no sound came.

"'Wot—wot were it? Wot we-ere it?' he brought out at last, with a gasp.

"The man behind, came to his side, and gesticulated.

"'What was what?' I asked sharply, and looking from one to the other. 'Where's the other man? What was that screaming?'

"The second man drew the palm of his hand across his brow; then flirted his fingers deckwards.

"'We don't know, Sir! We don't know! It were Jessop! Somethin's took 'im just as we was comin' forrid! We—we— He—he—HARK!'

"His head came forward with a jerk as he spoke, and then, for a space, no one stirred. A minute passed, and I was about to speak, when, suddenly, from somewhere out upon the deserted main-deck, there came a queer, subdued noise, as though something moved stealthily hither and thither. The man with the lamp caught me by the sleeve, and then, with an abrupt movement, slammed the door and fastened it.

"'That's IT, Sir!' he exclaimed, with a note of terror and conviction in his voice.

"I bade him be silent, while I listened; but no sound came to us through the door, and so I turned to the men and told them to let me have all they knew.

"It was little enough. They had been sitting in the galley, yarning, until, feeling tired, they had decided to go forrard and turn-in. They extinguished the light, and came out upon the deck, closing the door behind them. Then, just as they turned to go forrard, Jessop gave out a yell. The next instant they heard him screaming in the air above their heads, and, realising that some terrible thing was upon them, they took forthwith to their heels, and ran for the security of the fo'cas'le.

"Then I had come.

"As the men made an end of telling me, I thought I heard something outside, and held up my hand for silence. I caught the sound again. Someone was calling my name. It was Miss Knowles. Likely enough she was calling me to supper—and she had no knowledge of the dread thing which had happened. I sprang to the door. She might be coming along the main-deck in search of me. And there was Something out there, of which I had no conception—something unseen, but deadly tangible!

"'Stop, Sir!' shouted the men, together; but I had the door open.

"'Mr. Philips!' came the girl's voice at no great distance. 'Mr. Philips!'

"'Coming, Miss Knowles!' I shouted, and snatched the lamp from the man's hand.

"The next instant, I was running aft, holding the lamp high, and glancing fearfully from side to side. I reached the place where the mainmast had been, and spied the girl coming towards me.

"'Go back!' I shouted. 'Go back!'

"She turned at my shout, and ran for the poop ladder. I came up with her, and followed close at her heels. On the poop, she turned and faced me.

"'What is it, Mr. Philips?'

"I hesitated. Then:—

"'I don't know!' I said.

"'My father heard something,' she began. 'He sent me. He—'

"I put up my hand. It seemed to me that I had caught again the sound of something stirring on the main-deck.

"'Quick!' I said sharply. 'Down into the cabin!' And she, being a sensible girl, turned and ran down without waste of time. I followed, closing and fastening the companion-doors behind me.

"In the saloon, we had a whispered talk, and I told her everything. She bore up bravely, and said nothing; though her eyes were very wide, and her face pale. Then the Captain's voice came to us from the adjoining cabin.

"'Is Mr. Philips there, Mary?'

"'Yes, father.'

"'Bring him in.'

"I went in.

"'What was it, Mr. Philips?' he asked, collectedly.

"I hesitated; for I was willing to spare him the ill news; but he looked at me with calm eyes for a moment, and I knew that it was useless attempting to deceive him.

"'Something has happened, Mr. Philips,' he said, quietly. 'You need not be afraid to tell me.'

"At that, I told him so much as I knew, he listening, and nodding his comprehension of the story.

"'It must be something big,' he remarked, when I had made an end. 'And yet you saw nothing when you came aft?'

"'No,' I replied.

"'It is something in the weed,' he went on. 'You will have to keep off the deck at night.'

"After a little further talk, in which he displayed a calmness that amazed me, I left him, and went presently to my berth.

"The following day, I took the two men, and, together, we made a thorough search through the ship; but found nothing. It was evident to me that the Captain was right. There was some dread Thing hidden within the weed. I went to the side and looked down. The two men followed me. Suddenly, one of them pointed.

"'Look, Sir!' he exclaimed. 'Right below you, Sir! Two eyes like blessed great saucers! Look!'

"I stared; but could see nothing. The man left my side, and ran into the galley. In a moment, he was back with a great lump of coal.

"'Just there, Sir,' he said, and hove it down into the weed immediately beneath where we stood.

"Too late, I saw the thing at which he aimed—two immense eyes, some little distance below the surface of the weed. I knew instantly to what they belonged; for I had seen large specimens of the octopus some years previously, during a cruise in Australasian waters.

"'Look out, man!' I shouted, and caught him by the arm. 'It's an octopus! Jump back!' I sprang down on to the deck. In the same instant, huge masses of weed were hurled in all directions, and half a dozen immense tentacles whirled up into the air. One lapped itself about his neck. I caught his leg; but he was torn from my grasp, and I tumbled backwards on to the deck. I heard a scream from the other man as I scrambled to my feet. I looked to where he had been; but of him there was no sign. Regardless of the danger, in my great agitation, I leapt upon the rail, and gazed down with frightened eyes. Yet, neither of him nor his mate, nor the monster, could I perceive a vestige.

"How long I stood there staring down bewilderedly, I cannot say; certainly some minutes. I was so bemazed that I seemed incapable of movement. Then, all at once, I became aware that a light quiver ran across the weed, and the next instant, something stole up out of the depths with a deadly celerity. Well it was for me that I had seen it in time, else should I have shared the fate of those two—and the others. As it was, I saved myself only by leaping backwards on to the deck. For a moment, I saw the feeler wave above the rail with a certain apparent aimlessness; then it sank out of sight, and I was alone.

"An hour passed before I could summon a sufficiency of courage to break the news of this last tragedy to the Captain and his daughter, and when I had made an end, I returned to the solitude of the poop; there to brood upon the hopelessness of our position.

"As I paced up and down, I caught myself glancing continuously at the nearer weed tufts. The happenings of the past two days had shattered my nerves, and I feared every moment to see some slender death-grapple searching over the rail for me. Yet, the poop, being very much higher out of the weed than the main-deck, was comparatively safe; though only comparatively.

"Presently, as I meandered up and down, my gaze fell upon the hulk of the ancient ship, and, in a flash, the reason for that great superstructure was borne upon me. It was intended as a protection against the dread creatures which inhabited the weed. The thought came to me that I would attempt some similar means of protection; for the feeling that, at any moment, I might be caught and lifted out into that slimy wilderness, was not to be borne. In addition, the work would serve to occupy my mind, and help me to bear up against the intolerable sense of loneliness which assailed me.

"I resolved that I would lose no time, and so, after some thought as to the manner in which I should proceed, I routed out some coils of rope and several sails. Then I went down on to the main-deck and brought up an armful of capstan bars. These I lashed vertically to the rail all round the poop. Then I knotted the rope to each, stretching it tightly between them, and over this framework stretched the sails, sewing the stout canvas to the rope, by means of twine and some great needles which I found in the Mate's room.

"It is not to be supposed that this piece of work was accomplished immediately. Indeed, it was only after three days of hard labour that I got the poop completed. Then I commenced work upon the main-deck. This was a tremendous undertaking, and a whole fortnight passed before I had the entire length of it enclosed; for I had to be continually on the watch against the hidden enemy. Once, I was very nearly surprised, and saved myself only by a quick leap. Thereafter, for the rest of that day, I did no more work; being too greatly shaken in spirit. Yet, on the following morning, I recommenced, and from thence, until the end, I was not molested.

"Once the work was roughly completed, I felt at ease to begin and perfect it. This I did, by tarring the whole of the sails with Stockholm tar; thereby making them stiff, and capable of resisting the weather. After that, I added many fresh uprights, and much strengthening ropework, and finally doubled the sailcloth with additional sails, liberally smeared with the tar.

"In this manner, the whole of January passed away, and a part of February. Then, it would be on the last day of the month, the Captain sent for me, and told me, without any preliminary talk, that he was dying. I looked at him; but said nothing; for I had known long that it was so. In return, he stared back with a strange intentness, as though he would read my inmost thoughts, and this for the space of perhaps two minutes.

"'Mr. Philips,' he said at last, 'I may be dead by this time tomorrow. Has it ever occurred to you that my daughter will be alone with you?'

"'Yes, Captain Knowles,' I replied, quietly, and waited.

"For a few seconds, he remained silent; though, from the changing expressions of his face, I knew that he was pondering how best to bring forward the thing which it was in his mind to say.

"'You are a gentleman—' he began, at last.

"'I will marry her,' I said, ending the sentence for him.

"A slight flush of surprise crept into his face.

"'You—you have thought seriously about it?'

"'I have thought very seriously,' I explained.

"'Ah!' he said, as one who comprehends. And then, for a little, he lay there quietly. It was plain to me that memories of past days were with him. Presently, he came out of his dreams, and spoke, evidently referring to my marriage with his daughter.

"'It is the only thing,' he said, in a level voice.

"I bowed, and after that, he was silent again for a space. In a little, however, he turned once more to me:—

"'Do you—do you love her?'

"His tone was keenly wistful, and a sense of trouble lurked in his eyes.

"'She will be my wife,' I said, simply; and he nodded.

"'God has dealt strangely with us,' he murmured, presently, as though to himself.

"Abruptly, he bade me tell her to come in.

"And then he married us.

"Three days later, he was dead, and we were alone.

"For a while, my wife was a sad woman; but gradually time eased her of the bitterness of her grief.

"Then, some eight months after our marriage, a new interest stole into her life. She whispered it to me, and we, who had borne our loneliness uncomplainingly, had now this new thing to which to look forward. It became a bond between us, and bore promise of some companionship as we grew old. Old! At the idea of age, a sudden flash of thought darted like lightning across the sky of my mind:— FOOD! Hitherto, I had thought of myself, almost as of one already dead, and had cared naught for anything beyond the immediate troubles which each day forced upon me. The loneliness of the vast Weed World had become an assurance of doom to me, which had clouded and dulled my faculties, so that I had grown apathetic. Yet, immediately, as it seemed, at the shy whispering of my wife, was all this changed.

"That very hour, I began a systematic search through the ship. Among the cargo, which was of a 'general' nature, I discovered large quantities of preserved and tinned provisions, all of which I put carefully on one side. I continued my examination until I had ransacked the whole vessel. The business took me near upon six months to complete, and when it was finished, I seized paper, and made calculations, which led me to the conclusion that we had sufficient food in the ship to preserve life in three people for some fifteen to seventeen years. I could not come nearer to it than this; for I had no means of computing the quantity the child would need year by year. Yet it is sufficient to show me that seventeen years *must* be the limit. Seventeen years! And then—

"Concerning water, I am not troubled; for I have rigged a great sailcloth tundish, with a canvas pipe into the tanks; and from every rain, I draw a supply, which has never run short.

"The child was born nearly five months ago. She is a fine little girl, and her mother seems perfectly happy. I believe I could be quietly happy with them, were it not that I have ever in mind the end of those seventeen years. True! we may be dead long before then; but, if not, our little girl will be in her teens—and it is a hungry age.

"If one of us died—but no! Much may happen in seventeen years. I will wait.

"My method of sending this clear of the weed is likely to succeed. I have constructed a small fire-balloon, and this missive, safely enclosed in a little barrel, will be attached. The wind will carry it swiftly hence.

"Should this ever reach civilised beings, will they see that it is forwarded to:—"

(Here followed an address, which, for some reason, had been roughly obliterated. Then came the signature of the writer)

"Arthur Samuel Philips."

The Captain of the schooner looked over at Jock, as the man made an end of his readinsg.

"Seventeen years pervisions," he muttered thoughtfully. "An' this' ere were written sumthin' like twenty-nine years ago!" He nodded his head several times. "Poor creetures!" he exclaimed. "It'd be er long while, Jock—a long while!"

From the Tideless Sea (Second Part)

(Further News of the *Homebird*)

In the August of 1902, Captain Bateman, of the schooner *Agnes*, picked up a small barrel, upon which was painted a half obliterated word; which, finally, he succeeded in deciphering as "Homebird," the name of a full-rigged ship, which left London in the November of 1873, and from thenceforth was heard of no more by any man.

Captain Bateman opened the barrel, and discovered a packet of Manuscript, wrapped in oilskin. This, on examination, proved to be an account of the losing of the *Homebird* amid the desolate wastes of the Sargasso Sea. The papers were written by one Arthur Samuel Philips, a passenger in the ship; and, from them, Captain Bateman was enabled to gather that the ship, mastless, lay in the very heart of the dreaded Sargasso; and that all of the crew had been lost—some in the storm which drove them thither, and some in attempts to free the ship from the weed, which locked them in on all sides.

Only Mr. Philips and the Captain's daughter had been left alive, and they two, the dying Captain had married. To them had been born a daughter, and the papers ended with a brief but touching allusion to their fear that, eventually, they must run short of food.

There is need to say but little more. The account was copied into most of the papers of the day, and caused widespread comment. There was even some talk of fitting out a rescue expedition; but this fell through, owing chiefly to lack of knowledge of the whereabouts of the ship in all the vastness of the immense Sargasso Sea. And so, gradually, the matter has slipped into the background of the Public's memory.

Now, however, interest will be once more excited in the lonesome fate of this lost trio; for a second barrel, identical, it would seem, with that found by Captain Bateman, has been picked up by a Mr. Bolton, of Baltimore, master of a small brig, engaged in the South American coast-trade. In this barrel was enclosed a further message from Mr. Philips—the fifth that he has sent abroad to the world; but the second, third and fourth, up to this time, have not been discovered.

This "fifth message" contains a vital and striking account of their lives during the year 1879, and stands unique as a document informed with human lonesomeness and longing. I have seen it, and read it through, with the most intense and painful interest. The writing, though faint, is very legible; and the whole manuscript bears the impress of the same hand and mind that wrote the piteous account of the losing of the *Homebird*, of which I have already made mention, and with which, no doubt, many are well acquainted.

In closing this little explanatory note, I am stimulated to wonder whether, somewhere, at some time, those three missing messages ever shall be found. And then there may be others. What stories of human, strenuous fighting with Fate may they not contain. We can but wait and wonder. Nothing more may we ever learn; for what is this one little tragedy among the uncounted millions that the silence of the sea holds so remorselessly. And yet, again, news may come to us out of the Unknown—out of the lonesome silences of the dread Sargasso Sea—the loneliest and the most inaccessible place of all the lonesome and inaccessible places of this earth.

And so I say, let us wait. W. H. H.

The Fifth Message

"This is the fifth message that I have sent abroad over the loathsome surface of this vast Weed-World, praying that it may come to the open sea, ere the lifting power of my fire-balloon begone, and yet, if it come there—the which I could now doubt—how shall I be the better for it? Yet write I must, or go mad, and so I choose to write, though feeling as I write that no living creature, save it be the giant octopi that live in the weed about me, will ever see the thing I write.

"My first message I sent out on Christmas Eve, 1875, and since then, each eve of the birth of Christ has seen a message go skywards upon the winds, towards the open sea. It is as though this approaching time, of festivity and the meeting of parted loved ones, overwhelms me, and drives away the half apathetic peace that has been mine through spaces of these years of lonesomeness; so that I seclude myself from my wife and the little one, and with ink, pen, and paper, try to ease my heart of the pent emotions that seem at times to threaten to burst it.

"It is now six completed years since the Weed-World claimed us from the World of the Living—six years away from our brothers and sisters of the human and living world—It has been six years of living in a grave! And there are all the years ahead! Oh! My God! My God! I dare not think upon them! I must control myself—

"And then there is the little one, she is nearly four and a half now, and growing wonderfully, out among these wilds. Four and a half years, and the little woman has never seen a human face besides ours—think of it! And yet, if she lives four and forty years, she will never see another. . . . Four and forty years! It is foolishness to trouble about such a space of time; for the future, for us, ends in ten years—eleven at the utmost. Our food will last no longer than that. . . . My wife does not know;

70

for it seems to me a wicked thing to add unnecessarily to her punishment. She does but know that we must waste no ounce of food-stuff, and for the rest she imagines that the most of the cargo is of an edible nature. Perhaps, I have nurtured this belief. If anything happened to me, the food would last a few extra years; but my wife would have to imagine it an accident, else would each bite she took sicken her.

"I have thought often and long upon this matter, yet I fear to leave them; for who knows but that their very lives might at any time depend upon my strength, more pitifully, perhaps, than upon the food which they must come at last to lack. No, I must not bring upon them, and myself, a *near* and *certain* calamity, to defer one that, though it seems to have but little less certainty, is yet at a further distance.

"Until lately, nothing has happened to us in the past four years, if I except the adventures that attended my mad attempt to cut away through the surrounding weed to freedom, and from which it pleased God that I and those with me should be preserved.[1] Yet, in the latter part of this year, an adventure, much touched with grimness, came to us most unexpectedly, in a fashion quite unthought of—an adventure that has brought into our lives a fresh and more active peril; for now I have learned that the weed holds other terrors besides that of the giant octopi.

"Indeed, I have grown to believe this world of desolation capable of holding *any* horror, as well it might. Think of it—an interminable stretch of dank, brown loneliness in all directions, to the distant horizon; a place where monsters of the deep and the weed have undisputed reign; where never an enemy may fall upon them; but from which they may strike with sudden deadliness! No human can ever bring an engine of destruction to bear upon them, and the humans whose fate it is to have sight of them, do so only from the decks of lonesome derelicts, whence they stare lonely with fear, and without ability to harm.

"I cannot describe it, nor can any hope ever to imagine it! When the wind falls, a vast silence holds us girt, from horizon to horizon, yet it is a silence through which one seems to feel the pulse of hidden things all about us, watching and waiting— waiting and watching; waiting but for the chance to reach forth a huge and sudden death-grapple. . . . It is no use! I cannot bring it home to any; nor shall I be better able to convey the frightening sound of the wind, sweeping across these vast, quaking plains—the shrill whispering of the weed-fronds, under the stirring of the winds. To hear it from beyond our canvas screen, is like listening to the uncounted dead of the mighty Sargasso wailing their own requiems. Or again, my fancy, diseased with much loneliness and brooding, likens it to the advancing rustle of armies of the great monsters that are always about us—waiting.

"And so to the coming of this new terror:—

"It was in the latter end of October that we first had knowledge of it—a tapping in the night time against the side of the vessel, below the water-line; a noise that came distinct, yet with a ghostly strangeness in the quietness of the night. It

---

[1] This is evidently a reference to something which Mr. Philips has set forth in an earlier message—one of the three lost messages—W. H. H.

was on a Monday night when first I heard it. I was down in the lazarette, overhauling our stores, and suddenly I heard it—tap—tap—tap—against the outside of the vessel upon the starboard side, and below the water-line. I stood for a while listening; but could not discover what it was that should come a-tapping against our side, away out here in this lonesome world of weed and slime. And then, as I stood there listening, the tapping ceased, and so I waited, wondering, and with a hateful sense of fear, weakening my manhood, and taking the courage out of my heart. . . .

"Abruptly, it recommenced; but now upon the opposite side of the vessel, and as it continued, I fell into a little sweat; for it seemed to me that some foul thing out in the night was tapping for admittance. Tap—tap—tap—it went, and continued, and there I stood listening, and so gripped about with frightened thoughts, that I seemed without power to stir myself; for the spell of the Weed-World, and the fear bred of its hidden terrors and the weight and dreeness of its loneliness have entered into my marrow, so that I could, then and now, believe in the likelihood of matters which, ashore and in the midst of my fellows, I might laugh at in contempt. It is the dire lonesomeness of this strange world into which I have entered, that serves so to take the heart out of a man.

"And so, as I have said, I stood there listening, and full of frightened, but undefined, thoughts; and all the while the tapping continued, sometimes with a regular insistence, and anon with a quick spasmodic tap, tap, tap-a-tap, as though some Thing, having Intelligence, signalled to me.

"Presently, however, I shook off something of the foolish fright that had taken me, and moved over to the place from which the tapping seemed to sound. Coming near to it, I bent my head down, close to the side of the vessel, and listened. Thus, I heard the noises with greater plainness, and could distinguish easily, now, that something knocked with a hard object upon the outside of the ship, as though someone had been striking her iron side with a small hammer.

"Then, even as I listened, came a thunderous blow close to my ear, so loud and astonishing, that I leaped sideways in sheer fright. Directly afterwards there came a second heavy blow, and then a third, as though someone had struck the ship's side with a heavy sledge-hammer, and after that, a space of silence, in which I heard my wife's voice at the trap of the lazaretto, calling down to me to know what had happened to cause so great a noise.

"'Hush, My Dear!' I whispered; for it seemed to me that the thing outside might hear her; though this could not have been possible, and I do but mention it as showing how the noises had set me off my natural balance.

"At my whispered command, my wife turned her about and came down the ladder into the semi-darkness of the place.

"'What is it, Arthur?' she asked, coming across to me, and slipping her hand between my arm and side.

"As though in reply to her query, there came against the outside of the ship, a fourth tremendous blow, filling the whole of the lazarette with a dull thunder.

"My wife gave out a frightened cry, and sprang away from me; but the next instant, she was back, and gripping hard at my arm.

"'What is it, Arthur? What is it?' she asked me; her voice, though no more than a frightened whisper, easily heard in the succeeding silence.

"'I don't know, Mary,' I replied, trying to speak in a level tone. 'It's—'

"'There's something again,' she interrupted, as the minor tapping noises recommenced.

"For about a minute, we stood silent, listening to those eerie taps. Then my wife turned to me:—

"'Is it anything dangerous, Arthur—tell me? I promise you I shall be brave.'

"'I can't possibly say, Mary,' I answered. 'I can't say; but I'm going up on deck to listen . . . Perhaps,' I paused a moment to think; but a fifth tremendous blow against the ship's side, drove whatever I was going to say, clean from me, and I could do no more than stand there, frightened and bewildered, listening for further sounds. After a short pause, there came a sixth blow. Then my wife caught me by the arm, and commenced to drag me towards the ladder.

"'Come up out of this dark place, Arthur,' she said. 'I shall be ill if we stay here any longer. Perhaps the—the thing outside can hear us, and it may stop if we go upstairs.'

"By this, my wife was all of a shake, and I but little better, so that I was glad to follow her up the ladder. At the top, we paused for a while to listen, bending down over the open hatchway. A space of, maybe, some five minutes passed away in silence; then there commenced again the tapping noises, the sounds coming clearly up to us where we crouched. Presently, they ceased once more, and after that, though we listened for a further space of some ten minutes, they were not repeated. Neither were there any more of the great bangs.

"In a little, I led my wife away from the hatch, to a seat in the saloon; for the hatch is situated under the saloon table. After that, I returned to the opening, and replaced the cover. Then I went into our cabin—the one which had been the Captain's, her father,—and brought from there a revolver, of which we have several. This, I loaded with care, and afterwards placed in my side pocket.

"Having done this, I fetched from the pantry, where I have made it my use to keep such things at hand, a bull's-eye lantern, the same having been used on dark nights when clearing up the ropes from the decks. This, I lit, and afterwards turned the dark-slide to cover the light. Next, I slipped off my boots; and then, as an afterthought, I reached down one of the long-handled American axes from the rack about the mizzenmast—these being keen and very formidable weapons.

"After that, I had to calm my wife and assure her that I would run no unnecessary risks, if, indeed, there were any risks to run; though, as may be imagined, I could not say what new peril might not be upon us. And then, picking up the lantern, I made my way silently on stockinged feet, up the companionway. I had reached the top, and was just stepping out on to the deck, when something caught my arm. I turned swiftly, and perceived that my wife had followed me up the steps, and from the shaking of her hand upon my arm, I gathered that she was very much agitated.

"'Oh, My Dear, My Dear, don't go! don't go!' she whispered, eagerly. 'Wait until it is daylight. Stay below to-night. You don't know what may be about in this horrible place.'

"I put the lantern and the axe upon the deck beside the companion; then bent towards the opening, and took her into my arms, soothing her, and stroking her hair; yet with ever an alert glance to and fro along the indistinct decks. Presently, she was more like her usual self, and listened to my reasoning, that she would do better to stay below, and so, in a little, left me, having made me promise afresh that I would be very wary of danger.

"When she had gone, I picked up the lantern and the axe, and made my way cautiously to the side of the vessel. Here, I paused and listened very carefully, being just above that spot upon the port side where I had heard the greater part of the tapping, and all of the heavy bangs; yet, though I listened, as I have said, with much attention, there was no repetition of the sounds.

"Presently, I rose and made my way forrard to the break of the poop. Here, bending over the rail which ran across, I listened, peering along the dim main-decks; but could neither see nor hear anything; not that, indeed, I had any reason for expecting to see or hear ought unusual *aboard* of the vessel; for all of the noises had come from over the side, and, more than that, from beneath the water-line. Yet in the state of mind in which I was, I had less use for reason than fancy; for that strange thudding and tapping, out here in the midst of this world of loneliness, had set me vaguely imagining unknowable terrors, stealing upon me from every shadow that lay upon the dimly-seen decks.

"Then, as still I listened, hesitating to go down on to the main-deck, yet too dissatisfied with the result of my peerings, to cease from my search, I heard, faint yet clear in the stillness of the night, the tapping noises recommence.

"I took my weight from off the rail, and listened; but I could no longer hear them, and at that, I leant forward again over the rail, and peered down on to the main-deck. Immediately, the sounds came once more to me, and I knew now, that they were borne to me by the medium of the rail, which conducted them to me through the iron stanchions by which it is fixed to the vessel.

"At that, I turned and went aft along the poop-deck, moving very warily and with quietness. I stopped over the place where first I had heard the louder noises, and stooped, putting my ear against the rail. Here, the sounds came to me with great distinctness.

"For a little, I listened; then stood up, and slid away that part of the tarred canvas-screen which covers the port opening through which we dump our refuse;

they being made here for convenience, one upon each side of the vessel. This, I did very silently; then, leaning forward through the opening, I peered down into the dimness of the weed. Even as I did so, I heard plainly below me a heavy thud, muffled and dull by reason of the intervening water, against the iron side of the ship. It seemed to me that there was some disturbance amid the dark, shadowy masses of the weed. Then I had opened the dark-slide of my lantern, and sent a clear beam of light down into the blackness. For a brief instant, I thought I perceived a multitude of things moving. Yet, beyond that they were oval in shape, and showed white through the weed fronds, I had no clear conception of anything; for with the flash of the light, they vanished, and there lay beneath me only the dark, brown masses of the weed—demurely quiet.

"But an impression they did leave upon my over excited imagination—an impression that might have been due to morbidity, bred of too much loneliness; but nevertheless it seemed to me that I had seen momentarily a multitude of dead white faces, upturned towards me among the meshes of the weed.

"For a little, I leant there, staring down at the circle of illumined weed; yet with my thoughts in such a turmoil of frightened doubts and conjectures, that my physical eyes did but poor work, compared with the orb that looks inward. And through all the chaos of my mind there rose up weird and creepy memories— ghouls, the un-dead. There seemed nothing improbable, in that moment, in associating the terms with the fears that were besetting me. For no man may dare to say what terrors this world holds, until he has become lost to his brother men, amid the unspeakable desolation of the vast and slimy weed-plains of the Sargasso Sea.

"And then, as I leaned there, so foolishly exposing myself to those dangers which I had learnt did truly exist, my eyes caught and subconsciously noted the strange and subtle undulation which always foretells the approach of one of the giant octopi. Instantly, I leapt back, and whipped the tarred canvas-cover across the opening, and so stood alone there in the night, glancing frightenedly before and behind me, the beam from my lamp casting wavering splashes of light to and fro about the decks. And all the time, I was listening—listening; for it seemed to me that some Terror was brooding in the night, that might come upon us at any moment and in some unimagined form.

"Then, across the silence, stole a whisper, and I turned swiftly towards the companionway. My wife was there, and she reached out her arms to me, begging me to come below into safety. As the light from my lantern flashed upon her, I saw that she had a revolver in her right hand, and at that, I asked her what she had it for; whereupon she informed me that she had been watching over me, through the whole of the time that I had been on deck, save for the little while that it had taken her to get and load the weapon.

"At that, as may be imagined, I went and embraced her very heartily, kissing her for the love that had prompted her actions; and then, after that, we spoke a little together in low tones—she asking that I should come down and fasten up the companion-doors, and I demurring, telling her that I felt too unsettled to sleep; but would rather keep watch about the poop for a while longer.

"Then, even as we discussed the matter, I motioned to her for quietness. In the succeeding silence, she heard it, as well as I, a slow—tap! tap! tap! coming steadily along the dark main-decks. I felt a swift vile fear, and my wife's hold upon me became very tense, despite that she trembled a little. I released her grip from my arm, and made to go towards the break of the poop; but she was after me instantly, praying me at least to stay where I was, if I would not go below.

"Upon that, I bade her very sternly to release me, and go down into the cabin; though all the while I loved her for her very solicitude. But she disobeyed me, asserting very stoutly, though in a whisper, that if I went into danger, she would go with me; and at that I hesitated; but decided, after a moment, to go no further than the break of the poop, and not to venture on to the main-deck.

"I went very silently to the break, and my wife followed me. From the rail across the break, I shone the light of the lantern; but could neither see nor hear anything; for the tapping noise had ceased. Then it recommenced, seeming to have come near to the port side of the stump of the mainmast. I turned the lantern towards it, and, for one brief instant, it seemed to me that I saw something pale, just beyond the brightness of my light. At that, I raised my pistol and fired, and my wife did the same, though without any telling on my part. The noise of the double explosion went very loud and hollow sounding along the decks, and after the echoes had died away, we both of us thought we heard the tapping going away forrard again.

"After that, we stayed awhile, listening and watching; but all was quiet, and, presently, I consented to go below and bar up the companion, as my wife desired; for, indeed, there was much sense in her plea of the futility of my staying up upon the decks.

"The night passed quietly enough, and on the following morning, I made a very careful inspection of the vessel, examining the decks, the weed outside of the ship, and the sides of her. After that, I removed the hatches, and went down into the holds; but could nowhere find anything of an unusual nature.

"That night, just as we were making an end of our supper, we heard three tremendous blows given against the starboard side of the ship, whereat, I sprang to my feet, seized and lit the dark-lantern, which I had kept handy, and ran quickly and silently up on to the deck. My pistol, I had already in my pocket, and as I had soft slippers upon my feet, I needed not to pause to remove my footgear. In the companionway, I had left the axe, and this I seized as I went up the steps.

"Reaching the deck, I moved over quietly to the side, and slid back the canvas door; then I leant out and opened the slide of the lantern, letting its light play upon the weed in the direction from which the bangs had seemed to proceed; but nowhere could I perceive anything out of the ordinary, the weed seeming undisturbed. And so, after a little, I drew in my head, and slid-to the door in the canvas-screen; for it was but wanton folly to stand long exposed to any of the giant octopi that might chance to be prowling near, beneath the curtain of the weed.

"From then, until midnight, I stayed upon the poop, talking much in a quiet voice to my wife, who had followed me up into the companion. At times, we could hear the knocking; sometimes against one side of the ship, and again upon the other. And, between the louder knocks, and accompanying them, would sound the minor tap, tap, tap-a-tap, that I had first heard.

"About midnight, feeling that I could do nothing, and no harm appearing to result to us from the unseen things that seemed to be encircling us, my wife and I made our way below to rest, securely barring the companion-doors behind us.

"It would be, I should imagine, about two o'clock in the morning, that I was aroused from a somewhat troubled sleep, by the agonised screaming of our great boar, away forrard. I leant up upon my elbow, and listened, and so grew speedily wide awake. I sat up, and slid from my bunk to the floor. My wife, as I could tell from her breathing, was sleeping peacefully, so that I was able to draw on a few clothes without disturbing her.

"Then, having lit the dark-lantern, and turned the slide over the light, I took the axe in my other hand, and hastened towards the door that gives out of the forrard end of the saloon, on to the main-deck, beneath the shelter of the break of the poop. This door, I had locked before turning-in, and now, very noiselessly, I unlocked it, and turned the handle, opening the door with much caution. I peered out along the dim stretch of the main-deck; but could see nothing; then I turned on the slide of the lamp, and let the light play along the decks; but still nothing unusual was revealed to me.

"Away forrard, the shrieking of the pig had been succeeded by an absolute silence, and there was nowhere any noise, if I except an occasional odd tap-a-tap, which seemed to come from the side of the ship. And so, taking hold of my courage, I stepped out on to the main-deck, and proceeded slowly forrard, throwing the beam of light to and fro continuously, as I walked.

"Abruptly, I heard away in the bows of the ship a sudden multitudinous tapping and scraping and slithering; and so loud and near did it sound, that I was brought up all of a round-turn, as the saying is. For, perhaps, a whole minute, I stood there hesitating, and playing the light all about me, not knowing but that some hateful thing might leap upon me from out of the shadows.

"And then, suddenly, I remembered that I had left the door open behind me, that led into the saloon, so that, were there any deadly thing about the decks, it might chance to get in upon my wife and child as they slept. At the thought, I turned and ran swiftly aft again, and in through the door to my cabin. Here, I made sure that all was right with the two sleepers, and after that, I returned to the deck, shutting the door, and locking it behind me.

"And now, feeling very lonesome out there upon the dark decks, and cut off in a way from a retreat, I had need of all my manhood to aid me forrard to learn the wherefore of the pig's crying, and the cause of that manifold tapping. Yet go

I did, and have some right to be proud of the act; for the dreeness and lonesomeness and the cold fear of the Weed-World, squeeze the pluck out of one in a very woeful manner.

"As I approached the empty fo'cas'le, I moved with all wariness, swinging the light to and fro, and holding my axe very handily, and the heart within my breast like a shape of water, so in fear was I. Yet, I came at last to the pig-sty, and so discovered a dreadful sight. The pig, a huge boar of twenty-score pounds, had been dragged out on to the deck, and lay before the sty with all his belly ripped up, and stone dead. The iron bars of the sty—great bars they are too—had been torn apart, as though they had been so many straws; and, for the rest, there was a deal of blood both within the sty and upon the decks.

"Yet, I did not stay then to see more; for, all of a sudden, the realisation was borne upon me that this was the work of some monstrous thing, which even at that moment might be stealing upon me; and, with the thought, an overwhelming fear leapt upon me, overbearing my courage; so that I turned and ran for the shelter of the saloon, and never stopped until the stout door was locked between me and that which had wrought such destruction upon the pig. And as I stood there, quivering a little with very fright, I kept questioning dumbly as to what manner of wild-beast thing it was that could burst asunder iron bars, and rip the life out of a great boar, as though it were of no more account than a kitten. And then more vital questions:— How did it get aboard, and where had it hidden? And again:— *What was it?* And so in this fashion for a good while, until I had grown something more calmed.

"But through all the remainder of that night, I slept not so much as a wink.

"Then in the morning when my wife awoke, I told her of the happenings of the night; whereat she turned very white, and fell to reproaching me for going out at all on to the deck, declaring that I had run needlessly into danger, and that, at least, I should not have left her alone, sleeping in ignorance of what was towards. And after that, she fell into a fit of crying, so that I had some to-do comforting her. Yet, when she had come back to calmness, she was all for accompanying me about the decks, to see by daylight what had indeed befallen in the night-time. And from this decision, I could not turn her; though I assured her I should have told her nothing, had it not been that I wished to warn her from going to and fro between the saloon and the galley, until I had made a thorough search about the decks. Yet, as I have remarked, I could not turn her from her purpose of accompanying me, and so was forced to let her come, though against my desire.

"We made our way on deck through the door that opens under the break of the poop, my wife carrying her loaded revolver half-clumsily in both hands, whilst I had mine held in my left, and the long-handled axe in my right—holding it very readily.

"On stepping out on to the deck, we closed the door behind us, locking it and removing the key; for we had in mind our sleeping child. Then we went slowly forrard along the decks, glancing about warily. As we came fore-side of the pig-sty, and my wife saw that which lay beyond it, she let out a little exclamation of horror, shuddering at the sight of the mutilated pig, as, indeed, well she might.

"For my part, I said nothing; but glanced with much apprehension about us; feeling a fresh access of fright; for it was very plain to me that the boar had been molested since I had seen it the head having been torn, with awful might, from the body; and there were, besides, other new and ferocious wounds, one of which had come nigh to severing the poor brute's body in half. All of which was so much additional evidence of the formidable character of the monster, or Monstrosity, that had attacked the animal.

"I did not delay by the pig, nor attempt to touch it; but beckoned my wife to follow me up on to the fo'cas'le head. Here, I removed the canvas-cover from the small skylight which lights the fo'cas'le beneath; and, after that, I lifted off the heavy top, letting a flood of light down into the gloomy place. Then I leant down into the opening, and peered about; but could discover no signs of any lurking thing, and so returned to the main-deck, and made an entrance into the fo'cas'le through the starboard doorway. And now I made a more minute search; but discovered nothing, beyond the mournful array of sea-chests that had belonged to our dead crew.

"My search concluded, I hastened out from the doleful place, into the daylight, and after that made fast the door again, and saw to it that the one upon the port side was also securely locked. Then I went up again on to the fo'cas'le head, and replaced the skylight-top and the canvas-cover, battening the whole down very thoroughly.

"And in this wise, and with an incredible care, did I make my search through the ship, fastening up each place behind me, so that I should be certain that no Thing was playing some dread game of hide and seek with me.

"Yet I found *nothing*, and had it not been for the grim evidence of the dead and mutilated boar, I had been like to have thought nothing more dreadful than an over vivid Imagination had roamed the decks in the darkness of the past night.

"That I had reason to feel puzzled, may be the better understood, when I explain that I had examined the whole of the great, tarred canvas-screen, which I have built about the ship as a protection against the sudden tentacles of any of the roaming giant octopi, without discovering any torn place such as must have been made if any conceivable monster had climbed aboard out of the weed. Also, it must be borne in mind that the ship stands many feet out of the weed, presenting only her smooth iron sides to anything that desires to climb aboard.

"And yet there was the dead pig, lying brutally torn before its empty sty! An undeniable proof that, to go out upon the decks after dark, was to run the risk of meeting a horrible and mysterious death!

"Through all that day, I pondered over this new fear that had come upon us, and particularly upon the monstrous and unearthly power that had torn apart the stout iron bars of the sty, and so ferociously wrenched off the head of the boar. The result of my pondering was that I removed our sleeping belongings that evening from the cabin to the iron half-deck—a little, four-bunked house, standing fore-side of the stump of the mainmast, and built entirely of iron, even to the single door, which opens out of the after end.

"Along with our sleeping matters, I carried forrard to our new lodgings, a lamp, and oil, also the dark-lantern, a couple of the axes, two rifles, and all of the revolvers, as well as a good supply of ammunition. Then I bade my wife forage out sufficient provisions to last us for a week, if need be, and whilst she was so busied, I cleaned out and filled the water breaker which belonged to the half-deck.

"At half-past six, I sent my wife forrard to the little iron house, with the baby, and then I locked up the saloon and all of the cabin doors, finally locking after me the heavy, teak door that opened out under the break of the poop.

"Then I went forrard to my wife and child, and shut and bolted the iron door of the half-deck for the night. After that, I went round and saw to it that all of the iron storm-doors, that shut over the eight ports of the house, were in good working order, and so we sat down, as it were, to await the night.

"By eight o'clock, the dusk was upon us, and before half-past, the night hid the decks from my sight. Then I shut down all the iron port-flaps, and screwed them up securely, and after that, I lit the lamp.

"And so a space of waiting ensued, during which I whispered reassuringly to my wife, from time to time, as she looked across at me from her seat beside the sleeping child, with frightened eyes, and a very white face; for somehow there had come upon us within the last hour, a sense of chilly fright, that went straight to one's heart, robbing one vilely of pluck.

"A little later, a sudden sound broke the impressive silence—a sudden dull thud against the side of the ship; and, after that, there came a succession of heavy blows, seeming to be struck all at once upon every side of the vessel; after which there was quietness for maybe a quarter of an hour.

"Then, suddenly, I heard, away forrard, a tap, tap, tap, and then a loud rattling, slurring noise, and a loud crash. After that, I heard many other sounds, and always that tap, tap, tap, repeated a hundred times, as though an army of wooden-legged men were busied all about the decks at the fore end of the ship.

"Presently, there came to me the sound of something coming down the deck, tap, tap, tap, it came. It drew near to the house, paused for nigh a minute; then continued away aft towards the saloon:— tap, tap, tap. I shivered a little, and then, fell half consciously to thanking God that I had been given wisdom to bring my wife and child forrard to the security of the iron deckhouse.

"About a minute later, I heard the sound of a heavy blow struck somewhere away aft; and after that a second, and then a third, and seeming by the sounds to have been against iron—the iron of the bulkshead that runs across the break of the poop. There came the noise of a fourth blow, and it blended into the crash of broken woodwork. And therewith, I had a little tense quivering inside me; for the little one and my wife might have been sleeping aft there at that very moment, had it not been for the Providential thought which had sent us forrard to the half-deck.

"With the crash of the broken door, away aft, there came, from forrard of us, a great tumult of noises; and, directly, it sounded as though a multitude of wooden-legged men were coming down the decks from forrard. Tap, tap, tap; tap-a-tap, the noises came, and drew abreast of where we sat in the house, crouched and holding our breaths, for fear that we should make some noise to attract THAT which was without. The sounds passed us, and went tapping away aft, and I let out a little breath of sheer easement. Then, as a sudden thought came to me, I rose and turned down the lamp, fearing that some ray from it might be seen from beneath the door. And so, for the space of an hour, we sat wordless, listening to the sounds which came from away aft, the thud of heavy blows, the occasional crash of wood, and, presently the tap, tap, tap, again, coming forrard towards us.

"The sounds came to a stop, opposite the starboard side of the house, and, for a full minute, there was quietness. Then suddenly, "Boom!" a tremendous blow had been struck against the side of the house. My wife gave out a little gasping cry, and there came a second blow; and, at that, the child awoke and began to wail, and my wife was put to it, with trying to soothe her into immediate silence.

"A third blow was struck, filling the little house with a dull thunder of sound, and then I heard the tap, tap, tap, move round to the after end of the house. There came a pause, and then a great blow right upon the door. I grasped the rifle, which I had leant against my chair, and stood up; for I did not know but that the thing might be upon us in a moment, so prodigious was the force of the blows it struck. Once again it struck the door, and after that went tap, tap, tap, round to the port side of the house, and there struck the house again; but now I had more ease of mind for it was its direct attack upon the door, that had put such horrid dread into my heart.

"After the blows upon the port side of the house, there came a long spell of silence, as though the thing outside were listening; but, by the mercy of God, my wife had been able to soothe the child, so that no sound from us, told of our presence.

"Then, at last, there came again the sounds:— tap, tap, tap, as the voiceless thing moved away forrard. Presently, I heard the noises cease aft; and, after that, there came a multitudinous tap-a-tapping, coming along the decks. It passed the house without so much as a pause, and receded away forrard.

"For a space of over two hours, there was an absolute silence; so that I judged that we were now no longer in danger of being molested. An hour later, I whispered to my wife; but, getting no reply, knew that she had fallen into a doze, and so I sat on, listening tensely; yet making no sort of noise that might attract attention.

"Presently, by the thin line of light from beneath the door, I saw that the day was breaking; and, at that, I rose stiffly, and commenced to unscrew the iron port-covers. I unscrewed the forrard ones first, and looked out into the wan dawn; but could discover nothing unusual about so much of the decks as I could see from there.

"After that, I went round and opened each, as I came to it, in its turn; but it was not until I had uncovered the port which gave me a view of the port side of the after main-deck, that I discovered anything extraordinary. Then I saw, at first dimly, but more clearly as the day brightened, that the door, leading from beneath the break of the poop into the saloon, had been broken to flinders, some of which lay scattered upon the deck, and some of which still hung from the bent hinges; whilst more, no doubt, were strewed in the passage beyond my sight.

"Turning from the port, I glanced towards my wife, and saw that she lay half in and half out of the baby's bunk, sleeping with her head besides the child's, both upon one pillow. At the sight, a great wave of holy thankfulness took me, that we had been so wonderfully spared from the terrible and mysterious danger that had stalked the decks in the darkness of the preceding night. Feeling thus, I stole across the floor of the house, and kissed them both very gently, being full of tenderness, yet not minded to waken them. And, after that, I lay down in one of the bunks, and slept until the sun was high in the heaven.

"When I awoke, my wife was about and had tended to the child and prepared our breakfast, so that I had naught to do but tumble out and set to, the which I did with a certain keenness of appetite, induced, I doubt not, by the stress of the night. Whilst we ate, we discussed the peril through which we had just passed; but without coming any the nearer to a solution of the weird mystery of the Terror.

"Breakfast over, we took a long and final survey of the decks, from the various ports, and then prepared to sally out. This we did with instinctive caution and quietness, both of us armed as on the previous day. The door of the half-deck we closed and locked behind us, thereby ensuring that the child was open to no danger whilst we were in other parts of the ship.

"After a quick look about us, we proceeded aft towards the shattered door beneath the break of the poop. At the doorway, we stopped, not so much with the intent to examine the broken door, as because of an instinctive and natural hesitation to go forward into the saloon, which but a few hours previous had been visited by some incredible monster or monsters. Finally, we decided to go up upon the poop and peer down through the skylight. This we did, lifting the sides of the dome for that purpose; yet though we peered long and earnestly, we could perceive no signs of any lurking thing. But broken woodwork there appeared to be in plenty, to judge by the scattered pieces.

"After that, I unlocked the companion, and pushed back the big, over-arching slide. Then, silently, we stole down the steps and into the saloon. Here, being now able to see the big cabin through all its length, we discovered a most extraordinary scene; the whole place appeared to be wrecked from end to end; the six cabins that line each side had their bulksheading driven into shards and slivers of broken wood in places. Here, a door would be standing untouched, whilst the bulkshead beside it was in a mass of flinders—There, a door would be driven completely from its hinges, whilst the surrounding woodwork was untouched. And so it was, wherever we looked.

"My wife made to go towards our cabin; but I pulled her back, and went forward myself. Here the desolation was almost as great. My wife's bunk-board had been ripped out, whilst the supporting side-batten of mine had been plucked forth, so that all the bottom-boards of the bunk had descended to the floor in a cascade:

"But it was neither of these things that touched us so sharply, as the fact that the child's little swing cot had been wrenched from its standards, and flung in a tangled mass of white-painted ironwork across the cabin. At the sight of that, I glanced across at my wife, and she at me, her face grown very white. Then down she slid to her knees, and fell to crying and thanking God together, so that I found myself beside her in a moment, with a very humble and thankful heart.

"Presently, when we were more controlled, we left the cabin, and finished our search. The pantry, we discovered to be entirely untouched, which, somehow, I do not think was then a matter of great surprise to me; for I had ever a feeling that the things which had broken a way into our sleeping cabin, had been looking for us.

"In a little while, we left the wrecked saloon and cabins, and made our way forrard to the pig-sty; for I was anxious to see whether the carcass of the pig had been touched. As we came round the corner of the sty, I uttered a great cry; for there, lying upon the deck, on its back, was a gigantic crab, so vast in size that I had not conceived so huge a monster existed. Brown it was in colour, save for the belly part, which was of a light yellow.

"One of its pincer-claws, or mandibles, had been torn off in the fight in which it must have been slain (for it was all disembowelled). And this one claw weighed so heavy that I had some to-do to lift it from the deck; and by this you may have some idea of the size and formidableness of the creature itself.

"Around the great crab, lay half a dozen smaller ones, no more than from seven or eight to twenty inches across, and all white in colour, save for an occasional mottling of brown. These had all been killed by a single nip of an enormous mandible, which had in every case smashed them almost into two halves. Of the carcass of the great boar, not a fragment remained.

"And so was the mystery solved; and, with the solution, departed the superstitious terror which had suffocated me through those three nights, since the tapping had commenced. We had been attacked by a wandering shoal of giant crabs, which, it is quite possible, roam across the weed from place to place, devouring aught that comes in their path.

"Whether they had ever boarded a ship before, and so, perhaps, developed a moustrous lust for human flesh, or whether their attack had been prompted by curiosity, I cannot possibly say. It may be that, at first, they mistook the hull of the vessel for the body of some dead marine monster, and hence their blows upon her sides, by which, possibly, they were endeavouring to pierce through our somewhat unusually tough hide!

"Or, again, it may be that they have some power of scent, by means of which they were able to smell our presence aboard the ship; but this (as they made no general attack upon us in the deckhouse) I feel disinclined to regard as probable.

And yet—I do not know. Why their attack upon the saloon, and our sleeping-cabin? As I say, I cannot tell, and so must leave it there.

"The way in which they came aboard, I discovered that same day; for, having learned what manner of creature it was that had attacked us, I made a more intelligent survey of the sides of the ship; but it was not until I came to the extreme bows, that I saw how they had managed. Here, I found that some of the gear of the broken bowsprit and jibboom, trailed down on to the weed, and as I had not extended the canvas-screen across the heel of the bowsprit, the monsters had been able to climb up the gear, and thence aboard, without the least obstruction being opposed to their progress.

"This state of affairs, I very speedily remedied; for, with a few strokes of my axe, I cut through the gear, allowing it to drop down among the weed; and, after that, I built a temporary breastwork of wood across the gap, between the two ends of the screen; later on making it more permanent.

"Since that time, we have been no more molested by the giant crabs; though for several nights afterwards, we heard them knocking strangely against our sides. Maybe, they are attracted by such refuse as we are forced to dump overboard, and this would explain their first tappings being aft, opposite to the lazarette; for it is from the openings in this part of the canvas-screen that we cast our rubbish.

"Yet, it is weeks now since we heard aught of them, so that I have reason to believe that they have betaken themselves elsewhere, maybe to attack some other lonely humans, living out their short span of life aboard some lone derelict, lost even to memory in the depth of this vast sea of weed and deadly creatures.

"I shall send this message forth on its journey, as I have sent the other four, within a well-pitched barrel, attached to a small fire-balloon. The shell of the severed claw of the monster crab, I shall enclose,[1] as evidence of the terrors that beset us in this dreadful place. Should this message, and the claw, ever fall into human hands, let them, contemplating this vast mandible, try to imagine the size of the other crab or crabs that could destroy so formidable a creature as the one to which this claw belonged.

"What other terrors does this hideous world hold for us?

"I had thought of inclosing, along with the claw, the shell of one of the white smaller crabs. It must have been some of these moving in the weed that night, that set my disordered fancy to imagining of ghouls and the Un-Dead. But, on thinking it over, I shall not; for to do so would be to illustrate nothing that needs illustration, and it would but increase needlessly the weight which the balloon will have to lift.

"And so I grow wearied of writing. The night is drawing near, and I have little more to tell. I am writing this in the saloon, and, though I have mended and carpentered so well as I am able, nothing I can do will hide the traces of that night when the vast crabs raided through these cabins, searching for—WHAT?

[1]Captain Bolton makes no mention of the claw, in the covering letter which he has enclosed with the MS. —W. H. H.

"There is nothing more to say. In health, I am well, and so is my wife and the little one, but. . . .

"I must have myself under control, and be patient. We are beyond all help, and must bear that which is before us, with such bravery as we are able. And with this, I end; for my last word shall not be one of complaint.

"ARTHUR SAMUEL PHILIPS."

"Christmas Eve, 1879."

The Derelict

"It's the *Material*," said the old ship's doctor. . . . "The *Material*, plus the Conditions; and, maybe," he added slowly, " a third factor—yes, a third factor; but there, there. . . ." He broke off his half-meditative sentence, and began to charge his pipe.

"Go on, Doctor," we said, encouragingly, and with more than a little expectancy. We were in the smoke-room of the *Sand-a-lea*, running across the North Atlantic; and the Doctor was a character. He concluded the charging of his pipe, and lit it; then settled himself, and began to express himself more fully:—

"The *Material*," he said, with conviction, "is inevitably the medium of expression of the Life Force—the fulcrum, as it were; lacking which, it is unable to exert itself, or, indeed, to express itself in any form or fashion that would be intelligible or evident to us.

"So potent is the share of the *Material* in the production of that thing which we name Life, and so eager the Life-Force to express itself, that I am convinced it would, if given the right Conditions, make itself manifest even through so hopeless-seeming a medium as a simple block of sawn wood; for I tell you, gentlemen, the Life-Force is both as fiercely urgent and as indiscriminate as Fire— the Destructor; yet which some are now growing to consider the very essence of Life rampant. . . . There is a quaint seeming paradox there," he concluded, nodding his old grey head.

"Yes, Doctor," I said. "In brief, your argument is that Life is a thing, state, fact, or element, call-it-what-you-like, which requires the *Material* through which to manifest itself, and that given the *Material*, plus the Conditions, the result is Life. In other words, that Life is an evolved product, manifested through Matter and bred of Conditions—Eh?"

"As we understand the word," said the old Doctor. "Though, mind you, there *may* be a third factor. But, in my heart, I believe that it is a matter of chemistry; Conditions and a suitable medium; but given the Conditions, the Brute is so almighty that it will seize upon anything through which to manifest itself. It is a Force generated by Conditions; but nevertheless this does not bring us one iota nearer to its *explanation*, any more than to the explanation of Electricity or Fire. They are, all three, of the Outer Forces—Monsters of the Void. Nothing we can do will *create* any one of them; our power is merely to be able, by providing the Conditions, to make each one of them manifest to our physical senses. Am I clear?"

"Yes, Doctor, in a way you are," I said. "But I don't agree with you; though I think I understand you. Electricity and Fire are both what I might call natural things; but Life is an abstract something—a kind of all-permeating Wakefulness. Oh, I can't explain it; who could! But it's spiritual; not just a thing bred out of a Condition, like Fire, as you say, or Electricity. It's a horrible thought of yours. Life's a kind of spiritual mystery. . . ."

" Easy, my boy!" said the old Doctor, laughing gently to himself; "or else I may be asking you to demonstrate the spiritual mystery of life of the limpet, or the crab, shall we say."

He grinned at me, with ineffable perverseness. "Anyway," he continued, "as I suppose you've all guessed, I've a yarn to tell you in support of my impression that Life is no more a mystery or a miracle than Fire or Electricity. But, please to remember, gentlemen, that because we've succeeded in naming and making good use of these two Forces, they're just as much mysteries, fundamentally, as ever. And, anyway, the thing I'm going to tell you, won't explain the mystery of Life; but only give you one of my pegs on which I hang my feeling that Life is, as I have said, a Force made manifest through Conditions (that is to say, natural Chemistry), and that it can take for its purpose and Need, the most incredible and unlikely Matter; for without Matter, it cannot come into existence—it cannot become manifest. . . ."

"I don't agree with you, Doctor," I interrupted. "Your theory would destroy all belief in life after death. It would. . . ."

"Hush, sonny," said the old man, with a quiet little smile of comprehension. "Hark to what I've to say first; and, anyway, what objection have you to material life, after death; and if you object to a material framework, I would still have you remember that I am speaking of Life, as we understand the word in this our life. Now do be a quiet lad, or I'll never be done:—

"It was when I was a young man, and that is a good many years ago, gentlemen. I had passed my examinations; but was so run down with overwork, that it was decided that I had better take a trip to sea. I was by no means well off, and very glad, in the end, to secure a nominal post as Doctor in a sailing passenger-clipper, running out to China.

"The name of the ship was the *Bheotpte*, and soon after I had got all my gear aboard, she cast off, and we dropped down the Thames, and next day were well away out in the Channel.

"The Captain's name was Gannington, a very decent man; though quite illiterate. The First Mate, Mr. Berlies, was a quiet, sternish, reserved man, very well-read. The Second Mate, Mr. Selvern, was, perhaps, by birth and upbringing, the most socially cultured of the three; but he lacked the stamina and indomitable pluck of the two others. He was more of a sensitive; and emotionally and even mentally, the most alert man of the three.

"On our way out, we called at Madagascar, where we landed some of our passengers; then we ran Eastward, meaning to call at North West Cape; but about a hundred degrees East, we encountered very dreadful weather, which carried away all our sails, and sprung the jibboom and fore t'gallant mast.

"The storm carried us Northward for several hundred miles, and when it dropped us finally, we found ourselves in a very bad state. The ship had been strained, and had taken some three feet of water through her seams; the main top-mast had been sprung, in addition to the jibboom and fore t'gallant mast; two of our boats had gone, as also one of the pigsties (with three fine pigs), this latter having been washed overboard but some half hour before the wind began to ease, which it did quickly; though a very ugly sea ran for some hours after.

"The wind left us just before dark, and when morning came, it brought splendid weather; a calm, mildly undulating sea, and a brilliant sun, with no wind. It showed us also that we were not alone; for about two miles away to the Westward, was another vessel, which Mr. Selvern, the Second Mate, pointed out to me.

"'That's a pretty rum looking packet, Doctor, he said, and handed me his glass. I looked through it, at the other vessel, and saw what he meant; at least, I thought I did.

"Yes, Mr. Selvern,' I said, 'she's got a pretty old-fashioned look about her.'

"He laughed at me, in his pleasant way.

"'It's easy to see you're not a sailor, Doctor,' he remarked. 'There's a dozen rum things about her. She's a derelict, and has been floating round, by the look of her, for many a score of years. Look at the shape of her counter, and the bows and cutwater. She's as old as the hills, as you might say, and ought to have gone down to Davy Jones a long time ago. Look at the growths on her, and the thickness of her standing rigging; that's all salt encrustations, I fancy, if you notice the white colour. She's been a small barque; but don't you see she's not a yard left aloft. They've all dropped out of the slings; everything rotted away; wonder the standing rigging hasn't gone too. I wish the Old Man would let us take the boat, and have a look at her; she'd be well worth it.'

"There seemed little chance, however, of this; for all hands were turned-to and kept hard at it all day long, repairing the damage to the masts and gear, and this took a long while, as you may think. Part of the time, I gave a hand, heaving on one of the deck-capstans; for the exercise was good for my liver. Old Captain Gannington approved, and I persuaded him to come along and try some of the same medicine, which he did; and we grew very chummy over the job.

"We got talking about the derelict, and he remarked how lucky we were not to have run full tilt on to her, in the darkness; for she lay right away to leeward of us, according to the way that we had been drifting in the storm. He also was of the opinion that she had a strange look about her, and that she was pretty old; but on this latter point, he plainly had far less knowledge than the Second Mate; for he was, as I have said, an illiterate man, and knew nothing of sea-craft, beyond what experience had taught him. He lacked the book-knowledge which the Second Mate had, of vessels previous to his day, which it appeared the derelict was.

"'She's an old 'un, Doctor,' was the extent of his observations in this direction.

"Yet, when I mentioned to him that it would be interesting to go aboard, and give her a bit of an overhaul, he nodded his head, as if the idea had been already in his mind, and accorded with his own inclinations.

"'When the work's over, Doctor,' he said. 'Can't spare the men now, ye know. Got to get all shipshape an' ready as smart as we can. But we'll take my gig, an' go off in the Second Dog Watch. The glass is steady, an' it'll be a bit of gam for us.'

"That evening, after tea, the captain gave orders to clear the gig and get her overboard. The Second Mate was to come with us, and the Skipper gave him word to see that two or three lamps were put into the boat, as it would soon fall dark. A little later, we were pulling across the calmness of the sea, with a crew of six at the oars, and making very good speed of it.

"Now, gentlemen, I have detailed to you with great exactness, all the facts, both big and little, so that you can follow step by step each incident in this extraordinary affair; and I want you now to pay the closest attention.

"I was sitting in the stern-sheets, with the Second Mate, and the Captain, who was steering; and as we drew nearer and nearer to the stranger, I studied her with an ever growing attention, as, indeed, did Captain Gannington and the Second Mate. She was, as you know, to the Westward of us, and the sunset was making a great flame of red light to the back of her, so that she showed a little blurred and indistinct, by reason of the halation of the light, which almost defeated the eye in any attempt to see her rotting spars and standing-rigging, submerged as they were in the fiery glory of the sunset.

"It was because of this effect of the sunset, that we had come quite close, comparatively, to the derelict, before we saw that she was all surrounded by a sort of curious scum, the colour of which was difficult to decide upon, by reason of the red light that was in the atmosphere; but which afterwards we discovered to be brown. This scum spread all about the old vessel for many hundreds of yards, in a huge, irregular patch, a great stretch of which reached out to the Eastward, upon our starboard side, some score, or so, fathoms away.

"'Queer stuff,' said Captain Gannington, leaning to the side, and looking over. 'Something in the cargo as 'as gone rotten an' worked out through 'er seams.'

"'Look at her bows and stern,' said the Second Mate; 'just look at the growth on her.'

"There were, as he said, great clumpings of strange-looking sea-fungi under the bows and the short counter astern. From the stump of her jibboom and her cutwater, great beards of rime and marine-growths hung downward into the scum that held her in. Her blank starboard side was presented to us, all a dead, dirtyish white, streaked and mottled vaguely with dull masses of heavier colour.

"'There's a steam or haze rising off her,' said the Second Mate, speaking again; 'you can see it against the light. It keeps coming and going. Look!'

"I saw then what he meant—a faint haze or steam, either suspended above the old vessel, or rising from her; and Captain Gannington saw it also:—

"'Spontaneous combustion!' he exclaimed. 'We'll 'ave to watch w'en we lift the 'atches; 'nless it's some poor devil that's got aboard of 'er; but that ain't likely.'

"We were now within a couple of hundred yards of the old derelict, and had entered into the brown scum. As it poured off the lifted oars, I heard one of the men mutter to himself:—'dam treacle!' and, indeed, it was something like it. As the boat continued to forge nearer and nearer to the old ship, the scum grew thicker and thicker; so that, at last, it perceptibly slowed us.

"'Give way, lads! Put some beef to it!' sung out Captain Gannington; and thereafter there was no sound, except the panting of the men, and the faint, reiterated suck, suck, of the sullen brown scum upon the oars, as the boat was forced ahead. As we went, I was conscious of a peculiar smell in the evening air, and whilst I had no doubt that the puddling of the scum, by the oars, made it rise, I felt that in some way, it was vaguely familiar; yet I could give it no name.

"We were now very close to the old vessel, and presently she was high above us, against the dying light. The Captain called out then to:—'in with the bow oars, and stand-by with the boat-hook,' which was done.

"'Aboard there! Ahoy! Aboard there! Ahoy!' shouted Captain Gannington; but there came no answer, only the flat sound of his voice going lost into the open sea, each time he sung out.

"'Ahoy! Aboard there! Ahoy!' he shouted, time after time; but there was only the weary silence of the old hulk that answered us; and, somehow as he shouted, the while that I stared up half expectantly at her, a queer little sense of oppression, that amounted almost to nervousness, came upon me. It passed; but I remember how I was suddenly aware that it was growing dark. Darkness comes fairly rapidly in the tropics; though not so quickly as many fiction-writers seem to think; but it was not that the coming dusk had perceptibly deepened in that brief time, of only a few moments, but rather that my nerves had made me suddenly a little hyper-sensitive. I mention my state particularly; for I am not a nervy man, normally; and my abrupt touch of nerves is significant, in the light of what happened.

"'There's no one aboard there!' said Captain Gannington. 'Give way, men!' For the boat's crew had instinctively rested on their oars, as the Captain hailed the old craft. The man gave way again; and then the Second Mate called out excitedly:—'Why, look there, there's our pigsty! See, it's got *Bheotpte* painted on the end. It's drifted down here, and the scum's caught it. What a blessed wonder!'

"It was, as he had said, our pigsty that had been washed overboard in the storm; and most extraordinary to come across it there.

"'We'll tow it off with us, when we go,' remarked the Captain, and shouted to the crew to get-down to their oars; for they were hardly moving the boat, because the scum was so thick, close in around the old ship, that it literally clogged the boat from going ahead. I remember that it struck me, in a half-conscious sort of way, as curious that the pigsty, containing our three dead pigs, had managed to drift in so far, unaided, whilst we could scarcely manage to *force* the boat in, now that we had come right into the scum. But the thought passed from my mind; for so many things happened within the next few minutes.

"The men managed to bring the boat in alongside, within a couple of feet of the derelict, and the man with the boat-hook, hooked on.

"''Ave ye got 'old there, forrard?' asked Captain Gannington.

"'Yessir!' said the bow-man; and as he spoke, there came a queer noise of tearing.

"'What's that?' asked the Captain.

"'It's tore, Sir. Tore clean away!' said the man; and his tone showed that he had received something of a shock.

"'Get a hold again then!' said Captain Gannington, irritably. 'You don't s'pose this packet was built yesterday! Shove the hook into the main chains.' The man did so, gingerly, as you might say; for it seemed to me, in the growing dusk, that he put no strain on to the hook; though, of course, there was no need; you see, the boat could not go very far, of herself, in the stuff in which she was embedded. I remember thinking this, also, as I looked up at the bulging side of the old vessel. Then I heard Captain Gannington's voice:—

"'Lord! but she's old! An' what a colour, Doctor! She don't half want paint, do she! . . . Now then, somebody, one of them oars.'

"An oar was passed to him, and he leant it up against the ancient, bulging side; then he paused, and called to the Second Mate to light a couple of the lamps, and stand-by to pass them up; for darkness had settled down now upon the sea.

"The Second Mate lit two of the lamps, and told one of the men to light a third, and keep it handy in the boat; then he stepped across, with a lamp in each hand, to where Captain Gannington stood by the oar against the side of the ship.

"'Now, my lad,' said the Captain, to the man who had pulled stroke, 'up with you, an' we'll pass ye up the lamps.'

"The man jumped to obey; caught the oar, and put his weight upon it, and as he did so, something seemed to give a little.

"'Look!' cried out the Second Mate, and pointed, lamp in hand. . . . 'It's sunk in!'

"This was true. The oar had made quite an indentation into the bulging, somewhat slimy side of the old vessel.

"'Mould, I reckon,' said Captain Gannington, bending towards the derelict, to look. Then, to the man:—

"'Up you go, my lad, and be smart. . . . Don't stand there waitin'!'

"At that, the man, who had paused a moment as he felt the oar give beneath his weight, began to shin up, and in a few seconds he was aboard, and leant out over the rail for the lamps. These were passed up to him, and the Captain called to him to steady the oar. Then Captain Gannington went, calling to me to follow, and after me the Second Mate.

"As the Captain put his face over the rail, he gave a cry of astonishment:—

91

"'Mould, by gum! Mould. . . . Tons of it! . . . Good Lord!'

"As I heard him shout that, I scrambled the more eagerly after him, and in a moment or two, I was able to see what he meant—Everywhere that the light from the two lamps struck, there was nothing but smooth great masses and surfaces of a dirty-white mould.

"I climbed over the rail, with the Second Mate close behind, and stood upon the mould-covered decks. There might have been no planking beneath the mould, for all that our feet could feel. It gave under our tread, with a spongy, puddingy feel. It covered the deck-furniture of the old ship, so that the shape of each article and fitment was often no more than suggested through it.

"Captain Gannington snatched a lamp from the man, and the Second Mate reached for the other. They held the lamps high, and we all stared. It was most extraordinary, and, somehow, most abominable. I can think of no other word, gentlemen, that so much describes the predominant feeling that affected me at the moment.

"'Good Lord!' said Captain Gannington, several times. 'Good Lord!' But neither the Second Mate nor the man said anything, and for my part I just stared, and at the same time began to smell a little at the air; for there was again a vague odour of something half familiar, that somehow brought to me a sense of half-known fright.

"I turned this way and that, staring, as I have said. Here and there, the mould was so heavy as to entirely disguise what lay beneath; converting the deck-fittings into indistinguishable mounds of mould, all dirty-white, and blotched and veined with irregular, dull purplish markings.

"There was a strange thing about the mould, which Captain Gannington drew attention to—it was that our feet did not crush into it and break the surface, as might have been expected; but merely indented it.

"'Never seen nothin' like it before! . . . Never!' said the Captain, after having stooped with his lamp to examine the mould under our feet. He stamped with his heel, and the stuff gave out a dull, puddingy sound. He stooped again, with a quick movement, and stared, holding the lamp close to the deck. 'Blest, if it ain't a reg'lar skin to it!' he said.

"The Second Mate and the man and I all stooped, and looked at it. The Second Mate progged it with his forefinger, and I remember I rapped it several times with my knuckles, listening to the dead sound it gave out, and noticing the close, firm texture of the mould.

"'Dough!' said the Second Mate. 'It's just like blessed dough! . . . Pouf!' He stood up with a quick movement. 'I could fancy it stinks a bit,' he said.

"As he said this, I knew suddenly what the familiar thing was, in the vague odour that hung about us—It was that the smell had something animal-like in it; something of the same smell, only *heavier*, that you will smell in any place that is infested with mice. I began to look about with a sudden very real uneasiness. . . . There might be vast numbers of hungry rats aboard. . . . They might prove exceedingly dangerous, if in a starving condition; yet, as you will understand, somehow I hesitated to put forward my idea as a reason for caution; it was too fanciful.

"Captain Gannington had begun to go aft, along the mould-covered maindeck, with the Second Mate; each of them holding his lamp high up, so as to cast a good light about the vessel. I turned quickly and followed them, the man with me keeping close to my heels, and plainly uneasy. As we went, I became aware that there was a feeling of moisture in the air, and I remembered the slight mist, or smoke, above the hulk, which had made Captain Gannington suggest spontaneous combustion, in explanation.

"And always, as we went, there was that vague, animal smell; and, suddenly, I found myself wishing we were well away from the old vessel.

"Abruptly, after a few paces, the Captain stopped and pointed at a row of mould-hidden shapes on either side of the maindeck . . . 'Guns,' he said. 'Been a privateer in the old days, I guess; maybe worse! We'll 'ave a look below, Doctor; there may be something worth touchin'. She's older than I thought. Mr. Selvern thinks she's about three hundred year old; but I scarce think it.'

"We continued our way aft, and I remember that I found myself walking as lightly and gingerly as possible; as if I were subconsciously afraid of treading through the rotten, mould-hid decks. I think the others had a touch of the same feeling, from the way that they walked. Occasionally, the soft mould would grip our heels, releasing them with a little, sullen suck.

"The Captain forged somewhat ahead of the Second Mate; and I know that the suggestion he had made himself, that perhaps there might be something below, worth the carrying away, had stimulated his imagination. The Second Mate was, however, beginning to feel somewhat the same way that I did; at least, I have that impression. I think, if it had not been for what I might truly describe as Captain Gannington's sturdy courage, we should all of us have just gone back over the side very soon; for there was most certainly an unwholesome feeling abroad, that made one feel queerly lacking in pluck; and you will soon perceive that this feeling was justified.

"Just as the Captain reached the few, mould-covered steps, leading up on to the short half-poop, I was suddenly aware that the feeling of moisture in the air had grown very much more definite. It was perceptible now, intermittently, as a sort of thin, moist, fog-like vapour, that came and went oddly, and seemed to make the decks a little indistinct to the view, this time and that. Once, an odd puff of it beat up suddenly from somewhere, and caught me in the face, carrying a queer, sickly, heavy odour with it, that somehow frightened me strangely, with a suggestion of a waiting and half-comprehended danger.

"We had followed Captain Gannington up the three, mould-covered steps, and now went slowly aft along the raised after-deck.

"By the mizzen-mast, Captain Gannington paused, and held his lantern near to it. . . .

"'My word, Mister,' he said to the Second Mate, it's fair thickened up with the mould; why, I'll g'antee it's close on four foot thick.' He shone the light down to where it met the deck. 'Good Lord!' he said, 'look at the sea-lice on it!' I stepped up; and it was as he had said; the sea-lice were thick upon it, some of them huge; not less than the size of large beetles, and all a clear, colourless shade, like water, except where there were little spots of grey in them, evidently their internal organisms.

"'I've never seen the like of them,'cept on a live cod!' said Captain Gannington, in an extremely puzzled voice. 'My word! but they're whoppers!' Then he passed on; but a few paces farther aft, he stopped again, and held his lamp near to the mould-hidden deck.

"'Lord bless me, Doctor!' he called out, in a low voice, 'did ye ever see the like of that? Why, it's a foot long, if it's a hinch!'

"I stooped over his shoulder, and saw what he meant; it was a clear, colourless creature, about a foot long, and about eight inches high, with a curved back that was extraordinarily narrow. As we stared, all in a group, it gave a queer little flick, and was gone.

"'Jumped!' said the Captain. 'Well, if that ain't a giant of all the sea-lice that ever I've seen! I guess it's jumped twenty-foot clear.' He straightened his back, and scratched his head a moment, swinging the lantern this way and that with the other hand, and staring about us. 'Wot are *they* doin' aboard 'ere!' he said. 'You'll see 'em (little things) on fat cod, an' such-like. . . . I'm blowed, Doctor, if I understand.'

"He held his lamp towards a big mound of the mould, that occupied part of the after portion of the low poop-deck, a little foreside of where there came a two-foot high 'break' to a kind of second and loftier poop, that ran away aft to the taffrail. The mound was pretty big, several feet across, and more than a yard high. Captain Gannington walked up to it:—

"'I reck'n this 's the scuttle,' he remarked, and gave it a heavy kick. The only result was a deep indentation into the huge, whitish hump of mould, as if he had driven his foot into a mass of some doughy substance. Yet, I am not altogether correct in saying that this was the only result; for a certain other thing happened— From a place made by the Captain's foot, there came a little gush of a purplish fluid, accompanied by a peculiar smell, that was, and was not, half-familiar. Some of the mould-like substance had stuck to the toe of the Captain's boot, and from this, likewise, there issued a sweat, as it were, of the same colour.

"'Well!' said Captain Gannington, in surprise; and drew back his foot to make another kick at the hump of mould; but he paused, at an exclamation from the Second Mate:—

"'Don't, Sir!' said the Second Mate.

"I glanced at him, and the light from Captain Gannington's lamp showed me that his face had a bewildered, half-frightened look, as if he were suddenly and unexpectedly half-afraid of something, and as if his tongue had given away his sudden fright, without any intention on his part to speak.

"The Captain also turned and stared at him:—

"'Why, Mister?' he asked, in a somewhat puzzled voice, through which there sounded just the vaguest hint of annoyance. 'We've got to shift this muck, if we're to get below.'

"I looked at the Second Mate, and it seemed to me that, curiously enough, he was listening less to the Captain, than to some other sound.

"Suddenly, he said in a queer voice:— 'Listen, everybody!'

"Yet, we heard nothing, beyond the faint murmur of the men talking together in the boat alongside.

"'I don't hear nothin',' said Captain Gannington, after a short pause. 'Do you, Doctor?'

"'No,' I said.

"'Wot was it you thought you heard?' asked the Captain, turning again to the Second Mate. But the Second Mate shook his head, in a curious, almost irritable way; as if the Captain's question interrupted his listening. Captain Gannington stared a moment at him; then held his lantern up, and glanced about him, almost uneasily. I know I felt a queer sense of strain. But the light showed nothing, beyond the greyish dirty-white of the mould in all directions.

"'Mister Selvern,' said the Captain at last, looking at him, 'don't get fancying things. Get hold of your bloomin' self. Ye know ye heard nothin'?'

"'I'm quite sure I heard something, Sir!' said the Second Mate. 'I seemed to hear—' He broke off sharply, and appeared to listen, with an almost painful intensity.

"'What did it sound like?' I asked.

"'It's all right, Doctor,' said Captain Gannington, laughing gently. 'Ye can give him a tonic when we get back. I'm goin' to shift this stuff.'

"He drew back, and kicked for the second time at the ugly mass, which he took to hide the companionway. The result of his kick was startling; for the whole thing wobbled sloppily, like a mound of unhealthy-looking jelly.

"He drew his foot out of it, quickly, and took a step backward, staring, and holding his lamp towards it:—

"'By gum!' he said; and it was plain that he was genuinely startled, 'the blessed thing's gone soft!'

"The man had run back several steps from the suddenly flaccid mound, and looked horribly frightened. Though, of what, I am sure he had not the least idea. The Second Mate stood where he was, and stared. For my part, I know I had a most hideous uneasiness upon me. The Captain continued to hold his light towards the wobbling mound, and stare:—

"'It's gone squashy all through!' he said. 'There's no scuttle there. There's no bally woodwork inside that lot! Phoo! what a rum smell!'

"He walked round to the after-side of the strange mound, to see whether there might be some signs of an opening into the hull at the back of the great heap of mould-stuff. And then:—

95

"'LISTEN!' said the Second Mate, again, in the strangest sort of voice.

"Captain Gannington straightened himself upright, and there succeeded a pause of the most intense quietness, in which there was not even the hum of talk from the men alongside in the boat. We all heard it—a kind of dull, soft Thud! Thud! Thud! Thud! somewhere in the hull under us; yet so vague that I might have been half doubtful I heard it, only that the others did so, too.

"Captain Gannington turned suddenly to where the man stood:—

"'Tell them—' he began. But the fellow cried out something, and pointed. There had come a strange intensity into his somewhat unemotional face; so that the Captain's glance followed his action instantly. I stared, also, as you may think. It was the great mound, at which the man was pointing. I saw what he meant.

"From the two gapes made in the mould-like stuff by Captain Gannington's boot, the purple fluid was jetting out in a queerly regular fashion, almost as if it were being forced out by a pump. My word! but I stared! And even as I stared, a larger jet squirted out, and splashed as far as the man, spattering his boots and trouser-legs.

"The fellow had been pretty nervous before, in a stolid, ignorant sort of way; and his funk had been growing steadily; but, at this, he simply let out a yell, and turned about to run. He paused an instant, as if a sudden fear of the darkness that held the decks, between him and the boat, had taken him. He snatched at the Second Mate's lantern; tore it out of his hand, and plunged heavily away over the vile stretch of mould.

"Mr. Selvern, the Second Mate, said not a word; he was just standing, staring at the strange-smelling twin streams of dull purple, that were jetting out from the wobbling mound. Captain Gannington, however, roared an order to the man to come back; but the man plunged on and on across the mould, his feet seeming to be clogged by the stuff, as if it had grown suddenly soft. He zigzagged, as he ran, the lantern swaying in wild circles, as he wrenched his feet free, with a constant plop, plop; and I could hear his frightened gasps, even from where I stood.

"'Come back with that lamp!' roared the Captain again; but still the man took no notice, and Captain Gannington was silent an instant, his lips working in a queer, inarticulate fashion; as if he were stunned momentarily by the very violence of his anger at the man's insubordination. And in the silence, I heard the sounds again:—Thud! Thud! Thud! Thud! Quite distinctly now, beating, it seemed suddenly to me, right down under my feet, but deep.

"I stared down at the mould on which I was standing, with a quick, disgusting sense of the terrible all about me; then I looked at the Captain, and tried to say something, without appearing frightened. I saw that he had turned again to the mound, and all the anger had gone out of his face. He had his lamp out towards the mound, and was listening. There was a further moment of absolute silence; at least, I know that I was not conscious of any sound at all, in all the world, except that extraordinary Thud! Thud! Thud! Thud! down somewhere in the huge bulk under us.

"The Captain shifted his feet, with a sudden, nervous movement; and as he lifted them, the mould went plop! plop! He looked quickly at me, trying to smile, as if he were not thinking anything very much about it:—'What do you make of it, Doctor?' he said.

"'I think—' I began. But the Second Mate interrupted with a single word; his voice pitched a little high, in a tone that made us both stare instantly at him:—

"'Look!' he said, and pointed at the mound. The thing was all of a slow quiver. A strange ripple ran outward from it, along the deck, like you will see a ripple run inshore out of a calm sea. It reached a mound a little fore-side of us, which I had supposed to be the cabin-skylight; and in a moment, the second mound sank nearly level with the surrounding decks, quivering floppily in a most extraordinary fashion. A sudden, quick tremor took the mould, right under the Second Mate, and he gave out a hoarse little cry, and held his arms out on each side of him, to keep his balance. The tremor in the mould, spread, and Captain Gannington swayed, and spread his feet, with a sudden curse of fright. The Second Mate jumped across to him, and caught him by the wrist:—

"'The boat, Sir!' he said, saying the very thing that I had lacked the pluck to say. 'For God's sake—'

"But he never finished; for a tremendous, hoarse scream cut off his words. They hove themselves round, and looked. I could see without turning. The man who had run from us, was standing in the waist of the ship, about a fathom from the starboard bulwarks. He was swaying from side to side, and screaming in a dreadful fashion. He appeared to be trying to lift his feet, and the light from his swaying lantern showed an almost incredible sight. All about him, the mould was in active movement. His feet had sunk out of sight. The stuff appeared to be *lapping* at his legs; and abruptly his bare flesh showed. The hideous stuff had rent his trouser-legs away, as if they were paper. He gave out a simply sickening scream, and, with a vast effort, wrenched one leg free. It was partly destroyed. The next instant he pitched face downward, and the stuff heaped itself upon him, as if it were actually alive, with a dreadful savage life. It was simply infernal. The man had gone from sight. Where he had fallen was now a writhing, elongated mound, in constant and horrible increase, as the mould appeared to move towards it in strange ripples from all sides.

"Captain Gannington and the Second Mate were stone silent, in amazed and incredulous horror; but I had begun to reach towards a grotesque and terrific conclusion, both helped and hindered by my professional training.

"From the men in the boat alongside, there was a loud shouting, and I saw two of their faces appear suddenly above the rail. They showed clearly, a moment, in the light from the lamp which the man had snatched from Mr. Selvern; for, strangely enough, this lamp was standing upright and unharmed on the deck, a little way fore-side of that dreadful, elongated, growing mound, that still swayed and writhed with an incredible horror. The lamp rose and fell on the passing ripples of the mould, just—for all the world—as you will see a boat rise and fall on little swells. It is of some interest to me now, psychologically, to remember how that rising and falling lantern brought home to me, more than anything, the incomprehensible, dreadful strangeness of it all.

"The men's faces disappeared, with sudden yells, as if they had slipped, or been suddenly hurt; and there was a fresh uproar of shouting from the boat. The men were calling to us to come away; to come away. In the same instant, I felt my left boot drawn suddenly and forcibly downward, with a horrible, painful gripe. I wrenched it free, with a yell of angry fear. Forrard of us, I saw that the vile surface was all a-move; and abruptly I found myself shouting in a queer frightened voice:—
"'The boat, Captain! The boat, Captain!'

"Captain Gannington stared round at me, over his right shoulder, in a peculiar, dull way, that told me he was utterly dazed with bewilderment and the incomprehensibleness of it all. I took a quick, clogged, nervous step towards him, and gripped his arm and shook it fiercely.

"'The boat!' I shouted at him. 'The boat! For God's sake, tell the men to bring the boat aft!'

"Then the mould must have drawn his feet down; for, abruptly, he bellowed fiercely with terror, his momentary apathy giving place to furious energy. His thick-set, vastly muscular body doubled and writhed with his enormous effort, and he struck out madly, dropping the lantern. He tore his feet free, something ripping as he did so. The *reality* and necessity of the situation had come upon him, brutishly real, and he was roaring to the men in the boat :

"'Bring the boat aft! Bring 'er aft! Bring, 'er aft!'

"The Second Mate and I were shouting the same thing, madly.

"'For God's sake be smart, lads!' roared the Captain, and stooped quickly for his lamp, which still burned. His feet were gripped again, and he hove them out, blaspheming breathlessly, and leaping a yard high with his effort. Then he made a run for the side, wrenching his feet free at each step. In the same instant, the Second Mate cried out something, and grabbed at the Captain:—

"'It's got hold of my feet! It's got hold of my feet!' he screamed. His feet had disappeared up to his boot-tops; and Captain Gannington caught him round the waist with his powerful left arm, gave a mighty heave, and the next instant had him free; but both his boot-soles had almost gone.

"For my part, I jumped madly from foot to foot; to avoid the plucking of the mould; and suddenly I made a run for the ship's side, But before I could get there, a queer gape came in the mould, between us and the side, at least a couple of feet wide, and how deep I don't know. It closed up in an instant, and all the mould, where the gape had been, went into a sort of flurry of horrible ripplings, so that I ran back from it; for I did not dare to put my foot upon it. Then the Captain was shouting to me:—

"'Aft, Doctor! Aft, Doctor! This way, Doctor! Run!' I saw then that he had passed me, and was up on the after, raised portion of the poop. He had the Second

Mate thrown like a sack, all loose and quiet, over his left shoulder; for Mr. Selvern had fainted, and his long legs flogged, limp and helpless, against the Captain's massive knees as the Captain ran. I saw, with a queer, unconscious noting of minor details, how the torn soles of the Second Mate's boots flapped and jigged, as the Captain staggered aft.

"'Boat ahoy! Boat ahoy! Boat ahoy!' shouted the Captain; and then I was beside him, shouting also. The men were answering with loud yells of encouragement, and it was plain they were working desperately to force the boat aft, through the thick scum about the ship.

"We reached the ancient, mould-hid taffrail, and slewed about, breathlessly, in the half-darkness, to see what was happening. Captain Gannington had left his lantern by the big mound, when he picked up the Second Mate; and as we stood, gasping, we discovered suddenly that all the mould between us and the light was full of movement. Yet, the part on which we stood, for about six or eight feet forrard of us, was still firm.

"Every couple of seconds, we shouted to the men to hasten, and they kept on calling to us that they would be with us in an instant. And all the time, we watched the deck of that dreadful hulk, feeling, for my part, literally sick with mad suspense, and ready to jump overboard into that filthy scum all about us.

"Down somewhere in the huge bulk of the ship, there was all the time that extraordinary, dull, ponderous Thud! Thud! Thud! Thud! growing ever louder. I seemed to feel the whole hull of the derelict beginning to quiver and thrill with each dull beat. And to me, with the grotesque and monstrous suspicion of what made that noise, it was, at once, the most dreadful and incredible sound I have ever heard.

"As we waited desperately for the boat, I scanned incessantly so much of the grey-white bulk as the lamp showed. The whole of the decks seemed to be in strange movement. Forrard of the lamp, I could see, indistinctly, the moundings of the mould swaying and nodding hideously, beyond the circle of the brightest rays. Nearer, and full in the glow of the lamp, the mound which should have indicated the skylight, was swelling steadily. There were ugly, purple veinings on it, and as it swelled, it seemed to me that the veinings and mottlings on it, were becoming plainer—rising, as though embossed upon it, like you will see the veins stand out on the body of a powerful, full-blooded horse. It was most extraordinary. The mound that we had supposed to cover the companion-way, had sunk flat with the surrounding mould, and I could not see that it jetted out any more of the purplish fluid.

"A quaking movement of the mould began, away forrard of the lamp, and came flurrying away aft towards us; and at the sight of that, I climbed up on to the spongy-feeling taffrail, and yelled afresh for the boat. The men answered with a shout, which told me they were nearer; but the beastly scum was so thick that it was evidently a fight to move the boat at all. Beside me, Captain Gannington was shaking the Second Mate furiously, and the man stirred and began to moan. The Captain shook him again.

"'Wake up! Wake up, Mister!' he shouted.

"The Second Mate staggered out of the Captain's arms, and collapsed suddenly, shrieking:—'My feet! Oh, God! My feet!' The Captain and I lugged him up off the mould, and got him into a sitting position upon the taffrail, where he kept up a continual moaning.

"'Hold 'im, Doctor,' said the Captain, and whilst I did so, he ran forrard a few yards, and peered down over the starboard quarter rail. 'For God's sake, be smart, lads! Be smart! Be smart!' he shouted down to the men; and they answered him, breathless, from close at hand; yet still too far away for the boat to be any use to us on the instant.

"I was holding the moaning, half-unconscious officer, and staring forrard along the poop decks. The flurrying of the mould was coming aft, slowly and noiselessly. And then, suddenly, I saw something closer:—

"'Look out, Captain!' I shouted; and even as I shouted, the mould near to him gave a sudden peculiar slobber. I had seen a ripple stealing towards him through the horrible stuff. He gave an enormous, clumsy leap, and landed near to us on the sound part of the mould; but the movement followed him. He turned and faced it, swearing fiercely. All about his feet there came abruptly little gapings, which made horrid sucking noises.

"'Come *back*, Captain!' I yelled. 'Come back, *quick*!'

"As I shouted, a ripple came at his feet—lipping at them; and he stamped insanely at it, and leaped back, his boot torn half off his foot. He swore madly with pain and anger, and jumped swiftly for the taffrail.

"'Come on, Doctor! Over we go!' he called. Then he remembered the filthy scum, and hesitated; roaring out desperately to the men to hurry. I stared down, also.

"'The Second Mate?' I said.

"'I'll take charge, Doctor,' said Captain Gannington, and caught hold of Mr. Selvern. As he spoke, I thought I saw something beneath us, outlined against the scum. I leaned out over the stern, and peered. There was something under the port quarter.

"'There's something down there, Captain!' I called, and pointed in the darkness.

"He stooped far over, and stared.

"'A boat, by gum! A BOAT!' he yelled, and began to wriggle swiftly along the taffrail, dragging the Second Mate after him. I followed.

"'A boat it is, sure!' he exclaimed, a few moments later; and, picking up the Second Mate clear of the rail, he hove him down into the boat, where he fell with a crash into the bottom.

"'Over ye go, Doctor!' he yelled at me, and pulled me bodily off the rail, and dropped me after the officer. As he did so, I felt the whole of the ancient, spongy rail give a peculiar, sickening quiver, and begin to wobble. I fell on to the Second Mate, and the Captain came after, almost in the same instant; but fortunately, he

100

landed clear of us, on to the fore thwart, which broke under his weight, with a loud crack and splintering of wood.

"'Thank God!' I heard him mutter. 'Thank God! . . . I guess that was a mighty near thing to goin' to hell.'

"He struck a match, just as I got to my feet, and between us we got the Second Mate straightened out on one of the after thwarts. We shouted to the men in the boat, telling them where we were, and saw the light of their lantern shining round the starboard counter of the derelict. They called back to us, to tell us they were doing their best; and then, whilst we waited, Captain Gannington struck another match, and began to overhaul the boat we had dropped into. She was a modern, two-bowed boat, and on the stern, there was painted 'CYCLONE Glasgow.' She was in pretty fair condition, and had evidently drifted into the scum and been held by it.

"Captain Gannington struck several matches, and went forrard towards the derelict. Suddenly he called to me, and I jumped over the thwarts to him.

"Look, Doctor,' he said; and I saw what he meant—a mass of bones, up in the bows of the boat. I stooped over them, and looked. There were the bones of at least three people, all mixed together, in an extraordinary fashion, and quite clean and dry. I had a sudden thought concerning the bones; but I said nothing; for my thought was vague, in some ways, and concerned the grotesque and incredible suggestion that had come to me, as to the cause of that ponderous, dull Thud! Thud! Thud! Thud! that beat on so infernally within the hull, and was plain to hear even now that we had got off the vessel herself. And all the while, you know, I had a sick, horrible, mental-picture of that frightful wriggling mound aboard the hulk.

"As Captain Gannington struck a final match, I saw something that sickened me, and the Captain saw it in the same instant. The match went out, and he fumbled clumsily for another, and struck it. We saw the thing again. We had not been mistaken. . . . A great lip of grey-white was protruding in over the edge of the boat—a great lappet of the mould was coming stealthily towards us; a live mass of *the very hull itself.* And suddenly Captain Gannington yelled out, in so many words, the grotesque and incredible thing I was thinking:—

"'SHE'S ALIVE!'

"I never heard such a sound of *comprehension* and terror in a man's voice. The very horrified assurance of it, made actual to me the thing that, before, had only lurked in my subconscious mind. I knew he was right; I knew that the explanation my reason and my training, both repelled and reached towards, was the true one . . . . . . I wonder whether anyone can possibly understand our feelings in that moment. . . . The unmitigable horror of it, and the *incredibleness.*

"As the light of the match burned up fully, I saw that the mass of living matter, coming towards us, was streaked and veined with purple, the veins standing out, enormously distended. The whole thing quivered continuously to each ponderous Thud! Thud! Thud! Thud! of that gargantuan organ that pulsed within the huge grey-white bulk. The flame of the match reached the Captain's fingers, and there came to me a little sickly whiff of burned flesh; but he seemed unconscious of any pain. Then the flame went out, in a brief sizzle; yet at the last moment, I had seen an extraordinary raw look, become visible upon the end of that monstrous, protruding lappet. It had become dewed with a hideous, purplish sweat. And with the darkness, there came a sudden charnel-like stench.

, "I heard the match-box split in Captain Gannington's hands, as he wrenched it open. Then he swore, in a queer frightened voice; for he had come to the end of his matches. He turned clumsily in the darkness, and tumbled over the nearest thwart, in his eagerness to get to the stern of the boat; and I after him; for we knew that thing was coming towards us through the darkness; reaching over that piteous mingled heap of human bones, all jumbled together in the bows. We shouted madly to the men, and for answer saw the bows of the boat emerge dimly into view, round the starboard counter of the derelict.

"'Thank God!' I gasped out; but Captain Gannington yelled to them to show a light. Yet this they could not do; for the lamp had just been stepped on, in their desperate efforts to force the boat round to us.

"'Quick! Quick!' I shouted.

"'For God's sake be smart, men!' roared the Captain; and both of us faced the darkness under the port counter, out of which we knew (but could not see) the thing was coming towards us.

"'An oar! Smart now; pass me an oar!' shouted the Captain; and reached out his hands through the gloom towards the oncoming boat. I saw a figure stand up in the bows, and hold something out to us, across the intervening yards of scum. Captain Gannington swept his hands through the darkness, and encountered it.

"'I've got it. Let go there!' he said, in a quick, tense voice.

"In the same instant, the boat we were in, was pressed over suddenly to starboard by some tremendous weight. Then I heard the Captain shout:—'Duck y'r head, Doctor;' and directly afterwards he swung the heavy, fourteen-foot ash oar round his head, and struck into the darkness. There came a sudden squelch, and he struck again, with a savage grunt of fierce energy. At the second blow, the boat righted, with a slow movement, and directly afterwards the other boat bumped gently into ours.

"Captain Gannington dropped the oar, and springing across to the Second Mate, hove him up off the thwart, and pitched him with knee and arms clear in over the bows among the men; then he shouted to me to follow, which I did, and he came after me, bringing the oar with him. We carried the Second Mate aft, and the Captain shouted to the men to back the boat a little; then they got her bows clear of the boat we had just left, and so headed out through the scum for the open sea.

"Where's Tom 'Arrison?' gasped one of the men, in the midst of his exertions. He happened to be Tom Harrison's particular chum; and Captain Gannington answered him, briefly enough:—

"'Dead! Pull! Don't talk!'"

"'Now, difficult as it had been to force the boat through the scum to our rescue, the difficulty to get clear seemed tenfold. After some five minutes pulling, the boat seemed hardly to have moved a fathom, if so much; and a quite dreadful fear took me afresh; which one of the panting men put suddenly into words:—

"'It's got us!' he gasped out; 'same as poor Tom!' It was the man who had inquired where Harrison was.

"Shut y'r mouth an' *pull*!' roared the Captain. And so another few minutes passed. Abruptly, it seemed to me that the dull, ponderous Thud! Thud! Thud! Thud! came more plainly through the dark, and I stared intently over the stern. I sickened a little; for I could almost swear that the dark mass of the monster was actually *nearer* . . . that it was coming nearer to us through the darkness. Captain Gannington must have had the same thought; for after a brief look into the darkness, he made one jump to the stroke-oar, and began to double-bank it.

"'Get forrid under the thwarts, Doctor!' he said to me, rather breathlessly. 'Get in the bows, an' see if you can't free the stuff a bit round the bows.'

"I did as he told me, and a minute later I was in the bows of the boat, puddling the scum from side to side with the boat-hook, and trying to break up the viscid, clinging muck. A heavy, almost animal-like odour rose off it, and all the air seemed full of the deadening smell. I shall never find words to tell anyone the whole horror of it all—the threat that seemed to hang in the very air around us; and, but a little astern, that incredible thing, coming, as I firmly believe, nearer, and the scum holding us like half melted glue.

"The minutes passed in a deadly, eternal fashion, and I kept staring back astern into the darkness; but never ceasing to puddle that filthy scum, striking at it and switching it from side to side, until I sweated.

"Abruptly, Captain Gannington sang out:—

"'We're gaining, lads. Pull!' And I felt the boat forge ahead perceptibly, as they gave way, with renewed hope and energy. There was soon no doubt of it; for presently that hideous Thud! Thud! Thud! Thud! had grown quite dim and vague somewhere astern, and I could no longer see the derelict; for the night had come down tremendously dark, and all the sky was thick overset with heavy clouds. As we drew nearer and nearer to the edge of the scum, the boat moved more and more freely, until suddenly we emerged with a clean, sweet, fresh sound, into the open sea.

"'Thank God!' I said aloud, and drew in the boat-hook, and made my way aft again to where Captain Gannington now sat once more at the tiller. I saw him looking anxiously up at the sky, and across to where the lights of our vessel burned, and again he would seem to listen intently; so that I found myself listening also.

"'What's that, Captain?' I said sharply; for it seemed to me that I heard a sound far astern, something between a queer whine and a low whistling. 'What's that?'

"'It's wind, Doctor,' he said, in a low voice. 'I wish to God we were aboard.'

"Then, to the men:—'Pull! Put y'r backs into it, or ye'll never put y'r teeth through good bread again!'

"The men obeyed nobly, and we reached the vessel safely, and had the boat safely stowed, before the storm came, which it did in a furious white smother out of the West. I could see it for some minutes beforehand, tearing the sea, in the gloom, into a wall of phosphorescent foam; and as it came nearer, that peculiar whining, piping sound, grew louder and louder, until it was like a vast steam whistle, rushing towards us across the sea.

"And when it did come, we got it very heavy indeed; so that the morning showed us nothing but a welter of white seas; and that grim derelict was many a score of miles away in the smother, lost as utterly as our hearts could wish to lose her.

"When I came to examine the Second Mate's feet, I found them in a very extraordinary condition. The soles of them had the appearance of having been partly digested. I know of no other word that so exactly describes their condition; and the agony the man suffered, must have been dreadful,

"Now," concluded the Doctor, "that is what I call a case in point. If we could know exactly what that old vessel had originally been loaded with, and the juxtaposition of the various articles of her cargo, plus the heat and time she had endured, plus one or two other only guessable quantities, we should have solved the chemistry of the Life-Force, gentlemen. Not necessarily the *origin*, mind you; but, at least, we should have taken a big step on the way. I've often regretted that gale, you know—in a way, that is, in a way! It was a most amazing discovery; but, at the time, I had nothing but thankfulness to be rid of it. . . . A most amazing chance. I often think of the way the monster woke out of its torpor. . . . And that scum . . . The dead pigs caught in it. . . . I fancy that was a grim kind of a net, gentlemen. . . . It caught many things. . . . It . . ."

The old Doctor sighed and nodded.

"If I could have had her bill of lading," he said, his eyes full of regret. "If— It might have told me something to help. But, anyway. . . ." He began to fill his pipe again. . . . "I suppose," he ended, looking round at us gravely, "I s'pose we humans are an ungrateful lot of beggars, at the best! . . . But . . . but what a chance! What a chance—eh?"

The Wild Man of the Sea

"The wild man of the sea!" the first mate called him as soon as he came aboard.

"Who's yon wild-looking chap ye've signed on, sir?" he asked the captain.

"Best sailorman that ever stepped, mister," replied the Master. "I had him with me four trips running out to Frisco, and then I lost him. He went spreeing and got shipped away. I dropped on him to-day up at the shipping office, and was glad to get him. You'd best pick him for your watch."

The mate nodded, and decided to take the master's advice, for the man must be something more than average smart at sailoring to win such praise from old Captain Gallington. And, indeed, he soon had proof that his choice of the lean, wild-looking, straggle-bearded A. B. was justified, for the man became almost at once, by general acknowledgement, the leading seaman of the port watch.

He was evidently soaked in all the lore of the sea life and all its practical arts. Nineteen different ways of splicing wire he demonstrated during one dog-watch argument, and from such practical matters went on to nautical fancywork, showing Jeb, the much-abused deck boy belonging to his watch, a queerly simple method of starting a four-stranded Turk's-head, and after that he demonstrated a manner of alternating square and half-moon sennit without the usual unsightliness that is so inevitable at the alternations.

By the end of the watch he had the whole crowd round him, staring with silent respect at the deft handiwork of this master sailorman, as he illustrated a score of lost and forgotten knots—fancy-whippings, grace-finishings and pointings, and many another phase of rope work that hardly a man aboard the *Pareek*, sailing ship, had even so much as heard the name of.

They were mostly of the inefficient "spade and shovel," half-trained class of seamen, with most of the faults of the old shellback, and too few of his virtues— the kind of sailorman who lays rash and unblushing claim to the title of A. B. with an effrontery so amazing that he will stand unabashed at the wheel which he cannot handle, and stare stupidly at the compass card, the very points of which he is unable to name.

No wonder that Captain Gallington was emphatic in his satisfaction at getting one genuine, finished sailorman signed on among the usual crowd of nautical ploughboys.

And yet Jesson was not popular in the fo'c's'le. He was respected, it is true, not only for his sailorman's skill, but because his six feet odd inches of wire-and-leather body very early made it clear to the others that its owner was the strongest man aboard, with a knowledge of the art of taking care of himself that silenced all possible doubts in a manner at once sufficiently painful to be obvious.

As a result the whole fo'c's'le was silent and deferent when he spoke, which was seldom. Had not his seamanship and his fighting powers been so remarkable, he would have been stamped by his insensate fellow A. B.'s as hopelessly "barmy."

His good nature was often manifest. For instance, he kept most of the other men's lookouts in his watch, when he was not at the wheel. He would go up and relieve the lookout man, much to that individual's delight and half contempt. And there, with his fiddle he would sit on the crown of the anchor playing almost inaudible airs of tremendous import to himself.

Sometimes he would pace round and round the head, chanting breathlessly to himself in a kind of wind-drunken delight, walking with swift, noiseless strides in his endless circling.

Behind all his taciturnity, Jesson was fiercely kind hearted in a queer, impulsive way. Once, when Jeb, the deck boy in his watch, was receiving a licking from one of the men, Jesson, who was eating his dinner, put down his plate, rose from his sea chest, and, walking across to the man, lugged him out on deck by his two elbows.

His treatment of the man was sufficiently emphatic to insure that Jeb was not in future kicked into submission. As a result the much-hazed lad grew to a curious sort of dumb worship of the big, wild-looking sailorman. And so grew a queer and rather beautiful friendship—a wordless intimacy between these two—the wild, silent, strangemooded seaman and the callow youth.

Often at night, in their watch on deck, Jeb would steal up silently on to the fo'c's'le head with a pannikin of hot and much stewed tea. The doctor—that is, the cook—had an arrangement with the deck boy in each watch by which the lads would have his fire ready lighted for him in the morning. In return they were allowed to slip into the galley at night for a pot of tea out of the unemptied boilers.

Jesson would take the tea without a word of thanks, and put it on the top of the capstan, and Jeb would then vanish to the maindeck where he would sit on the forehatch listening in a part-understanding dumbness to the scarcely audible wail of the violin on the fo'c's'le head.

At the end of the watch, when Jesson returned Jeb his pannikin, there would often be inside of it some half worked-out fancy knot for the boy to study, but never a word of thanks or comment on either side.

One night Jesson spoke to the lad as he took from him the accustomed pannikin of hot tea.

"Hark to the wind, Jeb," he said, as he put down the pannikin on the head of the capstan. "Go down, lad, an' sit on the hatch an' let the wind talk to ye."

He handed something across to the boy.

"Here's the starting of some double-moon sennit for ye to have a go at," he said.

Jeb took the sennit and went down to his usual place on the forehatch. Here, in the clear moonlight, he puzzled awhile over the fancy sennit, and speedily had it hopelessly muddled. After that, he just sat still with the sennit in a muddle on his knees, and began half-consciously to listen to the wind as Jesson had bid him.

Presently, for the first time in his life, he heard *consciously* the living note of the wind, booming in its eternal melody of the sailing-ship wind, out of the foot of the foresail.

With the sound of five bells, deep and sonorous in the moonlight, the spell of the uncertain enchantment was broken. But from that night it might be said that Jeb's development had its tangible beginning.

Now the days went slowly, with the peculiar, monotonous unheeding of sailing-ship days of wandering on and on and on across the everlasting waters. Yet, even for a sailing-ship voyage the outward passage became so abnormally prolonged that no one of the lesser shellbacks had ever been so long in crossing the line. It was not until their eighty-fourth day out that the equator was floated across, in something that approximated an unending calm, broken from hour to hour by a cat's-paw of wind that would shunt the *Pareek* along a few miles, and then drop her with a rustle of sails once more into calm.

"Us'll never reach Frisco this trip!" remarked Stensen, an English-bred Dutchman one night as he came into the fo'c's'le, after having been relieved at the wheel by Jesson.

At this there broke out a subdued murmur of talk against Jesson, which showed plainly that the big sailorman had grown steadily more and more unpopular, being less and less understood by those smaller natures and intellects.

"It's his blamed fiddlin'!" said a small cockney named George. No one remembered his other name, or indeed troubled to inquire it.

It was the inevitable, half-believed imputation of a "Jonah," and as will be understood, they omitted none of their simple and strictly limited adjectives in accentuating the epithet.

The talk passed to a discussion of the quality of beer sold down on the water front, and so on, through the very brief catalogue of their remembered and deferred pleasures. It finally fizzled out into sleepy silence, broken at last by Jeb putting his head through the port doorway and calling them out to man the braces. Whereat they rose and slouched out, grumbling dully.

And so the *Pareek* proceeded on her seemingly interminable voyage, the calm being succeeded and interleaved by a succession of heavy head gales that delayed them considerably.

In the daytime Jesson was merely a smart, vigorous wild-haired seaman, but at night, mounting his eternal lookout on the fo'c's'le head, he became once more the elemental man and poet, pacing and watching and dreaming. He was more and more boldly listened to by Jeb, who, day by day, was being admitted to a closer, though unobtrusive, intimacy with the big seaman.

One night when Jeb brought him the usual pannikin of tea, Jesson again spoke to him.

"Did you listen, Jeb, to the wind as I told you?"

"Yes, sir," replied the boy. He always gave him "sir." And, indeed, the title had more than once slipped out from the lips of some of the A. B.'s; as if, despite themselves, something about him won the significant term from them.

"It's a wonderful night to-night, Jeb," said the big seaman, holding the hot pannikin between his two hands on the capstan top, and staring away into the greyness to leeward.

"Yes, sir," replied Jeb, staring out in the same direction with a kind of faithful sympathy.

For maybe a full two minutes, the two stood there in silence, the man clasping and unclasping his hands around the hot pannikin, and the boy just quiet under the spell of sympathy and a vague understanding. Presently the big man spoke again:

"Have ye ever thought, Jeb, what a mysterious place the sea is?" he asked.

"No, sir," replied Jeb, and left it at that.

"Well," said the big man, "I want ye to think about it, lad. I want you to grow up to realize that your life is to be lived in the most wonderful and mysterious place in the world. It will be full of compensations in such lots of ways for the sordidness of the sea life, as it is to the sailorman."

"Yes, sir," said Jeb again, only partly comprehending. As a matter of fact, as compared with his previous gutter life, it had never struck him as being sordid. As for the mystery and wonderfulness of the sea, why, he had possibly been ever so vaguely conscious of them right down somewhere in the deep of his undeveloped mind and personality.

But consciously, his thoughts had run chiefly to keeping dry, to pleasing the men, his masters, to becoming an A. B.—a dream of splendour to him. For the rest, to having a good time ashore in Frisco, like a man! Poor sailor laddie! And now he had met a real man who was quietly and deliberately shifting his point of view.

"Never make a pattern of the men you sail with, Jeb," said the big man. "Live your own life, and let the sea be your companion. It'll make a man of ye, lad. It's a place where you could meet God Himself walking at nights, boy. Never pattern yourself on sailormen, Jeb. Poor devils!"

"No, sir," repeated Jeb earnestly. "*They* ain't sailormen, them lot!" He jerked his thumb downward to indicate the rest of the A. B.'s in the fo'c's'le beneath them. "But I'll try to be like you, sir—only I couldn't be so, no matter how I tried," he ended wistfully.

"Don't try to be like me, Jeb," said Jesson in a low voice. He paused a moment, then lifting the pannikin, he sipped a little of the hot tea, and spoke again.

"Take the sea, lad, to be your companion. You'll never lack. A sailor lives very near to God if he would only open his eyes. Aye! Aye! If only they would realize it. And all the time they're lookin' for the shore and the devil of degeneration. Good heavens!"

He put the pannikin down and took a stride or two away as if in strange agitation. Then he came back, drank a gulp of tea and turned to the lad.

"Get along down, Jeb, and stand by. I want to be alone. And remember, lad, what I have told ye. You're living in the most wonderful place in the world. Lad, lad, look out on the waters and ye may see God Himself walking in the greyness. Get close to the glory that is round ye, lad—get close to the glory—Run along, now, run along."

"Aye, aye, sir," replied Jeb obediently, and he went down noiselessly off the fo'c's'le head, confused, yet elated because his hero had condescended to talk with him. He felt sanctified in some strange fashion as if, somehow—as he would have put it—he "was jest comed out o' church."

And because of this feeling, he spent quite a while staring away into the greyness to leeward, not knowing what he wanted or expected to see.

Presently the wail of the violin stole to him through the darkness, and quietly mounting the lee steps to the head till his ear was on a level with the deck, he listened until the big man ceased his playing, and began to walk round and round the head in his curious fashion, muttering to himself in a low voice.

Jeb listened, attracted as he always was by these moods of the big sailorman. And on this night, in particular, Jesson walked round and round for a long time just muttering to himself. Once or twice stopping at the lee rail for some silent moments, during which he appeared to be staring eagerly into the grey gloom of the night. At such times Jeb stared also to leeward with a feeling that he might see something.

Then Jesson would resume his walk round and round the head with long, swift, noiseless strides, muttering, muttering as he went. And suddenly he broke out into a kind of hushed, ecstatic chant, so subdued that Jeb missed portions here and there, strive as he might to hear all.

When the man's voice trailed off into silence the sudden hush was broken by a muttered remark from the starboard side of the maindeck.

"'E's proper barmy!"

Jeb glanced quickly to windward, and saw dimly against the greyness of the weather night the forms of two of the men crouching upon the starboard steps leading up to the rail.

"A blamed Jonah!" said another voice.

Some of the men had been listening to Jesson, and certainly without appreciation. Down stole Jeb from the port ladder, and took up his accustomed seat on the forehatch. He had a kind of savage anger because the men were secretly jeering his sailor demigod. But he was far too much afraid of them to risk making himself evident, and so he crouched there, listening and wondering. And even as he waited to hear what more they had to say there came the mate's voice, sharp and sudden along the decks:

"Stand by the t'gallant halyards! Smart now!"

A heavy squall was coming down upon them, and Jeb, having called out the men in the fo'c's'le, raced away aft with the rest to stand by the gear in case they had to lower away. He stood staring to windward as he waited, seeing dimly the heavy, black arch of the squall against the lighter, grey murk of the night sky. Then, even as he stared, he heard in the utter quietness the curious *whine whine* of the distant rain upon the sea, breaking out into a queer hiss as it drove nearer at tremendous speed. Behind the swiftly coming hiss of the rain front there sounded a low, dull sound that grew into an uncomfortably nearing roar. Just as the first sheet of that tremendous rain smote down upon them, there was the mate's voice again:

"Sheets and halyards! Lower away! Clew lines and bunt lines! Lower away! Lower away! Lower away—"

His voice was lost in a volume of sound as the weight of the wind behind the rain took them. The vessel lay over to the squall, over, over, over, whilst the whole world seemed lost in the down-thundering rain and the mad roar of the storm.

Jeb caught the mate's voice, faintly, and knew that he was singing out to lower away the topsails. He fumbled his way aft, groped and found the pin. Then he cast off the turns and tried to lower, but the heavy yard would not come down. The pressure of the wind was so heavy that the parrel had jammed against the topmast, and the friction of this, combined with the horrible list of the ship, prevented the yard coming down.

A man came dashing through the reek, hurled the boy to one side, and threw off the final turns of the halyards, roaring out in a voice of frightened anger:

"It's that damned Jonah we've got on board!"

There came the vague shouting in the mate's powerful voice, of "Downhauls! Downhauls!" coming thin and lost through the infernal darkness, and the dazing yell of the squall and the boil of the rain. The vessel went over to a more dreadful angle, so that it seemed she must capsize. There was an indistinct crashing sound up in the night, and then another seemingly further aft, and fainter. Immediately after, the cant of the decks eased, and slowly the vessel righted.

"Carried away! Yes, sir! The main topmast! Carried away! Look out, there—mizzen—look out, there!"

A maze of shouting fore and aft, for the squall was easing now, and it was possible to hear the shouts that before had been scarcely audible, even close at hand. The other watch was out on deck, and Captain Gallington was singing out something from the break of the poop.

"Stand from under!"

There was a fierce loud crash almost in the same moment, and a man screaming, with the horrible screaming of a man mortally hurt. Everywhere in the darkness there was lumber, smashed timber, swinging blocks, wet canvas, and from

110

somewhere amid the wreckage on the dark decks the infernal screaming of the man, growing fainter and fainter, but never less horrible.

The squall passed away to leeward, and a few stars broke through the greyness. On the deck all hands were turned to with ships' lamps investigating the damage. They found that the main topmast had carried away just below the crosstrees, and also the mizzen t'gallant. On the maindeck, under the broken arm of the main t'gallant yard, one of the men, named Pemell, was found crushed and dead. One other man was badly hurt, and three had somewhat painful injuries, though superficial in character. Most of the rest had not escaped bad bruises and cuts from the falling gear.

The vessel herself had suffered considerably, for much of the heavy timber had fallen inboard, and the decks were stove in in two places, and badly shaken in others. The steel bulwarks were cut down almost to the scuppers where the falling mast had struck.

Through all that night and the next day into the dog watches, both watches were kept at it with only brief spells for food and a smoke. By the end of the second dog watch "Chips" had managed to repair and recaulk the decks, while the wreckage had all been cleared away, and the masts secured with preventer stays pending Chips getting ready the spare main topmast and mizzen t'gallant mast.

All that day while they worked, there had lain in the bos'n's locker, covered with some old sail-cloth, the man who had been killed by the falling spars. When, finally, the men had cleared up for the night, Captain Gallington held a brief but grimly piteous service to the dead, which ended in a splash overside, and a lot of superstitious sailormen going forward in a depressed and rather dangerous mood.

Here, over their biscuits and tea, one of them ventured openly to accuse Jesson of being a Jonah and the cause of all that had happened that night before, also of the calms and the head gales that had made the voyage already so interminable.

Jesson heard the man out without saying a word. He merely went on eating his tea as though the man had not spoken. When the stupid sea yokel, mistaking Jesson's silence for something different, ventured on further indiscretions, Jesson walked across to him, pulled him off his sea chest, and promptly knocked him down on to the deck of the fo'c's'le.

Immediately there was a growl from several of the others, and three of them started up to a simultaneous attack. But Jesson did not wait for them. He jumped towards the first man and landed heavily, and as the man staggered, he caught him by the shoulders and ran him backward into the other two, bringing the three of them down with a crash. Then, as they rose, he used his fists liberally, causing two of them to run out on deck in their efforts to escape him. After which Jesson went back to his unfinished tea.

Presently, the night being fine, he took his fiddle and went on the fo'c's'le head, where, as usual, he relieved the lookout man, who hurried below for a smoke.

Meanwhile, there was a low mutter of talk going on in the fo'c's'le—ignorant and insanely dangerous—dangerous because of the very ignorance that bred it and made it brutal. And listening silent and fierce to it all sat Jeb, registering unconscious and heroic determination as the vague wail of the violin on the dark fo'c's'le head drifted down to him, making a strange kinlike music with the slight night airs that puffed moodily across the grey seas.

"'Ark to 'im!" said one of the men. "'Ark to 'im! Ain't it enough to bloomin' well bring a 'urricane!"

"I was once with a Jonah," said the cockney. "'E near sunk us. We 'elda meetin', both watches, an' 'e got washed overboard one night with a 'eavy sea, 'e did! That's 'ow they logged it, though the mate knowed 'ow it was reely; but 'e never blamed us, or let on 'e knowed. We couldn't do nothin' else. And we'd a fair wind with us all the way out, after."

With heads close together, amid the clouds of thick tobacco smoke, the low talk continued till one of the men remembered Jeb was near, and the lad was ordered out on deck. The doors were closed, and ignorance with its consequent and appalling brutality, made heavy and morbid the atmosphere as the poor undeveloped creatures talked among themselves without any knowledge of their own insanity.

Up on the fo'c's'le head the violin had hushed, and Jesson was walking round and round in that curious, noiseless fashion, muttering to himself and at times breaking out into one of his low-voiced chants. On the lee ladder crouched Jeb, listening, full of his need to explain to the big man something of the vague fear that had taken him after hearing the men talk.

Suddenly, his attention was distracted from the man's strange ecstacy by a murmur from the direction of the weather ladder.

"'Ark to 'im. 'Ell, if it ain't enough to sink us. Just 'ark to that blimy Jonah— 'ark to 'im!"

Whether Jesson heard or felt the nearness of the men who had come sullenly out on deck it is impossible to say, but his low-voiced, half-chanting utterance ceased, and he seemed to Jeb, out there in the darkness, to be suddenly alert.

One by one the men of both watches came silently out on deck, and Jeb had nearly screwed up his courage to the point of calling out a vague warning to the unconscious Jesson when there came the sound of footsteps along the maindeck, and the flash of the mate's lantern shone on the lanyards of the preventer gear. He was making a final uneasy round of the temporary jurystays with which the masts had been made secure. As the men realized this, they slipped quietly away, one by one, back into the fo'c's'le.

The mate came forward and went up on to the fo'c's'le head, felt the tension of the forestay, and went out on to the jib boom, testing each stay in turn to make sure that nothing had given or surged when the main upper spars went. He returned, and with a friendly word to Jesson, came down the lee ladder and told Jeb he might turn in "all standing" and get a sleep.

But Jeb did not mean to turn in until he had spoken to Jesson. He looked about him, and then stole quietly up the lee ladder, and so across to where the big sailor was standing, leaning against the fore side of the capstan.

"Mister Jesson, sir!" he said, hesitating somewhat awkwardly abaft the capstan.

But the big man had not heard him, and the lad stole round to his elbow and spoke again.

"That you, Jeb?" said the A.B., looking down at him through the darkness.

"Yes, sir," replied Jeb. And then, after hesitating a few moments, all his fear came out in a torrent of uncouth words.

"An' they're goin' to dump you as soon as she's takin' any heavy water, sir," he ended. "An' they'll tell the mate as you was washed overboard."

"The grey rats destroy the white rat!" muttered the big sailorman as if to himself. "Kind to kind, and death to the unkind. The stranger that is not understood!" Then, almost in a whisper: "There would be peace of course, out here forever among the mysteries. I've wanted it to come out here, but the white rat must do justice to itself! Yes!"

And he stood up suddenly, swinging his arms as if in a strange exhilaration of expectancy. Abruptly, he turned to the deck boy.

"Thank ye, Jeb," he said. "I'll be on my guard. Go and get some sleep now."

He turned about to the capstan head, and picked up his fiddle. And as Jeb slipped away silently, barefooted, down the lee ladder, there came to him the low wailing of the violin, infinitely mournful, yet with the faint sob of a strange triumph coming with a growing frequence, changing slowly into a curious, grim undertone of subtle notes that spoke as plainly as Jesson's voice.

A fortnight went by and nothing happened. The lad was beginning to settle down again to a feeling of comfort that nothing horrible would happen while he was asleep. By the end of the fortnight they had hove both the new main topmast and new mizzen t'gallant mast into place, and had got up the main royal and t'gallant mast, and the rigging on both main and mizzen set up.

Then, in slinging the yards there were two bad accidents. The first occurred just as they got the upper topsail yard into place. One of the men, Bellard, fell in the act of shackling on the tie, and died at once. That night in the fo'c's'le there was an absolute silence during tea. Not a man spoke to Jesson. He was literally, in their dull minds, a condemned person; and his death merely a matter of the speediest arrangement possible.

Jesson was surely aware of their state of mind. However, he showed no outward signs of his awareness, and as soon as tea was over he took his violin and went away up to the fo'c's'le head, while down in the fo'c's'le the men sent Jeb out on deck, and talked hideous things together.

Three days later, when all the yards and gear were finally in place again, Dicky—the deck boy in the other watch—was lighting up the gear of the main royal when he slipped in some stupid fashion, and came down. Luckily for him, he brought up on the crosstrees with nothing worse than a broken forearm, which Captain Gallington and the mate tortured into position again, in the usual barbarous way that occurs at sea in those ships that do not carry a doctor.

On deck, every man was glancing covertly at Jesson, accusing him secretly and remorselessly with the one deadly thought—"Jonah!"

And as if the very elements were determined to give some foolish colour to the men's gloomy ignorance, the royal had not been set an hour before an innocent-looking squall developed unexpected viciousness, blowing the royal and the three t'gallants out of the bolt-ropes. The yards were lowered, and all made secure.

This was followed, in the afternoon watch, by a general shortening of sail, for the glass was falling in an uncomfortably hasty fashion. And surely enough, just at nightfall, they got the wind out of the north in a squall of actual hurricane pressure, which lasted an hour before it finally veered a little and settled down into a gale of grim intention.

When Jeb was called that night for the middle watch he found the ship thundering along under foresail and main lower-topsail, driving heavily before the gale, Captain Gallington having decided to run her, and take full advantage of the fair wind.

He struggled aft to a perfunctory roll call. The mate shouting the names into the windy darkness, but only occasionally able to hear any of the men's answering calls. Then the wheel and the lookout were relieved, and the watch below struggled forward through the heavy water upon the decks on their way to the fo'c's'le.

The mate gave orders that the watch on deck were to stand by handy, under the break of the poop, and this was done. All the men being there except Jesson who was on the look out, and Svensen who was at the wheel.

Until two bells the men stayed there under the break, talking and growling together in orthodox shellback fashion. An occasional flare of a match making an instantaneous picture of them all grouped about in their shining, wet oilskins and sou'westers. Outside, beyond the shelter of the break, the night, full of the ugly roar of the wind and the dull, heavy note of the sea.

A dark chaos of spray and the damp boom of the wind. And ever and again there would come a loud crash as a heavy sea broke aboard, and the water would burst into a kind of livid phosphorescent light, roaring fore and aft along the decks as it swirled in under the dark break among the waiting men in great floods of foam and water.

At two bells, which no one heard because of the infernal roaring of the wind and the constant fierce noises of the seas, Jeb discovered suddenly that several of the men had slipped away quietly forward through the darkness of the storm.

Sick with fright, he realized why they had gone, and fumbling his way out from under the break of the poop, he made a staggering run for the teak support of the skids. Here he held on as a heavy sea broke aboard, burying him entirely beneath a mountain of fierce brine. Gasping for breath, mouth and nostrils full of water, he caught the temporary life line that had been rigged, and scurried forward through the dazing roar and the unseen spray that stung and half blinded him from moment to moment.

Reaching the after end of the deck house where was the galley and the sleeping place of Chips, the bos'n, and the "Doc," he fumbled for the iron ladder and went up, for he knew that the lookout was being kept from the top of the deck house, owing to the fact that the fo'c's'le head was under water most of the time.

Once having warned Jesson, he felt quite confident that the big sailorman would be able to take care of himself. And Jeb meant to stay near in the lee of the galley skylight so as to be on hand if anything were attempted.

Creeping right on to the forward end of the house, he failed to find Jesson. He stared around him into the intolerable gloom of the storm that held them in on every side. He shouted Jesson's name, but his voice disappeared in the wind, and he became conscious of a dreadful terror, so that the whole of that shouting blackness of the night seemed one vast elemental voice of the thing that had been done. And then, suddenly, he knew that it was being done in those moments, even while he crept and searched upon the dark housetop.

The boy stood and raced across the top of the house. He knew just where to go. One blind leap to the deck, from the port forward corner of the house, and he went crashing into a huddle of fighting men whose shouts and curses he could only now hear for the first time in the tremendous sound of the elements. They were close to the port rail, and something was being heaved up in the gloom—something that struck and struck, and knocked a man backwards, half dead, as Jeb came down among them.

He caught a man by the leg, and was promptly kicked back against the teak side of the house. He lurched to the rail, all natural fear lost in fierce determination. He cast off the turns of the idle topsail halyards and wrenched madly at the heavy iron belaying pin. Then he sprang at the black, struggling mass of men, and struck. A man screamed, like a half-mad woman, so loud that his voice made a thin, agonized skirl away up through the storm.

The blow had broken his shoulder. Before Jeb could strike again, a kicking boot took him in the chest and drove him to the deck, and even as he fell a strange inner consciousness told him with sickening assurance that knives were being used. Sick, yet dogged, he scrambled to his feet. As he did so the black, gloom-merged, struggling mass became suddenly quiet, for the thing that they had fought to do was achieved.

An unheard splash over-side among the everlasting seas, and Jesson the sailorman, the white rat among the grey—had taken his place "out there among the mysteries."

Immediately Jeb was upon the suddenly stilled crowd of men, striking right and left with the heavy pin. Once, twice, three times! And with each blow the iron smashed the bone. Then, swiftly, he was gripped by fierce, strong hands, and a few minutes later the *Pareek*, sailing ship, was storming along in her own thunder, a mile away from the place where the developed man and the crude boy had ended their first friendship, and begun a second and ever-enduring one among the "sea palaces and the winds of God."

Jesson had killed two men outright with his fists in his fight for life. The rest of the crew—both watches had assisted—dumped these men, and afterward reported them as having been washed overboard by the same sea that took the man and the boy!

To the same cause they were able to attribute with safety the injuries they themselves had received during the fight.

And while the night went muttering things with the deep waters, in the fo'c's'le under the slush lamps the men played cards unemotionally.

"We'll have a fair wind to-morrow," they said. And they did! By some unknown and brutal law of Chance, they did!

But, in some strange, psychic fashion peculiar to men who have lived for months lean and wholesome among the winds and the seas, both the mate and the master suspected something of the truth that they could neither voice nor prove. And because of their suspicions they hazed the crew to such an extent, that when Frisco was reached all hands cleared out—without pay, sea-chests and discharges!

In the brine-haunted fo'c's'les of other old sailing ships they told the story to believing and sympathetic ears. And foolish, ignorant heads nodded a sober and uncondemnatory assent.

The Place of Storms

'Twas evening out at sea; and in the West
Rolled a black arch; while o'er the silent deep
Came from afar the calling of the sea,
The sad deep call that tells of corning woe,
As though the Ocean sorrowed in its soul,
And moaned, all helpless 'gainst its destined rage.
   Grim and tremendous loomed that rugged arch,
Fashioned of murky mistiness it seemed,
As though some giant had built himself a bridge
To span the dying glory of the sun;
Building it not with stones, but thunder-clouds,
Piled up in hideous grandeur to the sky.
   And I, upon a little bark afar,
Watched, as the wandering night leapt to the world,
That fierce and awful splendour in the West—
Blazing in lurid flamings 'neath the gloom
Of that stupendous omen of the storm.
   And as the night carne down upon the sea,
From the quiet surface of the glassy wave
Rose a drear moaning, as from dead men's throats;
While in the West sank low the flames of blood,
Leaving a core of red within the gloom,
To glow awhile like some vast smouldering ash,
Dying within the night. . . .
And now against the dusk of evening grew,
Running across the arch's crested height,
Wild, subtle, livid, serpent-twining flames
Of trickling green that sprang from dark to dark,
Across abysmal depths of shadowy vales;
From out the cavernous solitudes
That lurked within that monstrous hill of cloud,
Had leapt a multitude of wordless things,

Rejoicing in the corning tramp of death.
    And underneath those writhing, gleaming forms,
I saw the hollow blackness of the arch
Loom dreadful, like a doorway in the night,
Opening upon the awesome solitudes
Of some unknown and hungry waste of woe.
    And still around my little bark the calm
Held steadfastly, while ne'er a ripple broke
The silence of the ocean all around.
    Then, all at once, there came a sullen clang
Of far re-echoing sound, as though a world,
Full in its flight among the stars, had struck
Upon some other world with direful crash.
And wonderingly upon the deck I stood,
Amazed at that loud thunderous clap of noise;
And more afraid than e'er I'd been before.
Thus as I stayed all trembling in my fear,
I heard again the shaking of night air
Beneath the impact of that fearsome note:
And now, alert in cold expectancy,
Discerned the true direction of the sound
Amid the bestial answering howls that called
Their mocking echoes back across the sea.
It came from that dread arch within the West,
Rising and falling with a muffled boom,
Half stifled in creation's act.
    Then, at that second call, I saw the ship,
As though obedient to a master voice,
Move slowly round upon her keel until
Direct unto the mountain-pile her bows
Looked straight. Then, by some unseen force impelled,
She 'gan to gather way, so that the foam
Up-piled itself, a murmuring hill of surge
Beneath her forging prow; while driven wheals,
Formed half of water, half of new-born spume,
Spread round her hull and waked the calm
Of that cold silent sea to sudden life.
    And so on through the grey of night we drove
Towards the gaping darkness waiting there,
From whence, at times, the sombre mutter broke
Of that huge thunder-calling 'cross the dark.
    Time passed in moments, long as weary hours,
And all the sea was soundless, save for where

It broke protesting 'neath our surging bows.
And still we slid o'er that expectant sea,
'Cross many a glassy lair of crouching deaths,
Until, at last, the arch's highest crest
Almost o'erhung our masts, and then we *stayed*,
There just upon the verge that opened on
The darkness of a sunless, lightless gloom.

    An hour passed slowly by in silent dread,
Broken anon by that deep-throated call,
Which seemed so close, we felt, at times, the breath
Of some unholy Being just within
The mountain shades upon our starboard beam.

    And then, a glow of subtle green, there came,
Stealing beneath the chasmic arch like dawn;
But such a dawn as one might look to see
Lighting the morning of some Hell-born day.
Slowly it grew apace, until in time,
Detail by detail, all that had been hid
Showed with a strange distinctness that impressed
My wakened spirit with a sense of awe:
For 'neath that livid light there showed a sea
Tortured with storms—shaken with mighty winds;
And piled in frothing hills—carved in dank vales;
Or whirled in spouting towers of changeful light;
And other times pierced deep in noisome pits,
Whose glassy sides, bespecked with foam, revolved
With hideous churning sound, until it seemed
Some frightful Thing climbed growling from cold depths.

    And all this while, there grew upon mine ear
A distant shrieking clamour of fierce winds,
As though spent, gasping gales fought for the breath
With which to fill their mighty lungs again,
Ere they across the ocean madly rushed
To breathe their damp destruction far abroad.

    Awhile, I stood; my soul bemused with fright,
Until another sound broke loud and clear,
A vast cyclonic wailing, and a noise
Of many seas commingling in wild rage.
Nearer it seemed to come, until I saw
A huge rotating hill upon my left,
From which a blazing hyporact sprang far,
Of phosphorescent foam and flame, until
The blackness of that midnight dome it reached,

As though a tower of restless surge were stacked
Up to the very skies, a gleaming mount
Of frothy white, through which dark waters gloomed;
And stalked across the night, a whirling giant,
Built of wandering deaths, until at last
It burst asunder in its headlong flight,
Falling upon the ocean with impact
More hugely loud upon mine ear than e'er
Had broke the deepest thunders of this world.
    This gone, there came a hollow gurgling sob,
And scarce six cables' length away, I saw,
Upon our starboard beam, a sudden gape,
Amid the wearying turmoil of the seas,
A deep and raging gulf, whose mouth stretched out
As though it would engorge the very waves
That tumbled in mad chaos on its lips.
Quickly it vanished, as it had appeared,
And o'er the self-same place where it had yawned,
There roared an Iron Whirlwind, ploughing through,
And hurling far aside, the broken seas;
With such tempestuous force, it carved their crests
Into a maze of tattered wisps of spume,
That when it passed, a path of calm was left,
Paved with the crumbled fragments of the waves;
Yet, such a calm it was that one may see,
When some fierce beast veils anger in its breast;
For, in awhile, the calm departed hence,
And in its place, wild seas upreared their heads,
Grim seas, all mutilated with the blast,
And shaped like unto pyramids, so that I knew
I looked upon the Pyramidal Seas.
    Then, from the sea's far edge, upward there burst
A forest formed of fire, whose branches struck
Against the sky's black dome with muffled sound—
A strange and fearsome lightning, dull in hue,
And shedding all around a savage glare.
    This quickly died, and in its stead there grew,
Across the dim horizon's distant gloom,
A furious ruddy flare, from whence there rushed,
With mighty bellowings far across the sea,
The Fiery Tempest, which is scarcely seen,
Once in a thousand years, by mariners;
The fiery storm, in which the broad sky burns—

In which the very waves are flames of blood,
Upleaping to the night; while blazing clouds
Wrap the whole world in one red shroud of fire.
       With frightened wonder thus I stared awhile,
Until the vision faded in the night:
Then, all at once, a spectral thing beheld,
As from two mountains surging, upward drove
Dim minarets and castellated towers,
And all the ghostly splendour of the House
Where dead men's souls await the coming end—
The House of Storms, it was, formed 'mid the spume,
A strange nocturnal structure from the sea
Growing upon my vision, like a cloud
That forms above the evening sun—from whence
No man can tell, so subtle is its birth.
       Huge were its walls, and gloomy, formed of nights
Hurled from the blasted sea's deep silences.
       Awhile, I stood, all mazed with fear and doubt,
And looked with scarce believing eyes, until,
All in a moment's space, I saw a glow
Shining within the house, and suddenly
Forth out from windows and from doors there burst
A deep and lurid glare that streamed afar
Across the tumbled chaos of the Place.
And then there rose the panting sounds of wind,
As though within the house a giant-great smith
Tortured some vast volcanic forge with blasts
Until its fervent fire lit up the night.
And then there came a clangour loud and fierce,
The hissing sounds of water met with flame,
And the deep breathings of some breathless Thing
Working within the house.
                          Awhile, I harked,
Half mad with curious thoughts to look within
Those great and gloomy walls; and to this end,
I climbed among the rigging—thence aloft,
Until, at last, my staring eyes beheld
A strange and awful sight. For there, I saw,
The subterranean fires of earth gush up,
In radiant flames through one great fiery cone,
Around which hissed the sea in steamy wreaths.
And, in that ruddy glare, my vision showed,
Upstanding in the sea, a monstrous form,

Which bent near by the fire and seemed to toil,
Surging a wind-wrought hammer far on high.
   I climbed a little higher; there, I saw,
The huge and mighty shoulders of grim Storm
Heaving beneath the whirling of his sledge,
As 'mid a thunderous din of beaten brine,
And far up-spurting reek of shattered seas,
He forged gigantic ocean-waves, from base
Of solid steel-blue waters, to dire crests—
Arching their curved fierce fronts with awful skill,
And then, as finished, tossing each afar,
To roam o'er ceaseless miles, with hungry maw,
Until some hapless ship within their bowels,
They dive far to the deeps to glut their prey.
   And on Storm's head there perched an Albatross—
That lonely bird of death, whose ghostly shriek,
At night, 'mid gales is heard—an eldritch cry
Above the helmsman's struggling form, as though
It would remind him of death's near approach.
   While, in the sea, far down between Storm's knees,
I saw a bloated Horror watching there—
A waiting shape, a shark; and deeper still,
A hideous, loathsome writhing mass, that claimed
The Ocean's silent bed—a foul affront
To Nature's strange and wondrous handiwork,
Smirching the very deep with darker hue.
   And other things there were that drew my sight;
For round about, with curious eyes, there watched,
A crowding, peering host of sodden souls
Staring with fearful orbs upon huge Storm;
And whispering among themselves their grief
At each gaunt sea complete, and sent abroad.
   And ever through the doors, with noiseful tread,
Leapt the returning foam-maned steeds; and each
Bore a wet soul upon its spumy crest,
Scarcely unfleshed, and still all palpitant
With the warm life from which it had been wrenched.
   And, as each sea deposed its quivering load;
From the whole ghostly concourse, waiting, rose
Sadly a breathless moan of sympathy,
As in their midst they made a roomy place
For each poor 'wildered soul, while fluttering hands
Guided it thence with damp caressing touch.

Then, as I stared, Storm turned himself about,
So that I saw his face, and lo! his eyes
Were caverns, whence came echoing moans that seemed
Like unto hollow sounds within a vault,
As though the wordless dead groaned in their sleep.
    And as he bent beside that mighty forge,
His cheeks puffed out—two bellied thunder-clouds,
Forth from his mouth there came a shaking blast,
With a shrill screaming noise of unpent gales,
Through which a lower vulturous sound, I heard,
As though a ghoulish legion sang of death.
And all this time, his gale-born hammer beat
Upon the crying brine; while down his sides,
Gushed the foam-sweat in many a reeking stream.
    Then, all at once, from underneath our keel,
A wave belched upwards from the silent sea,
Like some huge, spume-gloved hand thrust from black depths,
And caught the little bark and hurled her out
Into the raging tumult 'neath the arch;
And in a moment, all around, I saw
A vast and dreadful wall encircling me—
A night-black thunder wall of tufted cloud,
Shutting from sight the wonders I had viewed;
As though an amphitheatre of gloom
Had closed around the ship, whence multitudes
Of unknown things, and watching spirits glared.
And in the centre grew a sudden tree,
Formed all its length of pale and quaking light.
No wind there was; yet without wind, the sea,
In jagg'd tremendous pyramids, uprose
Far to the sky, and fell whence they had leapt,
Running no whither; but just rising up
In monstrous heaps, to fall again in foam.
And with the churning of that horrid sea,
The ship was tossed most woefully about,
So that, at whiles, the up-hurled waves o'erhung
About my head in black and watery hills.
    An hour of terror passed; then, all at once,
I heard across the sea a moaning come,
Dreadful and sad, and terrible to hear;
And then a hollow rumble of deep sound,
With afterwards a full continuous roar
High in the air above; and then there rushed,

Down on the waiting craft, a howling gust,
Filled to the throat with vast unholy shrieks,
And leapt upon, and bore her down until
The milk-white smother of the boiling sea
Sprang all across our decks in frothing spume.

    There, in that anguished moment, from the sky,
Brilliant and clear, within a circle dark,
Shone the great Star of Peace, whose beams proclaim
The lulling of the tempest's furious breath.
And at that blessed omen, hope leapt up
Within mine anxious breast; till, in awhile,
The wind decreasing somewhat in its strength,
The ship uprose upon her keel, and lived,
Though loaded to her rails with seething brine
And beat with murderous seas, that madly leapt,
Boldly, in house-great clots, across her decks.

    Then, in a greater space, the storm grew less,
So that her hull was visible once more;
And far above, the peaceful stars shone out,
While I, with trembling heart raised up my voice,
In joy that life was mine, and gave my thanks,
Joining them with the dying Cyclone's blast.

    And then, across the failing waves, I saw,
Lighting the far-off East, the coming dawn,
Which grew and strengthened up, until at last
The great white maw of day devoured the stars;
And the red sun, all bearded with the storm,
Rose from below the sea's dark edge, and shone,
Over the cliffs of night, upon the world.

    And high the sea tossed up her rugged hills
Into the ruddy flame that blazed afar
And lit the seas with sombre wandering tints—
With crimson stains all flecked with froth and spume;
And the black terror of the night and storm
Had vanished, for awhile, in blazing light.

The Haunted *Pampero*

"Hurrah!" cried young Tom Pemberton, as he threw open the door and came forward into the room where his newlywed wife was busily employed about some sewing, "they've given me a ship. What ho!" and he threw his peaked uniform cap down on the table with a bang.

"A ship, Tom?" said his wife, letting her sewing rest idly in her lap.

"The *Pampero*!" said Tom proudly.

"What! The 'Haunted *Pampero*?'" cried his wife in a voice expressive of more dismay than elation.

"That's what a lot of fools call her," admitted Tom, unwilling to hear a word against his new kingdom. "It's all a lot of rot! She's no more haunted than I am!"

"And you've accepted?" asked Mrs. Tom, anxiously, rising to her feet with a sudden movement which sent the contents of her lap to the floor.

"You bet I have!" replied Tom. "It's not a chance to be thrown away, to be Master of a vessel before I've jolly well reached twenty-five."

He went toward her, holding out his arms happily; but he stopped suddenly as he caught sight of the dismayed look upon her face.

"What's up, little girl?" he asked. "You don't look a bit pleased." His voice denoted that her lack of pleasure in his news hurt him.

"I'm not, Tom. Not a bit. She's a dreadful ship! All sorts of horrible things happen to her—"

"Rot!" interrupted Tom, decisively. "What do you know about her anyway? She's one of the finest vessels in the company."

"Everybody knows," she said, with a note of tears in her voice. "Oh, Tom, can't you get out of it?"

"Don't want to!" crossly.

"Why didn't you come and ask me before deciding?"

"Wasn't any time!" gruffly. "It was 'Yes' or 'No'."

"Oh, why didn't you say 'No'?"

"Because I'm not a fool!" growing savage.

"I shall never be happy again," she said, sitting down abruptly, and beginning to cry.

Tears had their due effect, and the next instant Tom was kneeling beside her, libelling himself heartily. Presently, after sundry passages, her nose—a little pink—came out from the depth of *his* handkerchief.

"I shall come with you!" The words were uttered with sufficient determination to warn him that there was real danger of her threat being put into execution, and Tom, who was not entirely free from the popular superstition regarding the *Pampero*, began to feel uneasy as she combated every objection which he put forward. It was all very well going to sea in her himself; but to take his little girl, well—that was another thing. And so, like a sensible loving fellow, he fought every inch of the ground with her; the natural result being that at the end of an hour he retired—shall we say "retreated"—to smoke a pipe in his den and meditate on the perversity of womankind in general and his own wife in particular.

And she—well, she went to her bed room, and turned out all her pretty summer dresses, and, for a time, was quite happy. No doubt she was thinking of the tropics. Later, under Tom's somewhat disparaging guidance, she made selection among her more substantial frocks. And, in short, three weeks later saw her at sea in the haunted *Pampero*, along with her husband.

II

The first ten days, aided by a fresh fair wind, took them well clear of the Channel, and Mrs. Tom Pemberton was beginning to find her sea legs. Then, on the thirteenth day out they ran into dirty weather. Hitherto the *Pampero* had been lucky (for her), nothing special having occurred, save that one of the men was laid up through the starboard fore crane line having given way under him, letting him down on deck with a run. Yet because the man was alive and no limbs broken, there was a general feeling that the old packet was on her good behavior.

Then, as I have said, they ran into bad weather, and were hove to for three weary days under bare poles. On the morning of the fourth, the wind moderated sufficiently to allow of their setting the main topsail, storm foresail, and staysail, and running her off before the wind. During that day the weather grew steadily finer, the wind dropping and the sea going down; so that by evening they were bowling along before a comfortable six-knot breeze. Then, just before sunset, they had evidence once again that the *Pampero* was on her good behavior, and that there were other ships less lucky than she; for out of the red glare of sunset to starboard there floated to them the water-logged shell of a ship's lifeboat.

In passing, one of the men caught a glimpse of something crumpled up on a thwart, and sung out to the Mate who was in charge. He, having obtained permission from the Skipper, put the ship in irons, and lowered a boat. Reaching the wrecked craft, it was discovered that the something on the thwart was the still living form of a seaman, exhausted and scarcely in his right mind. Evidently they had been only just in time; for hardly had they removed him to their own boat before the other, with a slow, oily roll, disappeared from sight.

They returned with him to the ship, where he was made comfortable in a spare bunk, and on the next day, being sufficiently recovered, told how that he had been one of the A.B.'s in the *Cyclops*, and how that she had broached to while running before the gale two nights previously, and gone down with all hands. He had found himself floating beside her battered lifeboat, which had evidently been torn from its place on the skids as the ship capsized; he had managed to get hold of the lifelines and climb into her, and since then, how he had managed to exist, he could not say.

Two days later, the man who had fallen, through the breaking of the crane line, expired; at which some of the crew were uneasy, declaring that the old packet was going back on them.

"It's as I said," remarked one of the Ordinaries, "she's er bloomin', 'aunted tin kettle, an' if it weren't better bein' 'aunted 'n 'ungry, I'd bloomin' well stay ashore!" Wherein he may be said to have voiced the general sentiments of the rest.

With this man dying, Captain Tom Pemberton offered to sign on Tarpin— the man they had picked up—in his place. Tarpin thankfully accepted, and took the dead man's place in the forecastle; for though undeniably an old man, he was, as he had already shown on a couple of occasions, a smart sailor.

He was specially adept at rope splicing, and had a peculiarly shaped Marlinspike, from which he was never separated. It served him as a weapon too, and occasionally some of the crew thought he drew it too freely.

And now it appeared that the ship's bad genius was determined to prove it was by no means so black as it had been painted; for matters went on quietly and evenly for two complete weeks, during which the ship wandered across the line into the Southern Tropics, and there slid into one of those hateful calms which lurk there remorselessly awaiting their prey.

For two days Captain Tom Pemberton whistled vainly for wind; on the third he swore (under his breath when his wife was about, otherwise when she was below). On the evening of the fourth day he ceased to say naughty words about the lack of wind, for something happened, something altogether inexplicable, and frightening; so much so that he was careful to tell his wife nothing concerning the matter, she having been below at the time.

The sun had set some minutes and the evening was dwindling rapidly into night when from forward there came a tremendous uproar of pigs squealing and shrieking.

Captain Tom and the Second Mate, who were pacing the poop together, stopped in their promenade and listened.

"Damnation!" exclaimed the captain. "Who's messing with the pigs?"

The Second Mate was proceeding to roar out to one of the 'prentices to jump forward and see what was up when a man came running aft to say that there was something in the pigsty getting at the pigs, and would he come forward.

On hearing this, the Captain and the Second Mate went forward at a run. As they passed along the deck and came nearer to the sound of action, they distinctly heard the sound of savage snarling mingled with the squealing of the pigs.

"What the devil's that!" yelled the Second, as he tried to keep pace with the Skipper. Then they were by the pigsty, and, in the gathering gloom, found the crew grouped in a semicircle about the sty.

"What's up?" roared Captain Tom Pemberton. "What's up here?" He made a way through the men, and stooped and peered through the iron bars of the sty, but it was too dark to make out anything with certainty. Then, before he could take away his face, there came a deeper, fiercer growl, and something snapped between the bars. The Captain gave out a cry and jumped back among the men, holding his nose.

"Hurt, Sir?" asked the Second Mate, anxiously.

"N—no," said the Captain, in a scared, doubtful voice. He fingered his nose for a further moment or two. "I don't think so."

The Second Mate turned and caught the nearest man by the shoulder.

"Bring out one of your lamps, smart now!" Yet even as he spoke, one of the Ordinaries came running out with one ready lighted. The Second snatched it from him and held it toward the pigsty. In the same instant something wet and shiny struck it from his hand. The Second Mate gave a shout, and then there was an instant's quietness in which all caught a sound of something slithering curiously along the decks to leeward. Several of the men made a run to the forecastle; but the Second was on his knees groping for the lantern. He found it and struck a light. The pigs had stopped squealing, but were still grunting in an agitated manner. He held the lantern near the bars and looked.

Two of the pigs were huddled up in the starboard corner of the sty, and they were bleeding in several places. The third, a big fellow, was stretched upon his back; he had apparently been bitten terribly about the throat, and was quite dead.

The Captain put his hand on the Second's shoulder, and stooped forward to get a better view.

"My God, Mister Kasson, what's been here," he muttered with an air of consternation.

The men had drawn up close behind and around, and were now looking on, almost too astonished to venture opinions. Then a man's voice broke the momentary silence:

"Looks as if they 'ad been 'avin 'a 'op with a cussed great shark!"

The Second Mate moved the light along the bars.

"The door's shut and the toggel's on, sir," he said in a low voice.

The Skipper grasped his meaning, but said nothing.

"S'posin' it 'ad been one o' us," muttered a man behind him.

From the surrounding "crowd" there came a murmur of comprehension and some uneasy glancing from side to side and behind.

The Skipper faced round upon them.

He opened his mouth to speak; then shut it as though a sudden idea had come to him.

"That light, quickly, Mister Kasson!" he exclaimed, holding out his hand.

The Second passed him the lamp, and he held it above his head. He was counting the men. They were all there, watch below and watch on deck; even the man on the look-out had come running down. There was absent only the man at the wheel.

He turned to the Second Mate.

"Take a couple of the men aft with you, Mr. Kasson, and pass out some lamps. We must make a search!"

In a couple of minutes they returned with a dozen lighted lamps which were quickly distributed among the men; then a thorough search of the decks was commenced. Every corner was peered into; but nothing found, and so, at last, they had to give it up, unsuccessful.

"That'll do, men," said Captain Tom. "Hang one of those lamps up foreside the pigsty, and shove the others back in the locker." Then he and the Second Mate went aft.

At the bottom of the poop steps the Skipper stopped abruptly, and said "Hush!" For a half a minute they listened, but without being able to say that they had heard anything definite. Then Captain Tom Pemberton turned and continued his way up on to the poop.

"What was it, sir?" asked the Second, as he joined him at the top of the ladder.

"I'm hanged if I know!" replied Captain Tom. "I feel all adrift. I never heard there was anything—anything like *this*!"

"And we've no dogs aboard!"

"Dogs! More like tigers! Did you hear what one of the shellbacks said?"

"A shark, you mean, sir?" said the Second Mate, with some remonstrance in his tone.

"Have you ever seen a shark-bite Mister Kasson?"

"No, sir," replied the Second Mate.

"Well, I have."

"But—but—" began the Second Mate.

"Those are shark-bites, Mister Kasson! God help us! Those are shark-bites!"

III

After this inexplicable affair a week of stagnant calm passed without anything unusual happening, and Captain Tom Pemberton was gradually losing the sense of haunting fear which had been so acute during the nights following the death of the porker.

It was early night, and Mrs. Tom Pemberton was sitting in a deck chair on the weather side of the saloon skylight, near the forward end. The Captain and the First Mate were walking up and down, passing and repassing her. Presently the Captain stopped abruptly in his walk, leaving the Mate to continue along the deck. Then, crossing quickly to where his wife was sitting, he bent over her.

"What is it, dear?" he asked. "I've seen you once or twice looking to leeward as though you heard something. What is it?"

His wife sat forward and caught his arm.

"Listen!" she said in a sharp undertone. "There it is again! I've been thinking it must be my fancy; but it isn't. Can't you hear it?"

Captain Tom was listening, and just as his wife spoke, his strained sense caught a low, snarling growl from among the shadows to leeward. Though he gave a start, he said nothing; but his wife saw his hand steal to his side pocket.

"You heard it?" she asked eagerly. Then, without waiting for an answer: "Do you know, Tom, I've heard the sound three times already. It's just like an animal growling somewhere over there," and she pointed among the shadows. She was so positive about having heard it that her husband gave up all idea of trying to make her believe that her imagination had been playing tricks with her. Instead, he caught her hand and raised her to her feet.

"Come below, Annie," he said and led her to the companionway. There he left her for a moment and ran across to warn the First Mate to be on the look out; then back to her and led her down the stairs. In the saloon she turned and faced him.

"What was it, Tom? You're afraid of something, and you're keeping it from me. It's something to do with this horrible vessel!"

The Captain stared at her with a puzzled look. He did not know how much or how little to tell her. Then, before he could speak, she had stepped to his side and thrust her hand into the side pocket of his coat on the right.

"You've got a pistol!" she cried, pulling the weapon out with a jerk. 'That shows it's something you're frightened of! It's something dangerous, and you won't tell me. I shall come up on deck with you again!" She was almost tearful, and very much in earnest; so much so that the Captain turned-to and told her everything; which was, after all, the wisest thing he could have done under the circumstances.

"Now," he said, when he had made an end, "you must promise me never to come up on deck at night without me—now promise!"

"I will, dear, if you will promise to be careful and—and not run any risks. Oh, I wish you hadn't taken this horrid ship!" And she commenced to cry.

Later, she consented to be quieted, and the Captain left her, after having exacted a promise from her that she would "turn in" right away and get some sleep.

The first part she fulfilled without delay; but the latter was more difficult, and at least an hour went by tediously before at last, growing drowsy, she fell into an uneasy sleep. From this she was awakened some little time later with a start. She had seemed to hear some noise. Her bunk was up against the side of the ship, and a glass port opened right above it, and it was from this port that the noise proceeded. It was a queer slurring sort of noise, as though something were rubbing up against it, and she grew frightened as she listened; for though she had pushed to the port on getting into her bunk, she was by no means certain that she had slipped the screw-catch on properly. She was, however, a plucky little woman, and wasted no time; but made one jump to the floor, and ran to the lamp. Turning it up with a sudden, nervous movement, she glanced toward the port. Behind the thick circle of glass she made out something that seemed to be pressed up against it. A queer, curved indentation ran right across it. Abruptly, as she stared, it gaped, and teeth flashed into sight. The whole thing started to move up and down across the glass, and she heard again that queer slurring noise which had frightened her into wakefulness. The thought leaped across her mind, as though it was a revelation, that it was something *living*, and it was grubbing at the glass, trying to get in. She put a hand down on to the table to steady herself, and tried to think.

Behind her the cabin door opened softly, and some one came into the room. She heard her husband's voice say "Why, Annie—" in a tone of astonishment, and then stop dead. The next instant a sharp report filled the little cabin with sound and the glass of the port was starred all across, and there was no more anything of which to be afraid, for Captain Tom's arms were round her.

From the door there came a noise of loud knocking and the voice of the First Mate:

"Anything wrong, sir?"

"It's all right, Mister Stennings. I'll be with you in half a minute." He heard the Mate's footsteps retreat, and go up the companion ladder. Then he listened quietly as his wife told him her story. When she had made an end, they sat and talked a while gravely, with an infinite sense of being upon the borders of the Unknown. Suddenly a noise out upon the deck interrupted their talk, a man crying aloud with terror, and then a pistol shot and the Mate's voice shouting. Captain Pemberton leaped to his feet simultaneously with his wife.

"Stay here, Annie!" he commanded, and pushed her down on to the seat. He turned to the door; then an idea coming to him, he ran back and thrust his revolver into her hands. "I'll be with you in a minute," he said assuringly; then, seizing a heavy cutlass from a rack on the bulkhead, he opened the door and made a run for the deck.

His wife, on her part, at once hurried to make sure that the port catch was properly on. She saw that it was and made haste to screw it up tightly. As she did so, she noticed that the bullet had passed clean through the glass on the left-hand side, low down. Then she returned to her seat with the revolver, and sat listening and waiting.

On the main deck the Captain found the Mate and a couple of men just below the break of the poop. The rest of the watch were gathered in a clump a little foreside of them, and between them and the Mate stood one of the 'prentices, holding a binnacle lamp. The two men with the mate were Coalson and Tarpin. Coalson appeared to be saying something; Tarpin was nursing his jaw and seemed to be in considerable pain.

"What is it, Mister Stennings?" sung out the Skipper quickly.

The First Mate glanced up.

"Will you come down, sir," he said. "There's been some infernal devilment on!"

Even as he spoke, the Captain was in the act of running down the poop ladder. Reaching the Mate and the two men, he put a few questions rapidly and learned that Coalson had been on his way aft to relieve the "wheel," when all at once something had leaped out at him from under the lee pinrail. Fortunately, he had turned just in time to avoid it, and then, shouting at the top of his voice, had run for his life. The Mate had heard him, and thinking he saw something behind, had fired. Almost directly afterward they had heard Tarpin calling out further forward, and then he too had come running aft; but just under the skids he had caught his foot in a ringbolt, and come crashing to the deck, smashing his face badly against the sharp corner of the after hatch. He, too, it would appear, had been chased; but by what, he could not say. Both the men were greatly agitated and could only tell their stories jerkily and with some incoherence.

With a certain feeling of the hopelessness of it all, Captain Pemberton gave orders to get lanterns and search the decks; but, as he anticipated, nothing unusual was found. Yet the bringing out of the lanterns suggested a wise precaution; for he told them to keep out a couple, and carry them about with them when they went to and fro along the decks.

IV

Two nights later, Captain Tom Pemberton was suddenly aroused from a sound slumber by his wife.

"Shish!" she whispered, putting her fingers on his lips. "Listen."

He rose on his elbow, but otherwise kept quiet. The berth was full of shadows for the lamp was turned rather low. A minute of tense silence passed; then, abruptly, from the direction of the door, he heard a slow, gritty, rubbing noise. At that he sat upright, and sliding his hand beneath his pillow, brought out his revolver; then remained silent—waiting.

Suddenly he heard the latch of the door snicked softly out of its catch, and an instant later a breath of air swept through the berth, stirring the draperies. By that he knew that the door had been opened, and he leaned forward, raising his weapon. A moment of intense stillness followed; then, all at once, something dark slid between him and the little glimmer of flame in the lamp. Instantly he aimed and fired, once—twice. There came a hideous howling which seemed to be retreating toward the door, and he fired in the direction of the noise. He heard it pass into the saloon. Then came a quick slither of steps upon the companion stairway, and the noise died away into silence.

Immediately afterward the Skipper heard the Mate bellowing for the watch to lay aft, then his heavy tread came tumbling down into the saloon, and the Captain, who had left his bunk to turn up his lamp, met him in the doorway. A minute was sufficient to put the Mate in possession of such facts as the Skipper himself had gleaned, and after that, they lit the saloon lamp and examined the floor and companion stairs. In several places they found traces of blood, which showed that

132

one, at least, of Captain Tom's shots had got home. They were also found to lead a little way along the lee side of the poop; but ceased altogether nearly opposite the end of the skylight.

As may be imagined, this affair had given the Captain a big shaking up, and he felt so little like attempting further sleep that he proceeded to dress; an action which his wife imitated, and the two of them passed the rest of the night on the poop; for, as Mrs. Pemberton said: You felt safer up in the fresh air. You could at least feel that you were near help. A sentiment which, probably, Captain Tom *felt* more distinctly than he could have put into words. Yet he had another thought, of which he was much more acutely aware, and which he did manage to formulate in some shape to the Mates during the course of the following day. As he put it:

"It's my wife that I'm afraid for! That thing (whatever it is) seems to be making a dead set for her!" His face was anxious and somewhat haggard under the tan. The two Mates nodded.

"I should keep a man in the saloon at night, sir," suggested the Second Mate, after a moment's thought. "And let her keep with you as much as possible."

Captain Tom Pemberton nodded with a slight air of relief. The reasonableness of the precaution appealed to him. He would have a man in the saloon after dark, and he would see that the lamp was kept going; then, at least, his wife would be safe, for the only entrance to his cabin was through the saloon. As for the shattered port, it had been replaced the day after he had broken it, and now every dog watch he saw to it himself that it was securely screwed up, and not only that, but the iron storm-cover as well; so that he had no fears in that direction.

That night at eight o'clock, as the roll was being called, the Second Mate turned and beckoned respectfully to the Captain, who immediately left his wife and stepped up to him.

"About that man, sir," said the Second. "I'm up here till twelve o'clock. Who would you care to have out of my watch?"

"Just as you like, Mister Kasson. Who can you best spare?"

"Well, sir, if it comes to that, there's old Tarpin. He's not been much use on a rope since that tumble he got the other night. He says he hurt his arm as well, and he's not able to use it."

"Very well, Mr. Kasson. Tell him to step up."

This the Second Mate did, and in a few moments old Tarpin stood before them. His face was bandaged up, and his right arm was slipped out of the sleeve of his coat.

"You seem to have been in the wars, Tarpin," said the Skipper, eyeing him up and down.

"Yes, sir," replied the man, with a touch of grimness.

"I want you down in the saloon till twelve o'clock," the Captain went on. "If you—er—hear anything, call me, do you hear?"

The man gave out a gruff "aye, aye, sir," and went slowly aft.

"I don't expect he's best pleased, sir," said the Second with a slight smile.

"How do you mean, Mister Kasson?"

"Well, sir, ever since he and Coalson were chased, and he got the tumble he's taken to waiting around the decks at night. He seems a plucky old devil, and it's my belief he's waiting to get square with whatever it was that made him run."

"Then he's just the man I want in the saloon," said the Skipper. "It may just happen that he gets his chance of coming close to quarters with this infernal hell-thing that's knocking about. And by Jove, if he does, he and I'll be friends for evermore."

At nightfall Captain Tom Pemberton and his wife went below. They found old Tarpin sitting on one of the benches. At their entrance he rose to his feet and touched his cap awkwardly to them. The Captain stopped a moment and spoke to him:

"Mind, Tarpin, the least sound of anything about, and you call me! And see you keep the lamp bright."

"Aye, aye, sir," said the man quietly; and the Skipper left him, and followed his wife into their cabin.

V

The Captain had been asleep more than an hour, when abruptly something roused him. He reached for his revolver, and then sat upright; yet though he listened intently, no sound came to him save the gentle breathing of his wife. The lamp was low, but not so low that he could not make out the various details of the cabin. His glance roved swiftly round and showed him nothing unusual, until it came to the door; then, in a flash, he noted that no light from the saloon lamp came under the bottom. He jumped swiftly from his bunk with a sudden gust of anger. If Tarpin had gone to sleep and allowed the lamp to go out, well—! His hand was upon the key. He had taken the precaution to turn it before going to sleep. How providential this action had been he was soon to learn. In the very act of unlocking the door, he paused; for all at once a low grumbling purr came to him from beyond the door. Ah! That was the sound that had come to him in his sleep and wakened him. For a moment he stood, a multitude of frightened fancies coming to him. Then, realizing that now was such a chance as he might not again have, he turned the key with a swift movement, and flung the door wide open.

The first thing he noticed was that the saloon lamp had burned down and was flickering, sending uncomfortable splashes of light and darkness across the place. The next, that something lay at his feet across the threshold—something that started up with a snarl and turned upon him. He pushed the muzzle of his revolver against it and pulled the trigger twice. The Thing gave out a queer roar, and flung itself from him half way across the saloon floor; then rose to a semi-upright position, and darted howling through the doorway leading to the companion stairs. Behind him he heard his wife crying out in alarm; but he did not stay to answer her; instead, he followed the Thing voicing its pains so hideously. At the bottom of the stairs he glanced up and saw something outlined against the stars. It was only a glimpse, and he saw that it had two legs, like a man; yet he thought of a shark. It disappeared, and he leaped up the stairs. He stared to the leeward and saw something by the rail. As he fired, the Thing leaped, and a cry and a splash came almost simultaneously. The Second Mate joined him breathlessly, as he raced to the side.

"What was it, sir?" gasped the officer.

"Look!" shouted Captain Tom, pointing down into the dark sea.

He stared down into the glassy darkness. Something like a great fish showed below the surface. It was dimly outlined by the phosphorescence. It was swimming in an erratic circle, leaving an indistinct trail of glowing bubbles behind it. Something caught the Second Mate's eyes as he stared, and he leaned farther out so as to get a better view. He saw the Thing again. The fish had two tails, or—they might have been legs. The Thing was swimming downward. How rapidly, he could judge by the speed at which its apparent size diminished. He turned and caught the Captain by the wrist.

"Do you see its—its tails, sir?" he muttered excitedly.

Captain Tom Pemberton gave an unintelligible grunt, but kept his eyes fixed on the deep. The Second glanced back. Far below him he made out a little moving spot of phosphorescence. It grew fainter, and vanished in the immensity beneath them.

Some one touched the Captain on the arm. It was his wife.

"Oh, Tom, have you—have you—?" she began; but he said "Hush!" and turned to the Second Mate.

"Call all hands, Mister Kasson!" he ordered; then, taking his wife by the arm, he led her down with him into the saloon. Here they found the steward, in his shirt and trousers, trimming the lamp. His face was pale, and he started to question as soon as they entered; but the Captain quieted him with a gesture.

"Look in all the empty cabins!" the Skipper commanded, and while the steward was doing this, the Skipper himself made a search of the saloon floor. In a few minutes the steward came up to say that the cabins were as usual, whereupon the Captain led his wife on deck. Here the Second Mate met them.

"The hands are mustered, sir," he said.

"Very good, Mister Kasson. Call the roll!"

The roll was gone over, each man answering to his name in turn. The Second Mate reached the last three on the list:

"Jones!"

"Sir!"

"Smith!"

"Yessir!"

"Tarpin!"

But from the waiting crowd below, in the light of the Second Mate's lantern, no answer came. He called the name again, and then Captain Tom Pemberton touched him on the arm. He turned and looked at the Captain, whose eyes were full of incredible realization.

"It's no good, Mister Kasson!" the Captain said. "I had to make quite sure—" He paused, and the Second Mate took a step toward him.

"But—where is he?" he asked, almost stupidly.

The Captain leaned forward, looking him in the eyes.

"You saw him go, Mister Kasson!" he said in a low voice.

The Second Mate stared back, but he did not see the Captain. Instead, he saw again in his mind's eye two things that looked like legs—human legs!

There was no more trouble that voyage; no more strange happenings; nothing unusual; but Captain Tom Pemberton had no peace of mind until he reached port and his wife was safely ashore again.

The story of the *Pampero*, her bad reputation, and this latest extraordinary happening got into the papers. Among the many articles which the tale evoked was one which held certain interesting suggestions.

The writer quoted from an old manuscript entitled "Ghosts," the well-known legend of the sea ghoul—which, as will be remembered, asserts that those who "die by ye sea, live of ye sea, and do come upward upon lonely shores, and do eate, biting like ye shark or ye deyvel-fishe, and are dreydful in hunger for ye fleyshe of man, and moreover do strive in mid sea to board ye ships of ye deep water, that they shall saytisfy theire dreydful hunger."

The author of the article suggested seriously that the man Tarpin was some abnormal thing out of the profound deeps; that had destroyed those who had once been in the whaleboat, and afterward, with dreadful cunning, been taken aboard the *Pampero* as a cast-away, afterward indulging its monstrous appetite. What form of life the creature possessed the writer frankly could not indicate; but set out the uncomfortable suggestion that the case of the *Pampero* was not the first; nor would it be the last. He reminded the public of the many ships that vanish. He pointed out how a ship, thus dreadfully bereft of her crew, might founder and sink when the first heavy storm struck her.

He concluded his article by asserting his opinion that he did not believe the *Pampero* to be "haunted." It was, he held, simple chance that had associated a long tale of ill-luck with the vessel in question; and that the thing which had happened could have happened as easily to any other vessel which might have met and picked up the grim occupant of the derelict whaleboat.

Whatever may be the correctness of the writer's suggestions, they are at least interesting, in endeavoring to sum up this extraordinary and incomprehensible happening. But Captain Pemberton felt surer of his own sanity when he remembered (when he thought of the matter at all) that men often go mad from exposure in open boats, and that the Marlinspike which Tarpin always carried was sharpened much to the shape of a shark's tooth.

An Adventure of the Deep Waters

This is an extraordinary tale. We had come up from the Cape, and owing to the Trades heading us more than usual, we had made some hundreds of miles more westing than I ever did before or since.

I remember perfectly the particular night of the happening. I suppose what occurred stamped it solid into my memory with a thousand little details that in the ordinary way I should never have remembered an hour. And, of course, we talked it over so often among ourselves that this no doubt helped to fix it all past any forgetting.

I remember the Mate and I had been pacing the weather side of the poop and discussing various old shellbacks' superstitions. I was third mate, and it was between four and five bells in the first watch (i.e. between ten and half-past). Suddenly, he stopped in his walk and lifted his head and sniffed several times.

"My word, Mister," he said, "there's a rum kind of stink somewhere about. Don't you smell it?"

I sniffed once or twice at the light airs that were coming in on the beam; then I walked to the rail and leaned over, smelling again at the slight breeze. And abruptly I got a whiff of it, faint and sickly, yet vaguely suggestive of something I had once smelt before.

"I can smell something, Mr. Lammart," I said. "I could almost give it name; and yet, somehow I can't." I stared away into the dark, to windward. "What do you seem to smell?" I asked him.

"I can't smell anything now," he replied, coming over and standing beside me. "It's gone again—No! By Jove! there it is again. My goodness! Phoo—"

The smell was all about us now, filling the night air. It had still that indefinable familiarity about it, and yet it was curiously strange; and, more than anything else, it was certainly simply beastly.

The stench grew stronger, and presently the Mate asked me to go forward, and see whether the lookout man noticed anything. When I reached the break of the forecastle head, I called up to the man, to know whether he smelled anything.

"Smell anything, sir!" he sang out. "Jumpin'larks! I sh'ud think I do. I'm fair p'isoned with it!"

137

I ran up the weather steps, and stood beside him. The smell was certainly very plain up there; and after savouring it for a few moments, I asked him whether he thought it might be a dead whale. But he was very emphatic that this could not be the case; for, as he said, he had been nearly fifteen years in whaling ships, and knew the smell of a dead whale "like as you would the smell of bad whisky, sir," as he put it. "'Tain't no whale, yon; but the Lord He knows what 'tis. I'm thinkin' it's Davy Jones come up for a breather."

I stayed with him some minutes, staring out into the darkness, but could see nothing; for, even had there been something big close to us, I doubt whether I could have seen it, so black a night it was, without a visible star, and with a vague, dull haze breeding an indistinctness all about the ship.

I returned to the Mate and reported that the lookout complained of the smell; but that neither he nor I had been able to see anything in the darkness to account for it.

By this time the queer, disgusting odour seemed to be in all the air about us, and the Mate told me to go below and shut all the ports, so as to keep the beastly smell out of the cabins and the saloon.

When I returned he suggested that we should shut the companion doors; and after that we commenced to pace the poop again, discussing the extraordinary smell, and stopping from time to time to stare through our night glasses out into the night about the ship.

"I'll tell you what it smells like, Mister," the Mate remarked, once, "and that's like a mighty old derelict I once went aboard in the North Atlantic. She was a proper old-timer, an' she gave us all the creeps. There was just this funny, dank, rummy sort of smell about her, sort of century-old bilge-water and dead men an' seaweed. I can't stop thinkin' we're nigh some lonesome old packet out there; an' a good thing we've not much way on us!"

"Do you notice how almighty quiet everything's gone the last half hour or so?" I said, a little later. "It must be the mist thickening down."

"It is the mist," said the Mate, going to the rail and staring out. "Good Lord, what's that?" he added.

Something had knocked his hat from his head, and it fell with a sharp rap at my feet. And suddenly, you know, I got a premonition of something horrid.

"Come away from the rail, sir," I said, sharply, and gave one jump, and caught him by the shoulders and dragged him back. "Come away from the side!"

"What's up, Mister?" he growled at me, and twisted his shoulders free. "What's wrong with you? Was it you knocked off my cap?" He stooped and felt around for it; and as he did so I *heard* something unmistakably fiddling away at the rail, which the Mate had just left.

"My God, sir!" I said, "there's something there. Hark!"

The Mate stiffened up, listening; then he heard it. It was for all the world as if something was feeling and rubbing the rail, there in the darkness, not two fathoms away from us.

"Who's there?" said the Mate quickly. Then, as there was no answer: "What the devil's this hanky-panky? Who's playing the goat there?" He made a swift step through the darkness towards the rail, but I caught him by the elbow.

"Don't go, Mister!" I said, hardly above a whisper. "It's not one of the men. Let me get a light."

"Quick, then!" he said; and I turned and ran aft to the binnacle and snatched out the lighted lamp. As I did so I heard the Mate shout something out of the darkness, in a strange voice. There came a sharp, loud, rattling sound, and then a crash, and immediately the Mate roaring to me to hasten with the light. His voice changed, even whilst he shouted, and gave out something that was nearer a scream than anything else. There came two loud, dull blows, and an extraordinary gasping sound; and then, as I raced along the poop, there was a tremendous smashing of glass, and an immediate silence.

"Mr. Lammart!" I shouted. "Mr. Lammart!" And then I had reached the place where I had left the Mate, not forty seconds before; but the Mate was not there.

"Mr. Lammart!" I shouted again, holding the light high over my head, and turning quickly to look behind me. As I did so my foot glided on some slippery substance and I went headlong to the deck, with a tremendous thud, smashing the lamp and putting out the light.

I was on my feet again in an instant. I groped a moment for the lamp, and as I did so I heard the men singing out from the main-deck and the noise of their feet as they came running aft. I found the broken lamp and realised it was useless; then I jumped for the companionway, and in half a minute I was back, with the big saloon lamp glaring bright in my hands.

I ran forward again, shielding the upper edge of the glass chimney from the draught of my running, and the blaze of the big lamp seemed to make the weather side of the poop as bright as day, except for the mist, that gave something of a vagueness to things.

Where I had left the Mate there was blood upon the deck, but nowhere any signs of the man himself. I ran to the weather rail and held the lamp to it. There was blood upon it; and the rail itself seemed to have been wrenched by some huge force. I put out my hand and found that I could shake it. Then I leaned out-board and held the lamp at arm's length, staring down over the ship's side.

"Mr. Lammart!" I shouted into the night and the thick mist. "Mr. Lammart! Mr. Lammart!" But my voice seemed to go lost and muffled and infinitely small away into the billowy darkness.

I heard the men snuffling and breathing, waiting to leeward of the poop. I whirled round to them, holding the lamp high.

"We heard somethin', sir," said Tarpley, the leading seaman in our watch. "Is anything wrong, sir?"

"The Mate's gone," I said blankly. "We heard something, and I went for the binnacle lamp. Then he shouted, and I heard something smashing things; and when I got back he'd gone clean." I turned and held the light out again over the unseen sea; and the men crowded round along the rail, and stared, bewildered.

"Blood, sir," said Tarpley, pointing. "There's something almighty queer out there!" He waved a huge hand into the darkness. "That's what stinks—"

He never finished; for, suddenly, one of the men cried out something in a frightened voice: "Look out, sir! Look out, sir!"

I saw, in one brief flash of sight, something come in with an infernal flicker of movement; and then, before I could form any notion of what I had seen, the lamp was dashed to pieces across the poop deck. In that instant my perceptions cleared, and I saw the incredible folly of what we were doing; for there we were, standing up against the blank, unknowable night; and out there in the dark there surely lurked some thing of monstrousness; and we were at its mercy. I seemed to feel it hovering, hovering over us; so that I felt the sickening creep of gooseflesh all over me.

"Stand back from the rail!" I shouted. "Stand back from the rail!" There was a rush of feet as the men obeyed, in sudden apprehension of their danger; and I gave back with them. Even as I did so I felt some invisible thing brush my shoulder; and an indescribable smell was in my nostrils, from something that moved over me in the dark.

"Down into the saloon, everyone!" I shouted. "Down with you all! Don't wait a moment!"

There was a rush along the dark weather deck, and then the men went helter skelter down the companion steps, into the saloon, falling and cursing over one another in the darkness. I sung out to the man at the wheel to join them, and then I followed.

I came upon the men huddled at the foot of the stairs, and filling up the passage, all crowding each other in the darkness. The Skipper's voice was filling the saloon, and he was demanding in violent adjectives the cause of so tremendous a noise. From the steward's berth there came also a voice, and the splutter of a match; and then the glow of a lamp in the saloon itself.

I pushed my way through the men and found the Captain in the saloon, in his sleeping gear, looking both drowsy and angry, though perhaps bewilderment topped every other feeling. He held his cabin lamp in his hand, and shone the light over the huddle of men.

I hurried to explain, and told him of the incredible disappearance of the Mate, and of my conviction that some extraordinary thing was lurking near the ship, out in the mist and the darkness. I mentioned the curious smell, and told how the Mate had suggested that we had drifted down near some old-time, sea-rotted derelict. And, you know, even as I put it into awkward words, my imagination began to awaken to horrible discomforts—a thousand dreadful impossibilities of the sea became suddenly possible.

The Captain (Jeldy was his name) did not stop to dress, but ran back into his cabin, and came out in a few moments with a couple of revolvers and a handful of

140

cartridges. The second mate had come running out of his cabin at the noise, and had listed intensely to what I had to say. Now he jumped back into his berth and brought out his own lamp and a large-pattern revolver which was evidently ready loaded.

Captain Jeldy pushed one of his revolvers into my hands with some of the cartridges, and we began hastily to load the weapons. Then the Captain caught up his lamp and made for the stairway, ordering the men into the saloon out of his way.

"Shall you want them, sir?" I asked.

"No," he said. "It's no use their running any unnecessary risks." He threw a word over his shoulder: "Stay quiet here, men; if I want you, I'll give you a shout; then come spry!"

"Aye, aye, sir," said the watch, in a chorus; and then I was following the Captain up the stairs, with the second mate close behind.

We came up through the companionway on to the silence of the deserted poop. The mist had thickened up, even during the brief time that I had been below, and there was not a breath of wind. The mist was so dense that it seemed to press in upon us; and the two lamps made a kind of luminous halo in the mist, which seemed to absorb their light in a most peculiar way.

"Where was he?" the Captain asked me, almost in a whisper.

"On the port side, sir," I said, "a little foreside the charthouse, and about a dozen feet in from the rail. I'll show you the exact place."

We went forward along what had been the weather side, going quietly and watchfully; though, indeed, it was little enough that we could see because of the mist. Once, as I led the way, I thought I heard a vague sound somewhere in the mist; but was all unsure because of the creak, creak of the spars and gear as the vessel rolled slightly upon an odd, oily swell. Apart from this slight sound, and the far-up rustle of the canvas, slatting gently against the masts, there was no sound at all throughout the ship. I assure you, the silence seemed to me to be almost menacing, in the tense, nervous state in which I was.

"Hereabouts is where I left him," I whispered to the Captain, a few seconds later. "Hold your lamp low, sir. There's blood on the deck."

Captain Jeldy did so, and made a slight sound with his mouth at what he saw. Then, heedless of my hurried warning, he walked across to the rail, holding his lamp high up. I followed him; for I could not let him go alone; and the second mate came too, with his lamp. They leaned over the port rail, and held their lamps out into the mist and the unknown darkness beyond the ship's side. I remember how the lamps made just two yellow glares in the mist, ineffectual, yet serving somehow to make extraordinarily plain the vastitude of the night, and the *possibilities of the dark*. Perhaps that is a queer way to put it, but it gives you the effect of that moment upon my feelings. And all the time, you know, there was upon me the brutal, frightening expectancy of something reaching in at us from out of that everlasting darkness and mist that held all the sea and the night, so that we were just three mist-shrouded, hidden figures, peering nervously.

The mist was now so thick that we could not even see the surface of the water overside; and fore and aft of us the rail vanished away into the fog and the dark. And then, you know, as we stood here staring, I heard something moving down on the main deck. I caught Captain Jeldy by the elbow.

"Come away from the rail, sir," I said, hardly above a whisper; and he—with the swift premonition of danger—stepped back and allowed me to urge him well inboard. The second mate followed, and the three of us stood there in the mist, staring round about us and holding our revolvers handy, and the dull waves of the mist beating in slowly upon the lamps in vague wreathings and swirls of fog.

"What was it you heard, Mister?" asked the Captain, after a few moments.

"S-s-s-t!" I muttered. "There it is again. There's something moving, down on the main-deck!"

Captain Jeldy heard it himself, now; and the three of us stood listening intensely. Yet it was hard to know what to make of the sounds. And then, suddenly, there was the rattle of a deck ringbolt, and then again, as if something or someone were fumbling and playing with it.

"Down there on the main deck!" shouted the Captain, abruptly, his voice seeming hoarse close to my ear, yet immediately smothered by the fog. "Down there on the main deck! Who's there?"

But there came never an answering sound. And the three of us stood there, looking quickly this way and that, and listening. Try to imagine how we felt! Abruptly the second mate muttered something:

"The lookout, sir! The lookout!"

Captain Jeldy took the hint, on the instant.

"On the lookout there!" he shouted.

And then, far away and muffled-sounding, there came the answering cry of the lookout man from the fo'cas'le head:

"Sir-r-r?" A little voice, long drawn out, through unknowable alleys of fog.

"Go below into the fo'cas'le, and shut both doors, and don't stir out till you're told!" sung out Captain Jeldy, his voice going lost into the mist. And then the man's answering: "Aye, aye, sir!" came to us faint and mournful. And directly afterwards the clang of a steel door, hollow-sounding and remote; and immediately the sound of another.

"That puts them safe for the present, anyway," said the second mate. And even as he spoke, there came again that indefinite noise, down upon the main deck, of something moving with an incredible and unnatural stealthiness.

"On the main deck there!" shouted Captain Jeldy, sternly. "If there is anyone there, answer, or I shall fire!"

The reply was both amazing and terrifying; for, suddenly, a tremendous blow was stricken upon the deck, and then there came the dull rolling sound of some enormous weight going hollowly across the main-deck. And then an abominable silence.

"My God!" said Captain Jeldy, in a low voice, "what was *that*?" And he raised his pistol, but I caught him by the wrist. "Don't shoot, sir!" I whispered. "It'll do no good. That—that—whatever it is—I— I mean it's something enormous, sir. I—I really wouldn't shoot—" I found it impossible to put my vague idea into words; but I felt there was a Force aboard, down on the main-deck, that it would be futile to attack with so ineffectual a thing as a puny revolver bullet.

And then, as I held Captain Jeldy's wrist, and he hesitated, irresolute there came a sudden bleating of sheep, and the sound of lashings being burst and the cracking of wood; and the next instant a huge crash, followed by another and then another, and the anguished m-a-a-ma-a-a-ing of the sheep.

"My God!" said the second mate, "the sheep pen's being beaten to pieces against the deck. Good God! What sort of thing could do that!"

The tremendous beating ceased, and there was a splashing overside; and after that a silence so profound that it seemed as if the whole atmosphere of the night was full of an unbearable, tense quietness. And then the damp slatting of a sail, far up in the night, that made me start—a lonesome sound to break suddenly through that infernal silence, upon my raw nerves.

"Get below, both of you. Smartly now!" muttered Captain Jeldy. "There's something run either aboard us or alongside; and we can't do anything till daylight."

We went below, and shut the doors of the companionway, and there we lay in the wide Atlantic, without wheel or lookout or officer in charge, and something incredible down on the dark main-deck.

II

For some hours we sat in the Captain's cabin, talking the matter over, while the men slept, sprawled in a dozen attitudes on the floor of the saloon. Captain Jeldy and the second mate still wore their pajamas, and our loaded revolvers lay handy on the cabin table. And so we watched anxiously through the hours for the dawn to come in.

As the light strengthened, we endeavoured to get some view of the sea from the ports; but the mist was so thick about us that it was exactly like looking out into a grey nothingness, that became presently white, as the day came.

"Now," said Captain Jeldy, "we're going to look into this." He went out through the saloon, to the companion stairs. At the top he opened the two doors, and the mist rolled in on us, white and impenetrable. For a little while we stood there, the three of us, absolutely silent and listening, with our revolvers handy; but never a sound came to us except the odd, vague slatting of a sail, or the slight creaking of the gear as the ship lifted on some slow, invisible swell.

Presently the Captain stepped cautiously out on to the deck; he was in his cabin slippers, and therefore made no sound. I was wearing gum-boots, and followed him silently, and the second mate came after me, in his bare feet. Captain

Jeldy went a few paces along the deck and the mist hid him utterly. "Phoo!" I heard him mutter, "the stink's worse than ever!" His voice came odd and vague to me through the wreathing of the mist.

"The sun'll soon eat up all this fog," said the second mate, at my elbow, in a voice little above a whisper.

We stepped after the Captain, and found him a couple of fathoms away, standing shrouded in the mist in an attitude of tense listening.

"Can't hear a thing!" he whispered. "We'll go forrard to the break, as quiet as you like. Don't make a sound."

We went forward, like three shadows, and suddenly Captain Jeldy kicked his shin against something, and pitched headlong over it, making a tremendous noise. He got up quickly, swearing grimly, and the three of us stood there in silence, waiting lest any infernal thing should come upon us out of all that white invisibility. Once I felt sure I saw something coming towards me, and I raised my revolver; but saw in a moment that there was nothing. The tension of imminent, nervous expectancy eased from us, and Captain Jeldy stooped over the object on the deck.

"The port hencoop's been shifted out here!" he muttered. "It's all stove!"

"That must be what I heard last night, when the Mate went," I whispered. There was a loud crash, just before he sang out to me to hurry with the lamp."

Captain Jeldy left the smashed hencoop, and the three of us tiptoed silently to the rail across the break of the poop. Here we leaned over and stared down into the blank whiteness of the mist that hid everything.

"Can't see a thing," whispered the second mate; yet, as he spoke, I could fancy that I heard a slight, indefinite, slurring noise somewhere below us, and I caught them each by an arm to draw them back.

"There's something down there," I muttered. "For goodness' sake, come back from the rail."

We gave back a step or two, and then stopped to listen; and even as we did so there came a slight air playing through the mist.

"The breeze is coming!" said the second mate. "Look, the mist is clearing already!"

He was right. Already the look of white impenetrability had gone; and suddenly we could see the corner of the after hatch coamings through the thinning fog. Within a minute we could see as far forward as the mainmast, and then the stuff blew away from us, clear of the vessel, like a great wall of whiteness, that dissipated as it went.

"*Look*!" we all exclaimed together. The whole of the vessel was now clear to our sight; but it was not at the ship herself that we looked; for after one quick glance along the empty main-deck, we had seen something beyond the ship's side. All around the vessel there lay a submerged spread of weed, for maybe a good quarter of a mile upon every side.

"Weed!" sung out Captain Jeldy, in a voice of comprehension. "Weed! Look, by Jove! I guess I know now what got the Mate!"

He turned and ran to the port side and looked over. And suddenly he stiffened and beckoned silently over his shoulder to us to come and see. We had followed, and now we stood, one on each side of him, staring.

"Look!" whispered the Captain, pointing. "See the great brute! Do you see it? There! Look!"

At first I could see nothing except the submerged spread of the weed into which we had evidently run after dark. Then, as I stared intently, my gaze began to separate from the surrounding weed a leathery looking something that was somewhat darker in hue than the weed itself.

"My God!" said Captain Jeldy. "What a monster! What a monster! Just look at the brute! Look at the thing's eyes! That's what got the Mate. What a creature out of hell itself!"

I saw it plainly now. Three of the massive feelers lay twined in and out among the clumpings of the weed; and then, abruptly, I realised that the two extraordinary round disks, motionless and inscrutable, were the creature's eyes, just below the surface of the water. It appeared to be staring, expressionless, up at the steel side of the vessel. I traced, vaguely, the shapeless monstrosity of what must be termed its head. "My God!" I muttered. "It's an enormous squid of some kind! What an awful brute! What—"

The sharp report of the Captain's revolver came at that moment. He had fired at the thing; and instantly there was a most awful commotion alongside. The weed was hove upward, literally in tons. An enormous quantity was thrown aboard us by the thrashing of the monster's great feelers. The sea seemed almost to boil in one great cauldron of weed and water all about the brute, and the steel side of the ship resounded with the dull, tremendous blows that the creature gave in its struggle. And into all that whirling boil of tentacles, weed and sea water, the three of us emptied our revolvers as fast as we could fire and reload. I remember the feeling of fierce satisfaction I had in thus aiding to avenge the death of the Mate.

Suddenly the Captain roared out to us to jump back; and we obeyed on the instant. As we did so the weed rose up into a great mound, more than twenty feet in height, and more than a ton of it slopped aboard. The next instant three of the monstrous tentacles came in over the side, and the vessel gave a slow, sullen roll to port, as the weight came upon her; for the monster had literally hove itself up almost free of the sea against our port side, in one vast, leathery shape, all wreathed with weed fronds, and seeming drenched with blood and some curious black liquid.

The feelers that had come inboard thrashed around, here and there, and suddenly one of them curled in the most hideous, snake-like fashion around the base of the mainmast. This seemed to attract it; for immediately it curled the two others about the mast and forthwith wrenched upon it with such hideous violence that the whole towering length of spars, through all their height of a hundred and thirty feet, were shaken visibly, whilst the vessel herself vibrated with the stupendous efforts of the brute.

"It'll have the mast down, sir!" said the second mate, with a gasp. "My God! It'll strain her side open! My—"

"One of those blasting cartridges!" I said to Captain Jeldy almost in a shout, as the inspiration took me. "Blow the brute to pieces!"

"Get one, quick!" said the Captain, jerking his thumb toward the companion, "You know where they are."

In thirty seconds I was back with the cartridge. Captain Jeldy took out his knife and cut the fuse dead short; then, with a perfectly steady hand he lit the fuse and calmly held it until I backed away, shouting to him to throw it, for I knew it must explode in another couple of seconds.

Captain Jeldy threw the thing, like one throws a quoit, so that it fell into the sea, just on the outward side of the vast bulk of the monster. So well had he timed it that it burst, with a stunning report, just as it struck the water. The effect upon the squid was amazing. It seemed literally to collapse. The enormous tentacles released themselves from the mast and curled across the deck helplessly, and were drawn inertly over the rail as the enormous bulk sank away from the ship's side out of sight into the weed. The ship rolled slowly to starboard and then steadied. "Thank God!" I muttered, and looked at the two others. They were pallid and sweating, and I must have been the same.

"Here's the breeze again," said the second mate, a minute later. "We're moving." He turned, without another word, and raced aft to the wheel, while the vessel slid over and through the weed field.

Meanwhile, Captain Jeldy had sung out to the men, who had opened the port forecastle door, to keep under cover until he told them to come out. Then he turned to have a look at the vessel itself.

"Look where that brute broke up the sheep-pen!" cried Jeldy, pointing. "And here's the skylight of the sail locker smashed to bits!"

He walked across to it and glanced down. And suddenly he let out a thunderous shout of astonishment:

"Here's the Mate, down here!" he shouted. "He's not over board at all! He's *here*!"

He dropped himself down through the skylight on to the sails, and I after him; and, surely, there was the Mate, lying all huddled and insensible on a hummock of spare sails. In his right hand he held a drawn sheath knife, which he was in the habit of carrying, A.B. fashion, while his left hand was all caked with dried blood where he had been badly cut. Afterward we concluded he had cut himself in slashing at one of the tentacles of the squid, which had caught him round the left wrist, the tip of the tentacle being still curled, cruelly tight, about his arm, just as it had been when he hacked it through.

For the rest, it will please you, I am sure, to know that he was not seriously damaged; the creature having obviously flung him violently away, as he slashed at it, so that he had fallen in a stunned condition on to the pile of sails.

We got him on deck and down into his bunk, where we left the steward to attend to him. When we returned to the poop, the vessel had drawn clear of the weed field, and the Captain and I stopped for a few moments to stare astern over the taffrail. The second mate turned also, as he stood at the wheel, and the three of us looked in a silence at that Death Patch lying so quiet and sullen in the dawn.

As we stood and looked, something wavered up out of the heart of the weed— a long, tapering, sinuous thing, that curled and wavered against the dawn-light, and presently sank back again into the demure weed—a veritable spider of the deep, waiting in the great web that Dame Nature had spun for it, in the eddy of her tides and currents.

And we sailed away northward, with strengthening Trades, and left that patch of monstrousness to the loneliness of the sea.

Demons of the Sea

"Come out on deck and have a look, 'Darky!'" Jepson cried, rushing into the half deck. "The Old Man says there's been a submarine earthquake, and the sea's all bubbling and muddy!"

Obeying the summons of Jepson's excited tone, I followed him out. It was as he had said; the everlasting blue of the ocean was mottled with splotches of a muddy hue, and at times a large bubble would appear, to burst with a loud "pop." Aft, the skipper and the three mates could be seen on the poop, peering at the sea, through their glasses. As I gazed out over the gently heaving water, far off to windward something was hove up into the evening air. It appeared to be a mass of seaweed, but fell back into the water with a sullen plunge as though it were something more substantial. Immediately after this strange occurrence, the sun set with tropical swiftness, and in the brief afterglow things assumed a strange unreality.

The crew were all below, no one but the mate and the helmsman remaining on the poop. Away forward, on the topgallant forecastle head the dim figure of the man on lookout could be seen, leaning against the forestay. No sound was heard save the occasional jingle of a chain sheet, or the flog of the steering gear as a small swell passed under our counter. Presently the mate's voice broke the silence, and, looking up, I saw that the Old Man had come on deck, and was talking with him. From the few stray words which could be overheard, I knew they were talking of the strange happenings of the day.

Shortly after sunset, the wind which had been fresh during the day, died down, and with its passing the air grew oppressively hot. Not long after two bells, the mate sung out for me, and ordered me to fill a bucket from overside, and bring it to him. When I had carried out his instructions, he placed a thermometer in the bucket.

"Just as I thought," he muttered, removing the instrument and showing it to the skipper; "ninety-nine degrees. Why, the sea's hot enough to make tea with!"

"Hope it doesn't get any hotter," growled the latter; "if it does, we shall all be boiled alive."

At a sign from the mate, I emptied the bucket, and replaced it in the rack, after which I resumed my former position by the rail. The Old Man and the mate walked the poop side by side. The air grew hotter as the hours passed, and after a long period of silence broken only by the occasional "pop" of a bursting gas bubble, the moon arose. It shed but a feeble light, however, as a heavy mist had arisen from the sea, and through this, the moonbeams struggled weakly. The mist, we decided, was due to the excessive heat of the sea water; it was a very wet mist, and we were soon soaked to the skin. Slowly the interminable night wore on, and the sun arose, looking dim and ghostly through the mist which rolled and billowed about the ship. From time to time we took the temperature of the sea, although we found but a slight increase therein. No work was done, and a feeling as of something impending, pervaded the ship.

The fog horn was kept going constantly, as the lookout peered through the wreathing mists. The captain walked the poop in company with the mates and once the third-mate spoke and pointed out into the clouds of fog. All eyes followed his gesture; we saw what was apparently a black line, which seemed to cut the whiteness of the billows. It reminded us of nothing so much as an enormous cobra standing on its tail. As we looked it vanished. The grouped mates were evidently puzzled; there seemed to be a difference of opinion among them. Presently as they argued, I heard the second mate's voice:

"That's all rot," he said. "I've seen things in fogs before, but they've always turned out to be imaginary."

The third shook his head and made some reply which I could not overhear, but no further comment was made. Going below that afternoon, I got a short sleep, and on coming on deck at eight bells, I found that the steam still held us; if anything, it seemed to be thicker than ever. Hansard, who had been taking the temperatures during my watch below, informed me that the sea was three degrees hotter, and that the Old Man was getting into a rare old state. At three bells I went forward to have a look over the bows, and a chin with Stevenson, whose lookout it was. On gaining the forecastle head, I went to the side and looked down into the water. Steven son came over and stood beside me.

"Rum go, this," he grumbled.

He stood by my side for a time in silence; we seemed to be hypnotized by the gleaming surface of the sea. Suddenly out of the depths, right before us, there arose a monstrous black face. It was like a frightful caricature of a human countenance. For a moment we gazed petrified; my blood seemed to suddenly turn to ice water; I was unable to move. With a mighty effort of will, I regained my self-control and, grasping Stevenson's arm, I found I could do no more than croak, my powers of speech seemed gone. "Look!" I gasped. "Look!"

Stevenson continued to stare into the sea, like a man turned to stone. He seemed to stoop further over, as if to examine the thing more closely. "Lord," he exclaimed, "it must be the devil himself!"

As though the sound of his voice had broken a spell, the thing disappeared. My companion looked at me, while I rubbed my eyes, thinking that I had been asleep, and that awful visitation had been a frightful nightmare. One look at my friend, however, disabused me of any such thought. His face wore a puzzled expression.

"Better go aft and tell the Old Man," he faltered.

I nodded and left the forecastle head, making my way aft like one in a trance. The skipper and the mate were standing at the break of the poop, and running up the ladder I told them what we had seen.

"Bosh!" sneered the Old Man. "You've been looking at your own ugly reflection in the water."

Nevertheless, in spite of his ridicule, he questioned me closely. Finally he ordered the mate forward to see if he could see anything. The latter, however, returned in a few moments, to report that nothing unusual could be seen. Four bells were struck, and we were relieved for tea. Coming on deck afterward, I found the men clustered together forward. The sole topic of conversation with them was the thing which Stevenson and I had seen.

"I suppose, Darky, it couldn't have been a reflection by any chance, could it?" one of the older men asked.

"Ask Stevenson," I replied as I made my way aft.

At eight bells, my watch came on deck again, to find that nothing further had developed. But, about an hour before midnight, the mate, thinking to have a smoke, sent me to his room for a box of matches with which to light his pipe. It took me no time to clatter down the brass-treaded ladder, and back to the poop, where I handed him the desired article. Taking the box, he removed a match and struck it on the heel of his boot. As he did so, far out in the night a muffled screaming arose. Then came a clamor as of hoarse braying, like an ass but considerably deeper, and with a horribly suggestive human note running through it.

"Good God! Did you hear that, Darky?" asked the mate in awed tones.

"Yes, sir," I replied, listening—and scarcely noticing his question—for a repetition of the strange sounds. Suddenly the frightful bellowing broke out afresh. The mate's pipe fell to the deck with a clatter.

"Run for'ard!" he cried. "Quick, now, and see if you can see anything."

With my heart in my mouth, and pulses pounding madly I raced forward. The watch were all up on the forecastle head, clustered around the lookout. Each man was talking and gesticulating wildly. They became silent, and turned questioning glances toward me as I shouldered my way among them.

"Have you seen anything?" I cried.

Before I could receive an answer, a repetition of the horrid sounds broke out again, profaning the night with their horror. They seemed to have definite direction now, in spite of the fog which enveloped us. Undoubtedly, too, they were nearer. Pausing a moment to make sure of their bearing, I hastened aft and reported to the mate. I told him that nothing could be seen, but that the sounds apparently came from right ahead of us. On hearing this he ordered the man at the wheel to let the ship's head come off a couple of points. A moment later a shrill screaming tore its way through the night, followed by the hoarse braying sounds once more.

"It's close on the starboard bow!" exclaimed the mate, as he beckoned the helmsman to let her head come off a little more. Then, singing out for the watch, he ran forward, slacking the lee braces on his way. When he had the yards trimmed to his satisfaction on the new course, he returned to the poop and hung far out over the rail listening intently. Moments passed that seemed like hours, yet the silence remained unbroken. Suddenly the sounds began again, and so close that it seemed as though they must be right aboard us. At this time I noticed a strange booming note that mingled with the brays. And once or twice, there came a sound which can only be described as a sort of "gug, gug." Then would come a wheezy whistling, for all the world like an asthmatic person breathing.

All this while the moon shone wanly through the steam which seemed to me to be somewhat thinner. Once the mate gripped me by the shoulder as the noises rose and fell again. They now seemed to be coming from a point broad on our beam. Every eye on the ship was straining into the mist, but with no result. Suddenly one of the men cried out, as something long and black slid past us into the fog astern. From it there rose four indistinct and ghostly towers, which resolved themselves into spars and ropes, and sails.

"A ship! It's a ship!" we cried excitedly. I turned to Mr. Gray; he, too, had seen something, and was staring aft into the wake. So ghostlike, unreal, and fleeting had been our glimpse of the stranger, that we were not sure that we had seen an honest, material ship, but thought that we had been vouchsafed a vision of some phantom vessel like the *Flying Dutchman*. Our sails gave a sudden flap, the clew irons flogging the bulwarks with hollow thumps. The mate glanced aloft.

"Wind's dropping," he growled savagely. "We shall never get out of this infernal place at this gait!"

Gradually the wind fell until it was a flat calm, no sound broke the deathlike silence save the rapid patter of the reef points, as she gently rose and fell on the light swell. Hours passed, and the watch was relieved and I then went below. At seven bells we were called again, and as I went along the deck to the galley, I noticed that the fog seemed thinner, and the air cooler. When eight bells were struck, I relieved Hansard at coiling down the ropes. From him I learned that the steam had begun to clear about four bells, and that the temperature of the sea had fallen ten degrees.

In spite of the thinning mist, it was not until about half an hour later that we were able to get a glimpse of the surrounding sea. It was still mottled with dark patches, but the bubbling and popping had ceased. As much of the surface of the ocean as could be seen had a peculiarly desolate aspect. Occasionally a wisp of steam would float up from the nearer sea, and roll undulatingly across its silent surface, until lost in the vagueness which still held the hidden horizon. Here and there columns of steam rose up in pillars, which gave me the impression that the sea was hot in patches. Crossing to the starboard side and looking over, I found that conditions there were similar to those to port. The desolate aspect of the sea filled me with an idea of chilliness, although the air was quite warm and muggy. From the break of the poop the mate called to me to get his glasses.

When I had done this, he took them from me and walked to the taffrail. Here he stood for some moments, polishing them with his handkerchief. After a moment he raised them to his eyes, and peered long and intently into the mist astern. I stood for some time staring at the point on which the mate had focused his glasses. Presently, something shadowy grew upon my vision. Steadily watching it, I distinctly saw the outlines of a ship take form in the fog.

"See!" I cried, but even as I spoke, a lifting wraith of mist disclosed to view a great four-masted bark lying becalmed with all sails set, within a few hundred yards of our stern. As though a curtain had been raised, and then allowed to fall, the fog once more settled down, hiding the strange bark from our sight. The mate was all excitement, striding with quick, jerky steps, up and down the poop, stopping every few moments to peer through his glasses at the point where the four-master had disappeared in the fog. Gradually, as the mists dispersed again, the vessel could be seen more plainly, and it was then that we got an inkling of the cause of the dreadful noises during the night.

For some time the mate watched her silently, and as he watched the conviction grew upon me that, in spite of the mist, I could detect some sort of movement on board of her. After some time had passed, the doubt became a certainty, and I could also see a sort of splashing in the water alongside of her. Suddenly the mate put his glasses on top of the wheel box and told me to bring him the speaking trumpet. Running to the companionway, I secured the trumpet and was back at his side.

The mate raised it to his lips, and taking a deep breath, sent a hail across the water that should have awakened the dead. We waited tensely for a reply. A moment later a deep, hollow mutter came from the bark; higher and louder it swelled, until we realized that we were listening to the same sounds which we had heard the night before. The mate stood aghast at this answer to his hail; in a voice barely more than a hushed whisper, he bade me call the Old Man. Attracted by the mate's hail, and its unearthly reply, the watch had all come aft, and were clustered in the mizzen rigging, in order to see better.

After calling the captain, I returned to the poop, where I found the second and third mates talking with the chief. All were engaged in trying to pierce the clouds of mist which half hid our strange consort, and arrive at some explanation of the strange phenomena of the past few hours. A moment later the captain appeared carrying his telescope. The mate gave him a brief account of the state of affairs, and handed him the trumpet. Giving me the telescope to hold, the captain hailed the shadowy bark. Breathlessly we all listened, when again, in answer to the Old Man's hail, the frightful sounds rose on the still morning air. The skipper lowered the trumpet and stood with an expression of astonished horror on his face.

"Lord!" he exclaimed. "What an ungodly row!"

At this, the third, who had been gazing through his binoculars, broke the silence.

"Look," he ejaculated. "There's a breeze coming up astern." At his words the captain looked up quickly, and we all watched the ruffling water.

"That packet yonder is bringing the breeze with her," said the skipper. "She'll be alongside in half an hour!"

Some moments passed, and the bank of fog had come to within a hundred yards of our taffrail. The strange vessel could be distinctly seen just inside the fringe of the driving mist wreaths. After a short puff, the wind died completely, but we stared with hypnotic fascination, the water astern of the stranger ruffled again with a fresh cats-paw. Seemingly with the flapping of her sails, she drew slowly up to us. As the leaden seconds passed, the big four-master approached us steadily. The light air had now reached us and, with a lazy lift of our sails, we too began to forge slowly through that weird sea. The bark was now within fifty yards of our stern, and she was steadily drawing nearer, seeming to be able to outfoot us with ease. As she came on she luffed sharply and came into the wind with her weather leeches shaking.

I looked toward her poop, thinking to discern the figure of the man at the wheel, but the mist coiled around her quarter, and objects on the after end of her became indistinguishable. With a rattle of chain sheets on her iron yards, she filled away again. We meanwhile had gone ahead, but it was soon evident that she was the better sailor, for she came up to us hand over fist. The wind rapidly freshened, and the mist began to drift away before it, so that each moment her spars and cordage became more plainly visible. The skipper and the mates were watching her intently, when an almost simultaneous exclamation of fear broke from them.

"My God!"

And well they might show signs of fear, for crawling about the bark's deck were the most horrible creatures I had ever seen. In spite of their unearthly strangeness there was something vaguely familiar about them. Then it came to me that the face which Stevenson and I had seen during the night belonged to one of them. Their bodies had something of the shape of a seal's, but of a dead, unhealthy white. The lower part of the body ended in a sort of double-curved tail on which they appeared to be able to shuffle about. In place of arms they had two long, snaky feelers, at the ends of which were two very humanlike hands equipped with talons instead of nails. Fearsome indeed were these parodies of human beings!

Their faces which, like their tentacles, were black, were the most grotesquely human things about them, and the upper jaw closed into the lower, after the manner of the jaws of an octopus. I have seen men among certain tribes of natives who had faces uncommonly like theirs, but yet no native I had ever seen could have given me the extraordinary feeling of horror and revulsion which I experienced toward these brutal-looking creatures.

"What devilish beasts!" burst out the captain in disgust.

With this remark he turned to the mates and, as he did so, the expressions on their faces told me that they had all realized what the presence of these bestial-looking brutes meant. If, as was doubtless the case, these creatures had boarded the bark and destroyed her crew, what would prevent them from doing the same with us? We were a smaller ship and had a smaller crew, and the more I thought of it the less I liked it.

We could now see the name on the bark's bow with the naked eye. It read: *Scottish Heath*, while on her boats we could see the name bracketed with Glasgow, showing that she hailed from that port. It was a remarkable coincidence that she should have a slant from just the quarter in which yards were trimmed, as before we saw her she must have been drifting around with everything "aback." But now, in this light air, she was able to run along beside us with no one at her helm. But steering herself she was, and although at times she yawed wildly, she never got herself aback. As we gazed at her we noticed a sudden movement on board of her, and several of the creatures slid into the water.

"See! See! They've spotted us. They're coming for us!" cried the mate wildly.

It was only too true; scores of them were sliding into the sea, letting themselves' down by means of their long tentacles. On they came, slipping by scores and hundreds into the water, and swimming toward us in droves. The ship was making about three knots, otherwise they would have caught us in a very few minutes. But they persevered, gaining slowly but surely, and drawing nearer and nearer. The long tentacle-like arms rose out of the sea in hundreds, and the foremost ones were already within a score of yards of the ship, before the Old Man bethought himself to shout to the mates to fetch up the half dozen cutlasses which comprised the ship's armory. Then, turning to me, he ordered me to go down to his cabin and bring up the two revolvers out of the top drawer of the chart table, also a box of cartridges which was there.

When I returned with the weapons, he loaded them and handed one to the mate. Meanwhile the pursuing creatures were coming steadily nearer, and soon half a dozen of the leaders were directly under our counter. Immediately the captain leaned over the rail and emptied his pistol into them, but without any apparent effect. He must have realized how puny and ineffectual his efforts were, for he did not reload his weapon.

Some dozens of the brutes had reached us, and as they did so, their tentacles rose into the air and caught our rail. I heard the third mate scream suddenly, and turning, I saw him dragged quickly to the rail, with a tentacle wrapped completely around him. Snatching a cutlass, the second mate hacked off the tentacle where it joined the body. A gout of blood splashed into the third mate's face, and he fell to the deck. A dozen more of those arms rose and wavered in the air, but they now seemed some yards astern of us. A rapidly widening patch of clear water appeared between us and the foremost of our pursuers, and we raised a wild shout of joy. The cause was soon apparent; for a fine, fair wind had sprung up, and with the increase in its force, the *Scottish Heath* had got herself aback, while we were rapidly leaving the monsters behind us. The third mate rose to his feet with a dazed look, and as he did so something fell to the deck. I picked it up and found that it was the severed portion of the tentacle of the third's late adversary. With a grimace of disgust I tossed it into the sea, as I needed no reminder of that awful experience.

Three weeks later we anchored in San Francisco. There the captain made a full report of the affair to the authorities, with the result that a gunboat was despatched to investigate. Six weeks later she returned to report that she had been unable to find any signs, either of the ship herself or of the fearful creatures which had attacked her. And since then nothing, as far as I know, has ever been heard of the four-masted bark *Scottish Heath*, last seen by us in the possession of creatures which may rightly be called demons of the sea.

Whether she still floats, occupied by her hellish crew, or whether some storm has sent her to her last resting place beneath the waves, is purely a matter of conjecture. Perchance on some dark, fog-bound night, a ship in that wilderness of waters may hear cries and sounds beyond those of the wailing of the winds. Then let them look to it; for it may be that the demons of the sea are near them.

Through the Vortex of a Cyclone

(The Cyclone—"The most fearful enemy which the mariner's perilous calling
obliges him to encounter.")

It was in the middle of November that the four-masted barque, *Golconda*, came
down from Crockett and anchored off Telegraph Hill, San Francisco. She was
loaded with grain, and was homeward bound round Cape Horn. Five days later she
was towed out through the Golden Gates, and cast loose off the Heads, and so set
sail upon the voyage that was to come so near to being her last.

For a fortnight we had baffling winds; but after that time, got a good slant that
carried us down to within a couple of degrees of the Line. Here it left us, and over
a week passed before we had managed to tack and drift our way into the Southern
Hemisphere.

About five degrees South of the Line, we met with a fair wind that helped us
Southward another ten or twelve degrees, and there, early one morning, it dropped
us, ending with a short, but violent, thunder storm, in which, so frequent were the
lightning flashes, that I managed to secure a picture of one, whilst in the act of
snapshotting the sea and clouds upon our port side.

During the day, the wind, as I have remarked, left us entirely, and we lay
becalmed under a blazing hot sun. We hauled up the lower sails to prevent them
from chafing as the vessel rolled lazily on the scarce perceptible swells, and busied
ourselves, as is customary on such occasions, with much swabbing and cleaning of
paint-work.

As the day proceeded so did the heat seem to increase; the atmosphere lost its
clear look, and a low haze seemed to lie about the ship at a great distance. At times,
the air seemed to have about it a queer, unbreathable quality; so that one caught
oneself breathing with a sense of distress.

And, hour by hour, as the day moved steadily onward, the sense of oppression
grew ever more acute.

Then, it was, I should think, about three-thirty in the afternoon, I became
conscious of the fact that a strange, unnatural, dull, brick-red glare was in the sky.
Very subtle it was, and I could not say that it came from any particular place; but

rather it seemed to shine *in* the atmosphere. As I stood looking at it, the Mate came up beside me. After about half a minute, he gave out a sudden exclamation:—

"Hark!" he said. "Did you hear that?"

"No, Mr. Jackson," I replied. "What was it like?"

"Listen!" was all his reply, and I obeyed; and so perhaps for a couple of minutes we stood there in silence.

"There!—There it is again!" he exclaimed, suddenly; and in the same instant I heard it . . . a sound like low, strange growling far away in the North-East. It lasted for about fifteen seconds, and then died away in a low, hollow, moaning noise, that sounded indescribably dree.

After that, for a space longer, we stood listening; and so, at last, it came again . . . a far, faint, wild-beast growling, away over the North-Eastern horizon. As it died away, with that strange hollow note, the Mate touched my arm:—

"Go and call the Old Man," he said, meaning the Captain. "And while you're down, have a look at the barometer."

In both of these matters I obeyed him, and in a few moments the Captain was on deck, standing beside the Mate—listening.

"How's the glass?" asked the Mate, as I came up.

"Steady," I answered, and at that, he nodded his head, and resumed his expectant attitude. Yet, though we stood silent, maybe for the better part of half an hour, there came no further repetition of that weird, far-off growling, and so, as the glass was steady, no serious notice was taken of the matter.

That evening, we experienced a sunset of quite indescribable gorgeousness, which had, to me, an unnatural glow about it, especially in the way which it lit up the surface of the sea, which was, at this time, stirred by a slight evening breeze. Evidently, the Mate was of the opinion that it foreboded something in the way of ill weather; for he gave orders for the watch on deck to take the three royals off her.

By the time the men had got down from aloft, the sun had set, and the evening was fading into dusk; yet, despite that, all the sky to the North-East was full of the most vivid red and orange; this being, it will be remembered, the direction from which we had heard earlier that sullen growling.

It was somewhat later, I remember, that I heard the Mate remark to the Captain that we were in for bad weather, and that it was his belief a Cyclone was coming down upon us; but this, the Captain—who was quite a young fellow—poo-poohed; telling him that he pinned *his* faith to the barometer, which was perfectly steady. Yet, I could see that the Mate was by no means so sure; but forebore to press further his opinion against his superior's.

Presently, as the night came down upon the world, the orange tints went out of the sky, and only a sombre, threatening red was left, with a strangely bright rift of white light running horizontally across it, about twenty degrees above the North-*Eastern*, horizon.

This lasted for nigh on to half an hour, and so did it impress the crew with a sense of something impending, that many of them crouched, staring over the port rail, until long after it had faded into the general greyness.

That night, I recollect, it was my watch on deck from midnight until four in the morning. When the boy came down to wake me, he told me that it had been lightning during the past watch. Even as he spoke, a bright, bluish glare lit up the porthole; but there was no succeeding thunder.

I sprang hastily from my bunk, and dressed; then, seizing my camera, ran out on deck. I opened the shutter, and the next instant—flash! a great stream of electricity sprang out of the zenith.

Directly afterwards, the Mate called to me from the break of the poop to know whether I had managed to secure *that* one. I replied, Yes, I thought I had, and he told me to come up on to the poop, beside him, and have a further try from there; for he, the Captain and the Second Mate were much interested in my photographic hobby, and did all in their power to aid me in the securing of successful snaps.

That the Mate was uneasy, I very soon perceived; for, presently, a little while after he had relieved the Second Mate, he ceased his pacing of the poop deck, and came and leant over the rail, alongside of me.

"I wish to goodness the Old Man would have her shortened right down to lower topsails," he said, a moment later, in a low voice, "There's some rotten, dirty weather knocking around. I can smell it." And he raised his head, and sniffed at the air.

"Why not shorten her down, on your own?" I asked him

"Can't !" he replied. "The Old Man's left orders not to touch anything; but to call him if any change occurs. He goes *too* d—n much by the barometer, to suit me, and won't budge a rope's end, because it's steady."

All this time, the lightning had been playing at frequent intervals across the sky; but now there came several gigantic flashes, seeming extraordinarily near to the vessel, pouring down out of a great rift in the clouds—veritable torrents of electric fluid. I switched open the shutter of my camera, and pointed the lens upward; and the following instant, I secured a magnificent photograph of a great flash, which, bursting down from the same rift, divided to the East and West in a sort of vast electric arch.

For perhaps a minute afterwards, we waited, thinking that such a flash *must* be followed by thunder; but none came. Instead, from the darkness to the North-East, there sounded a faint, far-drawn-out wailing noise, that seemed to echo queerly across the quiet sea. And after that, silence.

The Mate stood upright, and faced round at me.

"Do you know," he said, "only once before in my life have I heard anything like that, and that was before the Cyclone in which the *Lancing* and the *Eurasian* were lost, in the Indian Ocean.

"Do you think then there's *really* any danger of a Cyclone now?" I asked him, with something of a little thrill of excitement.

"I think—" he began, and then stopped, and swore suddenly. "Look!" he said, in a loud voice. " Look! 'Stalk' lightning, as I'm a living man!" And he pointed to the North-East. "Photograph that, while you've got the chance; you'll never have another as long as you live!"

I looked in the direction which he indicated, and there, sure enough, were great, pale, flickering streaks and tongues of flame *rising apparently out of the sea*. They remained steady for some ten or fifteen seconds, and in that time I was able to take a snap of them.

This photograph, as I discovered when I came to develop the negative, has not, I regret to say, taken regard of a strange, indefinable dull-red glare that lit up the horizon at the same time; but, as it is, it remains to me a treasured record of a form of electrical phenomenon but seldom seen, even by those whose good, or ill, fortune has allowed them to come face to face with a Cyclonic Storm. Before leaving this incident, I would once more impress upon the reader that this strange lightning was *not* descending from the atmosphere; but *rising from the sea*.

It was after I had secured this last snap, that the Mate declared it to be his conviction that a great Cyclonic Storm was coming down upon us from the North-East, and, with that—for about the twentieth time that watch—he went below to consult the barometer.

He came back in about ten minutes, to say that it was still steady; but that he had called the Old Man, and told him about the upward "Stalk" lightning; yet the Captain, upon hearing from him that the glass was still steady, had refused to be alarmed, but had promised to come up and take a look round. This, in a while, he did; but, as Fate would have it, there was no further display of the "Stalk" lightning, and, as the other kind had now become no more than an occasional dull glare behind the clouds to the North-East, he retired once more, leaving orders to be called if there were any change either in the glass or the weather.

With the sunrise there came a change, a low, slow-moving scud driving down from the North-East, and drifting across the face of the newly-risen sun, which was shining with a queer, unnatural glare. Indeed, so stormy and be-burred looked the sun, that I could have applied to it with truth the line:—

"And the red Sun all bearded with the Storm,"

to describe its threatening aspect.

The glass also showed a change at last, rising a little for a short while, and then dropping about a tenth, and, at that, the Mate hurried down to inform the Skipper, who was speedily up on deck.

He had the fore and mizzen t'gallants taken off her; but nothing more; for he declared that he wasn't going to throw away a fine fair wind for any Old Woman's fancies.

Presently, the wind began to freshen; but the orange-red burr about the sun remained, and also it seemed to me that the tint of the water had a "bad weather" look about it. I mentioned this to the Mate, and he nodded agreement; but said nothing in so many words, for the Captain was standing near.

By eight bells (4 a.m.) the wind had freshened so much that we were lying over to it, with a big cant of the decks, and making a good twelve knots, under nothing higher than the main t'gallant.

We were relieved by the other watch, and went below for a short sleep. At eight o'clock, when again I came on deck, I found that the sea had begun to rise somewhat; but that otherwise the weather was much as it had been when I left the decks; save that the sun was hidden by a heavy squall to windward, which was coming down upon us.

Some fifteen minutes later, it struck the ship, making the foam fly, and carrying away the main topsail sheet. Immediately upon this, the heavy iron ring in the clew of the sail began to thrash and beat about, as the sail flapped in the wind, striking great blows against the steel yard; but the clewline was manned, and some of the men went aloft to repair the damage, after which the sail was once more sheeted home, and we continued to carry on.

About this time, the Mate sent me down into the saloon to take another look at the glass, and I found that it had fallen a further tenth. When I reported this to him, he had the main t'gallant taken in; but hung on to the mainsail, waiting for eight bells, when the whole crowd would be on deck to give a hand.

By that time, we, had begun to ship water, and most of us were speedily very thoroughly soused; yet, we got the sail off her, and she rode the easier for the relief.

A little after one o'clock in the afternoon, I went out on deck to have a final "squint" at the weather, before turning-in for a short sleep, and found that the wind had freshened considerably, the seas striking the counter of the vessel at times, and flying to a considerable height in foam.

At four o'clock, when once more I appeared on deck, I discovered the spray flying over us with a good deal of freedom, and the solid water coming aboard occasionally in odd tons.

Yet, so far there was, *to a sailorman*, nothing worthy of note in the severity of the weather. It was merely blowing a moderately heavy gale, before which, under our six topsails and foresail, we were making a good twelve knots an hour to the Southward. Indeed, it seemed to me, at this time, that the Captain was right in his belief that we were not in for any very dirty weather, and I said as much to the Mate; whereat he laughed somewhat bitterly.

"Don't you make any sort of mistake!" he said, and pointed to leeward, where continual flashes of lightning darted down from a dark bank of cloud. "We're already within the borders of the Cyclone. We are travelling, so I take it, about a knot slower an hour to the South than the bodily forward movement of the Storm; so that you may reckon it's overtaking us at the rate of something like a mile an hour. Later on, I expect, it'll get a move on it, and then a torpedo boat wouldn't catch it! This bit of a breeze that we're having now"—and he gestured to windward with his elbow—"is only fluff—nothing more than the outer fringe of the advancing Cyclone! Keep your eye lifting to the North-East, and keep your ears open. Wait until you hear the thing yelling at you as loud as a million mad tigers!"

He came to a pause, and knocked the ashes out of his pipe; then he slid the empty "weapon" into the side pocket of his long oilskin coat. And all the time, I could see that he was ruminating.

"Mark my words," he said, at last, and speaking with great deliberation. "Within twelve hours it'll be upon us!"

He shook his head at me. Then he added:—

"Within twelve hours, my boy, you and I and every other soul in this blessed packet maybe down there in the cold!" And the brute pointed downward into the sea, and grinned cheerfully at me.

It was our watch that night from eight to twelve; but, except that the wind freshened a trifle, hourly, nothing of note occurred during our watch. The wind was just blowing a good fresh gale, and giving us all we wanted, to keep the ship doing her best under topsails and foresail.

At midnight, I went below for a sleep. When I was called at four o'clock, I found a very different state of affairs. The day had broken, and showed the sea in a very confused state, with a tendency to run up into heaps, and there was a good deal less wind; but what struck me as most remarkable, and brought home with uncomfortable force the Mate's warning of the previous day, was the colour of the sky, which seemed to be everywhere one great glare of gloomy, orange-coloured light, streaked here and there with red. So intense was this glare that the seas, as they rose clumsily into heaps, caught and reflected the light in an extraordinary manner, shining and glittering gloomily, like vast moving mounds of liquid flame. The whole presenting an effect of astounding and uncanny grandeur.

I made my way up on to the poop, carrying my camera. There, I met the Mate.

"You'll not want that pretty little box of yours," he remarked, and tapped my camera. "I guess you'll find a coffin more useful."

"Then it's coming?" I said.

"Look!" was all his reply, and he pointed into the North-East.

I saw in an instant what it was at which he pointed. It was a great black wall of cloud that seemed to cover about seven points of the horizon, extending almost from North to East, and reaching upward some fifteen degrees towards the zenith. The intense, solid blackness of this cloud was astonishing, and threatening to the beholder, seeming, indeed, to be more like a line of great black cliffs standing out of the sea, than a mass of thick vapour.

I glanced aloft, and saw that the other watch were securing the mizzen upper topsail. At the same moment, the Captain appeared on deck, and walked over to the Mate.

"Glass has dropped another tenth, Mr. Jackson," he remarked, and glanced to windward. "I think we'd better have the fore and main upper topsails off her."

Scarcely had he given the order, before the Mate was down on the maindeck, shouting:— "Fore and main topsail hal'yards! Lower away! Man clewlines and spillinglines!" So eager was he to have the sail off her.

By the time that the upper topsails were furled, I noted that the red glare had gone out of the greater part of the sky to windward, and a stiffish looking squall was bearing down upon us. Away more to the North, I saw that the black rampart of cloud had disappeared, and, in place thereof, it seemed to me that the clouds in that quarter were assuming a hard, tufted appearance, and changing their shapes with surprising rapidity.

The sea also at this time was remarkable, acting uneasily, and hurling up queer little mounds of foam, which the passing squall caught and spread.

All these points, the Mate noted; for I heard him urging the Captain to take in the foresail and mizzen lower topsail. Yet, this, the Skipper seemed unwilling to do; but finally agreed to have the mizzen topsail off her. Whilst the men were up at this, the wind dropped abruptly in the tail of the squall, the vessel rolling heavily, and taking water and spray with every roll.

Now, I want the Reader to try and understand exactly how matters were at this particular and crucial moment. The wind had dropped entirely, and, with the dropping of the wind, a thousand different sounds broke harshly upon the ear, sounding almost unnatural in their distinctness, and impressing the ear with a sense of discomfort. With each roll of the ship, there came a chorus of creaks and groans from the swaying masts and gear, and the sails slatted with a damp, disagreeable sound. Beyond the ship, there was the constant, harsh murmur of the seas, occasionally changing to a low roar, as one broke near us. One other sound there was that punctuated all these, and that was the loud, slapping blows of the seas, as they hove themselves clumsily against the ship; and, for the rest, there was a strange sense of silence.

Then, as sudden as the report of a heavy gun, a great bellowing came out of the North and East, and died away into a series of monstrous grumbles of sound. It was not thunder. *It was the Voice of the approaching Cyclone.*

In the same instant, the Mate nudged my shoulder, and pointed, and I saw, with an enormous feeling of surprise, that a large waterspout had formed about four hundred yards astern, and was coming towards us. All about the base of it, the sea was foaming in a strange manner, and the whole thing seemed to have a curious luminous quality.

Thinking about it now, I cannot say that I perceived it to be in rotation; but nevertheless, I had the impression that it was revolving swiftly. Its general onward motion seemed to be about as fast as would be attained by a well-manned gig.

I remember, in the first moments of astonishment, as I watched it, hearing the Mate shout something to the Skipper about the foresail, then I realised suddenly that the spout was coming straight for the ship. I ran hastily to the taffrail, raised my camera, and snapped it, and then, as it seemed to tower right up above me, gigantic, I ran backwards in sudden fright. In the same instant, there came a blinding flash of lightning, almost in my face, followed instantaneously by a tremendous roar of thunder, and I saw that the thing had burst within about fifty yards of the ship. The sea, immediately beneath where it had been, leapt up in a great hummock of solid water, and foam, as though something as great as a house had been cast into the ocean. Then, rushing towards us, it struck the stern of the vessel, flying as high as our topsail yards in spray, and knocking me backwards on to the deck.

As I stood up, and wiped the water hurriedly from my camera, I heard the Mate shout out to know if I were hurt, and then, in the same moment, and before I could reply, he cried out:—

"It's coming! Up hellum! Up hellum! Look out everybody! Hold on for your lives!"

Directly afterwards, a shrill, yelling noise seemed to fill the whole sky with a deafening, piercing sound. I glanced hastily over the port quarter. *In that direction the whole surface of the ocean seemed to be torn up into the air in monstrous clouds of spray.* The yelling sound passed into a vast scream, and the next instant the Cyclone was upon us.

Immediately, the air was so full of flying spray that I could not see a yard before me, and the wind slapped me back against the teak companion, pinning me there for a few moments, helpless. The ship heeled over to a terrible angle, so that, for some seconds, I thought we were going to capsize. Then, with a sudden lurch, she hove herself upright, and I became able to see about me a little, by switching the water from my face, and shielding my eyes. Near to me, the helmsman—a little Dago—was clinging to the wheel, looking like nothing so much as a drowned monkey, and palpably frightened to such an extent that he could hardly stand upright.

From him, I looked round at so much of the vessel as I could see, and up at the spars, and so, presently, I discovered how it was that she had righted. The mizzen topmast was gone just below the heel of the t'gallantmast, and the fore topmast a little above the cap. The main topmast alone stood. It was the losing of these spars which had eased her, and allowed her to right so suddenly. Marvellously enough, the foresail—a small, new, No. 1 canvas stormsail—had stood the strain, and was now bellying out, with a high foot, the sheets evidently having surged under the wind pressure. What was more extraordinary, was that the fore and main lower topsails were standing,[1] and this, despite the fact that the bare upper spars, on both the fore and mizzen masts, had been carried away.

---

[1] I suggest the existence of smaller air vortices within the Cyclone. By air vortices, I mean vorticular air whorls—as it might be the upper portions of uncompleted waterspouts. How else explain the *naked* mizzen and fore topmasts and t'gallant masts being *twisted* off (as later appeared to have been the case), and yet the great spread of the lower topsails and the foresail not suffering? I am convinced that the unequal force of the first wind-burst is only thus to be explained.

And now, the first awful burst of the Cyclone having passed with the righting of the vessel, the three sails stood, though tested to their utmost, and the ship, under the tremendous urging force of the Storm, was tearing forward at a high speed through the seas.

I glanced down now at myself and camera. Both were soaked; yet, as I discovered later, the latter would still take photographs. I struggled forward to the break of the poop, and stared down on to the main deck. The seas were breaking aboard every moment, and the spray flying over us continually in huge white clouds. And in my ears was the incessant, wild, roaring-scream of the monster Whirl-Storm.

Then I saw the Mate. He was up against the lee rail, chopping at something with a hatchet. At times the water left him visible to his knees; anon he was completely submerged; but ever there was the whirl of his weapon amid the chaos of water, as he hacked and cut at the gear that held the mizzen t'gallant mast crashing against the side.

I saw him glance round once, and he beckoned with the hatchet to a couple of his watch who were fighting their way aft along the streaming decks. He did not attempt to shout; for no shout could have been heard in the incredible roaring of the wind. Indeed, so vastly loud was the noise made by this element, that I had not heard even the topmasts carry away; though the sound of a large spar breaking will make as great a noise as the report of a big gun. The next instant, I had thrust my camera into one of the hencoops upon the poop, and turned to struggle aft to the companionway; for I knew it was no use going to the Mate's aid without axes.

Presently, I was at the companion, and had the fastenings undone; then I opened the door, and sprang in on to the stairs. I slammed-to the door, bolted it, and made my way below, and so, in a minute, had possessed myself of a couple of axes. With these, I returned to the poop, fastening the companion doors carefully behind me, and, in a little, was up to my neck in water on the maindeck, helping to clear away the wreckage. The second axe, I had pushed into the hands of one of the men.

Presently, we had the gear cleared away.

Then we scrambled away forrard along the decks, through the boiling swirls of water and foam that swept the vessel, as the seas thundered aboard; and so we came to the assistance of the Second Mate, who was desperately busied, along with some of his watch, in clearing away the broken foretopmast and yards that were held by their gear, thundering against the side of the ship.

Yet, it must not be supposed that we were to manage this piece of work, without coming to some harm; for, just as we made an end of it, an enormous sea swept aboard, and dashed one of the men against the spare topmast that was lashed along, inside the bulwarks, below the pin-rail. When we managed to pull the poor senseless fellow out from underneath the spar, where the sea had jammed him, we found that his left arm and collar-bone were broken. We took him forrard to the fo'cas'le, and there, with rough surgery, made him so comfortable as we could; after which we left him, but half conscious, in his bunk.

After that, several wet, weary hours were spent in rigging rough preventer-stays. Then the rest of us, men as well as officers, made our way aft to the poop; there to wait, desperately ready to cope with any emergency where our poor, futile human strength might aid to our salvation.

With great difficulty, the Carpenter had managed to sound the well, and, to our delight, had found that we were not making any water; so that the blows of the broken spars had done us no vital harm.

By midday, the following seas had risen to a truly formidable height, and two hands were working half naked at the wheel; for any carelessness in steering would, most certainly, have had horrible consequences.

In the course of the afternoon, the Mate and I went down into the saloon to get something to eat, and here, out of the deafening roar of the wind, I managed to get a short chat with my senior officer.

Talking about the waterspout which had so immediately preceded the first rush of the Cyclone, I made mention of its luminous appearance; to which he replied that it was due probably to a vast electric action going on between the clouds and the sea.

After that, I asked him why the Captain did not heave to, and ride the Storm out, instead of running before it, and risking being pooped, or broaching to.

To this, the Mate made reply that we were right in the line of translation; in other words, that we were directly in the track of the vortex, or centre, of the Cyclone, and that the Skipper was doing his best to edge the ship to leeward, before the centre, with the awful Pyramidal Sea, should overtake us.

"If we can't manage to get out of the way," he concluded, grimly, "you'll probably have a chance to photograph something that you'll never have time to develop!"

I asked him how he knew that the ship was directly in the track of the vortex, and he replied that the facts that the wind was not hauling, but getting steadily worse, with the barometer constantly falling, were sure signs.

And soon after that we returned to the deck.

As I have said, at midday, the seas were truly formidable; but by four p.m. they were so much worse that it was impossible to pass fore or aft along the decks, the water breaking aboard, as much as a hundred tons at a time, and sweeping all before it.

All this time, the roaring and *howling* of the Cyclone was so incredibly loud, that no word spoken, or shouted, out on deck—even though right into one's ear—could be heard distinctly, so that the utmost we could do to convey ideas to one another, was to make signs. And so, because of this, and to get for a little out of the painful and exhausting pressure of the wind, each of the officers would, in turn (sometimes singly and sometimes two at once), go down to the saloon, for a short rest and smoke.

It was in one of these brief "smoke-ohs" that the Mate told me the vortex of the Cyclone was probably within about eighty or a hundred miles of us, and coming down on us at something like twenty or thirty knots an hour, which—as this speed enormously exceeded ours—made it probable that it would be upon us before midnight.

"Is there no chance of getting out of the way?" I asked. "Couldn't we haul her up a trifle, and cut across the track a bit quicker than we are doing?"

"No," replied the Mate, and shook his head, thoughtfully. "The seas would make a clean breach over us, if we tried that. It's a case of 'run till you're blind, and pray till you bust'!" he concluded, with a certain despondent brutalness.

I nodded assent; for I knew that it was true. And after that we were silent. A few minutes later, we went up on deck. There we found that the wind had increased, and blown the foresail bodily away; yet, despite the greater weight of the wind, there had come a rift in the clouds, through which the sun was shining with a queer brightness.

I glanced at the Mate, and smiled; for it seemed to me a good omen; but he shook his head, as one who should say:—"It is no good omen; but a sign of something worse coming."

That he was right in refusing to be assured, I had speedy proof; for within ten minutes the sun had vanished, and the clouds seemed to be right down upon our mast-heads—great bellying webs of black vapour, that seemed almost to mingle with the flying clouds of foam and spray. The wind appeared to gain strength minute by minute, rising into an abominable scream, so piercing at times as to seem to pain the ear drums.

In this wise an hour passed, the ship racing onward under her two topsails, seeming to have lost no speed with the losing of the foresail; though it is possible that she was more under water forrard than she had been.

Then, about five-thirty p.m., I heard a louder roar in the air above us, so deep and tremendous that it seemed to daze and stun one; and, in the same instant, the two topsails were blown out of the bolt-ropes, and one of the hen-coops was lifted bodily off the poop, and hurled into the air, descending with an *inaudible* crash on to the maindeck. Luckily, it was not the one into which I had thrust my camera.

With the losing of the topsails, we might be very truly described as running under bare poles; for now we had not a single stitch of sail set anywhere. Yet, so furious was the increasing wind, so tremendous the weight of it, that the vessel, though urged forward only by the pressure of the element upon her naked spars and hull, managed to keep ahead of the monstrous following seas, which now were grown to truly awesome proportions.

The next hour or two, I remember only as a time that spread out monotonously. A time miserable and dazing, and dominated always by the deafening, roaring scream of the Storm. A time of wetness and dismalness, in which I knew, more than saw, that the ship wallowed on and on through the interminable seas. And so, hour by hour, the wind increased as the Vortex of the Cyclone—the "Death-Patch"—drew nearer and ever nearer.

Night came on early, or, if not night, a darkness that was fully its equivalent. And now I was able to see how tremendous was the electric action that was going on all about us. There seemed to be no lightning flashes; but, instead, there came at times across the darkness, queer luminous shudders of light. I am not acquainted with any word that better describes this extraordinary electrical phenomenon, than 'shudders' of light—broad, dull shudders of light, that came in undefined belts across the black, thunderous canopy of clouds, which seemed so low that our maintruck must have "puddled" them with every roll of the ship.

A further sign of electric action was to be seen in the "corpse candles," which ornamented every yard-arm. Not only were they upon the yard-arms; but occasionally several at a time would glide up and down one or more of the fore and aft stays, at whiles swinging off to one side or the other, as the ship rolled. The sight having in it a distinct touch of weirdness.

It was an hour or so later, I believe a little after nine p.m., that I witnessed the most striking manifestation of electrical action that I have ever seen; this being neither more nor less than a display of Aurora Borealis lightning—a sight dree and almost frightening, with the sense of unearthliness and mystery that it brings.

I want you to be very clear that I am *not* talking about the Northern Lights—which, indeed, could never be seen at that distance to the Southward—; but of an extraordinary electrical phenomenon which occurred when the vortex of the Cyclone was within some twenty or thirty miles of the ship. It occurred suddenly. First, a ripple of "Stalk" lightning showed right away over the oncoming seas to the Northward; then, abruptly, a red glare shone out in the sky, and, immediately afterwards, vast streamers of greenish flame appeared above the red glare. These lasted, perhaps, half a minute, expanding and contracting over the sky with a curious quivering motion. The whole forming a truly awe-inspiring spectacle.

And then, slowly, the whole thing faded, and only the blackness of the night remained, slit in all directions by the phosphorescent crests of the seas.

I don't know whether I can convey to you any vivid impression of our case and chances at this time. It is so difficult—unless one had been through a similar experience—even to comprehend fully the incredible loudness of the wind. Imagine a noise as loud as the loudest thunder you have ever heard; then imagine this noise to last hour after hour, without intermission, and to have in it a hideously threatening hoarse note, and, blending with this, a constant yelling scream that rises at times to such a pitch that the very ear drums seem to experience pain, and then, perhaps, you will be able to comprehend merely the amount of *sound* that has to be endured during the passage of one of these Storms. And then, the *force* of the wind! Have you ever faced a wind so powerful that it splayed your lips apart, whether you would or not, laying your teeth bare to view? This is only a little thing; but it may help you to conceive something of the strength of a wind that will play

167

such antics with one's mouth. The sensation it gives is extremely disagreeable—a sense of foolish impotence, is how I can best describe it.

Another thing; I learned that, with my face to the wind, I could not breathe. This is a statement baldly put; but it should help me somewhat in my endeavour to bring home to you the force of the wind, as exemplified in the minor details of my experience.

To give some idea of the wind's power, as shown in a larger way, one of the lifeboats on the after skids was up-ended against the mizzen mast, and there crushed flat by the wind, as though a monstrous invisible hand had pinched it. Does this help you a little to gain an idea of wind-force never met with in a thousand ordinary lives?

Apart from the wind, it must be borne in mind that the gigantic seas pitch the ship about in a most abominable manner. Indeed, I have seen the stern of a ship hove up to such a height that I could see the seas ahead over the fore topsail yards, and when I explain that these will be something like seventy to eighty feet above the deck, you may be able to imagine what manner of Sea is to be met with in a great Cyclonic Storm.

Regarding this matter of the size and ferocity of the seas, I possess a photograph that was taken about ten o'clock at night. This was photographed by the aid of flashlight, an operation in which the Captain assisted me. We filled an old, percussion pistol with flashlight powder, with an air-cone of paper down the centre. Then, when I was ready, I opened the shutter of the camera, and pointed it over the stern into the darkness. The Captain fired the pistol, and, in the instantaneous great blaze of light that followed, I saw what manner of sea it was that pursued us. To say it was a mountain, is to be futile. *It was like a moving cliff.*

As I snapped-to the shutter of my camera, the question flashed into my brain:—"Are we going to live it out, after all?" And, suddenly, it came home to me that I was a little man in a little ship, in the midst of a very great sea.

And then fresh knowledge came to me; I knew, abruptly, that it would not be a difficult thing to be very much afraid. The knowledge was new, and took me more in the stomach than the heart. Afraid! I had been in so many storms that I had forgotten they might be things to fear. Hitherto, my sensation at the thought of bad weather had been chiefly a feeling of annoyed repugnance, due to many memories of dismal wet nights, in wetter oilskins; with everything about the vessel reeking with damp and cheerless discomfort. But *fear*—No! A sailor has no more normal fear of bad weather, than a steeple-jack fears height. It is, as you might say, his vocation. And now this hateful sense of insecurity!

I turned from the taffrail, and hurried below to wipe the lens and cover of my camera; for the whole air was full of driving spray, that soaked everything, and hurt the face intolerably; being driven with such force by the storm,

Whilst I was drying my camera, the Mate came down for a minute's breathing space.

"Still at it?" he said.

"Yes," I replied, and I noticed, half-consciously, that he made no effort to light his pipe, as he stood with his arm crooked over an empty, brass candle bracket.

"You'll never develop them," he remarked.

"Of course I shall!" I replied, half-irritably; but with a horrid little sense of chilliness at his words, which came so unaptly upon my mind, so lately perturbed by uncomfortable thoughts.

"You'll see," he replied, with a sort of brutal terseness. "We shan't be above water by midnight!"

"You *can't* tell," I said. "What's the use of meeting trouble! Vessels have lived through worse than this?"

"Have they?" he said, very quietly. "Not many vessels have lived through worse than what's to come. I suppose you realise we expect to meet the Centre in less than an hour?"

"Well," I replied, "anyway, I shall go on taking photos. I guess if we come through all right, I shall have something to show people ashore."

He laughed, a queer, little, bitter laugh.

"You may as well do that as anything else," he said. "We can't do anything to help ourselves. If we're not pooped before the Centre reaches us, IT'll finish us in quick time!"

Then that cheerful officer of mine turned slowly, and made his way on deck, leaving me, as may be imagined, particularly exhilarated by his assurances. Presently, I followed, and, having barred the companion-way behind me, struggled forward to the break of the poop, clutching blindly at any holdfast in the darkness.

And so, for a space, we waited in the Storm—the wind bellowing fiendishly, and our maindecks one chaos of broken water, swirling and roaring to and fro in the darkness.

It was a little later that some one plucked me hard by the sleeve, and, turning, I made out with difficulty that it was the Captain, trying to attract my attention. I caught his wrist, to show that I comprehended what he desired, and, at that, he dropped on his hands and knees, and crawled aft along the streaming poop deck, I following, my camera held between my teeth by the handle.

He reached the companion-way, and unbarred the starboard door; then crawled through, and I followed after him. I fastened the door, and made my way, in his wake, to the saloon. Here he turned to me. He was a curiously devil-may-care sort of man, and I found that he had brought me down to explain that the Vortex would be upon us very soon, and that I should have the chance of a life-time to get a snap of the much talked of Pyramidal Sea. And, in short, that he wished me to have everything prepared, and the pistol ready loaded with flashlight powder; for, as he remarked:—

"*If* we get through, it'll be a rare curiosity to show some of those unbelieving devils ashore."

In a little, we had everything ready, and then we made our way once more up on deck; the Captain placing the pistol in the pocket of his silk oilskin coat.

There, together, under the after weather-cloth, we waited. The Second Mate, I could not see; but occasionally I caught a vague sight of the First Mate, standing near the after binnacle,[1] and obviously watching the steering. Apart from the puny halo that emanated from the binnacle, all else was blind darkness, save for the phosphorescent lights of the overhanging crests of the seas.

And above us and around us, filling all the sky with sound, was the incessant mad yowling of the Cyclone; the noise so vast, and the volume and mass of the wind so enormous that I am impressed now, looking back, with a sense of having been in a semi-stunned condition through those last minutes.

I am conscious now that a vague time passed. A time of noise and wetness and lethargy and immense tiredness, Abruptly, a tremendous flash of lightning burst through the clouds. It was followed, almost directly, by another, which seemed to rive the sky apart. Then, so quickly that the succeeding thunderclap was *audible* to our wind-deafened ears, the wind ceased, and, in the comparative, but hideously unnatural, silence, I caught the Captain's voice shouting:—

"The Vortex—quick!"

Even as I pointed my camera over the rail, and opened the shutter, my brain was working with a preternatural avidity, drinking in a thousand uncanny sounds and echoes that seemed to come upon me from every quarter, brutally distinct against the background of the Cyclone's distant howling. There were the harsh, bursting, frightening, intermittent noises of the seas, making tremendous, slopping crashes of sound; and, mingling with these, the shrill, hissing scream of the foam;[2] the dismal sounds, that suggested dankness, of water swirling over our decks; and, oddly, the faintly-heard creaking of the gear and shattered spars; and then—*Flash*, in the same instant in which I had taken in these varied impressions, the Captain had fired the pistol, and I saw the Pyramidal Sea. . . . A sight never to be forgotten. A sight rather for the Dead than the Living. A sea such as I could never have imagined. Boiling and bursting upward in monstrous hillocks of water and foam as big as houses. I heard, without knowing I heard, the Captain's expression of amazement. Then a thunderous roar was in my ears. One of those vast, flying hills of water had struck the ship, and, for some moments, I had a sickening feeling that she was sinking beneath me. The water cleared, and I found myself clinging to the

---

[1] It occurs to me here, as showing in another way the unusual wind-strength, to mention that, having tried in vain every usual method of keeping the wind from blowing out the binnacle lamps; such as stuffing all the crevices with rags, and making temporary shields for the chimneys, the Skipper had at last resorted to a tiny electric watch light, which he fixed in the binnacle, and which now enabled me to get an odd vague glimpse of the Mate, as he hovered near the compass.

[2] A description absolute and without exaggeration. Who that has ever heard the weird, crisp screaming of the foam, in some momentary lull in a great storm, when a big sea has reared itself within a few fathoms of one; can ever forget it?

iron weather-cloth staunchion; the weather-cloth itself had gone. I wiped my eyes, and coughed dizzily for a little; then I stared round for the Captain. I could see something dimly up against the rail; something that moved and stood upright. I sung out to know whether it was the Captain, and whether he was all right? To which he replied, heartily enough, but with a gasp, that he was all right so far.

From him, I glanced across to the wheel. There was no light in the binnacle, and, later, I found that it had been washed away, and with it one of the helmsmen. The other man also was gone; but we discovered him, nigh an hour later, jammed half through the rail that ran round the poop. To leeward, I heard the Mate singing out to know whether we were safe; to which both the Captain and I shouted a reply, so as to assure him. It was then I became aware that my camera had been washed out of my hands. I found it eventually among a tangle of ropes and gear to leeward.

Again and again the great hills of water struck the vessel, seeming to rise up on every side at once—towering, live pyramids of brine, in the darkness, hurling upward with a harsh unceasing roaring.

From her taffrail to her knight-heads, the ship was swept, fore and aft, so that no living thing could have existed for a moment down upon the maindeck, which was practically submerged. Indeed, the whole vessel seemed at times to be lost beneath the chaos of water that thundered down and over her in clouds and cataracts of brine and foam, so that each moment seemed like to be our last.

Occasionally, I would hear the hoarse voice of the Captain or the Mate, calling through the gloom to one another, or to the figures of the clinging men. And then again would come the thunder of water, as the seas burst over us. And all this in an almost impenetrable darkness, save when some unnatural glare of lightning sundered the clouds, and lit the thirty-mile cauldron that had engulfed us.

And, anon, all this while, round about, seeming to come from every point of the horizon, sounded a vast, but distant, bellowing and screaming noise, that I caught sometimes above the harsh, slopping roarings of the bursting water-hills all about us. The sound appeared now to be growing louder upon our port beam. It was the Storm circling far round us.

Some time later, there sounded an intense roar in the air above the ship, and then came a far-off shrieking, that grew rapidly into a mighty whistling-scream, and a minute afterwards a most tremendous gust of wind struck the ship on her port side, hurling her over on to her starboard broadside. For many minutes she lay there, her decks under water almost up to the coamings of the hatches.[1] Then she righted, sullenly and slowly, freeing herself from, maybe, half a thousand tons of water.

Again there came a short period of windlessness, and then once more the yelling of an approaching gust. It struck us; but now the vessel had paid off before the wind, and she was not again forced over on to her side.

---

[1] The Second Mate, who was holding to the rail across the break of the poop, gave me this information later; he being in a position to see the maindecks at the time.

From no onward, we drove forward over vast seas, with the Cyclone bellowing and wailing over us in one unbroken roar. . . . *The Vortex had passed*, and could we but last out a few more hours, then might we hope to win through.

With the return of the wind, the Mate and one of the men had taken the wheel; but, despite the mast careful steering, we were pooped several times;[1] for the seas were hideously broken and confused, we being still in the wake of the Vortex, and the wind not having had time as yet to smash the Pyramidal Sea into the more regular storm waves, which, though huge in size, give a vessel a chance to rise to them.

It was later that some of us, headed by the Mate—who had relinquished his place at the wheel to one of the men—ventured down on to the maindeck with axes and knives, to clear away the wreckage of some of the spars which we had lost in the Vortex. Many a grim risk was run in that hour; but we cleared the wreck, and after that, scrambled back, dripping, to the poop, where the Steward, looking woefully white and scared, served out rum to us from the wooden deck-bucket.

It was decided now that we should bring her head to the seas, so as to make better weather of it. To reduce the risk as much as possible, we had already put out two fresh oil-bags, which we had prepared, and which, indeed, we ought to have done earlier; for though they were being constantly washed aboard again, we had begun at once to take less water.

Now, we took a hawser from the bows, outside of everything, and right away aft to the poop, where we bent on our sea-anchor, which was like an enormous log-bag, or drogue, made of triple canvas.

We bent on our two oil-bags to the sea-anchor, and then dropped the whole business over the side. When the vessel took the pull of it; we put down our helm, and came up into the wind, very quick, and without taking any great water. And a risk it was; but a deal less than some we had come through already.

Slowly, with an undreamt of slowness, the remainder of the night passed, minute by minute, and at last the day broke in a weary dawn; the sky full of a stormy, sickly light. One very side tumbled an interminable chaos of seas. And the vessel herself—! A wreck, she appeared. The mizzenmast had gone, some dozen feet above the deck; the main-topmast had gone, and so had the jigger-topmast. I struggled forrard to the break of the poop, and glanced along the decks. The boats had gone. All the iron scupper-doors were either bent, or had disappeared. On the starboard side, opposite to the stump of the mizzenmast, was a great ragged gap in the steel bulwarks, where the mast must have struck, when it carried away. In several other places, the t'gallant rail was smashed or bent, where it had been struck

---

[1]Possibly, our being pooped at this time, was due chiefly to the fact that our speed through the water had diminished, owing to our having lost more of our spars whilst in the Vortex, and some of the gear still towing. And a Mercy our sides were not stove a thousand times!

by falling spars. The side of the teak deck-house had been stove, and the water was roaring in and out with each roll of the ship. The sheep-pen had vanished, and so—as I discovered later—had the pigsty.

Further forrard, my glance went, and I saw that the sea had breached the bulkshead, across the after end of the fo'cas'le, and, with each biggish sea that we shipped, a torrent of water drove in, and then flowed out, sometimes bearing with it an odd board, or perhaps a man's boot, or some article of wearing apparel. In two places on the maindeck, I saw men's sea-chests, washing to and fro in the water that streamed over the deck. And, suddenly, there came into my mind a memory of the poor fellow who had broken his arm when we were cutting loose the wreck of the fore-topmast.

Already, the strength of the Cyclone was spent, so far, at least, as we were concerned; and I was thinking of making a try for the fo'cas'le, when, close beside me, I heard the Mate's voice. I turned, with a little start. He had evidently noticed the breach in the bulkshead; for he told me to watch a chance, and see if we could get forrard.

This, we did; though not without a further thorough sousing; as we were still shipping water by the score of tons. Moreover, the risk was considerably greater than might be conceived; for the doorless scupper-ports offered uncomfortable facilities for gurgling out into the ocean, along with a ton or two of brine from the decks.

We reached the fo'cas'le, and pulled open the lee door. We stepped inside. It was like stepping into a dank, gloomy cavern. Water was dripping from every beam and staunchion. We struggled across the slippery deck, to where we had left the sick man in his bunk. In the dim light, we saw that man and bunk, everything, had vanished; only the bare steel sides of the vessel remained. Every bunk and fitting in the place had been swept away, and all of the men's sea-chests. Nothing remained, save, it might be, an odd soaked rag of clothing, or a sodden bunk-board.

The Mate and I looked at one another, in silence.

"Poor devil!" he said. He repeated his expression of pity, staring at the place where had been the bunk. Then, grave of face, he turned to go out on deck. As he did so, a heavier sea than usual broke aboard; flooded roaring along the decks, and swept in through the broken bulkshead and the lee doorway. It swirled round the sides, caught us, and threw us down in a heap; then swept out through the breach and the doorway, carrying the Mate with it. He managed to grasp the lintel of the doorway, else, I do believe, he would have gone out through one of the open scupper traps. A doubly hard fate, after having come safely through the Cyclone.

Outside of the fo'cas'le, I saw that the ladders leading up to the fo'cas'le head had both gone; but I managed to scramble up. Here, I found that both anchors had been washed away, and the rails all round; only the bare staunchions remaining.

Beyond the bows, the jibboom had gone, and all the gear was draggled inboard over the fo'cas'le head, or trailing in the sea.

We made our way aft, and reported; then the roll was called, and we found that one else was missing, besides the two I have already mentioned, and the man we found jammed half through the poop rails, who was now under the Steward's care.

From that time on, the sea went down steadily, until, presently, it ceased to threaten us, and we proceeded to get the ship cleared up a bit; after which, one watch turned-in on the floor of the saloon, and the other was told to "stand easy."

Hour by hour, through that day and the next, the sea went down, until it was difficult to believe that we had so lately despaired for our lives. And so the second evening came, calm and restful, the wind no more than a light summer's breeze, and the sea calming steadily.

About seven bells that second night, a big steamer crossed our stern, and slowed down to ask us if we were in need of help; for, even by moonlight, it was easy to see our dismantled condition. This offer, however, the Captain refused; and with many good wishes, the big vessel swung off into the moon-wake, and so, presently, we were left alone in the quiet night; safe at last, and rich in a completed experience.

The Finding of the *Graiken*

When a year had passed, and still there was no news of the full-rigged ship *Graiken*, even the most sanguine of my old chum's friends had ceased to hope perchance, somewhere, she might be above water.

Yet Ned Barlow, in his inmost thoughts, I knew, still hugged to himself the hope that she would win home. Poor, dear old fellow, how my heart did go out towards him in his sorrow!

For it was in the *Graiken* that his sweetheart had sailed on that dull January day some twelve months previously.

The voyage had been taken for the sake of her health; yet since then—save for a distant signal recorded at the Azores—there had been from all the mystery of ocean no voice; the ship and they within her had vanished utterly.

And still Barlow hoped. He said nothing actually, but at times his deeper thoughts would float up and show through the sea of his usual talk, and thus I would know in an indirect way of the thing that his heart was thinking.

Nor was time a healer.

It was later that my present good fortune came to me. My uncle died, and I—hitherto poor—was now a rich man. In a breath, it seemed, I had become possessor of houses, lands, and money; also—in my eyes almost more important—a fine fore-and-aft-rigged yacht of some two hundred tons register.

It seemed scarcely believable that the thing was mine, and I was all in a scutter to run away down to Falmouth and get to sea.

In old times, when my uncle had been more than usually gracious, he had invited me to accompany him for a trip round the coast or elsewhere, as the fit might take him; yet never, even in my most hopeful moments, had it occurred to me that ever she might be mine.

And now I was hurrying my preparations for a good long sea trip—for to me the sea is, and always has been, a comrade.

Still, with all the prospects before me, I was by no means completely satisfied, for I wanted Ned Barlow with me, and yet was afraid to ask him.

I had the feeling that, in view of his overwhelming loss, he must positively hate the sea; and yet I could not be happy at the thought of leaving him, and going alone.

He had not been well lately, and a sea voyage would be the very thing for him, if only it were not going to freshen painful memories.

Eventually I decided to suggest it, and this I did a couple of days before the date I had fixed for sailing.

"Ned," I said, "you need a change."

"Yes," he assented wearily.

"Come with me, old chap," I went on, growing bolder. "I'm taking a trip in the yacht. It would be splendid to have—"

To my dismay, he jumped to his feet and came towards me excitedly.

"I've upset him now," was my thought. "I *am* a fool!"

"Go to sea!" he said. "My God! I'd give—" He broke off short, and stood suppressed opposite to me, his face all of a quiver with suppressed emotion. He was silent a few seconds, getting himself in hand; then he proceeded more quietly: "Where to?"

"Anywhere," I replied, watching him keenly, for I was greatly puzzled by his manner. "I'm not quite clear yet. Somewhere south of here—the West Indies, I have thought. It's all so new, you know—just fancy being able to go just where we like. I can hardly realise it yet."

I stopped, for he had turned from me and was staring out of the window.

"You'll come, Ned?" I cried, fearful that he was going to refuse me.

He took a pace away, and came back.

"I'll come," he said, and there was a look of strange excitement in his eyes that set me off on a tack of vague wonder; but I said nothing, just told him how he had pleased me.

II

We had been at sea a couple of weeks, and were alone upon the Atlantic—at least, so much of it as presented itself to our view.

I was leaning over the taffrail, staring down into the boil of the wake; yet I noticed nothing, for I was wrapped in a tissue of somewhat uncomfortable thought. It was about Ned Barlow.

He had been queer, decidedly queer, since leaving port. His whole attitude mentally had been that of a man under the influence of an all-pervading excitement. I had said that he was in need of a change, and had trusted that the splendid tonic of the sea breeze would serve to put him soon to rights mentally and physically; yet here was the poor old chap acting in a manner calculated to cause me anxiety as to his balance.

Scarcely a word had been spoken since leaving the Channel. When I ventured to speak to him, often he would take not the least notice, other times he would answer only by a brief word; but talk—never.

In addition, his whole time was spent on deck among the men, and with some of them he seemed to converse both long and earnestly; yet to me, his chum and true friend, not a word.

Another thing came to me as a surprise—Barlow betrayed the greatest interest in the position of the vessel, and the courses set, all in such a manner as left me no room to doubt but that his knowledge of navigation was considerable.

Once I ventured to express my astonishment at this knowledge, and ask a question or two as to the way in which he had gathered it, but had been treated with such an absurdly stony silence that since then I had not spoken to him.

With all this it may be easily conceived that my thoughts, as I stared down into the wake, were troublesome.

Suddenly I heard a voice at my elbow:

"I should like to have a word with you, sir." I turned sharply. It was my skipper, and something in his face told me that all was not as it should be.

"Well, Jenkins, fire away."

He looked round, as if afraid of being overheard; then came closer to me.

"Someone's been messing with the compasses, sir," he said in a low voice.

"What?" I asked sharply.

"They've been meddled with, sir. The magnets have been shifted, and by someone who's a good idea of what he's doing."

"What on earth do you mean?" I inquired. "Why should anyone mess about with them? What good would it do them? You must be mistaken."

"No, sir, I'm not. They've been touched within the last forty-eight hours, and by someone that understands what he's doing."

I stared at him. The man was so certain. I felt bewildered.

"But why should they?"

"That's more than I can say, sir; but it's a serious matter, and I want to know what I'm to do. It looks to me as though there were something funny going on. I'd give a month's pay to know just who it was, for certain."

"Well," I said, "if they have been touched, it can only be by one of the officers. You say the chap who has done it must understand what he is doing."

He shook his head. "No sir—" he began, and then stopped abruptly. His gaze met mine. I think the same thought must have come to us simultaneously. I gave a little gasp of amazement.

He wagged his head at me. "I've had my suspicions for a bit, sir," he went on; "but seeing that he's—he's—" He was fairly struck for the moment.

I took my weight off the rail and stood upright.

"To whom are you referring?" I asked curtly.

"Why, sir, to him—Mr. Ned—"

He would have gone on, but I cut him short.

"That will do, Jenkins!" I cried. "Mr. Ned Barlow is my friend. You are forgetting yourself a little. You will accuse me of tampering with the compasses next!"

I turned away, leaving little Captain Jenkins speechless. I had spoken with an almost vehement over-loyalty, to quiet my own suspicions.

All the same, I was horribly bewildered, not knowing what to think or do or say, so that, eventually, I did just nothing.

III

It was early one morning, about a week later, that I opened my eyes abruptly. I was lying on my back in my bunk, and the daylight was beginning to creep wanly in through the ports.

I had a vague consciousness that all was not as it should be, and feeling thus, I made to grasp the edge of my bunk, and situp, but failed, owing to the fact that my wrists were securely fastened by a pair of heavy steel handcuffs.

Utterly confounded, I let my head fall back upon the pillow; and then, in the midst of my bewilderment, there sounded the sharp report of a pistol-shot somewhere on the decks over my head. There came a second, and the sound of voices and footsteps, and then a long spell of silence.

Into my mind had rushed the single word—mutiny! My temples throbbed a little, but I struggled to keep calm and think, and then, all adrift, I fell to searching round for a reason. Who was it? and why?

Perhaps an hour passed, during which I asked myself ten thousand vain questions. All at once I heard a key inserted in the door. So I had been locked in! It turned, and the steward walked into the cabin. He did not look at me, but went to the arm-rack and began to remove the various weapons.

"What the devil is the meaning of all this, Jones?" I roared, getting up a bit on one elbow. "What's happening?"

But the fool answered not a word—just went to and fro carrying out the weapons from my cabin into the next, so that at last I ceased from questioning him, and lay silent, promising myself future vengeance.

When he had removed the arms, the steward began to go through my table drawers, emptying them, so it appeared to me, of everything that could be used as a weapon or tool.

Having completed his task, he vanished, locking the door after him.

Some time passed, and at last, about seven bells, he reappeared, this time bringing a tray with my breakfast. Placing it upon the table, he came across to me and proceeded to unlock the cuffs from off my wrists. Then for the first time he spoke.

"Mr. Barlow desires me to say, sir, that you have the liberty of your cabin so long as you will agree not to cause any bother. Should you wish for anything, I am under his orders to supply you." He retreated hastily toward the door.

On my part, I was almost speechless with astonishment and rage.

"One minute, Jones!" I shouted, just as he was in the act of leaving the cabin. "Kindly explain what you mean. You said Mr. Barlow. Is it to him that I owe all this?" And I waved my hand towards the irons which the man still held.

"It is by his orders," replied he, and turned once more to leave the cabin.

"I don't understand!" I said, bewildered. "Mr. Barlow is my friend, and this is my yacht! By what right do you dare to take your orders from him? Let me out!"

As I shouted the last command, I leapt from my bunk, and made a dash for the door, but the steward, so far from attempting to bar it, flung it open and stepped quickly through, thus allowing me to see that a couple of the sailors were stationed in the alleyway.

"Get on deck at once!" I said angrily. "What are you doing down here?"

"Sorry sir," said one of the men. "We'd take it kindly if you'd make no trouble. But we ain't lettin' you out, sir. Don't make no bloomin' error."

I hesitated, then went to the table and sat down. I would, at least, do my best to preserve my dignity.

After an inquiry as to whether he could do anything further, the steward left me to breakfast and my thoughts. As may be imagined, the latter were by no means pleasant.

Here was I prisoner in my own yacht, and by the hand of the very man I had loved and befriended through many years. Oh, it was too incredible and mad!

For a while, leaving the table, I paced the deck of my room; then, growing calmer, I sat down again and attempted to make some sort of a meal.

As I breakfasted, my chief thought was as to why my one-time chum was treating me thus; and after that I fell to puzzling *how* he had managed to get the yacht into his own hands.

Many things came back to me—his familiarity with the men, his treatment of me—which I had put down to a temporary want of balance—the fooling with the compasses; for I was certain now that he had been the doer of that piece of mischief. But why? That was the great point.

As I turned the matter over in my brain, an incident that had occurred some six days back came to me. It had been on the very day after the captain's report to me of the tampering with the compasses.

Barlow had, for the first time, relinquished his brooding and silence, and had started to talk to me, but in such a wild strain that he had made me feel vaguely uncomfortable about his sanity for he told me some yarn of an idea which he had got into his head. And then, in an overbearing way, he demanded that the navigation of the yacht should be put into his hands.

He had been very incoherent, and was plainly in a state of considerable mental excitement. He had rambled on about some derelict, and then had talked in an extraordinary fashion of a vast world of seaweed.

Once or twice in his bewilderingly disconnected speech he had mentioned the name of his sweetheart, and now it was the memory of her name that gave me the first inkling of what might possibly prove a solution of the whole affair.

I wished now that I had encouraged his incoherent ramble of speech, instead of heading him off; but I had done so because I could not bear to have him talk as he had.

Yet, with the little I remembered, I began to shape out a theory. It seemed to me that he might be nursing some idea that had formed—goodness knows how or when—that his sweetheart (still alive) was aboard some derelict in the midst of an enormous "world," he had termed it, of seaweed.

He might have grown more explicit had I not attempted to reason with him, and so lost the rest.

Yet, remembering back, it seemed to me that he must undoubtedly have meant the enormous Sargasso Sea—that great seaweed-laden ocean, vast almost as Continental Europe, and the final resting-place of the Atlantic's wreckage.

Surely, if he proposed any attempt to search through that, then there could be no doubt but that he was temporarily unbalanced. And yet I could do nothing. I was a prisoner and helpless.

IV

Eight days of variable but strongish winds passed, and still I was a prisoner in my cabin. From the ports that opened out astern and on each side—for my cabin runs right across the whole width of the stern—I was able to command a good view of the surrounding ocean, which now had commenced to be laden with great floating patches of Gulf weed—many of them hundreds and hundreds of yards in length.

And still we held on, apparently towards the nucleus of the Sargasso Sea. This I was able to assume by means of a chart which I found in one of the lockers, and the course I had been able to gather from the "tell-tale" compass let into the cabin ceiling.

And so another and another day went by, and now we were among weed so thick that at times the vessel found difficulty in forcing her way through, while the surface of the sea had assumed a curious oily appearance, though the wind was still quite strong.

It was later in the day that we encountered a bank of weed so prodigious that we had to up helm and run round it, and after that the same experience was many times repeated; and so the night found us.

The following morning found me at the ports, eagerly peering out across the water. From one of those on the starboard side I could discern at a considerable distance a huge bank of weed that seemed to be unending, and to run parallel with our broadside. It appeared to rise in places a couple of feet above the level of the surrounding sea.

For a long while I stared, then went across to the port side. Here I found that a similar bank stretched away on our port beam. It was as though we were sailing up an immense river, the low banks of which were formed of seaweed instead of land.

And so that day passed hour by hour, the weed-banks growing more definite and seeming to be nearer. Towards evening something came into sight—a far, dim hulk, the masts gone, the whole hull covered with growth, an unwholesome green, blotched with brown in the light from the dying sun.

I saw this lonesome craft from a port on the starboard side, and the sight roused a multitude of questions and thoughts.

Evidently we had penetrated into the unknown central portion of the enormous Sargasso, the Great Eddy of the Atlantic, and this was some lonely derelict, lost ages ago perhaps to the outside world.

Just at the going down of the sun, I saw another; she was nearer, and still possessed two of her masts. which stuck up bare and desolate into the darkening sky. She could not have been more than a quarter of a mile in from the edge of the weed. As we passed her I craned out my head through the port to stare at her. As I stared the dusk grew out of the abyss of the air, and she faded presently from sight into the surrounding loneliness.

Through all that night I sat at the port and watched, listening and peering; for the tremendous mystery of that inhuman weed-world was upon me.

In the air there rose no sound; even the wind was scarcely more than a low hum aloft among the sails and gear, and under me the oily water gave no rippling noise. All was silence, supreme and unearthly.

About midnight the moon rose away on our starboard beam, and from then until the dawn I stared out upon a ghostly world of noiseless weed, fantastic, silent, and unbelievable, under the moonlight.

On four separate occasions my gaze lit on black hulks that rose above the surrounding weeds—the hulks of long-lost vessels. And once, just when the strangeness of dawn was in the sky, a faint, long-drawn wailing seemed to come floating to me across the immeasurable waste of weed.

It startled my strung nerves, and I assured myself that it was the cry of some lone sea bird. Yet, my imagination reached out for some stranger explanation.

The eastward sky began to flush with the dawn, and the morning light grew subtly over the breadth of the enormous ocean of weed until it seemed to me to reach away unbroken on each beam into the grey horizons. Only astern of us, like a broad road of oil, ran the strange river-like gulf up which we had sailed.

Now I noticed that the banks of weed were nearer, very much nearer, and a disagreeable thought came to me. This vast rift that had allowed us to penetrate into the very nucleus of the Sargasso Sea—suppose it should close!

It would mean inevitably that there would be one more among the missing—another unanswered mystery of the inscrutable ocean. I resisted the thought, and came back more directly into the present.

Evidently the wind was still dropping, for we were moving slowly, as a glance at the ever-nearing weed-banks told me. The hours passed on, and my breakfast, when the steward brought it, I took to one of the ports, and there ate; for I would lose nothing of the strange surroundings into which we were so steadily plunging.

And so the morning passed.

V

It was about an hour after dinner that I observed the open channel between the weed-banks to be narrowing almost minute by minute with uncomfortable speed. I could do nothing except watch and surmise.

At times I felt convinced that the immense masses of weed were closing in upon us, but I fought off the thought with the more hopeful one that we were surely approaching some narrowing outlet of the gulf that yawned so far across the seaweed.

By the time the afternoon was half-through, the weed-banks had approached so close that occasional outjutting masses scraped the yacht's sides in passing. It was now with the stuff below my face, within a few feet of my eyes, that I discovered the immense amount of life that stirred among all the hideous waste.

Innumerable crabs crawled among the seaweed, and once, indistinctly, something stirred among the depths of a large outlying tuft of weed. What it was I could not tell, though afterwards I had an idea; but all I saw was something dark and glistening. We were past it before I could see more.

The steward was in the act of bringing in my tea, when from above there came a noise of shouting, and almost immediately a slight jolt. The man put down the tray he was carrying, and glanced at me, with startled expression.

"What is it, Jones?" I questioned.

"I don't know sir. I expect it's the weed," he replied.

I ran to the port, craned out my head, and looked forward. Our bow seemed to be embedded in a mass of weeds, and as I watched it came further aft.

Within the next five minutes we had driven through it into a circle of sea that was free from the weed. Across this we seemed to drift, rather than sail, so slow was our speed.

Upon its opposite margin we brought up, the vessel swinging broadside on to the weed, being secured thus with a couple of kedges cast from the bows and stern, though of this I was not aware until later. As we swung, and at last I was able from my port to see ahead, I saw a thing that amazed me.

There, not three hundred feet distant across the quaking weed, a vessel lay embedded. She had been a three-master; but of these only the mizzen was standing. For perhaps a minute I stared, scarcely breathing in my exceeding interest.

All around above her bulwarks, to the height of apparently some ten feet, ran a sort of fencing formed, so far as I could make out, from canvas, rope, and spars. Even as I wondered at the use of such a thing, I heard my chum's voice overhead. He was hailing her:

"*Graiken*, ahoy!" he shouted. "*Graiken*, ahoy!"

At that I fairly jumped. *Graiken!* What could he mean! I stared out of the port. The blaze of the sinking sun flashed redly upon her stern, and showed the lettering of her name and port; yet the distance was too great for me to read.

I ran across to my table to see if there were a pair of binoculars in the drawers. I found one in the first I opened; then I ran back to the port, racking them out as I went. I reached it, and clapped them to my eyes. Yes; I saw it plainly, her name *Graiken* and her port London.

From her name my gaze moved to that strange fencing about her. There was a movement in the aft part. As I watched a portion of it slid to one side, and a man's head and shoulders appeared.

I nearly yelled with the excitement of that moment. I could scarcely believe the thing I saw. The man waved an arm, and a vague hail reached us across the weed; then he disappeared. A moment later a score of people crowded the opening, and among them I made out distinctly the face and figure of a girl.

"He was right, after all!" I heard myself saying out loud in a voice that was toneless through very amazement.

In a minute, I was at the door, beating it with my fists. "Let me out, Ned! Let me out!" I shouted.

I felt that I could forgive him all the indignity that I had suffered. Nay, more; in a queer way I had a feeling that it was I who needed to ask *him* for forgiveness. All my bitterness had gone, and I wanted only to be out and give a hand in the rescue.

Yet though I shouted, no one came, so that at last I returned quickly to the port, to see what further developments there were.

Across the weed I now saw that one man had his hands up to his mouth shouting. His voice reached me only as a faint, hoarse cry; the distance was too great for anyone aboard the yacht to distinguish its import.

From the derelict my attention was drawn abruptly to a scene alongside. A plank was thrown down on to the weed, and the next moment I saw my chum swing himself down the side and leap upon it.

I had opened my mouth to call out to him that I would forgive all were I but freed to lend a hand in this unbelievable rescue.

But even as the words formed they died, for though the weed appeared so dense, it was evidently incapable of bearing any considerable weight, and the plank, with Barlow upon it, sank down into the weed almost to his waist.

He turned and grabbed at the rope with both hands, and in the same moment he gave a loud cry of sheer terror, and commenced to scramble up the yacht's side.

As his feet drew clear of the weed I gave a short cry. Something was curled about his left ankle—something oily, supple and tapered. As I stared another rose up out from the weed and swayed through the air, made a grab at his leg, missed and appeared to wave aimlessly. Others came towards him as he struggled upwards.

Then I saw hands reach down from above and seize Barlow beneath the arms. They lifted him by main force, and with a mass of weed that enfolded something leathery, from which numbers of curling arms writhed.

A hand slashed down with a sheath-knife, and the next instant the hideous thing had fallen back among the weed.

For a couple of seconds longer I remained, my head twisted upwards; then faces appeared once more over our rail, and I saw the men extending arms and fingers, pointing. From above me there rose a hoarse chorus of fear and wonder, and I turned my head swiftly to glance down and across that treacherous extraordinary weedworld.

The whole of the hitherto silent surface was all of a move in one stupendous undulation—as though life had come to all that desolation.

The undulatory movement continued, and abruptly, in a hundred places, the seaweed was tossed up into sudden, billowy hillocks. From these burst mighty arms, and in an instant the evening air was full of them, hundreds and hundreds, coming toward the yacht.

"Devil-fishes!" shouted a man's voice from the deck. "Octopuses! My Lord!"

Then I caught my chum shouting.

"Cut the mooring ropes!" he yelled.

This must have been done almost on the instant, for immediately there showed between us and the nearest weed a broadening gap of scummy water.

"Haul away, lads!" I heard Barlow shouting; and the same instant I caught the splash, splash of something in the water on our port side. I rushed across and looked out. I found that a rope had been carried across to the opposite seaweed, and that the men were now warping us rapidly from those invading horrors.

I raced back to the starboard port, and, lo! as though by magic, there stretched between us and the Graiken only the silent stretch of demure weed and some fifty feet of water. It seemed inconceivable that it was a covering to so much terror.

And then speedily the night was upon us, hiding all; but from the decks above there commenced a sound of hammering that continued long throughout the night—long after I, weary with my previous night's vigil, had passed into a fitful slumber, broken anon by that hammering above.

VI

"Your breakfast, sir," came respectfully enough in the steward's voice; and I woke with a start. Overhead, there still sounded that persistent hammering, and I turned to the steward for an explanation.

"I don't exactly know, sir," was his reply. "It's something the carpenter's doing to one of the lifeboats." And then he left me.

I ate my breakfast standing at the port, staring at the distant Graiken. The weed was perfectly quiet, and we were lying about the centre of the little lake.

As I watched the derelict, it seemed to me that I saw a movement about her side, and I reached for the glasses. Adjusting them, I made out that there were several of the cuttlefish attached to her in different parts, their arms spread out almost starwise across the lower portions of her hull.

Occasionally a feeler would detached itself and wave aimlessly. This it was that had drawn my attention. The sight of these creatures, in conjunction with that extraordinary scene the previous evening, enabled me to guess the use of the great screen running about the *Graiken*. It had obviously been erected as a protection against the vile inhabitants of that strange weed-world.

From that my thoughts passed to the problem of reaching and rescuing the crew of the derelict. I could by no means conceive how this was to be effected.

As I stood pondering, whilst I ate, I caught the voices of men chaunteying on deck. For a while this continued; then came Barlow's voice shouting orders, and almost immediately a splash in the water on the starboard side.

I poked my head out through the port, and stared. They had got one of the lifeboats into the water. To the gunnel of the boat they had added a superstructure ending in a roof, the whole somewhat resembling a gigantic dog-kennel.

From under the two sharp ends of the boat rose a couple of planks at an angle or thirty degrees. These appeared to be firmly bolted to the boat and the superstructure. I guessed that their purpose was to enable the boat to over-ride the seaweed, instead of ploughing into it and getting fast.

In the stern of the boat was fixed a strong ringbolt, into which was spliced the end of a coil of one-inch Manila rope. Along the sides of the boat, and high above the gunnel, the superstructure was pierced with holes for oars. In one side of the roof was placed a trapdoor. The idea struck me as wonderfully ingenious, and a very probable solution of the difficulty of rescuing the crew of the *Graiken*.

A few minutes later one of the men threw over a rope on to the roof of the boat. He opened the trap, and lowered himself into the interior. I noticed that he was armed with one of the yacht's cutlasses and a revolver.

It was evident that my chum fully appreciated the difficulties that were to be overcome. In a few seconds the man was followed by four others of the crew, similarly armed; and then Barlow.

Seeing him, I craned my head as far as possible, and sang out to him.

"Ned! Ned, old man!" I shouted. "Let me come along with you!"

He appeared never to have heard me. I noticed his face, just before he shut down the trap above him. The expression was fixed and peculiar. It had the uncomfortable remoteness of a sleep-walker.

"Confound it!" I muttered, and after that I said nothing; for it hurt my dignity to supplicate before the men.

From the interior of the boat I heard Barlow's voice, muffled. Immediately four oars were passed out through the holes in the sides, while from slots in the front and rear of the superstructure were thrust a couple of oars with wooden chocks nailed to the blades.

These, I guessed, were intended to assist in steering the boat, that in the bow being primarily for pressing down the weed before the boat, so as to allow her to surmount it the more easily.

Another muffled order came from the interior of the queer-looking craft, and immediately the four oars dipped, and the boat shot towards the weed, the rope trailing out astern as it was paid out from the deck above me.

The board-assisted bow of the lifeboat took the weed with a sort of squashy surge, rose up, and the whole craft appeared to leap from the water down in among the quaking mass.

I saw now the reason why the oar-holes had been placed so high. For of the boat itself nothing could be seen, only the upper portion of the superstructure wallowing amid the weed. Had the holes been lower, there would have been no handling the oars.

I settled myself to watch. There was the probability of a prodigious spectacle, and as I could not help, I would, at least, use my eyes.

Five minutes passed, during which nothing happened, and the boat made slow progress towards the derelict. She had accomplished perhaps some twenty or thirty yards, when suddenly from the *Graiken* there reached my ears a hoarse shout.

My glance leapt from the boat to the derelict. I saw that the people aboard had the sliding part of the screen to one side, and were waving their arms frantically, as though motioning the boat back.

Amongst them I could see the girlish figure that had attracted my attention the previous evening. For a moment I stared, then my gaze travelled back to the boat. All was quiet.

The boat had now covered a quarter of the distance, and I began to persuade myself that she would get across without being attacked.

Then, as I gazed anxiously, from a point in the weed a little ahead of the boat there came a sudden quaking ripple that shivered through the weed in a sort of queer tremor. The next instant, like a shot from a gun, a huge mass drove up clear through the tangled weed, hurling it in all directions, and almost capsizing the boat.

The creature had driven up rear foremost. It fell back with a mighty splash, and in the same moment its monstrous arms were reached out to the boat. They grasped it, enfolding themselves about it horribly. It was apparently attempting to drag the boat under.

From the boat came a regular volley of revolver shots. Yet, though the brute writhed, it did not relinquish its hold. The shots closed, and I saw the dull flash of cutlass blades. The men were attempting to hack at the thing through the oar holes, but evidently with little effect.

All at once the enormous creature seemed to make an effort to overturn the boat. I saw the half-submerged boat go over to one side, until it seemed to me that nothing could right it, and at the sight I went mad with excitement to help them.

I pulled my head in from the port, and glanced round the cabin. I wanted to break down the door, but there was nothing with which to do this.

Then my sight fell on my bunkboard, which fitted into a sliding groove. It was made of teak wood, and very solid and heavy. I lifted it out, and charged the door with the end of it.

The panels split from top to bottom, for I am a heavy man. Again I struck, and drove the two portions of the door apart. I hove down the bunk-board, and rushed through.

There was no one on guard; evidently they had gone on deck to view the rescue. The gunroom door was to my right, and I had the key in my pocket.

In an instant, I had it open, and was lifting down from its rack a heavy elephant gun. Seizing a box of cartridges, I tore off the lid, and emptied the lot into my pocket; then I leapt up the companionway on the deck.

The steward was standing near. He turned at my step; his face was white and he took a couple of paces towards me doubtfully.

"They're—they're—" he began; but I never let him finish.

"Get out of my way!" I roared and swept him to one side. I ran forward.

"Haul in on that rope!" I shouted. "Tail on to it! Are you going to stand there like a lot of owls and see them drown!"

The men only wanted a leader to show them what to do, and, without showing any thought of insubordination, they tacked on to the rope that was fastened to the stern of the boat, and hauled her back across the weed—cuttle-fish and all.

The strain on the rope had thrown her on an even keel again, so that she took the water safely, though that foul thing was straddled all across her.

"Vast hauling!" I shouted. "Get the doc's cleavers, some of you—anything that'll cut!"

"This is the sort, sir!" cried the bo'sun; from somewhere he had got hold of a formidable double-bladed whale lance.

The boat, still under the impetus given by our pull, struck the side of the yacht immediately beneath where I was waiting with the gun. Astern of it towed the body of the monster, its two eyes— monstrous orbs of the Profound—staring out vilely from behind its arms.

I leant my elbows on the rail, and aimed full at the right eye. As I pulled on the trigger one of the great arms detached itself from the boat, and swirled up towards me. There was a thunderous bang as the heavy charge drove its way through that vast eye, and at the same instant something swept over my head.

There came a cry from behind: "Lookout, sir!" A flame of steel before my eyes, and a truncated something fell upon my shoulder, and thence to the deck.

Down below, the water was being churned to a froth, and three more arms sprang into the air, and then down among us.

One grasped the bo'sun, lifting him like a child. Two cleavers gleamed, and he fell to the deck from a height of some twelve feet, along with the severed portion of the limb.

I had my weapons reloaded again by now, and ran forward along the deck somewhat, to be clear of the flying arms that flailed on the rails and deck.

I fired again into the hulk of the brute, and then again. At the second shot, the murderous din of the creature ceased, and, with an ineffectual flicker of its remaining tentacles, it sank out of sight beneath the water.

A minute later we had the hatch in the roof of the superstructure open, and the men out, my chum coming last. They had been mightily shaken, but otherwise were none the worse.

As Barlow came over the gangway, I stepped up to him and gripped his shoulder. I was strangely muddled in my feelings. I felt that I had no sure position aboard my own yacht. Yet all I said was:

"Thank God, you're safe, old man!" And I meant it from my heart.

He looked at me in a doubtful, puzzled sort of manner, and passed his hand across his forehead.

"Yes," he replied; but his voice was strangely toneless, save that some puzzledness seemed to have crept into it. For a couple of moments he stared at me in an unseeing way, and once more I was struck by the immobile, tensed-up expression of his features.

Immediately afterwards he turned away—having shown neither friendliness nor enmity—and commenced to clamber back over the side into the boat.

"Come up, Ned!" I cried. "It's no good. You'll never manage it that way. Look!" and I stretched out my arm, pointing. Instead of looking, he passed his hand once more across his forehead, with that gesture of puzzled doubt. Then, to my relief, he caught at the rope ladder, and commenced to make his way slowly up the side.

Reaching the deck, he stood for nearly a minute without saying a word, his back turned to the derelict. Then, still wordless, he walked slowly across to the opposite side, and leant his elbows upon the rail, as though looking back along the way the yacht had come.

For my part, I said nothing, dividing my attention between him and the men, with occasional glances at the quaking weed and the—apparently—hopelessly surrounded *Graiken*.

The men were quiet, occasionally turning towards Barlow, as though for some further order. Of me they appeared to take little notice. In this wise, perhaps a quarter of an hour went by; then abruptly Barlow stood upright, waving his arms and shouting:

"It comes! It comes!" He turned towards us, and his face seemed transfigured, his eyes gleaming almost maniacally.

I ran across the deck to his side, and looked away to port, and now I saw what it was that had excited him. The weed-barrier through which we had come on our inward journey was divided, a slowly broadening river of oil water showing clean across it.

Even as I watched it grew broader, the immense masses of weed being moved by some unseen impulsion.

I was still staring, amazed, when a sudden cry went up from some of the men to starboard. Turning quickly, I saw that the yawning movement was being continued to the mass of weed that lay between us and the *Graiken*.

Slowly, the weed was divided, surely as though an invisible wedge were being driven through it. The gulf of weed-clear water reached the derelict, and passed beyond. And now there was no longer anything to stop our rescue of the crew of the derelict.

VII

It was Barlow's voice that gave the order for the mooring ropes to be cast off, and then, as the light wind was right against us, a boat was out ahead, and the yacht was towed towards the ship, whilst a dozen of the men stood ready with their rifles on the fo'c's'le head.

As we drew nearer, I began to distinguish the features of the crew, the men strangely grizzled and old looking. And among them, white-faced with emotion, was my chum's lost sweetheart. I never expect to know a more extraordinary moment.

I looked at Barlow; he was staring at the white-faced girl with an extraordinary fixidity of expression that was scarcely the look of a sane man.

The next minute we were alongside, crushing to a pulp between our steel sides one of those remaining monsters of the deep that had continued to cling steadfastly to the *Graiken*.

Yet of that I was scarcely aware, for I had turned again to look at Ned Barlow. He was swaying slowly to his feet, and just as the two vessels closed he reached up both hands to his head, and fell like a log.

Brandy was brought, and later Barlow carried to his cabin; yet we had won clear of that hideous weed-world before he recovered consciousness.

During his illness I learned from his sweetheart how, on a terrible night a long year previously, the *Graiken* had been caught in a tremendous storm and dismasted, and how, helpless and driven by the gale, they at last found themselves surrounded by the great banks of floating weed, and finally held fast in the remorseless grip of the dread Sargasso.

She told me of their attempts to free the ship from the weed, and of the attacks of the cuttlefish. And later of various other matters; for all of which I have no room in this story.

In return I told her of our voyage, and her lover's strange behaviour. How he had wanted to undertake the navigation of the yacht, and had talked of a great world of weed. How I had—believing him unhinged—refused to listen to him.

How he had taken matters into his own hands, without which she would most certainly have ended her days surrounded by the quaking weed and those great beasts of the deep waters.

She listened with an evergrowing seriousness, so that I had, time and again, to assure her that I bore my old chum no ill, but rather held myself to be in the wrong. At which she shook her head, but seemed mightily relieved.

It was during Barlow's recovery that I made the astonishing discovery that he remembered no detail of his imprisoning of me.

I am convinced now that for days and weeks he must have lived in a sort of dream in a hyper state, in which I can only imagine that he had possibly been sensitive to more subtle understandings than normal bodily and mental health allows.

One other thing there is in closing. I found that the captain and the two mates had been confined to their cabins by Barlow. The captain was suffering from a pistol-shot in the arm, due to his having attempted to resist Barlow's assumption of authority.

When I released him he vowed vengeance. Yet Ned Barlow being my chum, I found means to slake both the captain's and the two mates' thirst for vengeance, and the slaking thereof is—well, another story.

A Tropical Horror

We are a hundred and thirty days out from Melbourne, and for three weeks we have lain in this sweltering calm.

It is midnight, and our watch on deck until four a.m. I go out and sit on the hatch. A minute later, Joky, our youngest 'prentice, joins me for a chatter. Many are the hours we have sat thus and talked in the night watches; though, to be sure, it is Joky who does the talking. I am content to smoke and listen, giving an occasional grunt at seasons to show that I am attentive.

Joky has been silent for some time, his head bent in meditation. Suddenly he looks up, evidently with the intention of making some remark. As he does so, I see his face stiffen with a nameless horror. He crouches back, his eyes staring past me at some unseen fear. Then his mouth opens. He gives forth a strangulated cry and topples backward off the hatch, striking his head against the deck. Fearing I know not what, I turn to look.

Great Heavens! Rising above the bulwarks, seen plainly in the bright moonlight, is a vast slobbering mouth a fathom across. From the huge dripping lips hang great tentacles. As I look the Thing comes further over the rail. It is rising, rising, higher and higher. There are no eyes visible; only that fearful slobbering mouth set on the tremendous trunk-like neck; which, even as I watch, is curling inboard with the stealthy celerity of an enormous eel. Over it comes in vast heaving folds. Will it never end? The ship gives a slow, sullen roll to starboard as she feels the weight. Then the tail, a broad, flat-shaped mass, slips over the teak rail and falls with a loud slump on to the deck.

For a few seconds the hideous creature lies heaped in writhing, slimy coils. Then, with quick, darting movements, the monstrous head travels along the deck. Close by the mainmast stand the harness casks, and alongside of these a freshly opened cask of salt beef with the top loosely replaced. The smell of the meat seems to attract the monster, and I can hear it sniffing with a vast indrawing breath. Then those lips open, displaying four huge fangs; there is a quick forward motion of the head, a sudden crashing, crunching sound, and beef and barrel have disappeared. The noise brings one of the ordinary seamen out of the fo'cas'le. Coming into the night, he can see nothing for a moment. Then, as he gets further aft, he *sees*, and with horrified cries rushes forward. Too late! From the mouth of the Thing there flashes forth a long, broad blade of glistening white, set with fierce teeth. I avert my eyes, but cannot shut out the sickening "Glut! Glut!" that follows.

The man on the "look-out," attracted by the disturbance, has witnessed the tragedy, and flies for refuge into the fo'cas'le, flinging to the heavy iron door after him.

The carpenter and sailmaker come running out from the half-deck in their drawers. Seeing the awful Thing, they rush aft to the cabin with shouts of fear. The second mate, after one glance over the break of the poop, runs down the companion-way with the helmsman after him. I can hear them barring the scuttle, and abruptly I realise that I am on the main deck alone.

So far I have forgotten my own danger. The past few minutes seem like a portion of an awful dream. Now, however, I comprehend my position and, shaking off the horror that has held me, turn to seek safety. As I do so my eyes fall upon Joky, lying huddled and senseless with fright where he has fallen. I cannot leave him there. Close by stands the empty half-deck—a little steel-built house with iron doors. The lee one is hooked open. Once inside I am safe.

Up to the present the Thing has seemed to be unconscious of my presence. Now, however, the huge barrel-like head sways in my direction; then comes a muffled bellow, and the great tongue flickers in and out as the brute turns and swirls aft to meet me. I know there is not a moment to lose, and, picking up the helpless lad, I make a run for the open door. It is only distant a few yards, but that awful shape is coming down the deck to me in great wreathing coils. I reach the house and tumble in with my burden; then out on deck again to unhook and close the door. Even as I do so something white curls round the end of the house. With a bound I am inside and the door is shut and bolted. Through the thick glass of the ports I see the Thing sweep round the house, in vain search for me.

Joky has not moved yet; so, kneeling down, I loosen his shirt collar and sprinkle some water from the breaker over his face. While I am doing this I hear Morgan shout something; then comes a great shriek of terror, and again that sickening "Glut! Glut!"

Joky stirs uneasily, rubs his eyes, and sits up suddenly.

"Was that Morgan shouting—?" He breaks off with a cry. "Where are we? I have had such awful dreams!"

At this instant there is a sound of running footsteps on the deck and I hear Morgan's voice at the door.

"Tom, open—!"

He stops abruptly and gives an awful cry of despair. Then I hear him rush forward. Through the porthole, I see him spring into the fore rigging and scramble madly aloft. Something steals up after him. It shows white in the moonlight. It wraps itself around his right ankle. Morgan stops dead, plucks out his sheath-knife, and hacks fiercely at the fiendish thing. It lets go, and in a second he is over the top and running for dear life up the t'gallant rigging.

A time of quietness follows, and presently I see that the day is breaking. Not a sound can be heard save the heavy gasping breathing of the Thing. As the sun rises higher the creature stretches itself out along the deck and seems to enjoy the warmth. Still no sound, either from the men forward or the officers aft. I can only suppose that they are afraid of attracting its attention. Yet, a little later, I hear the report of a pistol away aft, and looking out I see the serpent raise its huge head as though listening. As it does so I get a good view of the fore part, and in the daylight see what the night has hidden.

There, right about the mouth, is a pair of little pig-eyes, that seem to twinkle with a diabolical intelligence. It is swaying its head slowly from side to side; then, without warning, it turns quickly and looks right in through the port. I dodge out of sight; but not soon enough. It has seen me, and brings its great mouth up against the glass.

I hold my breath. My God! If it breaks the glass! I cower, horrified. From the direction of the port there comes a loud, harsh, scraping sound. I shiver. Then I remember that there are little iron doors to shut over the ports in bad weather. Without a moment's waste of time I rise to my feet and slam to the door over the port. Then I go round to the others and do the same. We are now in darkness, and I tell Joky in a whisper to light the lamp, which, after some fumbling, he does.

About an hour before midnight I fall asleep. I am awakened suddenly some hours later by a scream of agony and the rattle of a water-dipper. There is a slight scuffling sound; then that soul-revolting "Glut! Glut!"

I guess what has happened. One of the men forrard has slipped out of the fo'cas'le to try and get a little water. Evidently he has trusted to the darkness to hide his movements. Poor beggar! He has paid for his attempt with his life!

After this I cannot sleep, though the rest of the night passes quietly enough. Towards morning I doze a bit, but wake every few minutes with a start. Joky is sleeping peacefully; indeed, he seems worn out with the terrible strain of the past twenty-four hours. About eight a.m. I call him, and we make a light breakfast off the dry ship's biscuit and water. Of the latter happily we have a good supply. Joky seems more himself, and starts to talk a little—possibly somewhat louder than is safe; for, as he chatters on, wondering how it will end, there comes a tremendous blow against the side of the house, making it ring again. After this Joky is very silent. As we sit there I cannot but wonder what all the rest are doing, and how the poor beggars forrard are faring, cooped up without water, as the tragedy of the night has proved.

Towards noon, I hear a loud bang, followed by a terrific bellowing. Then comes a great smashing of woodwork, and the cries of men in pain. Vainly I ask myself what has happened. I begin to reason. By the sound of the report it was evidently something much heavier than a rifle or pistol, and judging from the mad roaring of the Thing, the shot must have done some execution. On thinking it over further, I become convinced that, by some means, those aft have got hold of the small signal cannon we carry, and though I know that some have been hurt, perhaps killed, yet a feeling of exultation seizes me as I listen to the roars of the Thing, and realise that it is badly wounded, perhaps mortally. After a while, however, the bellowing dies away, and only an occasional roar, denoting more of anger than aught else, is heard.

Presently I become aware, by the ship's canting over to starboard, that the creature has gone over to that side, and a great hope springs up within me that possibly it has had enough of us and is going over the rail into the sea. For a time all is silent and my hope grows stronger. I lean across and nudge Joky, who is sleeping with his head on the table. He starts up sharply with a loud cry.

"Hush!" I whisper hoarsely. "I'm not certain, but I do believe it's gone."

Joky's face brightens wonderfully, and he questions me eagerly. We wait another hour or so, with hope ever rising. Our confidence is returning fast. Not a sound can we hear, not even the breathing of the Beast. I get out some biscuits, and Joky, after rummaging in the locker, produces a small piece of pork and a bottle of ship's vinegar. We fall to with a relish. After our long abstinence from food the meal acts on us like wine, and what must Joky do but insist on opening the door, to make sure the Thing has gone. This I will not allow, telling him that at least it will be safer to open the iron port-covers first and have a look out. Joky argues, but I am immovable. He becomes excited. I believe the youngster is light-headed. Then, as I turn to unscrew one of the after-covers, Joky makes a dash at the door. Before he can undo the bolts I have him, and after a short struggle lead him back to the table. Even as I endeavour to quieten him there comes at the starboard door—the door that Joky has tried to open—a sharp, loud sniff, sniff, followed immediately by a thunderous grunting howl and a foul stench of putrid breath sweeps in under the door. A great trembling takes me, and were it not for the carpenter's tool-chest I should fall. Joky turns very white and is violently sick, after which he is seized by a hopeless fit of sobbing.

Hour after hour passes, and, weary to death, I lie down on the chest upon which I have been sitting, and try to rest.

It must be about half-past two in the morning, after a somewhat longer doze, that I am suddenly awakened by a most tremendous uproar away forrard—men's voices shrieking, cursing, praying; but in spite of the terror expressed, so weak and feeble; while in the midst, and at times broken off short with that hellishly suggestive "Glut! Glut!" is the unearthly bellowing of the Thing. Fear incarnate seizes me, and I can only fall on my knees and pray. Too well I know what is happening.

Joky has slept through it all, and I am thankful.

Presently, under the door there steals a narrow riband of light, and I know that the day has broken on the second morning of our imprisonment. I let Joky sleep on. I will let him have peace while he may. Time passes, but I take little notice. The Thing is quiet, probably sleeping. About midday I eat a little biscuit and drink some of the water. Joky still sleeps. It is best so.

A sound breaks the stillness. The ship gives a slight heave, and I know that once more the Thing is awake. Round the deck it moves, causing the ship to roll perceptibly. Once it goes forrard—I fancy to again explore the fo'cas'le. Evidently it finds nothing, for it returns almost immediately. It pauses a moment at the house, then goes on further aft. Up aloft, somewhere in the fore-rigging, there rings out a peal of wild laughter, though sounding very faint and far away. The Horror stops suddenly. I listen intently, but hear nothing save a sharp creaking beyond the after end of the house, as though a strain had come upon the rigging.

A minute later I hear a cry aloft, followed almost instantly by a loud crash on deck that seems to shake the ship. I wait in anxious fear. What is happening? The minutes pass slowly. Then comes another frightened shout. It ceases suddenly. The suspense has become terrible, and I am no longer able to bear it. Very cautiously I open one of the after port-covers, and peep out to see a fearful sight. There, with its tail upon the deck and its vast body curled round the mainmast, is the monster, its head above the topsail yard, and its great claw-armed tentacle waving in the air. It is the first proper sight that I have had of the Thing. Good Heavens! It must weigh a hundred tons! Knowing that I shall have time, I open the port itself, then crane my head out and look up. There on the extreme end of the lower topsail yard I see one of the able seamen. Even down here I note the staring horror of his face. At this moment he sees me and gives a weak, hoarse cry for help. I can do nothing for him. As I look the great tongue shoots out and licks him off the yard, much as might a dog a fly off the window-pane.

Higher still, but happily out of reach, are two more of the men. As far as I can judge they are lashed to the mast above the royal yard. The Thing attempts to reach them, but after a futile effort it ceases, and starts to slide down, coil on coil, to the deck. While doing this I notice a great gaping wound on its body some twenty feet above the tail.

I drop my gaze from aloft and look aft. The cabin door is torn from its hinges, and the bulkhead—which, unlike the half-deck, is of teak wood—is partly broken down. With a shudder I realise the cause of those cries after the cannon-shot. Turning I screw my head round and try to see the foremast, but cannot. The sun, I notice, is low, and the night is near. Then I draw in my head and fasten up both port and cover.

How will it end? Oh! how will it end?

After a while Joky wakes up. He is very restless, yet though he has eaten nothing during the day I cannot get him to touch anything.

Night draws on. We are too weary—too dispirited to talk. I lie down, but not to sleep. . . . Time passes.

*   *   *   *   *

A ventilator rattles violently somewhere on the maindeck, and there sounds constantly that slurring, gritty noise. Later I hear a cat's agonised howl, and then again all is quiet. Some time after comes a great splash alongside. Then, for some hours all is silent as the grave. Occasionally I sit up on the chest and listen, yet never a whisper of noise comes to me. There is an absolute silence, even the monotonous creak of the gear has died away entirely, and at last a real hope is springing up within me. That splash, this silence—surely I am justified in hoping. I do not wake Joky this time. I will prove first for myself that all is safe. Still I wait. I will run no unnecessary risks. After a time I creep to the after-port and listen; but there is no sound. I put up my hand and feel at the screw, then again I hesitate, yet not for long. Noiselessly I begin to unscrew the fastening of the heavy shield. It swings loose on its hinge, and I pull it back and peer out. My heart is beating madly. Everything seems strangely dark outside. Perhaps the moon has gone behind a cloud. Suddenly a beam of moonlight enters through the port, and goes as quickly. I stare out. Something moves. Again the light streams in, and now I seem to be looking into a great cavern, at the bottom of which quivers and curls something palely white.

My heart seems to stand still! It is the Horror! I start back and seize the iron port-flap to slam it to. As I do so, something strikes the glass like a steam ram, shatters it to atoms, and flicks past me into the berth. I scream and spring away. The port is quite filled with it. The lamp shows it dimly. It is curling and twisting here and there. It is as thick as a tree, and covered with a smooth slimy skin. At the end is a great claw, like a lobster's, only a thousand times larger. I cower down into the farthest corner. . . . It has broken the tool-chest to pieces with one click of those frightful mandibles. Joky has crawled under a bunk. The Thing sweeps round in my direction. I feel a drop of sweat trickle slowly down my face—it tastes salty. Nearer comes that awful death. . . . Crash! I roll over backwards. It has crushed the water breaker against which I leant, and I am rolling in the water across the floor. The claw drives up, then down, with a quick uncertain movement, striking the deck a dull, heavy blow, a foot from my head. Joky gives a little gasp of horror. Slowly the Thing rises and starts feeling its way round the berth. It plunges into a bunk and pulls out a bolster, nips it in half and drops it, then moves on. It is feeling along the deck. As it does so it comes across a half of the bolster. It seems to toy with it, then picks it up and takes it out through the port. . . .

A wave of putrid air fills the berth. There is a grating sound, and something enters the port again—something white and tapering and set with teeth. Hither and thither it curls, rasping over the bunks, ceiling, and deck, with a noise like that of a great saw at work. Twice it flickers above my head, and I close my eyes. Then off it goes again. It sounds now on the opposite side of the berth and nearer to Joky. Suddenly the harsh, raspy noise becomes muffled, as though the teeth were passing across some soft substance. Joky gives a horrid little scream, that breaks off into a bubbling, whistling sound. I open my eyes. The tip of the vast tongue is curled tightly round something that drips, then is quickly withdrawn, allowing the moonbeams to steal again into the berth. I rise to my feet. Looking round, I note in a mechanical sort of way the wrecked state of the berth—the shattered chests, dismantled bunks, and something else—

"Joky!" I cry, and tingle all over.

There is that awful Thing again at the port. I glance round for a weapon. I will revenge Joky. Ah! there, right under the lamp, where the wreck of the carpenter's chest strews the floor, lies a small hatchet. I spring forward and seize it. It is small, but so keen—so keen! I feel its razor edge lovingly. Then I am back at the port. I stand to one side, and raise my weapon. The great tongue is feeling its way to those fearsome remains. It reaches them. As it does so, with a scream of "Joky! Joky!" I strike savagely again and again and again, gasping as I strike; once more, and the monstrous mass falls to the deck, writhing like a hideous eel. A vast, warm flood rushes in through the porthole. There is a sound of breaking steel and an enormous bellowing. A singing comes in my ears and grows louder—louder. Then the berth grows indistinct and suddenly dark.

*   *   *   *   *

Extract from the log of the steamship *Hispaniola*:

June 24. —Lat. —N. Long. —W. 11 a.m. — Sighted four-masted barque about four points on the port bow, flying signal of distress. Ran down to her and sent a boat aboard. She proved to be the *Glen Doon*, homeward bound from Melbourne to London. Found things in a terrible state. Decks covered with blood and slime. Steel deck-house stove in. Broke open door, and discovered youth of about nineteen in last stage of inanition, also part remains of boy about fourteen years of age. There was a great quantity of blood in the place, and a huge curled-up mass of whitish flesh, weighing about half a ton, one end of which appeared to have been hacked through with a sharp instrument. Found forecastle door open and hanging from one hinge. Doorway bulged, as though something had been forced through. Went inside. Terrible state of affairs, blood everywhere, broken chests, smashed bunks, but no men nor remains. Went aft again and found youth showing signs of recovery. When he came round, gave the name of Thompson. Said they had been attacked by a huge serpent—thought it must have been sea-serpent. He was too weak to say much, but told us there were some men up the mainmast. Sent a hand aloft, who reported them lashed to the royal mast, and quite dead. Went aft to the cabin. Here we found the bulkhead smashed to pieces, and the cabin-door lying on the deck near the after-hatch. Found body of captain down lazarette, but no officers. Noticed amongst the wreckage part of the carriage of a small cannon. Came aboard again.

Have sent the second mate with six men to work her into port. Thompson is with us. He has written out his version of the affair. We certainly consider that the state of the ship, as we found her, bears out in every respect his story. (Signed)

William Norton (Master).
Tom Briggs (lst Mate).

Thou Living Sea

Thou broad, great, living sea;
    Great in thy boundless spread;
With many tongues thy voices speak to me,
    With voices from the dead.

The splendour of thy sights;
    The vastness of thy flood;
The dim, o'er-curving shadows; and the lights
    That cover thee with blood—

Or golden glory, seen
    When falls the evening sun
Behind that vivid edge of wat'ry green,
    Before the night's begun.

Yet ever speaks the gloom
    That lurks beneath thy waves;
And whisperings of mystery and doom
    Rise ghostly from thy graves.

The deepness of thy vasts
    Fills my poor soul with fright;
Fills me with fearfulness; O dreadful vasts!
    O caverns of the night!

Still, thy great peacefulness;
    Thy gently heaving breast;
The shimmering stillness of thy silent dress
    Speak words to me of rest.

So when in rage thy howls
    Go shrieking, 'cross the sky,
Thy very mountain-crests and briny bowels

Shout out and prophesy.
At night hast thou with tongue
        Of murmuring waters, spelt
Out stories that have saddened me and wrung
        My soul with sorrows felt.

At times I've heard thee speak
        Of unknown shining gold;
Of treasures in thy depths that none shall seek;
        And wonderland untold.

But better far than these,
        The things thou toldest me,
That came to me upon the crooning breeze
        That whispers o'er the sea.

The wisdom of the years
        Was in thy counselling:
And subtle thoughts spoke ever in thy tears;
        Fine thoughts to which I cling.

Thus thou, O Sea, and I,
        In storms and calms have grown
To greater, broader knowledge—thou and I;
        A knowledge of our own.

And thou, O Sea, at last;
        Thou whom I dread and love,
Shalt take me in thine arms when I have passed,
        And usher me above.

The Mystery of the Derelict

All the night had the four-masted ship, *Tarawak*, lain motionless in the drift of the Gulf Stream; for she had run into a "calm patch"—into a stark calm which had lasted now for two days and nights.

On every side, had it been light, might have been seen dense masses of floating gulf-weed, studding the ocean even to the distant horizon. In places, so large were the weed-masses that they formed long, low banks, that, by daylight, might have been mistaken for low-lying land.

Upon the lee side of the poop, Duthie, one of the 'prentices, leaned with his elbows upon the rail, and stared out across the hidden sea, to where in the Eastern horizon showed the first pink and lemon streamers of the dawn—faint, delicate streaks and washes of colour.

A period of time passed, and the surface of the leeward sea began to show—a great expanse of grey, touched with odd, wavering belts of silver. And everywhere the black specks and islets of the weed.

Presently, the red dome of the sun protruded itself into sight above the dark rim of the horizon; and, abruptly, the watching Duthie saw something—a great, shapeless bulk that lay some miles away to starboard, and showed black and distinct against the gloomy red mass of the rising sun.

"Something in sight to looard, Sir," he informed the Mate, who was leaning, smoking, over the rail that ran across the break of the poop. "I can't just make out what it is."

The Mate rose from his easy position, stretched himself, yawned, and came across to the boy.

"Whereabouts, Toby?" he asked, wearily, and yawning again.

"There, Sir," said Duthie—alias Toby—"broad away on the beam, and right in the track of the sun. It looks something like a big houseboat, or a haystack."

The Mate stared in the direction indicated, and saw the thing which puzzled the boy, and immediately the tiredness went out of his eyes and face.

"Pass me the glasses off the skylight, Toby," he commanded, and the youth obeyed.

After the Mate had examined the strange object through his binoculars for, maybe, a minute, he passed them to Toby, telling him to take a "squint," and say what he made of it.

"Looks like an old powder-hulk, Sir," exclaimed the lad, after awhile, and to this description the Mate nodded agreement.

Later, when the sun had risen somewhat, they were able to study the derelict with more exactness. She appeared to be a vessel of an exceedingly old type, mastless, and upon the hull of which had been built a roof-like superstructure; the use of which they could not determine. She was lying just within the borders of one of the weed-banks, and all her side was splotched with a greenish growth.

It was her position, within the borders of the weed, that suggested to the puzzled Mate, how so strange and unseaworthy looking a craft had come so far abroad into the greatness of the ocean. For, suddenly, it occurred to him that she was neither more nor less than a derelict from the vast Sargasso Sea—a vessel that had, possibly, been lost to the world, scores and scores of years gone, perhaps hundreds. The suggestion touched the Mate's thoughts with solemnity, and he fell to examining the ancient hulk with an even greater interest, and pondering on all the lonesome and awful years that must have passed over her, as she had lain desolate and forgotten in that grim cemetery of the ocean.

Through all that day, the derelict was an object of the most intense interest to those aboard the *Tarawak*, every glass in the ship being brought into use to examine her. Yet, though within no more than some six or seven miles of her, the Captain refused to listen to the Mate's suggestions that they should put a boat into the water, and pay the stranger a visit; for he was a cautious man, and the glass warned him that a sudden change might be expected in the weather; so that he would have no one leave the ship on any unnecessary business. But, for all that he had caution, curiosity was by no means lacking in him, and his telescope, at intervals, was turned on the ancient hulk through all the day.

Then, it would be about six bells in the second dog watch, a sail was sighted astern, coming up steadily but slowly. By eight bells they were able to make out that a small barque was bringing the wind with her; her yards squared, and every stitch set. Yet the night had advanced apace, and it was nigh to eleven o'clock before the wind reached those aboard the *Tarawak*. When at last it arrived, there was a slight rustling and quaking of canvas, and odd creaks here and there in the darkness amid the gear, as each portion of the running and standing rigging took up the strain.

Beneath the bows, and alongside, there came gentle rippling noises, as the vessel gathered way; and so, for the better part of the next hour, they slid through the water at something less than a couple of knots in the sixty minutes.

To starboard of them, they could see the red light of the little barque, which had brought up the wind with her, and was now forging slowly ahead, being better able evidently than the big, heavy *Tarawak* to take advantage of so slight a breeze.

201

About a quarter to twelve, just after the relieving watch had been roused, lights were observed to be moving to and fro upon the small barque, and by midnight it was palpable that, through some cause or other, she was dropping astern.

When the Mate arrived on deck to relieve the Second, the latter officer informed him of the possibility that something unusual had occurred aboard the barque, telling of the lights about her decks,[1] and how that, in the last quarter of an hour, she had begun to drop astern.

On hearing the Second Mate's account, the First sent one of the 'prentices for his night-glasses, and, when they were brought, studied the other vessel intently, that is, so well as he was able through the darkness; for, even through the night-glasses, she showed only as a vague shape, surmounted by the three dim towers of her masts and sails.

Suddenly, the Mate gave out a sharp exclamation; for, beyond the barque, there was something else shown dimly in the field of vision. He studied it with great intentness, ignoring for the instant, the Second's queries as to what it was that had caused him to exclaim.

All at once, he said, with a little note of excitement in his voice:—

"The derelict! The barque's run into the weed around that old hooker!"

The Second Mate gave a mutter of surprised assent, and slapped the rail.

"That's it!" he said. "That's why we're passing her. And that explains the lights. If they're not fast in the weed, they've probably run slap into the blessed derelict!"

"One thing," said the Mate, lowering his glasses, and beginning to fumble for his pipe, "she won't have had enough way on her to do much damage."

The Second Mate, who was still peering through his binoculars, murmured an absent agreement, and continued to peer. The Mate, for his part, filled and lit his pipe, remarking meanwhile to the unhearing Second, that the light breeze was dropping.

Abruptly, the Second Mate called his superior's attention, and in the same instant, so it seemed, the failing wind died entirely away, the sails settling down into runkles, with little rustles and flutters of sagging canvas.

"What's up?" asked the Mate, and raised his glasses.

"There's something queer going on over yonder," said the Second. "Look at the lights moving about, and—Did you see *that*?"

The last portion of his remark came out swiftly, with a sharp accentuation of the last word.

"What?" asked the Mate, staring hard.

"They're shooting," replied the Second. "Look! There again!"

"Rubbish!" said the Mate, a mixture of unbelief and doubt in his voice.

With the falling of the wind, there had come a great silence upon the sea. And, abruptly, from far across the water, sounded the distant, dullish thud of a gun,

---

[1]Unshaded lights are never allowed about the decks at night, as they are likely to blind the vision of the officer of the watch.—W. H. H.

followed almost instantly by several minute, but sharply defined, reports, like the cracking of a whip out in the darkness.

"Jove!" cried the Mate, "I believe you're right." He paused and stared. "There!" he said. "I saw the flashes then. They're firing from the poop, I believe. . . . I must call the Old Man."

He turned and ran hastily down into the saloon, knocked on the door of the Captain's cabin, and entered. He turned up the lamp, and, shaking his superior into wakefulness, told him of the thing he believed to be happening aboard the barque:—

"It's mutiny, Sir; they're shooting from the poop. We ought to do something—" The Mate said many things, breathlessly; for he was a young man; but the Captain stopped him, with a quietly lifted hand.

"I'll be up with you in a minute, Mr. Johnson," he said, and the Mate took the hint, and ran up on deck.

Before the minute had passed, the Skipper was on the poop, and staring through his night-glasses at the barque and the derelict. Yet now, aboard of the barque, the lights had vanished, and there showed no more the flashes of discharging weapons—only there remained the dull, steady red glow of the port sidelight; and, behind it, the night-glasses showed the shadowy outline of the vessel.

The Captain put questions to the Mates, asking for further details.

"It all stopped while the Mate was calling you, Sir," explained the Second. "We could hear the shots quite plainly."

They seemed to be using a gun as well as their revolvers," interjected the Mate, without ceasing to stare into the darkness.

For awhile the three of them continued to discuss the matter, whilst down on the maindeck the two watches clustered along the starboard rail, and a low hum of talk rose, fore and aft.

Presently, the Captain and the Mates came to a decision. If there had been a mutiny, it had been brought to its conclusion, whatever that conclusion might be, and no interference from those aboard the *Tarawak*, at that period, would be likely to do good. They were utterly in the dark—in more ways than one—and, for all they knew, there might not even have been any mutiny. If there had been a mutiny, and the mutineers had won, then they had done their worst; whilst if the officers had won, well and good. They had managed to do so without help. Of course, if the *Tarawak* had been a man-of-war with a large crew, capable of mastering any situation, it would have been a simple matter to send a powerful, armed boat's crew to inquire; but as she was merely a merchant vessel, under-manned, as is the modern fashion, they must go warily. They would wait for the morning, and signal. In a couple of hours it would be light. Then they would be guided by circumstances.

The Mate walked to the break of the poop, and sang out to the men:—

"Now then, my lads, you'd better turn in, the watch below, and have a sleep; we may be wanting you by five bells."

There was a muttered chorus of "i, i, Sir," and some of the men began to go forrard to the fo'cas'le; but others of the watch below remained, their curiosity overmastering their desire for sleep.

On the poop, the three officers leaned over the starboard rail, chatting in a desultory fashion, as they waited for the dawn. At some little distance hovered Duthie, who, as eldest 'prentice just out of his time, had been given the post of acting Third Mate.

Presently, the sky to starboard began to lighten with the solemn coming of the dawn. The light grew and strengthened, and the eyes of those in the *Tarawak* scanned with growing intentness that portion of the horizon where showed the red and dwindling glow of the barque's sidelight.

Then, it was in that moment when all the world is full of the silence of the dawn, something passed over the quiet sea, coming out of the East—a very faint, long-drawn-out, screaming, piping noise. It might almost have been the cry of a little wind wandering out of the dawn across the sea—a ghostly, piping skirl, so attenuated and elusive was it; but there was in it a weird, almost threatening note, that told the three on the poop it was no wind that made so dree and inhuman a sound.

The noise ceased, dying out in an indefinite, mosquito-like shrilling, far and vague and minutely shrill. And so came the silence again.

"I heard that, last night, when they were shooting," said the Second Mate, speaking very slowly, and looking first at the Skipper and then at the Mate. "It was when you were below, calling the Captain," he added.

"Ssh!" said the Mate, and held up a warning hand; but though they listened, there came no further sound; and so they fell to disjointed questionings, and guessed their answers, as puzzled men will. And ever and anon, they examined the barque through their glasses; but without discovering anything of note, save that, when the light grew stronger, they perceived that her jibboom had struck through the superstructure of the derelict, tearing a considerable gap therein.

Presently, when the day had sufficiently advanced, the Mate sung out to the Third, to take a couple of the 'prentices, and pass up the signal flags and the code book. This was done, and a "hoist" made; but those in the barque took not the slightest heed; so that finally the Captain bade them make up the flags and return them to the locker.

After that, he went down to consult the glass, and when he reappeared, he and the Mates had a short discussion, after which, orders were given to hoist out the starboard life-boat. This, in the course of half an hour, they managed; and, after that, six of the men and two of the 'prentices were ordered into her.

Then half a dozen rifles were passed down, with ammunition, and the same number of cutlasses. These were all apportioned among the men, much to the disgust of the two apprentices, who were aggrieved that they should be passed over; but their feelings altered when the Mate descended into the boat, and handed them each a loaded revolver, warning them, however, to play no "monkey tricks" with the weapons.

Just as the boat was about to push off, Duthie, the eldest 'prentice, came scrambling down the side ladder, and jumped for the after thwart. He landed, and sat down, laying the rifle which he had brought, in the stern; and, after that, the boat put off for the barque.

There were now ten in the boat, and all well armed, so that the Mate had a certain feeling of comfort that he would be able to meet any situation that was likely to arise.

After nearly an hour's hard pulling, the heavy boat had been brought within some two hundred yards of the barque, and the Mate sung out to the men to lie on their oars for a minute. Then he stood up and shouted to the people on the barque; but though he repeated his cry of "Ship ahoy!" several times, there came no reply.

He sat down, and motioned to the men to give way again, and so brought the boat nearer the barque by another hundred yards. Here, he hailed again; but still receiving no reply, he stooped for his binoculars, and peered for a while through them at the two vessels—the ancient derelict, and the modern sailing-vessel.

The latter had driven clean in over the weed, her stern being perhaps some two score yards from the edge of the bank. Her jibboom, as I have already mentioned, had pierced the green-blotched superstructure of the derelict, so that her cutwater had come very close to the grass-grown side of the hulk.

That the derelict was indeed a very ancient vessel, it was now easy to see; for at this distance the Mate could distinguish which was hull, and which superstructure. Her stern rose up to a height considerably above her bows, and possessed galleries, coming round the counter. In the window frames some of the glass still remained; but others were securely shuttered, and some missing, frames and all, leaving dark holes in the stern. And everywhere grew the dank, green growth, giving to the beholder a queer sense of repulsion. Indeed, there was that about the whole of the ancient craft, that repelled in a curious way—something elusive—a remoteness from humanity, that was vaguely abominable.

The Mate put down his binoculars, and drew his revolver, and, at the action, each one in the boat gave an instinctive glance to his own weapon. Then he sung out to them to give-way, and steered straight for the weed. The boat struck it, with something of a sog; and, after that, they advanced slowly, yard by yard, only with considerable labour.

They reached the counter of the barque, and the Mate held out his hand for an oar. This, he leaned up against the side of the vessel, and a moment later was swarming quickly up it. He grasped the rail, and swung himself aboard; then, after a swift glance fore and aft, gripped the blade of the oar, to steady it, and bade the rest follow as quickly as possible, which they did, the last man bringing up the painter with him, and making it fast to a cleat.

Then commenced a rapid search through the ship. In several places about the main-deck they found broken lamps, and aft on the poop, a shot-gun, three revolvers, and several capstan-bars lying about the poop-deck. But though they pried into every possible corner, lifting the hatches, and examining the lazarette, not a human creature was to be found—the barque was absolutely deserted.

After the first rapid search, the Mate called his men together; for there was an uncomfortable sense of danger in the air, and he felt that it would be better not to straggle. Then, he led the way forrard, and went up on to the t'gallant fo'cas'le head. Here, finding the port sidelight still burning, he bent over the screen, as it were mechanically, lifted the lamp, opened it, and blew out the flame; then replaced the affair on its socket.

After that, he climbed into the bows, and out along the jibboom, beckoning to the others to follow, which they did, no man saying a word, and all holding their weapons handily; for each felt the oppressiveness of the Incomprehensible about them.

The Mate reached the hole in the great superstructure, and passed inside, the rest following. Here they found themselves in what looked something like a great, gloomy barracks, the floor of which was the deck of the ancient craft. The superstructure, as seen from the inside, was a very wonderful piece of work, being beautifully shored and fixed; so that at one time it must have possessed immense strength; though now it was all rotted, and showed many a gape and rip. In one place, near the centre, or midships part, was a sort of platform, high up, which the Mate conjectured might have been used as a "look-out"; though the reason for the prodigious superstructure itself, he could not imagine.

Having searched the decks of this craft, he was preparing to go below, when, suddenly, Duthie caught him by the sleeve, and whispered to him, tensely, to listen. He did so, and heard the thing that had attracted the attention of the youth—it was a low, continuous, shrill whining that was rising from out of the dark hull beneath their feet, and, abruptly, the Mate was aware that there was an intensely disagreeable animal-like smell in the air. He had noticed it, in a subconscious fashion, when entering through the broken superstructure; but now, suddenly, he was *aware* of it.

Then, as he stood there hesitating, the whining noise rose all at once into a piping, screaming squeal, that filled all the space in which they were inclosed, with an awful, inhuman and threatening clamour. The Mate turned and shouted at the top of his voice to the rest, to retreat to the barque, and he, himself, after a further quick nervous glance round, hurried towards the place where the end of the barque's jibboom protruded in across the decks.

He waited, with strained impatience, glancing ever behind him, until all were off the derelict, and then sprang swiftly on to the spar that was their bridge to the other vessel. Even as he did so, the squealing died away into a tiny shrilling, twittering sound, that made him glance back; for the suddenness of the quiet was as effective as though it had been a loud noise. What he saw, seemed to him in that first instant so incredible and monstrous, that he was almost too shaken to cry out. Then he raised his voice in a shout of warning to the men, and a frenzy of haste shook him in every fibre, as he scrambled back to the barque, shouting ever to the men to get into the boat. For in that backward glance, he had seen the whole decks of the derelict a-move with living things—giant rats, thousands and tens of thousands of them; and so in a flash had come to an understanding of the disappearance of the crew of the barque.

He had reached the fo'cas'le head now, and was running for the steps, and behind him, making all the long slanting length of the jibboom black, were the rats, racing after him. He made one leap to the maindeck, and ran. Behind, sounded a queer, multitudinous pattering noise, swiftly surging upon him. He reached the poop steps, and as he sprang up them, felt a savage bite in his left calf. He was on the poop-deck now, and running with a stagger. A score of great rats leapt around him, and half a dozen hung grimly to his back, whilst the one that had gripped his calf, flogged madly from side to side as he raced on. He reached the rail, gripped it, and vaulted clean over and down into the weed.

The rest were already in the boat, and strong hands and arms hove him aboard, whilst the others of the crew sweated in getting their little craft round from the ship. The rats still clung to the Mate; but a few blows with a cutlass eased him of his murderous burden. Above them, making the rails and half-round of the poop black and alive, raced thousands of rats.

The boat was now about an oar's length from the barque, and, suddenly, Duthie screamed out that *they* were coming. In the same instant, nearly a hundred of the largest rats launched themselves at the boat. Most fell short, into the weed; but over a score reached the boat, and sprang savagely at the men, and there was a minute's hard slashing and smiting, before the brutes were destroyed.

Once more the men resumed their task of urging their way through the weed, and so in a minute or two, had come to within some fathoms of the edge, working desperately. Then a fresh terror broke upon them. Those rats which had missed their leap, were now all about the boat, and leaping in from the weed, running up the oars, and scrambling in over the sides, and, as each one got inboard, straight for one of the crew it went; so that they were all bitten and be-bled in a score of places.

There ensued a short but desperate fight, and then, when the last of the beasts had been hacked to death, the men lay once more to the task of heaving the boat clear of the weed.

A minute passed, and they had come almost to the edge, when Duthie cried out, to look; and at that, all turned to stare at the barque, and perceived the thing that had caused the 'prentice to cry out; for the rats were leaping down into the weed in black multitudes, making the great weed-fronds quiver, as they hurled themselves in the direction of the boat. In an incredibly short space of time, all the weed between the boat and the barque, was alive with the little monsters, coming at break-neck speed.

The Mate let out a shout, and, snatching an oar from one of the men, leapt into the stern of the boat, and commenced to thrash the weed with it, whilst the rest laboured infernally to pluck the boat forth into the open sea. Yet, despite their mad efforts, and the death-dealing blows of the Mate's great fourteen-foot oar, the black, living mass were all about the boat, and scrambling aboard in scores, before she was free of the weed. As the boat shot into the clear water, the Mate gave out a great curse, and, dropping his oar, began to pluck the brutes from his body with his bare hands, casting them into the sea. Yet, fast almost as he freed himself, others sprang upon him, so that in another minute he was like to have been pulled down, for the boat was alive and swarming with the pests, but that some of the men got to work with their cutlasses, and literally slashed the brutes to pieces, sometimes killing several with a single blow. And thus, in a while, the boat was freed once more; though it was a sorely wounded and frightened lot of men that manned her.

The Mate himself took an oar, as did all those who were able. And so they rowed slowly and painfully away from that hateful derelict, whose crew of monsters even then made the weed all of a-heave with hideous life.

From the *Tarawak* came urgent signals for them to haste; by which the Mate knew that the storm, which the Captain had feared, must be coming down upon the ship, and so he spurred each one to greater endeavour, until, at last they were under the shadow of their own vessel, with very thankful hearts, and bodies, bleeding, tired and faint.

Slowly and painfully, the boat's crew scrambled up the side-ladder, and the boat was hoisted aboard; but they had no time then to tell their tale; for the storm was upon them.

It came half an hour later, sweeping down in a cloud of white fury from the Eastward, and blotting out all vestiges of the mysterious derelict and the little barque which had proved her victim. And after that, for a weary day and night, they battled with the storm. When it passed, nothing was to be seen, either of the two vessels or of the weed which had studded the sea before the storm; for they had been blown many a score of leagues to the Westward of the spot, and so had no further chance—nor, I ween, inclination—to investigate further the mystery of that strange old derelict of a past time, and her habitants of rats.

Yet, many a time, and in many fo'cas'les has this story been told; and many a conjecture has been passed as to how came that ancient craft abroad there in the ocean. Some have suggested—as indeed I have made bold to put forth as fact—that she must have drifted out of the lonesome Sargasso Sea. And, in truth, I cannot but think this the most reasonable supposition. Yet, of the rats that evidently dwelt in her, I have no reasonable explanation to offer. Whether they were true ship's rats, or a species that is to be found in the weed-haunted plains and islets of the Sargasso Sea, I cannot say. It may be that they are the descendants of rats that lived in ships long centuries lost in the Weed Sea, and which have learned to live among the weed, forming new characteristics, and developing fresh powers and instincts. Yet, I cannot say; for I speak entirely without authority, and do but tell this story as it is told in the fo'cas'le of many an old-time sailing ship-that dark, brine-tainted place where the young men learn somewhat of the mysteries of the all mysterious sea.

The Stone Ship

Rum things!—Of course rum things happen at sea— As rum as ever there were. I remember when I was in the *Alfred Jessop*, a small barque, whose owner was her skipper, we came across a most extraordinary thing.

· We were twenty days out from London, and well down into the tropics. It was before I took my ticket, and I was in the fo'cas'le. The day had passed without a breath of wind, and the night found us with all the lower sails up in the buntlines.

Now, I want you to take good note of what I am going to say:—

When it was dark in the second dog watch, there was not a sail in sight; not even the far off smoke of a steamer, and no land nearer than Africa, about a thousand miles to the Eastward of us.

It was our watch on deck from eight to twelve, midnight, and my look-out from eight to ten. For the first hour, I walked to and fore across the break of the fo'cas'le head, smoking my pipe and just listening to the quiet. . . . Ever heard the kind of silence you can get away out at sea? You need to be in one of the old time wind-jammers, with all the lights dowsed, and the sea as calm and quiet as some queer plain of death. And then you want a pipe and the lonesomeness of the fo'cas'le head, with the caps'n to lean against while you listen and think. And all about you, stretching out into the miles, only and always the enormous silence of the sea, spreading out a thousand miles every way into the everlasting, brooding night. And not a light anywhere, out on all the waste of waters; nor ever a sound, as I have told, except the faint moaning of the masts and gear, as they chafe and whine a little to the occasional invisible roll of the ship.

And suddenly, across all this silence, I heard Jensen's voice from the head of the starboard steps, say:—

"Did you hear *that*, Duprey?"

"What?" I asked, cocking my head up. But as I questioned, I heard what he heard—the constant sound of running water, for all the world like the noise of a brook running down a hill-side. And the queer sound was surely not a hundred fathoms off our port bow!

"By gum!" said Jensen's voice, out of the darkness. "That's damned sort of funny!"

"Shut up!" I whispered, and went across, in my bare feet, to the port rail, where I leaned out into the darkness, and stared towards the curious sound.

The noise of a brook running down a hill-side continued, where there was no brook for a thousand sea-miles in any direction.

"What is it?" said Jensen's voice again, scarcely above a whisper now. From below him, on the main-deck, there came several voices questioning:—"Hark!" "Stow the talk!" "... there!" "Listen!" "Lord love us, what is it?" ... And then Jensen muttering to them to be quiet.

There followed a full minute, during which we all heard the brook, where no brook could ever run; and then, out of the night there came a sudden hoarse incredible sound:—ooaaze, oooaze, arrrr, arrrr, oooaze—a stupendous sort of croak, deep and somehow abominable, out of the blackness. In the same instant, I found myself sniffing the air. There was a queer rank smell, stealing through the night.

"Forrard there on the look-out!" I heard the mate singing out, away aft. "Forrard there! What the blazes are you doing!"

I heard him come clattering down the port ladder from the poop, and then the sound of his feet at a run along the main-deck. Simultaneously, there was a thudding of bare feet, as the watch below came racing out of the fo'cas'le beneath me.

"Now then! Now then! Now then!" shouted the Mate, as he charged up on to the fo'cas'le head. "What's up?"

"It's something off the port bow, Sir." I said. "Running water! And then that sort of howl. . . . Your night-glasses," I suggested.

"Can't see a thing," he growled, as he stared away through the dark. "There's a sort of mist. Phoo! what a devil of a stink!"

"Look!" said someone down on the main-deck. "What's that?"

I saw it in the same instant, and caught the Mate's elbow.

"Look, Sir," I said. "There's a light there, about three points off the bow. It's moving."

The Mate was staring through his night-glasses, and suddenly he thrust them into my hands:—

"See if you can make it out," he said, and forthwith put his hands round his mouth, and bellowed into the night:—"Ahoy there! Ahoy there! Ahoy there!" his voice going out lost into the silence and darkness all around. But there came never a comprehensible answer, only all the time the infernal noise of a brook running out there on the sea, a thousand miles from any brook of earth; and away on the port bow, a vague shapeless shining.

I put the glasses to my eyes, and stared. The light was bigger and brighter, seen through the binoculars; but I could make nothing of it, only a dull, elongated shining, that moved vaguely in the darkness, apparently a hundred fathoms or so away on the sea.

"Ahoy there! Ahoy there!" sung out the Mate again. Then, to the men below:— "Quiet there on the main-deck!"

There followed about a minute of intense stillness, during which we all listened; but there was no sound, except the constant noise of water running steadily.

I was watching the curious shining, and I saw it flick out suddenly at the Mate's shout. Then in a moment I saw three dull lights, one under the other, that flicked in and out intermittently.

"Here, give me the glasses! said the Mate, and grabbed them from me.

He stared intensely for a moment; then swore, and turned to me:—

"What do you make of them?" he asked, abruptly.

"I don't know, Sir," I said. "I'm just puzzled. Perhaps it's electricity, or something of that sort."

"Oh hell!" he replied, and leant far out over the rail, staring. "Lord!" he said, for the second time, "what a stink!"

As he spoke, there came a most extraordinary thing; for there sounded a series of heavy reports out of the darkness, seeming in the silence, almost as loud as the sound of small cannon.

"They're shooting!" shouted a man on the main-deck, suddenly.

The Mate said nothing; only he sniffed violently at the night air. "By Gum!" he muttered, "what is it?"

I put my hand over my nose; for there was a terrible, charnel-like stench filling all the night about us.

"Take my glasses, Duprey," said the Mate, after a few minutes further watching. "Keep an eye over yonder. I'm going to call the Captain."

He pushed his way down the ladder, and hurried aft. About five minutes later, he returned forrard with the Captain and the Second and Third Mates, all in their shirts and trousers.

"Anything fresh, Duprey?" asked the Mate.

"No, Sir," I said, and handed him back his glasses. "The lights have gone again, and I think the mist is thicker. There's still the sound of running water out there."

The Captain and the three Mates stood some time along the port rail of the fo'cas'le head, watching through their night-glasses, and listening. Twice the Mate hailed; but there came no reply.

There was some talk, among the officers; and I gathered that the Captain was thinking of investigating.

"Clear one of the life-boats, Mr. Gelt," he said, at last. The glass is steady; there'll be no wind for hours yet. Pick out half a dozen men. Take 'em out of either watch, if they want to come. I'll be back when I've got my coat."

"Away aft with you, Duprey, and some of you others" said the Mate. "Get the cover off the port life-boat, and bail her out."

" 'i, 'i, Sir," I answered, and went away aft with the others.

We had the boat into the water within twenty minutes, which is good time for a wind-jammer, where boats are generally used as storage receptacles for odd gear.

I was one of the men told off to the boat, with two others from our watch, and one from the starboard.

The Captain came down the end of the main tops'l halyards into the boat, and the Third after him. The Third took the tiller, and gave orders to cast off.

We pulled out clear of our vessel, and the Skipper told us to lie on our oars for a moment while he took his bearings. He leant forward to listen, and we all did the same. The sound of the running water was quite distinct across the quietness; but it struck me as seeming not so loud as earlier.

I remember now, that I noticed how plain the mist had become—a sort of warm, wet mist; not a bit thick; but just enough to make the night very dark, and to be visible, eddying slowly in a thin vapour round the port side-light, looking like a red cloudiness swirling lazily through the red glow of the big lamp.

There was no other sound at this time, beyond the sound of the running water; and the Captain, after handing something to the Third Mate, gave the order to give-way.

I was rowing stroke, and close to the officers, and so was able to see dimly that the Captain had passed a heavy revolver over to the Third Mate.

"Ho!" I thought to myself, "so the Old Man's a notion there's really something dangerous over there."

I slipped a hand quickly behind me, and felt that my sheath knife was clear.

We pulled easily for about three or four minutes, with the sound of the water growing plainer somewhere ahead in the darkness; and astern of us, a vague red glowing through the night and vapour, showed where our vessel was lying.

We were rowing easily, when suddenly the bow-oar muttered "G'lord!" Immediately afterwards, there was a loud splashing in the water on his side of the boat.

"What's wrong in the bows, there?" asked the Skipper, sharply.

"There's somethin' in the water, Sir, messing round my oar," said the man.

I stopped rowing, and looked round. All the men did the same. There was a further sound of splashing, and the water was driven right over the boat in showers. Then the bow-oar called out:—"There's somethin' got a holt of my oar, Sir!"

I could tell the man was frightened; and I knew suddenly that a curious nervousness had come to me—a vague, uncomfortable dread, such as the memory of an ugly tale will bring, in a lonesome place. I believe every man in the boat had a similar feeling. It seemed to me in that moment, that a definite, muggy sort of silence was all round us, and this in spite of the sound of the splashing, and the strange noise of the running water somewhere ahead of us on the dark sea.

"It's let go the oar, Sir!" said the man.

Abruptly, as he spoke, there came the Captain's voice in a roar:—"Back water all!" he shouted. "Put some beef into in now! Back all! Back all! . . . Why the devil was no lantern put in the boat! Back now! Back! Back!"

We backed fiercely, with a will; for it was plain that the Old Man had some good reason to get the boat away pretty quickly. He was right, too; though, whether it was guess-work, or some kind of instinct that made him shout out at that moment, I don't know; only I am sure he could not have seen anything in that absolute darkness.

As I was saying, he was right in shouting to us to back; for we had not backed more than half a dozen fathoms, when there was a tremendous splash right ahead of us, as if a house had fallen into the sea; and a regular wave of sea-water came at us out of the darkness, throwing our bows up, and soaking us fore and aft.

"Good Lord!" I heard the Third Mate gasp out. "What the devil's that?"

"Back all! Back! Back!" the Captain sung out again.

After some moments, he had the tiller put over, and told us to pull. We gave way with a will, as you may think, and in a few minutes were alongside our own ship again.

"Now then, men," the Captain said, when we were safe aboard, "I'll not order any of you to come; but after the steward's served out a tot of grog each, those who are willing, can come with me, and we'll have another go at finding out what devil's work is going on over yonder."

He turned to the Mate, who had been asking questions:—

"Say, Mister," he said, "it's no sort of thing to let the boat go without a lamp aboard. Send a couple of the lads into the lamp locker, and pass out a couple of the anchor-lights, and that deck bull's-eye you use at nights for clearing up the ropes."

He whipped round on the Third:—"Tell the steward to buck up with that grog, Mr. Andrews," he said, "and while you're there, pass out the axes from the rack in my cabin."

The grog came along a minute later; and then the Third Mate with three big axes from out the cabin rack.

"Now then, men," said the Skipper, as we took our tots off, "those who are coming with me, had better take an axe each from the Third Mate. They're mighty good weapons in any sort of trouble."

We all stepped forward, and he burst out laughing, slapping his thigh.

"That's the kind of thing I like!" he said. "Mr. Andrews, the axes won't go round. Pass out that old cutlass from the steward's pantry. It's a pretty hefty piece of iron!"

The old cutlass was brought, and the man who was short of an axe collared it. By this time, two of the 'prentices had filled (at least we supposed they had filled them!) two of the ship's anchor-lights; also they had brought out the bull's-eye lamp we used when clearing up the ropes on a dark night. With the lights and the axes and the cutlass, we felt ready to face anything, and down we went again into the boat, with the Captain and the Third Mate after us.

"Lash one of the lamps to one of the boat-hooks, and rig it out over the bows," ordered the Captain.

This was done, and in this way the light lit up the water for a couple of fathoms ahead of the boat; and made us feel less that something could come at us without our knowing. Then the painter was cast off, and we gave way again toward the sound of the running water, out in the darkness.

I remember now that it struck me that our vessel had drifted a bit; for the sounds seemed farther away.

The second anchor-light had been put in the stern of the boat, and the Third Mate kept it between his feet, while he steered. The Captain had the bull's-eye in his hand, and was pricking up the wick with his pocket-knife.

As we pulled, I took a glance or two over my shoulder; but could see nothing, except the lamp making a yellow halo in the mist round the boat's bows, as we forged ahead. Astern of us, on our quarter, I could see the dull red glow of our vessel's port light. That was all, and not a sound in all the sea, as you might say, except the roll of our oars in the rowlocks, and somewhere in the darkness ahead, that curious noise of water running steadily; now sounding, as I have said, fainter and seeming farther away.

"It's got my oar again, Sir!" exclaimed the man at the bow oar, suddenly, and jumped to his feet. He hove his oar up with a great splashing of water, into the air, and immediately something whirled and beat about in the yellow halo of light over the bows of the boat. There was a crash of breaking wood, and the boathook was broken. The lamp soused down into the sea, and was lost. Then, in the darkness, there was a heavy splash, and a shout from the bow-oar:—"It's gone, Sir. It's loosed off the oar!"

"Vast pulling, all!" sung out the Skipper. Not that the order was necessary; for not a man was pulling. He had jumped up, and whipped a big revolver out of his coat pocket.

He had this in his right hand, and the bull's-eye in his left. He stepped forrard smartly over the oars from thwart to thwart, till he reached the bows, where he shone his light down into the water.

"My word!" he said. "Lord in Heaven! Saw anyone ever the like!"

And I doubt whether any man ever did see what we saw then; for the water was thick and living for yards round the boat with the hugest eels I ever saw before or after.

"Give way, men," said the Skipper, after a minute. "Yon's no explanation of the almighty queer sounds out yonder we're hearing this night. Give way, lads!"

He stood right up in the bows of the boat, shining his bull's eye from side to side, and flashing it down on the water.

"Give way, lads!" he said again. "They don't like the light, that'll keep them from the oars. Give way steady now. Mr. Andrews, keep her dead on for the noise out yonder."

We pulled for some minutes, during which I felt my oar plucked at twice; but a flash of the Captain's lamp seemed sufficient to make the brutes loose hold.

The noise of the water running, appeared now quite near-sounding. About this time, I had a sense again of an added sort of silence to all the natural quietness of the sea. And I had a return of the curious nervousness that had touched me before. I kept listening intensely, as if I expected to hear some other sound than the noise of the water. It came to me suddenly that I had the kind of feeling one has in the aisle of a large cathedral. There was a sort of echo in the night—an incredibly faint reduplicating of the noise of our oars.

"Hark!" I said, audibly; not realizing at first that I was speaking aloud. "There's an echo—"

"That's it!" the Captain cut in, sharply. "I thought I heard something rummy!"

... "I thought I heard something rummy," said a thin ghostly echo, out of the night ... "thought I heard something rummy" ... "heard something rummy." The words went muttering and whispering to and fro in the night about us, in rather a horrible fashion.

"Good Lord!" said the Old Man, in a whisper.

We had all stopped rowing, and were staring about us into the thin mist that filled the night. The Skipper was standing with the bull's-eye lamp held over his head, circling the beam of light round from port to starboard, and back again.

Abruptly, as he did so, it came to me that the mist was thinner. The sound of the running water was very near; but it gave back no echo.

"The water doesn't echo, Sir," I said. That's dam funny!"

"That's dam funny," came back at me, from the darkness to port and starboard, in a multitudinous muttering. . . . "Dam funny! . . . funny . . . eeey!"

"Give way!" said the Old Man, loudly. "I'll bottom this!"

"I'll bottom this. . . . Bottom this . . . this!" The echo came back in a veritable rolling of unexpected sound. And then we had dipped our oars again, and the night was full of the reiterated rolling echoes of our rowlocks.

Suddenly the echoes ceased, and there was, strangely, the sense of a great space about us, and in the same moment the sound of the water running, appeared to be directly before us, but somehow up in the air.

"Vast rowing!" said the Captain, and we lay on our oars, staring round into the darkness ahead. The Old Man swung the beam of his lamp upwards, making circles with it in the night, and abruptly I saw something looming vaguely through the thinner-seeming mist.

"Look, Sir," I called to the Captain. "Quick, Sir, your light right above you! There's something up there!"

The Old Man flashed his lamp upwards, and found the thing I had seen. But it was too indistinct to make anything of, and even as he saw it, the darkness and mist seemed to wrap it about.

"Pull a couple of strokes, all!" said the Captain. "Stow your talk, there in the boat! . . . Again! . . . That'll do! Vast pulling!"

He was sending the beam of his lamp constantly across that part of the night where we had seen the thing, and suddenly I saw it again.

"There, Sir!" I said, quickly. "A little to starboard with the light."

He flicked the light swiftly to the right, and immediately we all saw the thing plainly—a strangely-made mast, standing up there out of the mist, and looking like no spar I had ever seen.

It seemed now that the mist must lie pretty low on the sea in places; for the mast stood up out of it plainly for several fathoms; but, lower, it was hidden in the mist, which, I thought, seemed heavier now all round us; but thinner, as I have said, above.

"Ship ahoy!" sang out the skipper suddenly. "Ship ahoy, there!" But for some moments there came never a sound back to us except the constant noise of the water running, not a score yards away; and then, it seemed to me that a vague echo beat back at us out of the mist, oddly:—"Ahoy! Ahoy! Ahoy!"

"There's something hailing us, Sir," said the Third Mate.

Now, that "something" was significant. It showed the sort of feeling that was on us all.

"That's na ship's mast as ever I've seen!" I heard the man next to me mutter. "It's got a unnatcheral look."

"Ahoy there!" shouted the Skipper again, at the top of his voice. "Ahoy there!"

With the suddenness of a clap of thunder there burst out at us a vast, grunting:—oooaze; arrrr; arrrr; oooaze—a volume of sound so great that it seemed to make the loom of the oar in my hand vibrate.

"Good Lord!" said the Captain, and levelled his revolver into the mist; but he did not fire.

I had loosed one hand from my oar, and gripped my axe. I remember thinking that the Skipper's pistol wouldn't be much use against whatever thing made a noise like that.

"It wasn't ahead, Sir," said the Third Mate, abruptly, from where he sat and steered. "I think it came from somewhere over to starboard."

"Damn this mist!" said the Skipper. "Damn it! What a devil of a stink! Pass that other anchor-light forrard."

I reached for the lamp, and handed it to the next man, who passed it on.

"The other boat-hook," said the Skipper; and when he'd got it, he lashed the lamp to the hook end, and then lashed the whole arrangement upright in the bows, so that the lamp was well above his head.

"Now," he said. "Give way gently! And stand by to back-water, if I tell you. . . . Watch my hand, Mister," he added to the Third Mate. "Steer as I tell you."

We rowed a dozen slow strokes, and with every stroke, I took a look over my shoulder. The Captain was leaning forward under the big lamp, with the bull's-eye in one hand and his revolver in the other. He kept flashing the beam of the lantern up into the night.

"Good Lord!" he said, suddenly, "Vast pulling."

We stopped, and I slewed round on the thwart, and stared.

He was standing up under a glow of the anchor-light, and shining the bull's-eye up at a great mass that loomed dully through the mist. As he flicked the light to and fro over the great bulk, I realised that the boat was within some three or four fathoms of the hull of a vessel.

"Pull another stroke," the Skipper said, in a quiet voice, after a few minutes of silence. "Gently now! Gently! . . . "Vast pulling!"

I slewed round again on my thwart and stared. I could see part of the thing quite distinctly now, and more of it, as I followed the beam of the Captain's lantern. She was a vessel right enough; but such a vessel as I had never seen. She was extraordinarily high out of the water, and seemed very short, and rose up into a queer mass at one end. But what puzzled me more, I think, than anything else, was the queer look of her sides, down which water was streaming all the time.

"That explains the sound of the water running," I thought to myself; "but what on earth is she built of?"

You will understand a little of my bewildered feelings, when I tell you that as the beam of the Captain's lamp shone on the side of this queer vessel, it showed stone everywhere—as if she were built out of stone. I never felt so dumb-founded in my life.

"She's stone, Cap'n!" I said. "Look at her, Sir!"

I realised, as I spoke, a certain horribleness, of the unnatural. . . . A stone ship, floating out there in the night in the midst of the lonely Atlantic!

"She's stone," I said again, in that absurd way in which one reiterates, when one is bewildered.

"Look at the slime on her!" muttered the man next but one forrard of me. "She's a proper Davy Jones Ship. By gum! she stinks like a corpse!"

"Ship ahoy!" roared the Skipper, at the top of his voice. "Ship ahoy! Ship ahoy!"

His shout beat back at us, in a curious, dank, yet metallic, echo, something the way one's voice sounds in an old disused quarry.

"There's no one aboard there, Sir," said the Third Mate. "Shall I put the boat alongside?"

"Yes, shove her up, Mister," said the Old Man. "I'll bottom this business. Pull a couple of strokes, aft there! In bow, and stand by to fend off."

The Third Mate laid the boat alongside, and we unshipped our oars. Then, I leant forward over the side of the boat, and pressed the flat of my hand upon the stark side of the ship. The water that ran down her side, sprayed out over my hand and wrist in a cataract; but I did not think about being wet, for my hand was pressed solid upon stone. . . . I pulled my hand back with a queer feeling.

"She's stone, right enough, Sir," I said to the Captain.

"We'll soon see what she is," he said. "Shove your oar up against her side, and shin up. We'll pass the lamp up to you as soon as you're aboard. Shove your axe in the back of your belt. I'll cover you with my gun, till you're aboard."

" 'i, 'i, Sir," I said; though I felt a bit funny at the thought of having to be the first aboard that damn rummy craft.

I put my oar upright against her side, and took a spring up it from the thwart, and in a moment I was grabbing over my head for her rail, with every rag on me soaked through with the water that was streaming down her, and spraying out over the oar and me.

I got a firm grip of the rail, and hoisted my head high enough to look over; but I could see nothing . . . what with the darkness, and the water in my eyes.

I knew it was no time for going slow, if there were danger aboard; so I went in over that rail in one spring, my boots coming down with a horrible, ringing, hollow stony sound on her decks. I whipped the water out of my eyes and the axe out of my belt, all in the same moment; then I took a good stare fore and aft; but it was too dark to see anything.

"Come along, Duprey!" shouted the Skipper. "Collar the lamp."

I leant out sideways over the rail, and grabbed for the lamp with my left hand, keeping the axe ready in my right, and staring inboard; for I tell you I was just mortally afraid in that moment of what might be aboard of her.

I felt the lamp-ring with my left hand, and gripped it. Then I switched it aboard, and turned fair and square to see where I'd gotten.

Now, you never saw such a packet as that, not in a hundred years, nor yet two hundred, I should think. She'd got a rum little main-deck, about forty feet long, and then came a step about two feet high, and another bit of a deck, with a little house on it.

That was the after end of her; and more I couldn't see, because the light of my lamp went no farther, except to show me vaguely the big, cocked-up stern of her, going up into the darkness. I never saw a vessel made like her; not even in an old picture of old-time ships.

Forrard of me, was her mast—a big lump of a stick it was too, for her size. And here was another amazing thing, the mast of her looked just solid stone.

"Funny, isn't she, Duprey?" said the Skipper's voice at my back, and I came round on him with a jump.

"Yes," I said. "I'm puzzled. Aren't you, Sir?"

"Well," he said, "I am. If we were like the shell-backs they talk of in books, we'd be crossing ourselves. But, personally, give me a good heavy Colt, or the hefty chunk of steel you're cuddling."

He turned from me, and put his head over the rail.

"Pass up the painter, Jales," he said, to the bow-oar. Then to the Third Mate:—

"Bring 'em all up, Mister. If there's going to be anything rummy, we may as well make a picnic party of the lot. . . . Hitch that painter round the cleet yonder, Duprey," he added to me. "It looks good solid stone! . . . That's right. Come along."

He swung the thin beam of his lantern fore and aft, and then forrard again.

"Lord!" he said. "Look at that mast. It's stone. Give it a whack with the back of your axe, man; only remember she's apparently a bit of an old-timer! So go gently."

I took my axe short, and tapped the mast, and it rang dull, and solid, like a stone pillar. I struck it again, harder, and a sharp flake of stone flew past my cheek. The Skipper thrust his lantern close up to where I'd struck the mast.

"By George," he said, "she's absolutely a stone ship—solid stone, afloat here out of Eternity, in the middle of the wide Atlantic. . . . Why! She must weigh a thousand tons more than she's buoyancy to carry. It's just impossible. . . . It's—"

He turned his head quickly, at a sound in the darkness along the decks. He flashed his light that way, across and across the after decks; but we could see nothing.

"Get a move on you in the boat!" he said sharply, stepping to the rail and looking down. "For once I'd really prefer a little more of your company. . . ." He came round like a flash. "Duprey, what was that?" he asked in a low voice.

"I certainly heard something, Sir," I said. "I wish the others would hurry. By Jove! Look! What's that—"

"Where?" he said, and sent the beam of his lamp to where I pointed with my axe.

"There's nothing," he said, after circling the light all over the deck. "Don't go imagining things. There's enough solid unnatural fact here, without trying to add to it."

There came the splash and thud of feet behind, as the first of the men came up over the side, and jumped clumsily into the lee scuppers, which had water in them. You see she had a cant to that side, and I supposed the water had collected there.

The rest of the men followed, and then the Third Mate. That made six men of us, all well armed; and I felt a bit more comfortable, as you can think.

"Hold up that lamp of yours, Duprey, and lead the way," said the Skipper. "You're getting the post of honour this trip!"

" 'i, 'i, Sir," I said, and stepped forward, holding up the lamp in my left hand, and carrying my axe half way down the haft, in my right.

"We'll try aft, first," said the Captain, and led the way himself, flashing the bull's-eye to and fro. At the raised portion of the deck, he stopped.

"Now," he said, in his queer way, "let's have a look at this. . . . Tap it with your axe, Duprey. . . . Ah!" he added, as I hit it with the back of my axe. "That's what we call stone at home, right enough. She's just as rum as anything I've seen while I've been fishing. We'll go on aft and have a peep into the deck-house. Keep your axes handy, men."

We walked slowly up to the curious little house, the deck rising to it with quite a slope. At the fore side of the little deck-house, the Captain pulled up, and shone his bull's-eye down at the deck. I saw that he was looking at what was plainly the stump of the after mast. He stepped closer to it, and kicked it with his foot; and it gave out the same dull, solid note that the foremast had done. It was obviously a chunk of stone.

I held up my lamp so that I could see the upper part of the house more clearly. The fore-part had two square window-spaces in it; but there was no glass in either of them; and the blank darkness within the queer little place just seemed to stare out at us.

And then I saw something suddenly . . . a great shaggy head of red hair was rising slowly into sight, through the port window, the one nearest to us.

"My God! What's that, Cap'n?" I called out. But it was gone, even as I spoke.

"What?" he asked, jumping at the way I had sung out.

"At the port window, Sir," I said. "A great red-haired head. It came right up to the window-place; and then it went in a moment."

The Skipper stepped right up to the little dark window, and pushed his lantern through into the blackness. He flashed the light round; then withdrew the lantern.

"Bosh, man!" he said. "That's twice you've got fancying things. Ease up your nerves a bit!"

"I did see it!" I said, almost angrily. "It was like a great red-haired head. . . ."

"Stow it, Duprey!" he said, though not sneeringly. The house is absolutely empty. Come round to the door, if the Infernal Masons that built her, went in for doors! Then you'll see for yourself. All the same, keep your axes ready, lads. I've a notion there's something pretty queer aboard here."

We went up round the after-end of the little house; and here we saw what appeared to be a door.

The Skipper felt at the queer, odd-shapen handle, and pushed at the door; but it had stuck fast.

"Here, one of you!" he said, stepping back. "Have a whack at this with your axe. Better use the back."

One of the men stepped forward, and we stood away to give him room. As his axe struck, the door went to pieces with exactly the same sound that a thin slab of stone would make, when broken.

"Stone!" I heard the Captain mutter, under his breath. "By Gum! What *is* she?"

I did not wait for the Skipper. He had put me a bit on edge, and I stepped bang in through the open doorway, with the lamp high, and holding my axe short and ready; but there was nothing in the place, save a stone seat running all round, except where the doorway opened on to the deck.

"Find your red-haired monster?" asked the Skipper, at my elbow.

I said nothing. I was suddenly aware that he was all on the jump with some inexplicable fear. I saw his glance going everywhere about him. And then his eye caught mine, and he saw that I realised. He was a man almost callous to fear, that is the fear of danger in what I might call any normal sea-faring shape. And this palpable nerviness affected me tremendously. He was obviously doing his best to throttle it; and trying all he knew to hide it. I had a sudden warmth of understanding for him, and dreaded lest the men should realise his state. Funny that I should be able at that moment to be aware of anything but my own bewildered fear and expectancy of intruding upon something monstrous at any instant. Yet I describe exactly my feelings, as I stood there in the house.

"Shall we try below, Sir?" I said, and turned to where a flight of stone steps led down into an utter blackness, out of which rose a strange, dank scent of the sea . . . an imponderable mixture of brine and darkness.

"The worthy Duprey leads the van!" said the Skipper; but I felt no irritation now. I knew that he must cover his fright, until he had got control again; and I think he felt, somehow, that I was backing him up. I remember now that I went down those stairs into that unknowable and ancient cabin, as much aware in that moment of the Captain's state, as of that extraordinary thing I had just seen at the little window, or of my own half-funk of what we might see any moment.

The Captain was at my shoulder, as I went, and behind him came the Third Mate, and then the men, all in single file; for the stairs were narrow.

I counted seven steps down, and then my foot splashed into water on the eighth. I held the lamp low, and stared. I had caught no glimpse of a reflection, and I saw now that this was owing to a curious, dull, greyish scum that lay thinly on the water, seeming to match the colour of the stone which composed the steps and bulksheads.

"Stop!" I said. "I'm in water!"

I let my foot down slowly, and got the next step. Then sounded with my axe, and found the floor at the bottom. I stepped down and stood up to my thighs in water.

"It's all right, Sir," I said, suddenly whispering. I held my lamp up, and glanced quickly about me. "It's not deep. There's two doors here. . . ."

I whirled my axe up as I spoke; for, suddenly, I had realised that one of the doors was open a little. It seemed to move, as I stared, and I could have imagined that a vague undulation ran towards me, across the dull scum-covered water.

"The door's opening!" I said, aloud, with a sudden sick feeling. "Look out!"

I backed from the door, staring; but nothing came. And abruptly, I had control of myself; for I realised that the door was not moving. It had not moved at all. It was simply ajar.

"It's all right, Sir," I said. "It's not opening."

I stepped forward again a pace towards the doors, as the Skipper and the Third Mate came down with a jump, splashing the water all over me.

The Captain still had the "nerves" on him, as I think I could feel, even then; but he hid it well.

"Try the door, Mister. I've jumped my dam lamp out!" he growled to the Third Mate; who pushed at the door on my right; but it would not open beyond the nine or ten inches it was fixed ajar.

"There's this one here, Sir," I whispered, and held my lantern up to the closed door that lay on my left.

"Try it," said the Skipper, in an undertone. We did so, but it also was fixed. I whirled my axe suddenly, and struck the door heavily in the centre of the main panel, and the whole thing crashed into flinders of stone, that went with hollow sounding splashes into the darkness beyond.

"Goodness!" said the Skipper, in a startled voice; for my action had been so instant and unexpected. He covered his lapse, in a moment, by the warning:—

"Look out for bad air!" But I was already inside with the lamp, and holding my axe handily. There was no bad air; for right across from me, was a split clean through the ship's side, that I could have put my two arms through, just above the level of the scummy water.

The place I had broken into, was a cabin, of a kind; but seemed strange and dank, and too narrow to breathe in; and wherever I turned, I saw stone. The Third Mate and the Skipper gave simultaneous expressions of disgust at the wet dismalness of the place.

"It's all stone," I said, and brought my axe hard against the front of a sort of squat cabinet, which was built into the after bulkshead. It caved in, with a crash of splintered stone.

"Empty!" I said, and turned instantly away.

The Skipper and the Third Mate, with the men who were now peering in at the door, crowded out; and in that moment, I pushed my axe under my arm, and thrust my hand into the burst stone-chest. Twice I did this, with almost the speed of lightning, and shoved what I had seen, into the side-pocket of my coat. Then, I was following the others; and not one of them had noticed a thing. As for me, I was quivering with excitement, so that my knees shook; for I had caught the unmistakable gleam of gems; and had grabbed for them in that one swift instant.

I wonder whether anyone can realise what I felt in that moment. I knew that, if my guess were right, I had snatched the power in that one miraculous moment, that would lift me from the weary life of a common shellback, to the life of ease that had been mine during my early years. I tell you, in that instant, as I staggered almost blindly out of that dark little apartment, I had no thought of any horror that might be held in that incredible vessel, out there afloat on the wide Atlantic.

I was full of the one blinding thought, that possibly I was *rich*! And I wanted to get somewhere by myself as soon as possible, to see whether I was right. Also, if I could, I meant to get back to that strange cabinet of stone, if the chance came; for I knew that the two handfuls I had grabbed, had left a lot behind.

Only, whatever I did, I must let no one guess; for then I should probably lose everything, or have but an infinitesimal share doled out to me, of the wealth that I believed to be in those glittering things there in the side-pocket of my coat.

I began immediately to wonder what other treasures there might be aboard; and then, abruptly, I realised that the Captain was speaking to me:—

"The light, Duprey, damn you!" he was saying, angrily, in a low tone. "What's the matter with you! Hold it up."

I pulled myself together, and shoved the lamp above my head. One of the men was swinging his axe, to beat in the door that seemed to have stood so eternally ajar; and the rest were standing back, to give him room. Crash! went the axe, and half the door fell inward, in a shower of broken stone, making dismal splashes in the darkness. The man struck again, and the rest of the door fell away, with a sullen slump into the water.

"The lamp," muttered the Captain. But I had hold of myself once more, and I was stepping forward slowly through the thigh-deep water, even before he spoke.

I went a couple of paces in through the black gape of the doorway, and then stopped and held the lamp so as to get a view of the place. As I did so, I remember how the intense silence struck home on me. Every man of us must surely have been holding his breath; and there must have been some heavy quality, either in the water, or in the scum that floated on it, that kept it from rippling against the sides of the bulksheads, with the movements we had made.

At first, as I held the lamp (which was burning badly), I could not get its position right to show me anything, except that I was in a very large cabin for so small a vessel. Then I saw that a table ran along the centre, and the top of it was no more than a few inches above the water. On each side of it, there rose the backs of what were evidently two rows of massive, olden looking chairs. At the far end of the table, there was a huge, immobile, humped something.

I stared at this for several moments; then I took three slow steps forward, and stopped again; for the thing resolved itself, under the light from the lamp, into the figure of an enormous man, seated at the end of the table, his face bowed forward upon his arms. I was amazed, and thrilling abruptly with new fears and vague impossible thoughts. Without moving a step, I held the light nearer at arm's length. . . . The man was of stone, like everything in that extraordinary ship.

That foot!" said the Captain's voice, suddenly cracking. "Look at that foot!" His voice sounded amazingly startling and hollow in that silence, and the words seemed to come back sharply at me from the vaguely seen bulkheads.

I whipped my light to starboard, and saw what he meant—a huge human foot was sticking up out of the water, on the right hand side of the table. It was enormous. I have never seen so vast a foot. And it also was of stone.

And then, as I stared, I saw that there was a great head above the water, over by the bulkshead.

"I've gone mad!" I said, out loud, as I saw something else, more incredible.

"My God! Look at the hair on the head!" said the Captain. . . . "It's growing! It's growing!" His voice cracked again.

"Look at it! It's growing!" he called out once more. I was looking. On the great head, there was becoming visible a huge mass of red hair, that was surely and unmistakably rising up, as we watched it.

"It's what I saw at the window!" I said. "It's what I saw at the window! I told you I saw it!"

"Come out of that, Duprey," said the Third Mate, quietly.

"Let's get out of here!" muttered one of the men. Two or three of them called out the same thing; and then, in a moment, they began a mad rush up the stairway.

I stood dumb, where I was. The hair rose up in a horrible living fashion on the great head, waving and moving. It rippled down over the forehead, and spread abruptly over the whole gargantuan stone face, hiding the features completely. Suddenly, I swore at the thing madly, and I hove my axe at it. Then I was backing crazily for the door, slumping the scum as high as the deck-beams, in my fierce haste. I reached the stairs, and caught at the stone rail, that was modelled like a rope; and so hove myself up out of the water. I reached the little deck-house, where I had seen the great head of hair. I jumped through the doorway, out on to the decks, and I felt the night air sweet on my face. . . . Goodness! I ran forward along the decks. There was a Babel of shouting in the waist of the ship, and a thudding of feet running. Some of the men were singing out, to get into the boat; but the Third Mate was shouting that they must wait for me.

"He's coming," called someone. And then I was among them. "Turn that lamp up, you idiot," said the Captain's voice. "This is just where we want light!"

I glanced down, and realised that my lamp was almost out. I turned it up, and it flared, and began again to dwindle.

"Those damned boys never filled it," I said. "They deserve their necks breaking."

The men were literally tumbling over the side, and the Skipper was hurrying them.

"Down with you into the boat," he said to me. "Give me the lamp. I'll pass it down. Get a move on you!"

The Captain had evidently got his nerve back again. This was more like the man I knew. I handed him the lamp, and went over the side. All the rest had now gone, and the Third Mate was already in the stern, waiting.

As I landed on the thwart, there was a sudden, strange noise from aboard the ship—a sound, as if some stone object were trundling down the sloping decks, from aft. In that one moment, I got what you might truly call the "horrors." I seemed suddenly able to believe incredible possibilities.

"The stone men!" I shouted. "Jump, Captain! Jump! Jump!" The vessel seemed to roll oddly.

Abruptly, the Captain yelled out something, that not one of us in the boat understood. There followed a succession of tremendous sounds, aboard the ship, and I saw his shadow swing out huge against the thin mist, as he turned suddenly with the lamp.   He fired twice with his revolver.

"The hair!" I shouted. "Look at the hair!"

We all saw it—the great head of red hair that we had seen grow visibly on the monstrous stone head, below in the cabin. It rose above the rail, and there was a moment of intense stillness, in which I heard the Captain gasping. The Third Mate fired six times at the thing, and I found myself fixing an oar up against the side of that abominable vessel, to get aboard.

As I did so, there came one appalling crash, that shook the stone ship fore and aft, and she began to cant up, and my oar slipped and fell into the boat. Then the Captain's voice screamed something in a choking fashion above us. The ship lurched forward, and paused. Then another crash came, and she rocked over towards us; then away from us again. The movement away from us continued, and the round of the vessel's bottom showed, vaguely. There was a smashing of glass above us, and the dim glow of light aboard, vanished. Then the vessel fell clean over from us, with a giant splash. A huge wave came at us, out of the night, and half filled the boat.

The boat nearly capsized, then righted and presently steadied.

"Captain!" shouted the Third Mate. "Captain!" But there came never a sound; only presently, out of all the night, a strange murmuring of waters.

"Captain!" he shouted once more; but his voice just went lost and remote into the darkness.

"She's foundered!" I said.

"Out oars," sung out the Third. "Put your backs into it. Don't stop to bail!"

For half an hour we circled the spot slowly. But the strange vessel had indeed foundered and gone down into the mystery of the deep sea, with her mysteries.

Finally we put about, and returned to the *Alfred Jessop*.

Now, I want you to realise that what I am telling you is a plain and simple tale of fact. This is no fairy tale, and I've not done yet; and I think this yarn should prove to you that some mighty strange things do happen at sea, and always will while the world lasts. It's the home of all the mysteries; for it's the one place that is really difficult for humans to investigate. Now just listen:—

"The Mate had kept the bell going, from time to time, and so we came back pretty quickly, having as we came, a strange repetition of the echoey reduplication of our oar-sounds; but we never spoke a word; for not one of us wanted to hear those beastly echoes again, after what we had just gone through. I think we all had a feeling that there was something a bit hellish abroad that night.

We got aboard, and the Third explained to the Mate what had happened; but he would hardly believe the yarn. However, there was nothing to do, but wait for daylight; so we were told to keep about the deck, and keep our eyes and ears open.

One thing the Mate did, showed he was more impressed by our yarn, than he would admit. He had all the ships' lanterns lashed up round the decks, to the sheerpoles; and he never told us to give up either the axes or the cutlass.

It was while we were keeping about the decks, that I took the chance to have a look at what I had grabbed. I tell you, what I found, made me nearly forget the Skipper, and all the rummy things that had happened. I had twenty-six stones in my pocket and four of them were diamonds, respectively 9, 11, 13 1/2 and 17 carats in weight, uncut, that is. I know quite something about diamonds. I'm not going to tell you how I learnt what I know; but I would not have taken a thousand pounds for the four, as they lay there, in my hand. There was also a big, dull stone, that looked red inside. I'd have dumped it over the side, I thought so little of it: only,

I argued that it must be something, or it would never have been among that lot. Lord! but I little knew what I'd got; not then. Why, the thing was as big as a fair-sized walnut. You may think it funny that I thought of the four diamonds first; but you see, I *know* diamonds when I see them. They're things I understand; but I never saw a ruby, in the rough, before or since. Good Lord! And to think I'd have thought nothing of heaving it over the side!

You see, a lot of the stones were not anything much; that is, not in the modern market. There were two big topaz, and several onyx and cornelians—nothing much. There were five hammered slugs of gold about two ounces each they would be. And then a prize—one winking green devil of an emerald. You've got to know an emerald to look for the "eye" of it, in the rough; but it is there—the eye of some hidden devil staring up at you. Yes, I'd seen an emerald before, and I knew I held a lot of money in that one stone alone.

And then I remembered what I'd missed, and cursed myself for not grabbing a third time. But that feeling lasted only a moment. I thought of the beastly part that had been the Skipper's share; while there I stood safe under one of the lamps, with a fortune in my hands. And then, abruptly, as you can understand, my mind was filled with the crazy wonder and bewilderment of what had happened. I felt how absurdly ineffectual my imagination was to comprehend anything understandable out of it all, except that the Captain had certainly gone, and I had just as certainly had a piece of impossible luck.

Often, during that time of waiting, I stopped to take a look at the things I had in my pocket; always careful that no one about the decks should come near me, to see what I was looking at.

Suddenly the Mate's voice came sharp along the decks:—

"Call the doctor, one of you," he said. "Tell him to get the fire in and the coffee made."

" 'i, 'i, Sir," said one of the men; and I realised that the dawn was growing vaguely over the sea.

Half an hour later, the "doctor" shoved his head out of the galley doorway, and sung out that coffee was ready.

The watch below turned out, and had theirs with the watch on deck, all sitting along the spar that lay under the port rail.

As the daylight grew, we kept a constant watch over the side; but even now we could see nothing; for the thin mist still hung low on the sea.

"Hear that?" said one of the men, suddenly. And, indeed, the sound must have been plain for half a mile round.

"Ooaaze, ooaaze, arrr, arrrr, oooaze——"

"By George!" said Tallett, one of the other watch; "that's a beastly sort of thing to hear."

"Look!" I said. "What's that out yonder?"

The mist was thinning under the effect of the rising sun, and tremendous shapes seemed to stand towering half-seen, away to port. A few minutes passed, while we stared. Then, suddenly, we heard the Mate's voice:—

"All hands on deck!" he was shouting, along the decks.

I ran aft a few steps.

"Both watches are out, Sir," I called.

"Very good!" said the Mate. "Keep handy all of you. Some of you have got the axes. The rest had better take a caps'n-bar each, and stand-by till I find what this devilment is, out yonder."

" 'i, 'i, Sir," I said, and turned forrard. But there was no need to pass on the Mate's orders; for the men had heard, and there was a rush for the capstan-bars, which are a pretty hefty kind of cudgel, as any sailorman knows. We lined the rail again, and stared away to port.

"Look out, you sea-divvils," shouted Timothy Galt, a huge Irishman, waving his bar excitedly, and peering over the rail into the mist, which was steadily thinning, as the day grew.

Abruptly there was a simultaneous cry:—"*Rocks!*" shouted everyone.

I never saw such a sight. As at last the mist thinned, we could see them. All the sea to port was literally cut about with far-reaching reefs of rock. In places the reefs lay just submerged; but in others they rose into extraordinary and fantastic rock-spires, and arches, and islands of jagged rock.

"Jehoshaphat!" I heard the Third Mate shout. "Look at that, Mister! Look at that! Lord! how did we take the boat through that, without stoving her?"

Everything was so still for the moment, with all the men just staring and amazed, that I could hear every word come along the decks.

"There's sure been a submarine earthquake somewhere," I heard the First Mate say. "The bottom of the sea's just riz up here, quiet and gentle, during the night; and God's mercy we aren't now a-top of one of those ornaments out there."

And then, you know, I saw it all. Everything that had looked mad and impossible, began to be natural; though it was, none the less, all amazing and wonderful.

There had been during the night, a slow lifting of the sea-bottom, owing to some action of the Internal Pressures. The rocks had risen so gently that they had made never a sound; and the stone ship had risen with them out of the deep sea. She had evidently lain on one of the submerged reefs, and so had seemed to us to be just afloat in the sea. And she accounted for the water we heard running. She was naturally bung full, as you might say, and took longer to shed the water than she did to rise. She had probably some biggish holes in her bottom. I began to get my "soundings" a bit, as I might call it in sailor talk. The natural wonders of the sea, beat all made-up yarns that ever were!

The Mate sung out to us to man the boat again, and told the Third Mate to take her out to where we lost the Skipper, and have a final look round, in case there might be any chance to find the Old Man's body anywhere about.

"Keep a man in the bows to look out for sunk rocks, Mister," the Mate told the Third, as we pulled off. "Go slow. There'll be no wind yet awhile. See if you can fix up what made those noises, while you're looking round."

We pulled right across about thirty fathoms of clear water, and in a minute we were between two great arches of rock. It was then I realised that the re-duplicating of our oar-roll was the echo from these on each side of us. Even in the sunlight, it was queer to hear again that same strange cathedral echoey sound that we had heard in the dark.

We passed under the huge arches, all hung with deep-sea slime. And presently we were heading straight for a gap, where two low reefs swept in to the apex of a huge horseshoe. We pulled for about three minutes, and then the Third gave the word to "vast pulling."

"Take the boat-hook, Duprey," he said, "and go forrard, and see we don't hit anything."

" 'i, 'i, Sir," I said, and drew in my oar.

"Give way again gently!" said the Third; and the boat moved forward for another thirty or forty yards.

"We're right on to a reef, Sir," I said, presently, as I stared down over the bows. I sounded with the boat-hook. "There's about three feet of water, Sir," I told him.

"Vast pulling," ordered the Third. "I reckon we are right over the rock, where we found that rum packet last night." He leant over the side, and stared down.

"There's a stone cannon on the rock, right under the bows of the boat," I said. Immediately afterwards I shouted:—

"There's the hair, Sir! There's the hair! It's on the reef. There's two! There's three! There's one on the cannon!"

"All right! All right, Duprey! Keep cool," said the Third Mate. "I can see them. You've enough intelligence not to be superstitious now the whole thing's explained. They're some kind of big hairy sea-caterpillar. Prod one with your boat-hook."

I did so; a little ashamed of my sudden bewilderment. The thing whipped round like a tiger, at the boat-hook. It lapped itself round and round the boat-hook, while the hind portions of it kept gripped to the rock, and I could no more pull the boathook from its grip, than fly; though I pulled till I sweated.

"Take the point of your cutlass to it, Varley," said the Third Mate. "Jab it through."

The bow-oar did so, and the brute loosed the boat-hook, and curled up round a chunk of rock, looking like a great ball of red hair.

I drew the boat-hook up, and examined it.

"Goodness!" I said. "That's what killed the Old Man—one of those things! Look at all those marks in the wood, where it's gripped it with about a hundred legs."

I passed the boat-hook aft to the Third Mate to look at.

"They're about as dangerous as they can be, Sir, I reckon," I told him. "Makes you think of African centipedes, only these are big and strong enough to kill an elephant, I should think."

"Don't lean all on one side of the boat!" shouted the Third Mate, as the men stared over. "Get back to your places. Give way there! . . . Keep a good look-out for any signs of the ship or the Captain, Duprey."

For nearly an hour, we pulled to and fro over the reef; but we never saw either the stone ship or the Old Man again. The queer craft must have rolled off into the profound depths that lay on each side of the reef.

As I leant over the bows, staring down all that long while at the submerged rocks, I was able to understand almost everything, except the various extraordinary noises.

The cannon made it unmistakably clear that the ship which had been hove up from the sea-bottom, with the rising of the reef, had been originally a normal enough wooden vessel of a time far removed from our own. At the sea-bottom, she had evidently undergone some natural mineralizing process, and this explained her stony appearance. The stone men had been evidently humans who had been drowned in her cabin, and their swollen tissues had been subjected to the same natural process, which, however, had also deposited heavy encrustations upon them, so that their size, when compared with the normal, was prodigious.

The mystery of the hair, I had already discovered; but there remained, among other things, the tremendous bangs we had heard. These were, possibly, explained later, while we were making a final examination of the rocks to the Westward, prior to returning to our ship. Here we discovered the burst and swollen bodies of several extraordinary deep-sea creatures, of the eel variety. They must have had a girth, in life, of many feet, and the one that we measured roughly with an oar, must have been quite forty feet long. They had, apparently, burst on being lifted from the tremendous pressure of the deep sea, into the light air pressure above water, and hence might account for the loud reports we had heard; though, personally, I incline to think these loud bangs were more probably caused by the splitting of the rocks under new stresses.

As for the roaring sounds, I can only conclude that they were caused by a peculiar species of grampus-like fish, of enormous size, which we found dead and hugely distended on one of the rocky masses. This fish must have weighed at least four or five tons, and when prodded with a heavy oar, there came from its peculiar snout-shaped mouth, a low, hoarse sound, like a weak imitation of the tremendous sounds we had heard during the past night.

Regarding the apparently carved handrail, like a rope up the side of the cabin stairs, I realise that this had undoubtedly been actual rope at one time.

Recalling the heavy, trundling sounds aboard, just after I climbed down into the boat, I can only suppose that these were made by some stone object, possibly a fossilized gun-carriage, rolling down the decks, as the ship began to slip off the rocks and her bows sank lower in the water.

The varying lights must have been the strongly phosphorescent bodies of some of the deep-sea creatures, moving about on the upheaved reefs. As for the giant splash that occurred in the darkness ahead of the boat, this must have been due to some large portion of heaved-up rock, overbalancing and rolling back into the sea.

No one aboard ever learnt about the jewels. I took care of that! I sold the ruby badly, so I've heard since; but I do not grumble even now. Twenty-three thousand pounds I had for it alone, from a merchant in London. I learned afterwards he made double that on it; but I don't spoil my pleasure by grumbling. I wonder often how the stones and things came where I found them; but she carried guns, as I've told, I think; and there's rum doings happen at sea; yes, by George!

The smell—oh, that I guess was due to heaving all that deep-sea slime up for human noses to smell at.

This yarn is, of course, known in nautical circles, and was briefly mentioned in the old Nautical Mercury of 1879. The series of volcanic reefs (which disappeared in 1883) were charted under the name of the "Alfred Jessop Shoals and Reefs"; being named after our Captain who discovered them and lost his life on them.

The *Shamraken* Homeward-Bounder

The old *Shamraken*, sailing-ship, had been many days upon the waters. She was old—older than her masters, and that was saying a great deal. She seemed in no hurry; as she lifted her bulging, old, wooden sides through the seas. What need for hurry! She would arrive some time, in some fashion, as had been her habit heretofore.

Two matters were especially noticeable among her crew—who were also her masters—; the first the agedness of each and everyone; the second the *family* sense which appeared to bind them, so that the ship seemed manned by a crew, all of whom were related one to the other; yet it was not so.

A strange company were they, each man bearded, aged and grizzled; yet there was nothing of the inhumanity of old age about them, save it might be in their freedom from grumbling, and the calm content which comes only to those in whom the more violent passions have died.

Had anything to be done, there was nothing of the growling, inseparable from the average run of sailor men, They went aloft to the "job"—whatever it might be—with the wise submission which is brought only by age and experience. Their work was gone through with a certain slow pertinacity—a sort of tired steadfastness, born of the knowledge that such work *had* to be done. Moreover, their hands possessed the ripe skill which comes only from exceeding practice, and which went far to make amends for the feebleness of age. Above all, their movements, slow as they might be, were remorseless in their lack of faltering. They had so often performed the same kind of work, that they had arrived, by the selection of utility, at the shortest and most simple methods of doing it.

They had, as I have said, been many days upon the water, though I am not sure that any man in her knew to a nicety the number of those days. Though Skipper Abe Tombes—addressed usually as Skipper Abe—may have had some notion; for he might be seen at times gravely adjusting a prodigious quadrant, which suggests that he kept some sort of record of time and place.

Of the crew of the *Shamraken*, some half dozen were seated, working placidly at such matters of seamanship as were necessary. Besides these, there were others about the decks. A couple who paced the lee side of the main deck, smoking, and exchanging an occasional word. One who sat by the side of a worker, and made odd remarks between draws at his pipe. Another, out upon the jibboom, who fished, with a line, hook and white rag, for bonito. This last was Nuzzie, the ship's' boy. He was grey-bearded, and his years numbered five and fifty. A boy of fifteen he had been, when he joined the *Shamraken*, and "boy" he was still, though forty years had passed into eternity, since the day of his "signing on"; for the men of the *Shamraken* lived in the past, and thought of him only as the "boy" of that past.

It was Nuzzie's watch below—his time for sleeping. This might have been said also of the other three men who talked and smoked; but for themselves they had scarce a thought of sleep. Healthy age sleeps little, and they were in health, though so ancient.

Presently, one of those who walked the lee side of the main deck, chancing to cast a glance forrard, observed Nuzzie still to be out upon the jibboom, jerking his line so as to delude some foolish bonito into the belief that the white rag was a flying fish.

The smoker nudged his companion.

"Time that b'y 'ad 'is sleep."

"i, i, mate," returned the other, withdrawing his pipe, and giving a steadfast look at the figure seated out upon the jibboom,

For the half of a minute they stood there, very effigies of Age's implacable determination to rule rash Youth. Their pipes were held in their hands, and the smoke rose up in little eddies from the smouldering contents of the bowls.

"Thar's no tamin' of thet b'y!" said the first man, looking very stern and determined. Then he remembered his pipe, and took a draw.

"B'ys is tur'ble queer critters," remarked the second man, and remembered his pipe in turn.

"Fishin' w'en 'e orter be sleepin'," snorted the first man.

"B'ys needs a tur'ble lot er sleep," said the second man. "I 'member w'en I wor a b'y. I reckon it's ther growin'."

And all the time poor Nuzzie fished on.

"Guess I'll, jest step up an' tell 'im ter come in outer thet," exclaimed the first man, and commenced to walk towards the steps leading up on to the fo'cas'le head.

"B'y!" he shouted, as soon as his head was above the level of the fo'cas'le deck. "B'y!"

Nuzzie looked round, at the second call.

"Eh?" he sung out.

"Yew come in outer thet," shouted the older man, in the somewhat shrill tone which age had brought to his voice. "Reckon we'll be 'avin' yer sleepin' at ther wheel ter night."

"i," joined in the second man, who had followed his companion up on to the fo'cas'le' head. "Come in, b'y, an' get ter yer bunk."

"Right," called Nuzzie, and commenced to coil up his line. It was evident that he had no thought of disobeying. He came in off the spar, and went past them without a word, on the way to turn in.

They, on their part, went down slowly off the fo'cas'le head, and resumed their walk fore and aft along the lee side of the main deck.

II

"I reckon, Zeph" said the man who sat upon the hatch and smoked, "I reckon as Skipper Abe's 'bout right. We've made a trifle o' dollars outer the ole 'ooker, an' we don't get no younger."

"Ay, thet's so, right 'nuff," returned the man who sat beside him, working at the stropping of a block.

"An' it's 'bout time's we got inter the use o' bein' ashore," went on the first man, who was named Job.

Zeph gripped the block between his knees, and fumbled in his hip pocket for a plug. He bit off a chew and replaced the plug.

"Seems cur'ous this is ther last trip, w'en yer comes ter think uv it," he remarked, chewing steadily, his chin resting on his hand.

Job took two or three deep draws at his pipe before he spoke.

"Reckon it had ter come sumtime," he said, at length. "I've a purty leetle place in me mind w'er' I'm goin' ter tie up. 'Ave yer thought erbout it, Zeph?"

The man who held the block between his knees, shook his head, and stared away moodily over the sea.

"Dunno, Job, as I know what I'll do w'en ther old 'ooker's sold," he muttered. "Sence M'ria went, I don't seem nohow ter care 'bout bein' 'shore."

"I never 'ad no wife," said Job, pressing down the burning tobacco in the bowl of his pipe. "I reckon seafarin' men don't ought ter have no truck with wives."

"Thet's right 'nuff, Job, fer yew. Each man ter 'is taste. I wer' tur'ble fond uv M'ria—" he broke off short, and continued to stare out over the sea.

"I've allus thought I'd like ter settle down on er farm o' me own. I guess the dollars I've arned 'll do the trick," said Job.

Zeph made no reply, and, for a time, they sat there, neither speaking.

Presently, from the door of the fo'cas'le, on the starboard side, two figures emerged. They were also of the "watch below." If anything, they seemed older than the rest of those about the decks; their beards, white, save for the stain of tobacco juice, came nearly to their waists. For the rest, they had been big vigorous men; but were now sorely bent by the burden of their years. They came aft, walking slowly. As they came opposite to the main hatch, Job looked up and spoke:—

"Say, Nehemiah, thar's Zeph here's been thinkin' 'bout M'ria, an' I ain't bin able ter peek 'im up nohow."

The smaller of the two newcomers shook his head slowly.

"We hev oor trubbles," he said. "We hev oor trubbles. I hed mine w'en I lost my datter's gell. I wor powerful took wi' thet gell, she wor that winsome; but it wor like ter be—it wor like ter be, an' Zeph's hed his trubble sence then."

234

"M'ria wer' a good wife ter me, she wer'," said Zeph, speaking slowly. "An' now th' old 'ooker's goin', I'm feared, as I'll find it mighty lonesome ashore yon," and he waved his hand, as though suggesting vaguely that the shore lay anywhere beyond the starboard rail.

"Ay," remarked the second of the newcomers. "It's er weary thing tu me as th' old packet's goin'. Six and sixty year hev I sailed in her. Six and sixty year!" He nodded his head, mournfully, and struck a match with shaky hands.

"It's like ter be," said the smaller man. "It's like ter be."

And, with that, he and his companion moved over to the spar that lay along under the starboard bulwarks, and there seated themselves, to smoke and meditate.

III

Skipper Abe, and Josh Matthews, the First Mate, were standing together beside the rail which ran across the break of the poop. Like the rest of the men of the *Shamraken*, their age had come upon them, and the frost of eternity had touched their beards and hair.

Skipper Abe was speaking:—

"It's harder 'n I'd thought," he said, and looked away from the Mate, staring hard along the worn, white-scoured decks.

"Dunno w'at I'll du, Abe, w'en she's gone," returned the old Mate. "She's been a 'ome fer us, these sixty years an' more." He knocked out the old tobacco from his pipe, as he spoke, and began to cut a bowl-full of fresh.

"It's them durned freights!" exclaimed the Skipper. "We're jest losin' dollars every trip. It's them steam packets as hes knocked us out."

He sighed wearily, and bit tenderly at his plug.

"She's been a mighty comfortable ship," muttered Josh, in soliloquy. "An' sence thet b'y o' mine went, I sumhow thinks less o' goin' ashore 'n I used ter. I ain't no folk left on all thar 'arth."

He came to an end, and began with his old trembling fingers to fill his pipe.

Skipper Abe said nothing. He appeared to be occupied with his own thoughts. He was leaning over the rail across the break of the poop, and chewing steadily. Presently, he straightened himself up and walked over to leeward. He expectorated, after which he stood there for a few moments, taking a short look round—the result of half a century of habit. Abruptly, he sung out to the Mate. . . .

"W'at d'yer make outer it?" he queried, after they had stood awhile, peering.

"Dunno, Abe, less'n it's some sort o' mist, riz up by ther 'eat."

Skipper Abe shook his head; but having nothing better to suggest, held his peace for awhile.

Presently, Josh spoke again:—

"Mighty cur'us, Abe. These are strange parts."

Skipper Abe nodded his assent, and continued to stare at that which had come into sight upon the lee bow. To them, as they looked, it seemed that a vast wall of rose-coloured mist was rising towards the zenith. It showed nearly ahead, and at first had seemed no more than a bright cloud upon the horizon; but already had reached a great way into the air, and the upper edge had taken on wondrous flame-tints.

"It's powerful nice-lookin'," said Josh. "I've allus 'eard as things was diff'rent out 'n these parts"

Presently, as the *Shamraken* drew near to the mist, it appeared to those aboard that it filled all the sky ahead of them, being spread out now far on either bow. And so in a while they entered into it and, at once, the aspect of all things was changed. . . . The mist, in great rosy wreaths, floated all about them, seeming to soften and beautify every rope and spar, so that the old ship had become, as it were, a fairy craft in an unknown world.

"Never seen nothin' like it, Abe—nothin'!" said Josh. "Ey! but it's fine! It's fine! Like 's ef we'd run inter ther sunset."

"I'm mazed, just mazed!" exclaimed Skipper Abe, "but I'm 'gree'ble as it's purty, mighty purty."

For a further while, the two old fellows, stood without speech, just gazing and gazing. With their entering into the mist, they had come into a greater quietness than had been theirs out upon the open sea. It was as though the mist muffled and toned down the creak, creak, of the spars and gear; and the big, foamless seas that rolled past them, seemed to have lost something of their harsh whispering roar of greeting.

"Sort o' unarthly, Abe," said Josh, later, and speaking but little above a whisper. "Like as ef yew was in church."

"Ay," replied Skipper Abe. "It don't' seem nat'rel."

"Shouldn't think as 'eaven was all thet diff'rent," whispered Josh. And Skipper Abe said nothing in contradiction.

IV

Sometime later, the wind began to fail, and it was decided that, when eight-bells was struck, all hands should set the main t'gallant. Presently, Nuzzie having been called (for he was the only one aboard who had turned in) eight bells went, and all hands put aside their pipes, and prepared to tail on to the ha'lyards; yet no one of them made to go up to loose the sail. That was the b'y's job, and Nuzzie was a little late in coming out on deck. When, in a minute, he appeared, Skipper Abe spoke sternly to him.

"Up now, b'y, an' loose thet sail. D'y think to let er grown man dew suchlike work! Shame on yew!"

And Nuzzie, the grey-bearded "b'y" of five and fifty years, went aloft humbly, as he was bidden.

Five minutes later, he sung out that all was ready for hoisting, and the string of ancient Ones took a strain on the ha'lyards. Then Nehemiah, being the chaunty man: struck up in his shrill quaver:—

"Thar wor an ole farmer in Yorkshire did dwell"

And the shrill piping of the ancient throats took up the refrain:—

"Wi' me ay, ay, blow thar lan' down."

Nehemiah caught up the story:—

" 'e 'ad 'n ole wife, 'n 'e wished 'er in 'ell."

"Give us some time ter blow thar lan' down," came the quavering chorus of old voices.

"O, thar divvel come to 'im one day at thar plough," continued old Nehemiah; and the crowd of ancients followed up with the refrain: —"Wi' me ay, ay, blow thar lan' down."

"I've comed fer th' ole woman, I mun 'ave 'er now," sang Nehemiah. And again the refrain:—"Give us some time ter blow thar lan' down," shrilled out.

And so on to the last couple of stanzas. And all about them, as they chaunteyed, was that extraordinary, rose-tinted mist; which, above, blent into a marvellous radiance of flame-colour, as though, just a little higher than their mastheads, the sky was one red ocean of silent fire.

"Thar wor three leetle divvels chained up ter thar wall," sang Nehemiah, shrilly.

"Wi' me ay, ay, blow thar lan' down," came the piping chorus.

"She tuk off 'er clog, 'n she walloped 'em all," chaunted old Nehemiah, and again followed the wheezy, age-old refrain.

"These three leetle divvels fer marcy did bawl," quavered Nehemiah, cocking one eye upward to see whether the yard was nearly mast-headed.

"Wi' me ay, ay, blow thar lan' down," came the chorus.

"Chuck out this ole hag, or she'll mur—"

"Belay," sung out Josh, cutting across the old sea song, with the sharp command. The chaunty had ceased with the first note of the Mate's voice, and, a couple of minutes later, the ropes were coiled up, and the old fellows back to their occupations.

It is true that eight bells had gone, and that the watch was supposed to be changed; and changed it was, so far as the wheel and look-out were concerned; but otherwise little enough difference did it make to those sleep-proof ancients. The only change visible in the men about the deck, was that those who had previously only smoked, now smoked and worked; while those who had hitherto worked and smoked, now only smoked. Thus matters went on in all amity; while the old *Shamraken* passed onward like a rose-tinted shadow through the shining mist, and only the great, silent, lazy seas that came at her, out from the enshrouding redness, seemed aware that she was anything more than the shadow she appeared.

Presently, Zeph sung out to Nuzzie to get their tea from the galley, and so, in a little, the watch below were making their evening meal. They ate it as they sat upon the hatch or spar, as the chance might be; and, as they ate, they talked with their mates, of the watch on deck, upon the matter of the shining mist into which they had plunged. It was obvious, from their talk, that the extraordinary phenomenon had impressed them vastly, and all the superstition in them seemed to have been waked to fuller life. Zeph, indeed, made no bones of declaring his belief that they were nigh to something more than earthly. He said that he had a feeling that "M'ria" was somewhere near to him.

"Meanin' ter say as we've come purty near ter 'eaven?" said Nehemiah, who was busy thrumming a paunch mat, for chafing gear.

"Dunno," replied Zeph; "but"—making a gesture towards the hidden sky—"yew'll 'low as it's mighty wonnerful, 'n I guess ef 'tis 'eaven, thar's some uv us as is growin' powerful wearied uv 'arth. I guess I'm feelin' peeky fer a sight uv M'ria."

Nehemiah nodded his head slowly; and the nod seemed to run round the group of white-bearded ancients.

"Reckon my datter's gell 'll be thar," he said, after a space of pondering. "Be s'prisin' ef she 'n M'ria 'd made et up ter know one anuther."

"M'ria wer' great on makin' friends," remarked Zeph, meditatively, "an' gells wus awful friendly wi' 'er. Seemed as she hed er power thet way."

"I never 'ad no wife," said Job, at this point, somewhat irrelevantly. It was a fact of which he was proud, and he made a frequent boast of it.

"Thet's naught ter cocker thysel on, lad," exclaimed one of the white-beards, who, until this time, had been silent. "Thou'lt find less folk in heaven t' greet thee."

"Thet's trewth, sure 'nuff, Jock," assented Nehemiah, and fixed a stern look on Job; whereat Job retired into silence.

Presently, at three bells, Josh came along and told them to put away their work for the day.

V

The second dog watch came, and Nehemiah and the rest of his side, made their tea out upon the main hatch, along with their mates. When this was finished, as though by common agreement, they went everyone and sat themselves upon the pinrail running along under the t'gallant bulwarks; there, with their elbows upon the rail, they faced outward to gaze their full at the mystery of colour which had wrapped about them. From time to time, a pipe would be removed, and some thought given an utterance.

Eight bells came and went; but, save for changing of the wheel and lookout, none moved from his place.

Nine o'clock, and the night came down upon the sea; but to those within the mist, the only result was a deepening of the rose colour into an intense red, which seemed to shine with a light of its own creating. Above them, the unseen sky seemed to be one vast blaze of silent, blood-tinted flame.

"Piller uv cloud by day, 'n er piller uv fire by night," muttered Zeph to Nehemiah, who crouched near.

"I reckon's them's Bible words," said Nehemiah.

"Dunno," replied Zeph; "but them's thar very words as I heerd passon Myles a sayin' w'en thar timber wor afire down our way. 'Twer' mostly smoke 'n daylight; but et tarned ter 'n etarnal fire w'en thar night comed."

At four bells, the wheel and look-out were relieved, and a little later, Josh and Skipper Abe came down on to the main deck.

"Tur'ble queer," said Skipper Abe, with an affectation of indifference.

"Aye, 'tes, sure," said Nehemiah.

And after that, the two old men sat among the others, and watched.

At five bells, half-past ten, there was a murmur from those who sat nearest to the bows, and a cry from the man on the look-out. At that, the attention of all was turned to a point nearly right ahead. At this particular spot, the mist seemed to be glowing with a curious, unearthly red brilliance; and, a minute later, there burst upon their vision a vast arch, formed of blazing red clouds.

At the sight, each and everyone cried out their amazement, and immediately began to run towards the fo'cas'le head. Here they congregated in a clump, the Skipper and the Mate among them. The arch appeared now to extend its arc far beyond either bow, so that the ship was heading to pass right beneath it.

"'Tis 'eaven fer sure," murmured Josh to himself; but Zeph heard him.

"Reckon 's them's ther Gates uv Glory thet M'ria wus allus talkin' 'bout," he replied.

"Guess I'll see thet b'y er mine in er little," muttered Josh, and he craned forward, his eyes very bright and eager.

All about the ship was a great quietness. The wind was no more now than a light steady breath upon the port quarter; but from right ahead, as though issuing from the mouth of the radiant arch, the long-backed, foamless seas rolled up, black and oily.

Suddenly, amid the silence, there came a low musical note, rising and falling like the moan of a distant æolian harp. The sound appeared to come from the direction of the arch, and the surrounding mist seemed to catch it up and send it sobbing and sobbing in low echoes away into the redness far beyond sight.

"They'm singin'," cried Zeph. "M'ria wer' allus tur'ble fond uv singin'. Hark ter—"

"'Sh!" interrupted Josh. "Thet's my b'y!" His shrill old voice had risen almost to a scream.

"It's wunnerful—wunnerful; just mazin'!" exclaimed Skipper Abe.

Zeph had gone a little forrard of the crowd. He was shading his eyes with his hands, and staring intently, his expression denoting the most intense excitement.

"B'lieve I see 'er. B'lieve I see 'er," he was muttering to himself, over and over again.

Behind him, two of the old men were steadying Nehemiah, who felt, as he put it, "a bit mazy at thar thought o' seein' thet gell."

Away aft, Nuzzie, the "b'y," was at the wheel. He had heard the moaning; but, being no more than a boy, it must be supposed that he knew nothing of the *nearness* of the next world, which was so evident to the men, his masters.

A matter of some minutes passed, and Job, who had in mind that farm upon which he had set his heart, ventured to suggest that heaven was less near than his mates supposed; but no one seemed to hear him, and he subsided into silence.

It was the better part of an hour later, and near to midnight, when a murmur among the watchers announced that a fresh matter had come to sight. They were yet a great way off from the arch; but still the thing showed clearly—a prodigious umbel, of a deep, burning red; but the crest of it was black, save for the very apex which shone with an angry red glitter.

"Thar Throne uv God!" cried out Zeph, in a loud voice, and went down upon his knees. The rest of the old men followed his example, and even old Nehemiah made a great effort to get to that position.

"Simly we'm a'most 'n 'eaven," he muttered huskily.

Skipper Abe got to his feet, with an abrupt movement. He had never heard of that extraordinary electrical phenomenon, seen once perhaps in a hundred years— the "Fiery Tempest" which precedes certain great Cyclonic Storms; but his experienced eye had suddenly discovered that the red-shining umbel was truly a low, whirling water-hill reflecting the red light. He had no theoretical knowledge to tell him that the thing was produced by an enormous air-vortice; but he had often seen a water-spout form. Yet, he was still undecided. It was all so beyond him; though, certainly, that monstrous gyrating hill of water, sending out a reflected glitter of burning red, appealed to him as having no place in his ideas of Heaven. And then, even as he hesitated, came the first, wild-beast bellow of the coming Cyclone. As the sound smote upon their ears, the old men looked at one another with bewildered, frightened eyes.

"Reck'n thet's God speakin'," whispered Zeph. "Guess we're on'y mis'rable sinners."

The next instant, the breath of the Cyclone was in their throats, and the *Shamraken*, homeward-bounder, passed in through the everlasting portals.

Farewell

And, now it is farewell,
    Forever, O great Sea!
        Yet in some distant world, my soul
Shall dream of thee.
        For now, a far-off toll,
I hear—It is my knell
            Rung out by solemn waves on mist-bound shores,
              While overhead, the groan
        Of opening, monstrous doors
Comes echoing down to me,
              And streams of awful light
Shine o'er thy tumult, Sea,
           As I pass up across the night
        Into the great Unknown.

Source Notes

The texts in this volume have been reprinted mainly from one of two sources: a book by Hodgson in which each piece was first collected (that is, a book published during Hodgson's life, or, in the case of his verse, as published by his wife soon after his death); or, from the item's first publication in a periodical. The texts of some of these stories differ considerably from the versions published in the 1960s in volumes edited by August Derleth. The Derleth-edited versions of four titles in particular are much inferior to the earlier magazine versions selected for this volume. The four stories are "The Voice in the Dawn" (re-titled by Derleth "The Call of the Dawn"); "The Wild Man of the Sea"; "Demons of the Sea" (drastically re-written and re-titled "The Crew of the Lancing"); and "An Adventure of the Deep Waters" (Derleth evidently did not know of this revised and extended version, and he simply reprinted Hodgson's earlier version, titled "The Thing in the Weeds").

Specific source details for each item in this book are given below, arranged alphabetically by title.

"An Adventure of the Deep Waters." First published as "The Thing in the Weeds" in *The Story-Teller*; reprinted from *Short Stories*, February 1916, where a subsequently revised and re-titled version appeared

"Demons of the Sea." Reprinted from *Sea Stories*, 5 October 1923

"The Derelict." First published in *The Red Magazine*, 1 December 1912; reprinted from *Men of the Deep Waters* (1914)

"Farewell" [verse]. Reprinted from *The Lost Poetry of William Hope Hodgson* (2005), edited by Jane Frank, by kind permission of Jane Frank.

"The Finding of the *Graiken*." Reprinted from *The Red Magazine*, 15 February 1913

"From the Tideless Sea (First Part)." First published in *Monthly Story Magazine*, April 1906; reprinted from *Men of the Deep Waters* (1914)

"From the Tideless Sea (Second Part)." First published as "More News from the *Homebird*" in *Blue Book Magazine*, August 1907; reprinted from *Men of the Deep Waters* (1914)

"Grey Seas are Dreaming of My Death" [verse]. First published in *"Poems" and "The Dream of X"* (1912); reprinted from *The Calling of the Sea* (1920)

"The Haunted *Jarvee*." Reprinted from *Premier Magazine*, March 1929

"The Haunted *Pampero*." Reprinted from *Short Stories*, February 1918

"The Mystery of the Derelict." First published in *The Story-Teller*, July 1907; reprinted from *Men of the Deep Waters* (1914)

"On the Bridge." First published in *Saturday Westminster Gazette*, 20 April 1912; reprinted from *Men of the Deep Waters* (1914)

"Out of the Storm." Reprinted from *Putnam's Monthly*, February 1909

"The Place of Storms" [verse]. Reprinted from *The Calling of the Sea* (1920)

"The *Shamraken* Homeward-Bounder." First published in *Putnam's Monthly*, April 1908; reprinted from *Men of the Deep Waters* (1914)

"The Stone Ship." First published in abridged form in *The Red Magazine*, 1 July 1914; reprinted from the first complete publication in *The Luck of the Strong* (1916)

"Thou Living Sea" [verse]. Reprinted from *The Calling of the Sea* (1920)

"Through the Vortex of a Cyclone." First published in *Cornhill Magazine*, November 1907; reprinted from *Men of the Deep Waters* (1914)

"A Tropical Horror." Reprinted from *The Grand Magazine*, June 1905

"The Voice in the Dawn." Reprinted from *Premier Magazine*, 5 November 1920

"The Voice in the Night." First published in *Blue Book Magazine*, November 1907; reprinted from *Men of the Deep Waters* (1914)

"The Wild Man of the Sea." Reprinted from *Sea Stories*, May 1926

Read the short stories that inspired and awed H. P. Lovecraft! This volume represents horror's classic stories – the roots of modern horror as selected by Lovecraft himself.

$14.00
ISBN 1-59360-056-9

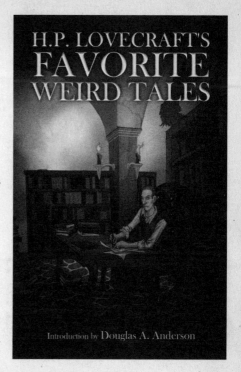

H. P. LOVECRAFT'S FAVORITE WEIRD TALES
Introduction by Douglas A. Anderson

Selected by the master of horror, these stories were Lovecraft's favorite tales of the weird. Compiled from his own lists – augmented with comments from Lovecraft's own extensive correspondence, essays, and newspaper interviews – this unique collection makes for a truly landmark Lovecraftian anthology. Contributors include Edgar Allan Poe, Ambrose Bierce, Clark Ashton Smith, Arthur Machen, Henry S. Whitehead, Algernon Blackwood, H.F. Arnold, and other leading masters of the horror genre.

THE
100
BEST WRITERS OF
FANTASY AND HORROR

J.R.R. Tolkien, Stephen King, Phillip Pullman,
J.K. Rowling, Clive Barker, H.P. Lovecraft,
Terry Pratchett, Ursula K. Le Guin, Bram Stoker,
and many more

Douglas A. Anderson

A Readers Guide for fantasy and horror fans – discover the men and women who spun these fantastic and enduring tales, from J.R.R. Tolkien to Stephen King, J. K. Rowling to L. Frank Baum!

$16.95
ISBN 1-59360-040-2

THE 100 BEST WRITERS OF FANTASY AND HORROR
by Douglas A. Anderson

A unique assemblage of the English language's top hundred fantasy and horror writers! Each entry features a short biography, detailed accounts of the author's best books in the genre, notable editions, some representative quotes, and brief accounts of similar worthy writers. Key authors featured include J.R.R. Tolkien, Stephen King, Phillip Pullman, J.K. Rowling, Lucius Shepard, Clive Barker, Thomas Ligotti, John Crowley, L. Frank Baum, Jack Finney, H. P. Lovecraft, Terry Pratchett, Ursula K. Le Guin, Kenneth Morris, M. R. James, Bram Stoker, Robert E. Howard – among many others!

*Read fantasy's best short stories,
with biographical notes on each
contributor by fantasy scholar
Douglas A. Anderson.*

$14.00
ISBN 1-59360-048-8

FANTASY'S BEST SHORT STORIES
Featuring Bram Stoker, L. Frank Baum, Jonathan Carroll, Thomas
Ligotti, H.P. Lovecraft, Lord Dunsany, Peter S. Beagle, and more

SEEKERS OF DREAMS
Masterpieces of Fantasy
Introduction and Biographical Notes by Douglas A. Anderson

This anthology showcases the spectrum of fantasy: light and
dark, with masterpieces by famous authors such as L. Frank
Baum, Lord Dunsany, H.P. Lovecraft, Leonard Cline, Clark
Ashton Smith, Henry S. Whitehead, Bram Stoker and more.
Contemporary writers included are Peter S. Beagle, Jonathan
Carroll, Thomas Ligotti, Verlyn Flieger and Andy Duncan.

Cold Spring Press

An Imprint of Open Road Publishing
P.O. Box 284
Cold Spring Harbor, NY 11724
E-mail: jopenroad@aol.com

Nonfiction:

The Science of Middle-earth, by Henry Gee, $14.00

More People's Guide to J.R.R. Tolkien, by TheOneRing.net, $14.00

The People's Guide to J.R.R. Tolkien, by TheOneRing.net, $16.95

The Tolkien Fan's Medieval Reader, by Turgon, $14.95

Tolkien in the Land of Heroes, by Anne C. Petty, $16.95

Dragons of Fantasy, by Anne C. Petty, $14.95

Myth & Middle-earth, by Leslie Ellen Jones, $14.95

The 100 Best Writers of Fantasy and Horror, by Douglas A. Anderson, $16.95

Fiction:

Book of the Three Dragons, by Kenneth Morris, $11.95

Lud-in-the-Mist, by Hope Mirrlees, $11.00

Thin Line Between: Book One of the Wandjina Quartet, by M.A.C. Petty, $11.00

The Sillymarillion, by D.R. Lloyd, $11.00

Seekers of Dreams: Classic Short Stories of Fantasy & Horror, selected by Douglas A. Anderson, $14.00

Adrift on the Haunted Seas: The Best Short Stories of William Hope Hodgson, $11.00

The Dark Chamber, by Leonard Cline, $6.99

H.P. Lovecraft's Favorite Weird Tales, $14.00

The Shadow at the Bottom of the World, by Thomas Ligotti, $13.00

For US orders, include $5.00 for postage and handling for the first book ordered; for each additional book, add $1.00. Orders outside US, inquire first about shipping charges (money order payable in US dollars on US banks only for overseas shipments). We also offer bulk discounts. Note: Checks or money orders must be made out to Open Road Publishing.